HELLO, DEAR READERS!

I'm Harley Laroux! Some of you may be familiar with me and my writing already, but to those who don't know me yet, I'm an author, cat guardian, candle enthusiast, and plant collector. Whether you've been reading me for a while or are new, I can't thank you enough for your interest in my work.

The Souls Trilogy got its start in April 2021, when I self-published my first full-length novel, *Her Soul to Take*. Since its initial release, the Souls Trilogy has been truly life-changing. It has introduced me to amazing readers and creators around the world and helped to bring together an incredible community of folks who enjoy their reads spicy and romantic, spooky and thrilling.

I've gotten to watch this trilogy grow and reach readers around the world. So I'm absolutely thrilled for what's coming next!

for these gorgeous print editions of the Souls Trilogy. Each book will feature an all-new bonus epilogue, and beautiful updates to the covers' original designs! It's such a joy to be able to bring you paperbacks that are as much a pleasure to collect as they are to read.

Inspired by the stunning natural beauty of Washington State and my fascination with all things spooky, the Souls Trilogy follows three fierce women and the demons who love them as they fight to survive in a small town full of monsters, magic, and mystery. These adult paranormal romances are extra spicy, with a diverse cast of queer characters and themes that are sex- and kink-positive. They are stand-alone but interconnected, each following a different couple as they unravel the dark mysteries of their town's past.

I've always been interested in the role demons play in mythology, and including demons as the love interests in this series fit perfectly. To me, demons represent the ultimate in freedom, self-acceptance, and passion— all themes that I love to touch on throughout the Souls Trilogy. Like humans, demons are flawed beings, but when their immortal power clashes with humanity's curiosity and desperation, sparks are sure to fly.

In book 1, *Her Soul to Take*, you'll meet a paranormal investigator named Raelynn and the demon she mistakenly summons, Leon. Known to kill anyone who dares summon him, Leon instead finds himself enraptured by the stubborn, curious woman who called to him. When a cult wants Rae as the next sacrifice

HER SOUL TO TAKE

BY HARLEY LAROUX

The Souls Trilogy
Her Soul to Take
Her Soul for Revenge
Soul of a Witch

Losers
The Dare (prequel)
Losers: Part 1
Losers: Part 2

Dirty First Dates (short erotica series)
Halloween Haunt
The Arcade
The Museum

HER SOUL TO TAKE

Harley Laroux

KENSINGTON
PUBLISHING CORP.

kensingtonbooks.com

KENSINGTON BOOKS are published by:

Kensington Publishing Corp.
119 West 40th Street
New York, NY 10018

All Kensington titles, imprints, and distributed lines are available at special quantity discounts for bulk purchases for sales promotions, premiums, fundraising, educational, or institutional use.

Special book excerpts or customized printings can also be created to fit specific needs. For details, write or phone the office of the Kensington sales manager: Kensington Publishing Corp., 119 West 40th Street, New York, NY 10018, attn: Sales Department; phone 1-800-221-2647.

The K with book logo Reg US Pat. & TM Off.

First Kensington Trade Paperback Printing: January 2024

ISBN 978-1-4967-5289-5 (trade paperback)

10 9 8 7 6 5 4 3 2 1

Printed in the United States of America

CONTENT NOTICE: This book contains graphic violence and sexual content. It is not intended for anyone under the age of legal adulthood. All characters depicted herein are over eighteen years of age. This book is not to be used as a resource for sexual education, or as an informational guide to sex or BDSM. The activities depicted within this book are dangerous and the scenes within this book are not meant to depict realistic expectations of BDSM or fetish-related activities.

Some contents within this book may be triggering or disturbing to some readers. Reader discretion is strongly advised.

The kinks/fetishes within this book: consensual non-consent (CNC), breath play/ choking, bloodplay, spit, swallowing bodily fluids, needle play (body modification fetish), pain play, fear play, public play, bondage, restraint, spanking/impact play, erotic humiliation/degradation, raw sex/sex without a condom.

To my husband.
My light in the darkness.

for the ancient deity they worship, Leon and Rae must work together to survive. But Leon doesn't just want her heart—he wants her soul.

Whether you've read this series before or are picking it up for the first time, I can't thank you enough for your interest in my books. I'm so grateful for the opportunity to share my stories with you. I hope you find just as much love, adventure, and excitement while reading these books as I did while writing them.

WITH LOVE,

Harley
Laroux

LEON

"BLOOD HAS BEEN spilled in Its name. It is awake."

I'd felt the stirring before he announced it. Damned mortals always stating the obvious, as if I couldn't feel the ground trembling and the old roots tensing—*tensing*, like a body preparing to be hit. As if I couldn't hear the whispers growing louder in the dark, tendrils of ancient, incomprehensible thought reaching out and prodding for vulnerabilities.

The concrete surrounding me—burying me alive— couldn't hide the disturbance. I didn't need Kent's pompous ass strutting in here, making declarations as if I was supposed to grovel at the news. Seated cross-legged in my wretched binding circle, sharpening my nails against the concrete floor, I barely gave him more than a glance when he came into the room with his cronies in tow. At his declaration, I merely grunted, and that hardly seemed to satisfy him.

"Did you hear me, demon?" he snapped, and his fingers tightened upon the leather surface of his grimoire. That damned worn-out book was always in his grip, the hammer he had raised over my head. A non-magical man like Kent couldn't control me without his little spell book.

"I heard you." I sighed heavily, and leaned back so I could tap my nails upon the floor. "Pardon me for not jumping in joy, Kenny-boy. The fact that you're here to gloat about your Old God stretching Its limbs only tells me It hasn't woken up enough to give you all that delicious power you seek." His expression darkened dangerously, and I knew I was walking the edge of enticing him to hurt me.

Captivity was so endlessly boring that seeing how far I could push my master before pain resulted had become a real thrill.

I shrugged. "So, you're here with a task. Here to send me off on some petty errand before locking me in the dark again. Thrilling."

Kent's knuckles had gone white. He had a certain aristocratic look about him; he would have been just as at home in Victorian London as he was mingling among Seattle's business elite. Dark-gray suit, a subtle pinstripe on his black tie, perfectly cut and combed gray hair. He was as muted as Washington's cloudy skies, and about as unpredictable in his moods.

"I would save your strength for the work ahead, demon," he said, his voice tight, rage barely restrained.

"Rather than wasting it on that petty tongue of yours. Unless you'd like me to rip it out again?"

There was a snicker from one of the white-cloaked figures behind him, and I glowered but kept my mouth shut. Kent had them wear the cloaks and the stag-skull masks, but I knew the two faceless beings that accompanied him down here were his adult spawns. Victoria, smelling of bitter artificial-vanilla fragrance and all the chemicals in her makeup. And Jeremiah, reeking of cheap body spray and hair gel.

"Tonight, at midnight, you will go to Westchurch Cemetery. You will go silently and ensure no one detects you along the way. There, find the grave of Marcus Kynes. Dig up his body, and refill the grave. Then bring his body to White Pine. Is that understood?"

I rather liked my tongue in my mouth. Growing a new one was nasty business. "Understood."

THERE WAS NO clock in that wretched little room, but I could feel midnight arrive nonetheless. The world changed slightly, moving just a little closer to the boundary separating it from Heaven and Hell. Midnight always made me feel good, as did finally stretching my legs and leaving the binding circle.

Kent kept me in that circle so often he'd had it carved into the floor. Like his father, and his grandfather before him, Kent feared that if he released me from his service when he had no immediate need of me, I would somehow manage to escape from him forever. A lovely thought, but an unlikely outcome. Kent had the grimoire, the only remaining record of my name on the Earth. He alone could summon me because of it.

I suppose he also feared that, in my considerable amount of hatred for him, I'd bend the rules and seek vengeance by murdering him and his entire family after being dismissed from his service. Again, a lovely thought, and a far more likely outcome. I'd risk the wrath of my superiors in Hell if it meant being able to demolish this whole family.

But it had been over a century, and in all that time I'd been in service to the Hadleigh family. It was impressive, honestly—no one else had ever managed to keep me in captivity for so long without losing their lives. There was a good reason there was only one remaining record of my name. Summoners throughout the years had learned quickly that I wasn't an easy one to command, and thought it best to discourage summoning me at all.

I'd left a trail of dead magicians in my wake, and was eager to add a few more.

The night was cold and foggy, the pines dripping with dew. Westchurch Cemetery was surrounded by trees, all but invisible from the quiet road that ran alongside it. Rows of headstones, some over a century old, lined the wide untrimmed lawn. It didn't take me long to find Marcus. The plot of disturbed dirt gave him away, his grave freshly filled. A flat, simple headstone marked him.

Marcus Kynes. Twenty-one years old. The "spilled blood" that had awakened Hadleigh's God. Odd that Marcus had been buried at all. A sacrifice was meant to be done in the cathedral, with the corpse offered up immediately—or offered alive, if possible, for God to toy with at Its leisure. The fact that Marcus had been buried seemed messy.

It didn't take me long to dig down to him, using my bare hands and claws to wrench up the loose dirt. The coffin was a plain wooden box, utterly unadorned. The moment I tugged up the lid, the stench of formaldehyde rushed in my nose. Marcus had been buried in a cheap suit, his youthful face waxen with the amount of makeup that had been coated onto it.

"Wakey, wakey." I hauled him over my shoulder and crawled up from the grave, dumping him beside the pile of dirt I'd just dug out. "Just give me a minute here, buddy. Can't have your mother knowing her son's grave has been desecrated."

I quickly filled back in the grave, then, with the corpse over my shoulder, began to make my way toward White Pine. The area of forest, and the mine shaft that lay within it, was a quick enough run to make, but cumbersome with Marcus flopping over my back. Still, running through the trees with a corpse was preferable to my concrete prison.

The witching hour neared as I reached White Pine. A misting rain had begun to fall, and Marcus was smelling worse by the second. But beyond his stench and the aroma of wet earth, I could smell smoke. A bonfire somewhere in the woods.

Deep in the trees, and a little way up the hillside, I found Kent and his merry band awaiting me near the flames.

They'd all donned their white cloaks and stag masks. There were at least two dozen of them scattered among the trees, speaking softly beneath black umbrellas. It was no wonder this little town was booming with cryptid sightings. Thanks to Kent's little cult, who called themselves the Libiri, nearly the entirety of Abelaum's population had some fantastical story about seeing a monster in the woods.

They weren't exactly wrong. They *were* seeing monsters, but of the human variety.

The only one not in uniform was Everly, Kent Hadleigh's bastard daughter. A few months older than her half-siblings, Victoria and Jeremiah, Everly was blonde, willowy, and garbed in her usual black ensemble. The fledgling witch looked absolutely petrified to be there, and when her blue eyes fell on me and the corpse I came bearing, she looked as if she would vomit.

"Brothers, Sisters, the sacrifice comes," Kent spoke in a bizarrely theatrical voice when he was in front of his band of zealots. Somewhere between a fire-and-brimstone Southern preacher and a kindergarten teacher who had bodies buried in his garden. It grated on my nerves, that voice, as did the way he snapped his fingers at me and pointed to the ground at Everly's feet. "Here. Put him down."

I let Marcus flop down unceremoniously at the young witch's feet, and a flicker of pain went across her face. Had she known him? A fellow student at the university perhaps? Or had her heart gone suddenly tender when all her father's preaching about the beauty of death became a very ugly reality?

"Remove his clothes," Kent said, and I promptly stripped the corpse down, ripping the cheap suit like paper. With his chest laid bare, I found the wounds that no amount of mortuary makeup could have covered: multiple stab wounds were gashed haphazardly across his chest, and scrawled among them were the lines and runes of the sacrificial offering.

Messy. Very messy. Unplanned, if I had to guess. Spontaneous even.

I tweaked an eyebrow at Kent, a silent question I knew he wouldn't answer. He gave Everly a brisk nod, and the young witch, looking sickly pale, knelt and began to examine the marks across Marcus's chest.

"They'll work," she said at last. She hurriedly got to her feet and averted her eyes from the body. "The marks are crude but efficient." Her eyes flickered among the crowd in a brief moment of worry. She thought what she'd said might offend, and offense could bring consequences.

"Very good," Kent said softly. Then, louder, all theatrics once more, "Long have we waited for this day, my children. Long has the Deep One waited for this, waited with utter patience and mercy. Today, the first of three go to Its depths. May two more follow."

"May two more follow," the crowd murmured, save for Everly, whose lips were pressed into a thin, hard line on her pretty face.

"Servant, bear the sacrifice up to the mine," Kent said. *Servant*. Fucking hell. I wanted to gag him with his own tongue. "Jeremiah will accompany you. This sacrifice is his to offer."

A figure stepped forward, reeking of body spray. Jeremiah, of course. This messy, unplanned, absolute botchery of a sacrifice was all thanks to Kent's dear son. I rolled my eyes, but hauled naked Marcus up off the ground and, without a word to Jeremiah, stalked away into the trees, away from the fire's light.

Jeremiah tried to make a point of walking ahead of me, but I kept my pace just fast enough that he couldn't. The boy had even less patience than his father.

"Slow the fuck down, Leon," he said. "Or I swear I'll have Dad rip your balls off next time."

"Temper, temper." I shook my head, but slowed. I'd let the asshole lead, let him revel in his little power trip. Staring at the back of his head at least let me fantasize about cracking it open. "So, this one's yours, eh? Have a little trouble with him?"

"Bastard tried to run," he said, then laughed darkly. "He didn't get far. Squealed like a pig. I think I understand why you enjoy killing so much, Leon. It's a fucking rush."

I grit my teeth. "Don't think you understand death from one messy murder. Just wait until your God wakes up. It'll teach you a thing or two about death."

I'm sure he would have loved to snap back at me, but we'd arrived. There, in the shadows of the trees, was the White Pine mine shaft. Boarded up for nearly a century, the stained wood framing of the entrance had been covered with numerous runes: some carved, some painted, some branded. A metal sign dangled from the wood on a broken chain, reading: *CAUTION: OPEN MINE. DO*

NOT ENTER. The ground was mossy, and numerous white-capped mushrooms grew in thick clusters around the shaft's opening.

The ground itself was vibrating. The trees were restless. An odd smell, like deep water and rotting algae, permeated the air. Somewhere, deep in those flooded tunnels beneath our feet, an ancient God was stirring.

I didn't spook easily, but I still got a chill.

"Well, here you go." I shoved Marcus into Jeremiah's arms, who leapt back with a yelp and let poor Marcus thump down into the mud.

"What the fuck is wrong with you?" His voice shot up in pitch. He wasn't sounding so cocky anymore. "I don't want to touch that!"

"It's *your* sacrifice." I shrugged. "You really want a demon to claim your offering to the Deep One by tossing him in?"

Jeremiah wavered, his eyes flickering between the corpse and the mine. His throat clenched as he gulped. I really didn't give a fuck how the damn body got down there, but if I had the opportunity to make Jeremiah squirm, I'd take it.

Finally, with a groan of disgust, Jeremiah hauled Marcus up into his arms; no easy task, considering the dead man was nearly his same size. He trudged toward the mine, and stopped just outside the entrance, peering into the utter blackness beyond.

How much would I suffer if I just shoved him in? Two sacrifices for the price of one. Kent should consider it a real bargain.

But I resisted. Vengeance would come, someday.

Or the Deep One would wake and kill me first.

With a grunt, Jeremiah threw Marcus down into the darkness. His body hit the ground with a thud, there was a shuffle as he rolled, and then a splash as he hit the water in the flooded tunnel below. The smell of seawater intensified, and the wind picked up, rattling the pine needles above. My stomach lurched unpleasantly, and Jeremiah quickly stumbled back from the mine, wiping his hands on his cloak. He didn't say a word to me, just marched back down the hill.

I stayed for a moment, staring into the darkness. My toes curled at the rumbling below, my skull vibrating with the force of it. The tides would be high tomorrow. These trees would begin the long, slow process of trying to pull their roots up from the dirt, as if they could walk away from the thing below that felt so *wrong*.

Then, from the darkness, there came a howl. Like the scream of a fox, but drawn out into such an agonized cry that it made the hairs on the back of my neck stand up.

It was time to leave. I didn't feel like dealing with that now. Or ever.

The God wasn't the only thing waking up.

RAE

THERE WAS SOMETHING magical about going back to a place I hadn't stepped foot in since childhood. Those early memories felt hazy, like a feverish dream, an entirely different world than what I'd gotten used to in Oceanside. Smoking joints and drinking Modelo on the beach had been my teen years, but when I was little? My world was those deep green forests that seemed to go on forever, full of fairies and unicorns, my little kid brain bursting with so much imagination that my dad thought I'd never manage to settle down and just exist in the real world.

He wasn't wrong. The real world was boring and involved office jobs, stiff-collared blouses, and way too many uncomfortable shoes. It also involved getting to retire to Spain—hence why I was driving back to my childhood home, while my parents finished the process of selling their house in Southern California to retire luxuriously on the Spanish coast.

I could have gone with them, sure. But choosing to stay and finish my last year at university was responsible and very *adult*, as my dad would say, which I needed to start acting like considering I was on the verge of no longer being a college student.

It was a long drive toward north. My butt was sore, my back hurt, and my chubby kitty, Cheesecake, was absolutely livid to be back in the car for the second day in a row. Not even the fries I kept tossing him from my fast food bag were keeping him placated any longer. I drove through a world awash in wet grays and soaked dark greens until, finally, I passed the *Welcome* sign for the town of Abelaum, population 6,223—or 6,224 now, thanks to me. The downpour became a drizzle, and the watercolor world deepened its tones until the forest took shape: tall pines surrounded by a thick undergrowth of ferns and saplings, with mushroom caps sprouting pale and ghostly among their roots.

I should have stayed at the house to unpack. Instead, after hurriedly hauling my boxes into the living room and making sure Cheesecake got his food and water, I got back into my car and made the short drive into town, to Main Street. Right in the corner shop of a three-story brick building, I met my best friend of nearly fifteen years, Inaya, in Golden Hour Books.

Her Golden Hour Books. My best friend had made her dream a reality and was the proud owner of the cutest damn bookstore I'd ever seen.

"Almost finished," she said, her fingers flying over her laptop keys. Her hands were adorned with delicate gold rings that shone brightly against her deep brown skin, the rings bejeweled with little bees and flowers that matched the cute floral patches stitched on her pink jacket. She was the brightest ray of sunshine I'd seen since passing San Francisco, and I felt warmer just being in her presence.

"No rush, girl, take your time." We'd originally agreed to meet later that night, but I'd been too impatient to see her and too eager to shirk off the tedious task of unpacking my entire life from cardboard boxes to wait. I felt guilty now that I'd popped in on her when she was in the middle of cataloguing such a large new shipment of books.

I picked up one of the stacks she'd finished inputting and balanced them carefully against my chest. "Should I take these to the back?"

"That stack is as big as you!" She laughed. "You don't have to do anything."

I couldn't exactly see her around the book stack, and my glasses had slipped down my nose. But I insisted. "To the back?"

"Yeah, there's a yellow cart back there," she said. "Thank you!"

Unfortunately, gravity and I had always had a strained relationship—pretty toxic, actually. Between my untied boot laces, slipping glasses, and too-large book stack, I tripped over my own feet halfway to the back and sent the books flying.

"Everything is fine!" I called as Inaya loudly burst out laughing. I scrambled on my hands and knees to collect the books—until my fingers brushed over the cracking leather-bound cover of a thin volume and I jerked back in shock. The book was *cold*.

I turned it over curiously. The lettering and filigree design on the front looked as if it had been burned into the leather, and the words were foreign to me: Latin, if I had to guess. I pulled out my phone and typed in the search engine for a translation.

It *was* Latin, and it read: *Magical Work and Conjuring*.

"Find something good?" Inaya's voice made me jump. There was a sound in my ears like the distant roar of waves through a long tunnel, and my stomach felt hollow, like the sensation of falling.

"Yeah, check this out. This one looks really old." I handed the book over to her, and there was a jolt as it left my fingers: a tiny rush of fear that made me want to snatch it back. Inaya opened it, frowning.

"Wow." Her eyes went wide as her fingers moved reverently over the page. "This isn't a printed book. This is *handwritten*."

I got to my feet and leaned against her shoulder so I could see. She'd opened the book to the center. On one page was a sketch of a bizarre mutated zombie dog, ragged and skeletal. The other page was covered in rows of neat Latin text. It reminded me of an explorer's journal, like something Charles Darwin would have carried around as he explored the Galápagos—if the Galápagos had been filled with monsters and magic.

"I think it's a grimoire," I said softly. She glanced at me in confusion, so I explained. "A book of spells and rituals, like the *Key of Solomon*. An original like this is rare. Really, *really* rare."

Inaya shook her head as she shut the book carefully, a wry grin on her face. "Sounds like it'll be right at home with you then. Do you want it?"

"Inaya, that thing has to be priceless! I have to pay you something—"

She ignored me as she carried the book toward the front counter. "Consider it part of your bridesmaid's gift," she said. Moving with the utmost care, she pulled out a roll of brown paper from beneath the counter and wrapped the book, finishing it with a bit of tape and a bow of twine. "All these books were donations from the Abelaum Historical Society, so don't worry about money. These volumes had just been sitting in storage." She held it out to me and I took it delicately into my hands, as if she'd gifted me a holy relic. "A creepy book for my favorite creepy girl. Now, I think we could both use a break. What do you say to some coffee?"

"SHE JUST *DUMPED* you? The week before you move and she's just like, *Peace out, good luck, bye*?" Inaya shook her head, pink nails tapping irritably on her coffee mug. "You have a really bad habit of dating assholes, Rae."

I nodded with a heavy sigh. The sting of Rachel dumping me because I'd chosen to move out of state was still potent, needling into my side like a thorn. I hadn't exactly thought we'd be together forever, but our shared interest in the paranormal and urban exploration had managed to gloss over our deeper issues for the six months we'd dated.

Inaya added quickly, "I love the post-breakup haircut though! So mod. Very '60s. It suits you."

I brushed a hand over my hair, smiling widely at the compliment. It was a lot shorter and darker than the last time she'd seen me—I'd dyed my naturally reddish-brown hair black and cut it into a blunt bob the same night Rachel broke it off. It felt good. Fresh. A clean slate.

"I feel like I can call myself a Library Goth now," I joked, pushing my black-rimmed glasses a little further up my nose. Inaya raised an eyebrow skeptically. "Nerd Goth, maybe?"

"You're still my Ghost Girl Goth, honey, no matter what you do with your hair," she said with a giggle, and we sat in silence for a few moments as we sipped our coffees. The shop we sat in, La Petite Baie, was just next door to Golden Hour Books. The decor was a pleasantly eclectic mix of local artists' work, odd bronze sculptures, and a variety of cushy chairs and upcycled tables. Inaya and I had taken two seats by the window, where we could look out and see the forest pressing close against the opposite side of the street.

"How are you liking being back in the cabin?" Inaya said, taking a sip of her latte. "Have you seen your old ghost yet? What did we used to call him?" She thought for a moment. "Oh yeah, the Nighttime Cowboy!"

I smiled at the nickname we'd given to my childhood ghost. I hadn't thought of it in years. "I haven't seen him yet, but we'll see how the first night goes." I tapped my chin thoughtfully. "Maybe I'll set up a few thermal cameras, and see if I can finally get a full-body apparition recorded."

"How's that going, by the way? The ghost vlog?"

I giggled at Inaya's apt description of my "ghost vlog," even though the question made me wince internally. "Oh, you know. The channel is growing."

"You caught anything big lately? Apparitions, or . . ."

"Caught some disembodied voices. Orbs."

"Oh. That's cool."

That's cool. Yeah, that underwhelmed response was exactly what was going to happen with my vlog audience soon too. The internet just wasn't the place for genuine paranormal investigations—not when all the other "paranormal" channels were pretending to summon The Midnight Man and using special effects and mediocre acting to draw in an audience looking for instant gratification. In comparison, my lengthy recordings and vague captures of electronic voice phenomena were boring.

I needed something big. Something shocking.

I needed something *real.*

But spirits operated on their own time, not mine, and continually coming away from my investigations of "haunted" locales with nothing to show for it was frustrating. The time and effort I'd been dumping into my passion would soon have to go toward finding myself a "real" job. Ad revenue from the channel wasn't going to bring in enough to keep me going on my own, not once my parents sold the cabin they'd given me a year to stay in while I finished school.

"I'm sure you'll be able to find some good places to record up here," Inaya said, snapping me from my mental pit of despair. "All the legends in this town . . . girl, it must be a treasure trove for you."

I nodded. Growing up in Abelaum was like getting raised surrounded by ghosts—not real ones, necessarily, but ghosts of the past. Once one of the most lucrative mining towns of the Pacific Northwest, boarded-up mining shafts could still be found throughout Abelaum's surrounding forests. Dozens of its original buildings were still standing, carefully restored and maintained by a passionately dedicated local historical society.

There was a lot of history to be found here, and with history, came tragedy.

"Oh shit, have you seen Mrs. Kathy yet? She still lives just down the street from your place," Inaya said. "Remember how angry your dad was when she told us about the whole tragedy of '99 thing?"

"Girl, that story got me addicted to horror, of course I remember! Honestly though, who goes and tells a story like that to their first-grade class?" I put on my best imitation of our former teacher, making my voice high-pitched as I wagged my finger at an imaginary room full of kids. "Oh, children! Do you want to hear about the miners who were trapped in the flooded mine and ate each other to survive? If cannibalism doesn't give you brats nightmares, what if I tell you about the monster who lives down there too?"

"The *Old God*." Inaya air-quoted with her fingers, shaking her head. "She believed it though. Mrs. Kathy was batty."

"She did not . . ."

"Uh, yeah, she did. Don't you remember all those fishbones and silver spoons she hung around her house? She told my mom it kept away the evil eye or some shit." Inaya shrugged, finishing off the last of her latte. "I love this town, but people can get really weird when they live out in the woods for too long. Mrs. Kathy wasn't the only person who believed those old legends."

"Speaking of legends . . ." I tapped my fingers on my cup, trying to look innocent. "Is that old church still up there? Near the shaft that they pulled the last three miners out of?"

"St. Thaddeus? I think so." Inaya frowned. "I doubt Mr. Hadleigh would let them demolish it. He's really protective of those historical sites." Seeing my look of confusion, she said, "Kent Hadleigh is the head of the Historical Society. Super nice, super wealthy. I'm in some of the same classes as his daughter, Victoria. I'll introduce you on Monday."

I mouthed an "oh" at her explanation, my brain still focused on the fantastic potential of a hundred-year-old abandoned church with a tragic backstory. She didn't miss it and narrowed her eyes.

"It's condemned, by the way," she deadpanned. "The church is condemned. Like, *not safe to go inside.*"

"Oh, sure, sure." I nodded quickly. "Old, probably haunted, abandoned church? Wouldn't even think of going inside it."

Inaya sighed. "You're crazy, girl. You're gonna get yourself into real trouble one of these days."

I laid my hand over my heart in mock offense. "Me? Get into trouble? Never."

RAE

MY EARLIEST MEMORIES were in this old cabin. The single bedroom house had been big enough for two newlyweds when my parents first bought it. But then I came along, and my dad's corner office became my childhood bedroom. Eventually, we just outgrew the place, and my dad had been eager to escape the small town he'd spent his entire life in. We'd moved down to Southern California when I was seven, and I'd been there ever since. The cabin had become our vacation home, and Dad rented it out to other vacationers the rest of the year.

Nostalgia clung to the wooden walls as bright as their glossy finish. Childhood memories held an entirely different feeling than my memories as a teen—they felt softer, richer, like streaks of acrylic paint across a canvas.

The forest had been my fairy kingdom, the stairway that led up to the master bedroom was the grand path

I'd lead my army of imaginary friends along. On one of the baseboards, hidden under the kitchen cabinets, was a little sketch of a dog I'd drawn with red pen when I was five. Mom had never found it, and it still brought me a little thrill to see it was there, my inner child convinced she'd pulled off a master crime of vandalization.

The corner office turned bedroom held wild memories of its own. That was where I'd seen my first ghost.

The *Nighttime Cowboy*, as I'd called him. Mom said I'd been only four when I first mentioned him. He'd appear through the wall, walk past the foot of my bed, pause, and then disappear just beside my window. A hazy figure, as if he was made of smoke, in boots, denim overalls, and a wide-brimmed hat—hence why I called him a cowboy as a kid. He wasn't scary, just interesting.

And he started my life's obsession.

CLASSES DIDN'T START until Monday, so I had the whole weekend to try to reassemble my life from the stacks of cardboard boxes. The gray sky had darkened after I'd parted from Inaya at the coffee shop, and rain tapped against the windows in a sporadic shower. I lit the fireplace and pulled back all the curtains, basking in the pale natural light that made its way through the clouds.

I couldn't stay here forever. Sooner rather than later, I'd have to begin the search for an apartment, but the idea felt daunting.

I fit my books onto the empty shelves, placed my collection of potted succulents in the kitchen window, and left my laptop and recording equipment scattered across the desk in the downstairs bedroom. Organizing was exhausting. I connected my Bluetooth to the portable speaker on the coffee table and put my playlist on shuffle, dancing through the tedious work to "Monsters" by All Time Low.

Night had fallen, and the cloud cover made it pitch black outside. There was a pause as the next song buffered, leaving only the tapping of the rain on the glass, the soft wind, and the crickets chirping. The window panes had become one-way mirrors: my reflection stared back at me, glasses slipping down my nose, oversized sweater draped over my hands. Outside, in the dark, I wouldn't know if something was staring back.

Someone could have stood right outside the glass, and I wouldn't be able to see them.

The next song began to play right as a chill went up my spine. The cabin seemed inconsequential in the night, as if its bare wooden walls and large windows could do nothing to hold back the dark. Instead of me observing from the inside, I felt like something out there was looking in. Observing *me*.

I jumped as my phone buzzed on the coffee table. I snatched it up, my music paused, and smiled when I saw the caller ID.

"Hey, Mom."

"Hi, sweetheart! How're you settling in? Was the drive okay?"

I could hear something sizzling in the background and my smile widened. Mom would be cooking dinner, Dad would be in the living room with his glass of scotch and his latest mystery novel. My parents had been, as they put it, "free-range parents," mostly leaving me to my own devices unless I was about to do something catastrophically dangerous or destructive. Mom was the epitome of a Woodstock hippie all grown up, while Dad had more of the quiet, studious thing going on.

"Long drive," I said, and snickered as a pan clattered and my mom swore softly. Mom and I shared a love for talking each other's ears off when we probably should have been concentrating on other tasks, like cooking—or unpacking. "But it was really gorgeous."

We chattered on as she caught me up on all the gossip she'd gathered in the mere two days I'd been gone. Dad was, as usual, meticulously planning every aspect of their international move, while Mom remained far less concerned about having a perfect itinerary—yet more proof that I was truly my mother's daughter.

"I forgot how nice this town is," I said, having abandoned unpacking altogether in favor of munching chips on the couch. "The people are friendly, there are no chain businesses. There's cute little mom-and-pop shops everywhere. Why did we ever move anyway?"

My mother chuckled, but lowered her voice a bit as she responded. "Oh, you know your father. All his superstitions, his . . . anxieties . . . small-town life wasn't for him. He felt like people were too up in our business, whatever that means. It got worse when you started grade school." She paused, as if there was more she was about to say—but she seemed to think better of it. "California had more opportunities for his line of work."

"Ah, Dad's good old superstitions." I laughed. "The one trait I was lucky enough to inherit from him. Let me guess: he's checked the history of every house you've looked at buying to make sure no one has died there?"

I could practically hear my mother's eye roll. "Naturally."

"Good call." I nodded. "You don't need your retirement interrupted by vengeful ghosts."

"Oh, don't start." I could hear the clink of plates, and knew she wouldn't put down the phone to eat unless I forced her.

"I'll let you go, Mom. I love you. Miss you."

"Miss you too, sweetheart!" There was a murmur in the background, and she added, "Dad says to stay safe out there."

The house felt even emptier once I'd hung up the phone. I was grateful for Cheesecake, who sauntered over from the kitchen meowing loudly for his dinner. He was a bossy roommate, but he was so damn cute I had to forgive him.

On my way back to the couch with some dip for my chips, the brown paper parcel poking out of my bag caught my eye. The book Inaya had gifted me, the grimoire. Excitement squeezed its fingers around my stomach, a feeling not unlike walking into a haunting investigation for the first time: a thrill, mingled with trepidation.

I unwrapped the book on the coffee table. I probably should have worn gloves; the thing was so old it should have been in a museum. A signature was scrawled in the corner on the inside cover, but the calligraphy was too fancy for me to make out.

I flipped through the pages, marveling at the detailed sketches and tiny, neat Latin. There were drawings of herbs and plants, and some quick use of an online translator told me that the text described the greenery's magical properties. Then there were the sketches of monsters: the boney wolf zombie; a lean, faceless creature draped in seaweed with tentacle-like legs; a multi-limbed thing that looked like a spider with a bird's beak made out of broken tree branches. The art was amazing, the kind of design that would have inspired creepypastas and indie video game developers.

There were pages on purifications, clothing, prayers, astrological events—I only had the patience to translate bits and pieces, but the sheer amount of information was mind-blowing. This grimoire was an absolute treasure. Every time I turned the page, my heart beat a little faster.

Then I found a drawing unlike the others. It was a sketch of a man, around my own age I guessed. His hair lay in waves that curled around his ears, soft pencil strokes portraying a lightness to it. He was shirtless, the muscles of his lean chest starkly outlined but marred with what I could only think were meant to be scars and the vague outlines of tattoos. His lips were full, his chin dimpled. Beneath dark, heavily drawn brows, his eyes had been colored gold.

It was the only spot of color I'd encountered in the book so far. It made his eyes look alive, as if they were watching me, and there was a texture to them as if they'd been formed with flakes of gold leaf.

The adjoining page read, *Operation for the Summoning and Binding of the Killer.*

The Killer . . . summoning and binding . . .

These were instructions for summoning a demon.

I leaned back from the book, the trepidation that had been lurking at the edge of my excitement taking center stage. I wasn't sure if I believed in demons and magic. Ghosts were one thing: the remnants of departed souls, lingering energy, stranded spirits. But demons were something else entirely, one of the many creatures that had lurked in the shadows of human fears for centuries, for millennia. I didn't deny the possibility they *could* exist—but like Gods and angels, I usually assigned them to the realm of mythos.

Demons were exciting, fascinating. The possibility of a place not being merely haunted, but possessed by demonic forces was the driving entertainment value behind numerous horror stories. They played perfectly on human fears: unexplained, terrifyingly powerful, tempting and seductive, representative of sin.

I'd walked through places where demons were said to play. I'd found them no more frightening than anywhere else.

I COULDN'T GET those eyes out of my head. Golden, glowing, piercing in the dark. I was still awake at nearly 2:00 a.m., lying in bed with my laptop open, trying to use my body's refusal to sleep as an opportunity to brainstorm new vlog ideas.

My subscriber count was being swiftly surpassed by newer channels, channels that played up the drama rather than the science of careful investigations. *WE*

USE A OUIJA BOARD IN MASSACHUSETTS' MOST HAUNTED FOREST! ATTACKED BY A DEMON! Millions of views for this shitty clickbait. It had only been up a few days.

Shot in the green lens of night vision, I watched the group pretend to be possessed. I watched them run through the woods shrieking, move a planchet around a Ouija board to form threatening messages they all gaped at. It was fake, all fake. I think the audience knew it was fake too, but judging from the comments, no one really cared. It was exciting, it was funny. It was *entertaining.* Dozens of channels pumped out content like this while mine wallowed behind on views because I insisted on authenticity.

I snatched up my vape pen from the bedside table, inhaling irritably. If I didn't turn something around soon, I wouldn't be able to keep up the channel. Pretty soon I'd have to face reality, get the office job, and settle down. Every fiber of my being cringed away from that possibility, but I wasn't a teenager anymore. I had bills to pay, and this adult thing seemed determined to crush every last dream down to a pulp.

The Killer. Golden eyes in the dark.

I'd bookmarked that page, and I wasn't sure why yet. It became even harder to sleep knowing that downstairs on the coffee table, the grimoire sat closed—but within those pages, in the dark, those golden eyes still shone.

Watching.

Waiting.

RAE

MONDAY MORNING BROUGHT more gray skies and drizzling rain. I walked to school under the black brim of my umbrella, boots splashing through the puddles along my narrow driveway to the road. As I reached the mailboxes, I caught sight of Mrs. Kathy grabbing her mail. As my first-grade teacher, nearly fourteen years ago, her blonde hair had been streaked with gray—now it had gone straight silver.

"Hi, Mrs. Kathy!" I waved to her cheerfully from under my umbrella. She narrowed her eyes at me, blinked rapidly behind her large horn-rimmed glasses, and then hurriedly walked back toward her driveway.

Well, damn. Okay then.

It was only a fifteen-minute walk to campus, but the cold made it feel longer. Then Abelaum University's Gothic peaks and tall windows loomed up behind the trees, cloaked with creeping vines and spackled with moss. It looked as if it should have been abandoned and decaying, not swarming with students carrying iPhones and Starbucks cups. Umbrellas definitely weren't the thing here: the misting rain didn't seem to bother anyone but me. Everyone else merely had hooded raincoats.

Southern California didn't require raincoats—there wasn't a single one in my closet. I'd have to go shopping soon if I didn't want to keep sticking out like a very cold sore thumb.

I wandered down the wide stone hallways in search of my first class, squinting for the tiny gold numbers affixed beside every dark wooden door. The rain increased and drizzled in slow rivulets down the narrow windows that lined one side of the hall. The view was obscured by aspen and spruce, but beyond the needles I could still see the university's tall, sharp spires. The temptation to stop every few yards and pull my camera from my bag was barely resistible, and when I finally made it to class on time, I considered it a massive achievement.

Classes were the typical first day affair of going over the syllabus, but with one stark difference: both my morning professors addressed the recent "tragic loss of a student's life." There were reassurances of safety, of increased security, of local police doing "everything they could." I was in the dark until I did a quick Google check.

Student Found Dead on University Campus: Investigation Ongoing.

Just before the semester started, a student's body had been found brutally murdered in one of the university buildings. The true-crime junkie in me kept searching for more, but there was little to go off. No suspects. No leads. No statements by local police. I was honestly stunned that a murder could occur in such a quiet small town and not result in an absolute explosion of press and speculation.

THE MORNING MIST lingered, seeping between the old buildings and dampening the stones to a darker shade of gray. The mossy roots of the evergreens were enveloped like a slowly rolling tide. But despite the weather, ASB had set up booths all across the quad to greet new students, as had a few dozen of the campus clubs. The excitement of a new semester felt at odds with the dampening fog, as if nature was trying everything in her power to silence the loud, chattering students.

With time to spare before my next class, I gave in and pulled out my camera. Everything from the bell tower above the library to the low, crooked stone walls that boxed in the hedges carried a pleasing aesthetic from behind my lens. The damp, the greenery, the Gothic drama of it all—I felt as if I had stepped into a Grimm fairy tale, right back into my childhood fairy kingdom.

But death had come to the kingdom, and it announced its presence with the sudden shock of yellow caution tape cordoning off the entrance to one of the northwest halls.

I wandered closer. *CALGARY* was affixed in rusting letters above the building's closed double doors, with an *H* and awkwardly spaced *L* following. The trees had grown close to it, their limbs snaking around the building's steep roof as if slowly enfolding it in a living cocoon.

I knew that name from the news articles I'd read that morning: this was the hall in which the student's body had been found. I snapped another photo, capturing the juxtaposition of the glaring plastic tape against the old pockmarked stone. It was beautiful, in a dreadfully grim way.

"Are you fucking lost?"

Don't judge me, but there was something about a mean voice that got me hot—and the voice that spoke from behind me was as mean as they come. I turned, to find a man standing at the foot of Calgary's stairs, his arms folded and his light-green eyes sliding over me. He couldn't have been more than a few years older than me, dressed all in black, with a tight long-sleeved athletic shirt, cargo pants, and laced-up military boots.

Shit. Exactly my type of too-pretty-for-their-own-good asshole.

"Not lost," I said, pinning my best please-fuck-off smile on my face. "It's hard to miss the bright yellow tape pasted across the scene of a murder."

He answered my smile with one of his own; but where mine was bitchy, his was the kind of smile you could imagine seeing outside your window at night, with canines sharp enough to tear me apart. "Oh, *good,* you didn't miss the tape. Then I'll take it that you just can't *read,* since you decided to hang around."

I had to force myself to keep my feet planted and not shuffle them. Something about his face looked *off*. His high cheekbones could cut a girl with their razor edge, if his piercing green eyes didn't get her first. His full lips made him look boyish, almost innocent—but that innocence stopped at his eyes. They were deep set below thick brows the same color as his honey-blond hair, which was shaved short above his ears and long and messy on top.

He was absurdly attractive. My stomach was already in knots, which meant my voice only got sharper as I said, "I'm pretty sure the tape says *Caution,* not *Stay Back Twenty Feet.* I don't see a sign telling me to stay away."

His smile faded. It melted away from his face like icicles shattering from a roof in winter, and he climbed the steps toward me. I folded my arms, regretting that I hadn't just walked away as I spotted a logo stitched into his shirt: *PNW Security Services.*

Damn it. I was mouthing off to a security guard.

He *towered* over me. He had to lean down to get his face in mine.

"What's your name?" His voice was low, the words wrapping threateningly around my throat as surely as his big hands could have. I began to chew nervously on my lower lip, and pushed my glasses up my nose.

"Alex," I said. If he was going to report me to some authority figure, then there was no way I was going to risk getting a mark on my record the first day here. But he shook his head with a languidly slow, patient blink.

"No. It's not."

That feeling of fingers wrapping around my throat intensified. I had to resist reaching my hand up to ensure nothing was squeezing me. What was this guy's problem? Maybe if I'd just watched my attitude to begin with, then he wouldn't be pissed off, but it was a little late for that now.

My back was to Calgary's closed doors, and this guy was entirely blocking my path down the stairs. As I hesitated to answer, he straightened up and leaned one hand above me against the door. Now it wasn't just the feeling of a hand around my throat; it was also the sensation of a boot pressing down on my skull, pushing me against concrete, whispering incomprehensible threats in my ear—

"It's Raelynn," I muttered hurriedly. Instantly the feeling vanished. What the hell? Did I have low blood sugar, or was this asshole really that intimidating? I tugged my book bag a little closer. "If you're going to be such a dick about it, I'll just leave then."

He sniffed harshly, something that easily could have been either amusement or disgust. His rock-hard expression was impossible to read, but having that much intensity fixated on me was uncomfortable. He pushed off the wall and stepped aside, clearing the way for my hurried escape.

"Watch where you wander, girl," he said, refusing to use my name even now that he'd gotten it out of me. "Curiosity can get you in trouble."

Part of me desperately wanted to know what kind of "trouble" he was talking about, because a man that beautiful could cause me a lot of trouble indeed. Embarrassing that a pair of bright eyes and a deep voice could make my vow to stop being attracted to assholes go flying out the window.

I stalked away from the building onto the lawn, those light-green eyes needling into the back of my skull. I tossed my hair back, trying to add some determination in my step to cover up how flustered he'd gotten me. But something strange happened. It felt like a rope snaking around my ankle, higher and higher, tighter and tighter—

That toxic relationship of mine with gravity? Yeah, it was back to bite me in the ass.

I tripped over my own feet, and at the same time, my old pin-covered book bag finally gave out. The frayed shoulder strap snapped and the bag fell open. My textbooks splayed themselves across the wet grass, loose papers drifted down into puddles, and my to-go cup of iced coffee that I'd wedged—foolishly—into the corner of the bag burst open and sent watered-down coffee splashing across my shoes.

I had to take a moment of silence before I knelt and began to collect my things. I could feel the eyes of passing students, staring: torn between feeling guilty enough to help and awkward enough to just quicken their pace. Cheeks burning, I glanced back over my shoulder, and found the guard watching me.

A small, crooked smile was on his face, and he glanced down at my sodden belongings in the grass as if to say, *I told you so*. That smile would have been charming if he wasn't such a jerk.

Who was I kidding? His smile was *still* charming and my traitorous body was getting tummy flutters from him staring at me.

"Aw, Rae, what happened?"

I looked up with a book halfway stuffed back into my useless bag. Inaya was jogging over the lawn toward me, her bright yellow raincoat a sharp contrast to the gloom. She made a sympathetic noise when she saw the state of me: trying to kneel in the grass without giving everyone a look up my skirt, the knees of my black leggings damp and muddy, glasses sliding down my nose.

"It's the First Day Curse, I swear," she said. "Things always go wrong." She knelt beside me, making quick work of collecting my books as I snatched up the ruined papers. She helped me to my feet, and I did my best to tie the bag's shoulder strap back together. "It'll be smooth sailing from here, don't even worry about it."

I pouted up at her, but couldn't keep up the expression and gave into laughter as she pulled me into a hug. I looped my arm through hers, walking with her across the quad.

"I see you've already met our lovely new security guard, Leon," she said, giving a slight glance back.

"Oh, he's a piece of work," I grumbled, but I had more on my mind than just a disturbingly hot asshole. I gave her arm a playful slap. "Why didn't you tell me there was a *murder* on campus, Inaya?"

She groaned, rolling her eyes. "Because *most* people would get freaked out and I didn't want to make your move any harder, you weirdo!" She shook her head at me. "It was pretty grim, girl. I've never heard of anything like that happening here."

We made our way toward a square of four stone benches sitting beneath some tall red alders. Several students were seated there, and Inaya waved to them excitedly as we approached.

"I finally get to introduce you to everyone!" she whispered excitedly as a tall, familiar man in a gray peacoat rose up from his seat on the bench and extended his arms.

"Miss Raelynn Lawson!" His big voice boomed, and he picked me up for a tight squeeze as Inaya laughed. "It's been so long, I swear you've grown."

"Oh, ha-ha, very funny!" I smiled as he set me down. Trent, Inaya's fiancé, had graduated two years ago from Abelaum University and—from what Inaya had told me—was already doing well for himself at an investment firm in Seattle. "It's the boots, I wore them specifically so I could reach your waistline."

Trent chuckled and reached over to give Inaya a quick kiss on the forehead. Inaya motioned to the man and woman still seated beside us.

"Rae, this is Jeremiah and Victoria Hadleigh." They were obviously twins. Light-brown hair, dark-blue eyes, pale skin, and freckled noses. They looked like they would have been the popular ones in high school. Victoria's hair was perfectly straight, her black nails long and coffin-shaped, her lips glossed pale nude. Her brother seemed like a jock: muscular, tall, square-jawed, with a cocky smile that managed not to come off as annoying.

"Their dad pretty much owns the school, so if you have any complaints, just go straight to them," Inaya said, which got a groan out of Victoria, and a shake of the head from Jeremiah.

"No, no, no," Jeremiah said. "We don't *own* the school."

"Technically, Dad only owns three buildings," Victoria said, taking a drag from a slim silver vape she pulled from within her black raincoat. "And the only building that really matters is Hadleigh Library." She motioned behind her, toward the large structure that occupied the entire east side of the quad. She gave me a wink. "If you have any book requests, you can totally bring that to us."

"That's awesome, thank you!" I made a mental note of that, as having a library's worth of knowledge at my fingertips was extremely helpful for investigations. Not everything could be found on the internet, especially when it came to particularly old or rare texts. The library was lined with trees, and a massive arch of stained-glass windows crowned its entrance. "It's gorgeous."

"Thanks." Victoria shrugged, as if having your father's library complimented was something she heard every day. "But enough about *us*. What about you, Miss California? What's your sign, what do you like, what do you do?"

"Oh, uh, Sagittarius," I cleared my throat, fiddling with the knot in my bag's strap. "I'm a Radio-TV-Film major, I like photography, uh . . ."

"Film, huh?" said Jeremiah. "Need any actors for upcoming projects?"

I laughed nervously, but Inaya spared me from answering as she said, "Tell them about your YouTube channel! Your investigations!"

"Investigations?" Victoria rested her chin on her palm. "Are you, like, a detective?"

I smiled tightly, bracing for the incoming weird looks. "Well, kind of. I do vlogs, talk about local legends, creepy stories . . . I do paranormal investigations."

"She's a ghost hunter," Inaya said.

I was relieved to see both Jeremiah and Victoria look intrigued, instead of repulsed. "Oh, yeah?" Jeremiah leaned forward on the bench. "Have you caught stuff on camera? Ghosts?"

"I mean, I've caught some weird voices. Orbs, shadows." I shrugged and plopped down on the bench beside Inaya. "I'm still hoping for that big sighting: a full-body apparition, or, shit, I'd take some vaguely human-shaped mist."

"Well, you've come to the right place for spooky shit." Victoria narrowed her eyes as she looked at me, her nails tapping on her vape. "You were born around here, right? Like, your family is from here?"

I nodded. "Yep. My dad's side, the Lawsons. They'd lived here for, hell, probably a century."

"Just like our family." Victoria smiled, but the expression seemed a little too *tight* to be real. Weird. "Then you probably already have an idea of just how *interesting* this place can be. Ghosts, poltergeists, demons, cryptids"— she glanced to the side, behind me, toward Calgary Hall—"even murders now, apparently."

The five of us glanced back. Calgary Hall would have looked so normal if it wasn't for all that caution tape, and the painfully hot asshole standing guard in front of it. I hurriedly turned back around.

"Rumor is they're just keeping the building closed because they can't get all the bloodstains out of the stone," Victoria said. "Some freshmen found the body and called the cops. He was a sophomore—"

"Junior," Jeremiah corrected. "Marcus was a junior."

"Okay, yeah, junior, whatever," Victoria waved him off. "A guy named Marcus Kynes. He was stabbed eight times—"

"Nine times," Jeremiah interjected.

"Ugh, God, Jerry, would you let me say it? He was stabbed *nine* times. There was blood everywhere, the kid's body was just *destroyed*. Someone even got a video."

"Of the murder?" I gasped.

"Oh, no. No one knows who did it . . . or at least, they're not giving names yet." She smirked. "No, they got a video of the body when it was found, before the cops showed up. It was so gross."

"I have it saved on my phone if you want to see it," said Jeremiah, pulling out the device. "It's crazy how much blood there is in people."

"Oh my God, you guys, don't be so disgusting!" said Inaya, shoving Jeremiah's phone away as he leaned forward to show me. "Too soon, okay, way too soon. The poor kid is barely in the ground."

Jeremiah sat back, staring at his phone in such a way that my morbid curiosity only increased. "He must've really pissed someone off," he muttered. "Right in the middle of the hall."

I dared another glance back. Right there in that unassuming old building, someone's life had come to its brutal end. Why? What could spur such a rage to stab a person *nine* times?

I frowned. The security guard, Leon, was still standing at the foot of the building's steps, and I noticed the students walking past gave him a wide berth. Even from all the way across the quad, as I pushed my glasses up my nose, I could have sworn he was looking at me. At that distance, his pale-green eyes caught the light peeking through the clouds and flashed, like gold leaf caught in the sun.

In French, there's a phrase for the random urge to jump from high places, the irrational desire to swerve into traffic despite imminent destruction: *l'appel du vide,* the call of the void. Those sudden feral impulses tend to be shoved away immediately, but humans still experience them. *What if you jumped? What if you touched the fire? What if? What if?*

When I looked at him, staring at me, the void called. What if?

"Oh, shit. I gotta get to class." Inaya jumped up, staring at the time on her phone. She gave me a quick hug, and Trent helped her gather her things before he took her hand to walk her to class. "I'll see you guys later! Rae, text me, we gotta do something fun soon."

"Investigation!" I called after her. "We need to go somewhere haunted; I need content!"

"Rae, what's your number?" Victoria pulled out her phone, the sparkling blue case sporting a dangling silver crown charm. "That way I can give you a heads-up if there's anything fun going on." She gave me a sweet smile. "I know it can be intimidating making new friends."

I gave her my number, glad to see her so willing to be friendly. Out of the corner of my eye as I rattled off my digits, I noticed Jeremiah typing at the same time on his phone. I could have been wrong, but it seemed like he took my number too.

When I turned to head for my next class, my eyes swept along the sidewalk in front of Calgary Hall, but this time, Leon was gone.

5

LEON

THERE WAS ONLY so long I could jack off in that vile concrete room before I began to feel more than a little feral. Demons have needs: the drive to hunt pleasure, to seek stimulation, is as necessary as food and water to a human. So as much as I hated the man, when Kent told me I was to guard the university campus when the semester started, I could have kissed his goddamn boots.

Could have. I didn't. But it had been far too many years since I'd felt so free.

Kent's sacrifice hadn't just stirred his God. It had awakened the Eld, the ancient beasts of the forest who were sustained only by blood, magic, and pain. The God's awakening was making them restless, and soon enough they would begin to creep from the darkest depths of the forest to hunt.

Kent didn't need panic sweeping through Abelaum. It was my duty to keep the Eld away from the students, away from town. I was to dispose of the beasts when I found them, which wasn't an easy task, but it wasn't as if I could refuse Kent's orders. I'd gladly kill any Eld I laid eyes on if it meant having their hunting grounds for myself.

The Eld would consume the flesh of humans if they could, but I would consume them in another way. Through pleasure, pain, and blood. Corruption. Temptation. Utterly perverse intoxication. Humans were the most pitifully willing prey. Too many of them lived such constrained lives, binding themselves to moralities that only served to limit their enjoyment of their short mortal existence.

Offer one an easy path to perversion, tempt them with pleasure's darkest desires, and they made for easy prey. A feast of curious college students had been put before me, and I intended to eat well.

They were all wary, at first. Primal instinct told them what their eyes did not: I was dangerous. A predator. They kept their distance from me even when they couldn't keep their eyes from roaming over me. It meant that the steps up to Calgary Hall's closed doors, where I had set up my primary post to watch everyone milling across the quad, remained vacant.

Until *she* skipped up the steps without a care in the world, wide-eyed, vibrating with energy, smelling of sage and mint and warm skin.

She didn't even glance in my direction, as if whatever primal instinct that drove her fellow students was utterly vacant from her, the feral guardian for self-preservation shrugging its shoulders and letting the little thing run wild. She *was* little—in stature but not in energy. She had a large camera held close beneath her chin, as if she was ready to lift it to her eye at any moment. Her black denim jacket looked too large, as did the leather boots on her feet and the stuffed book bag she carried. She wasn't tall enough to reach my shoulder, but beneath her oversized jacket I spotted the pleasing curve of her breasts, her hips, thighs that begged to be gripped and left bruised.

Heat flushed through me. If I wasn't careful, if I let myself give in too quickly to that *need* to hunt, to pursue, to tempt, my human disguise would slip and these poor mortals wouldn't just be giving me space—they'd be running, screaming.

But I wasn't about to let her simply walk away.

"Are you fucking lost?"

She turned slowly, wide brown eyes now narrowed, to look me over skeptically from behind thick-rimmed glasses. Her eyes lingered, her body's sudden flood of nervous hormones turning the air pungently sweet.

Perfect.

"Not lost. It's hard to miss the bright yellow tape pasted across the scene of a murder."

She'd tried to sound bothered, but her tone shot up in pitch and betrayed her lie. She was nervous, intrigued. Just frightened enough to be wary. The bitchy smile she plastered on those black-painted lips was yet another falsehood.

I rather liked liars. It meant they were afraid of telling the truth, and I loved making humans face their fears.

I smiled back, and it seemed to awaken that sleepy primal guardian of hers. Instinct finally kicked a bit more fear into her as she caught a glimpse of my teeth. She probably saw them a bit sharper than she should have, but I was excited, and maintaining a "normal" human appearance was difficult.

"Oh, *good*, you didn't miss the tape. Then I'll take it that you just can't *read*, since you decided to hang around."

Would she push back, despite that instinct to flee? There was something vicious in her stance, like a cornered cat prepared to fight. She was sizing me up, her eyes moving slowly over me. A bitchy attitude couldn't mask fear, and it couldn't mask desire. Her voice grew sharper, just a little bit more desperate. "I'm pretty sure the tape says *Caution*, not *Stay Back Twenty Feet*. I don't see a sign telling me to stay away."

There was a spark of hellfire in her. Bratty. Brave. Oh, I *liked* that.

Have you ever wondered why humans buy their dogs toys that squeak? It's because the squeak mimics the sound of an animal fighting for its life, and the dog gets excited.

Sometimes those squeaky, desperate sounds of struggle just make a predator want to bite even more.

Her face fell as I climbed the steps toward her. She folded her arms and shuffled her feet into a wider stance as I stood over her and leaned down. We demons couldn't control the minds of humans, but we could *nudge* them. We could implant influences to stir feelings or sensations. Easy enough to ignore if a human tried, but not when they were so distracted as she was.

Her eyes kept wandering, naughty little thing. I nudged her mind just enough to let her imagine a subtle squeeze around her neck.

"What's your name?"

She was fidgeting now. Nervous, aroused, confused. If I'd touched her, she might have combusted, and that was exactly how I wanted it. The pursuit was no fun if the victim wasn't willing, and the longer she lingered in the tease of it, the temptation, the more curious she'd be.

"Alex."

Liar.

"No. It's not." A little bit more of a squeeze, a little more of a nudge. I did love making brats quiver—certain former lovers would attest that it was because I was a brat myself, but those former lovers would be *wrong*. I only gave her mind a push, and her imagination did the rest. Confusion flickered across her face, and she gulped. A curious mind would begin to wander in the direction of dark lusts, the sins they'd tried to hide. What were hers?

"It's Raelynn," she said, and this time, she wasn't lying. "If you're going to be such a dick about it, I'll just leave then."

Raelynn. It suited her, felt right for her. Satisfied, I widened the gap between us and stepped aside, giving her an easy escape. She hurried down the steps, body tight and tense, her scent wafting over me again.

"Watch where you wander, girl," I said. "Curiosity can get you in trouble."

Her shoulders tensed even more. She flipped her short hair over her shoulder, stomping her boots across the grass as if I'd just *ruined* her morning.

Brats need to learn their lessons somehow, don't they?

I didn't push her. I just nudged her mind in the direction it was apt to go anyway. Unfortunately for her, she was already rather clumsy.

Her feet tangled, and the jolt made the strap on her bag snap. Books tumbled across the grass and papers settled into lingering puddles, her coffee burst and sent its contents dribbling everywhere. I had to clench my jaw to hold back the laughter that wanted to come out. Posted up directly in front of the steps she'd just left, I folded my arms and watched her attempt to crouch down in her skirt, one hand awkwardly clutching the back of it to keep it down. Her head twitched back, curious eyes searching, and they met mine for only a brief moment before she looked away again.

She looked even cuter with her freckled cheeks reddened in embarrassment.

Her friend came to collect her, and they left together. I watched her walk across the quad, but my eyes narrowed as she reached her group and sat down. The Hadleighs— what in Lucifer's name was she doing with the Hadleighs? I'd never seen her with them before. Did she even have any idea who they were? What they were capable of?

It didn't matter. It shouldn't have mattered. She'd be my prey regardless. But the peculiar urge to warn her needled at the back of my mind. It was an urge I quickly shoved away. I hadn't earned a reputation as a guardian, I was known only for one thing among human kind.

I was a killer. A hunter. Not a protector. Not even for tiny mortal girls with no sense of self-preservation.

IT WAS EVENING when I found her again. I'd gotten away from the monotony of the quad for a while and walked through one of the far corners of the campus. Benches and tables were scattered under the trees, where students sat hunched over their laptops. I recognized her immediately, sitting cross-legged at a picnic table with her laptop open in front of her. There was now a massive knot in the strap of her book bag, and she had yet another coffee in her right hand. Did this girl run entirely on caffeine? No wonder her heart rate was so high.

Maybe I'd make it a little higher.

I lingered behind her, just out of her line of sight. Her internet browser was open to a webpage with the title *Mass Deaths, Madness, and Cryptids: Abelaum's Creepy History*. She rubbed her eyes before she went back to reading and highlighted a passage that she copied and pasted into another document.

Abelaum is host to a menagerie of haunted locales and historical monuments, it read. *One such place is St. Thaddeus Church, located one mile from the infamous White Pine mine shaft, where the survivors of the 1899 disaster were freed.*

What the hell was she looking into St. Thaddeus for? "History homework already?"

She jumped at the sound of my voice, and turned her head to look up at me. That nervous glance, the uptick in her heart rate, the rapid blink before she looked away—it was enough to make me suck in my breath and hold it in an effort not to move in any closer.

I'd been locked away *far* too long if a mere glance from a human was having me feel this way.

But I'd had plenty of glances. Plenty of longing looks. It was *her* gaze. Her scent. Tempting me. I wasn't usually the tempted one.

"How do you know it's for history?" she muttered. She turned the laptop slightly, as if to hide the screen from me, and her hand clenched on her lap. Maybe I'd get to see that little bit of hellfire come out in her again. Her hackles were already raised.

I shrugged, sauntering over to the table to lean against it, my shadow looming over her. Fuck, she smelled good. Warm blood, mint and sage, coffee, and something like granola. This girl was flat-out dangerous to be around. "Just a guess. Maybe you like researching condemned churches for fun."

She slammed her laptop shut. The glare she directed toward me brought a smile to my face. "Are you *fucking* lost?" she said, echoing my earlier words to her. So much sass in such a small body.

"Unfriendly little thing, aren't you?" I said. "I patrol the whole campus, doll. It's my job to check secluded corners."

"Okay, well, patrol *away*. That way, preferably." She made a show of pulling out her phone and turning her back to me, but she was just idly scrolling through text messages. As if she could dismiss me that easily. It was too fun to watch her squirm to leave now.

But besides the fun of it, unease had grown in me to see her looking into that damned church. She was already spending time with the Hadleighs, which was bad enough, but something told me this woman didn't have the slightest clue what she was meddling with.

"You're not from here, are you?" Even if they didn't know the true nature of it, locals would steer clear of St. Thaddeus and White Pine. Too many legends. Too many stories.

"Why do you say that?" she said suspiciously, slowly turning back to me. At least she was wary. She needed to turn that wariness on her little friend group.

I shrugged, and tucked my hands into the pockets of my pants. "Oh, I don't know. You smell different."

"I *smell* different? What does Southern California smell like, hmm? Brush fires and avocado toast?" She ended her outburst with a wince, as if she regretted giving that little bit of information away. Flustered, she shoved her laptop into her bag and got up, keeping her back turned to me. Her skirt brushed against her thighs and her movement flooded me not just with another whiff of her shampoo, but a faint and far more primal scent.

I grinned wider. Stubborn little thing, resisting her own arousal. That was why she was trying so hard not to look at me. She stalked off, bag slung hurriedly over her shoulder, boots stomping. I lingered near the table, but called, "I can't say St. Thaddeus makes for a good tourist attraction. I'd stay away from the church, if I were you."

That made her stop. She whirled back around, snapping, "Oh, I'm sorry, I thought you were the *campus* guard. Are you the church guard too?"

Goddamn, every time she snapped it had my mind spiraling into all the ways I could turn those snippy words into moans. I should have been more focused on that, rather than whatever white-knight crusade had me saying bullshit like, "It's a dangerous place. Condemned, locked. Any local would know better than to visit there."

Something about this unassuming new girl casually involving herself with the most dangerous parts of Abelaum just didn't sit right with me. Victoria and Jeremiah were popular, certainly, but they rarely showed anyone special attention.

What did they want with this girl?

She was nodding, slowly. Her anger had moved into confusion, but there was a curious gleam in her eyes. "Thanks for the warning. I'll keep that in mind." She kicked at a pebble on the sidewalk, and added casually, "What else do you know about the church? What have you heard about it? Have you been there?"

"I've heard it's old, dirty, and not worth seeing." *And haunted by damned souls fed to a wicked God.* But that was the last thing a curious woman like her needed to hear.

"But what about the stories?" she pried, betraying her enthusiasm. "About the miners and—Hey! Where are you going?"

I'd lingered there with her long enough, and I didn't like the impulsive feelings that were poking against my ribs like sharp accusing fingers. I wanted her away from that church. I wanted her away from the Hadleighs. She was too ignorant, too curious for her own good.

But goddammit, that was *not* my responsibility.

"I've got a job to do, doll." I gave her a little wave over my shoulder. Her boots stomped again, this time to rush after me and pop up at my side like an eager puppy. I fully halted in surprise, staring down at her. She'd pulled out her phone, and seemed to be recording.

"Look, maybe I could just get a quick statement from you about the church. A spooky story you've heard, something!" she spoke rapidly, leaving her out of breath. Fucking hell, she was one of *those*: a social media attention chaser who wanted everything posted, everything live. Now I *knew* she'd be trouble.

I snorted, sidestepping her to continue on my way. "I'm not interested in being in your little documentary, or whatever it is you're doing. Stay away from St. Thaddeus."

"Oh, come *on*." Her tone changed. She'd lightened it—she was attempting to sweet-talk me. "It'll sound more authentic coming from a local. You seem like the kind of guy who would have some great stories."

It took no small amount of self-control not to grin. I had to hand it to her, she was determined. "Is that so? What kinds of stories do you think I have?" I stepped closer, and this time I couldn't hold back the smile as her heart rate quickened. "Do you think I'll tell stories of monsters in the woods? Mad old men who think they're going to resurrect God? Ghosts of the long-dead and endlessly tormented?"

She was hanging onto my every word, eyes wide, sweet lips just slightly parted.

"Well, doll, I'm sorry to disappoint you," I said softly. "But the only good story I have about that old church is about the last couple I took there."

She blinked rapidly. "About . . . what?"

"If you've never been fucked bent over a pulpit with one man in your ass and another in your mouth, I'm sure the woman would highly recommend it. But if you'd like, I can tell you the story myself in graphic detail."

She blinked rapidly, her brain practically steaming as she processed how to react. Hot and bothered as hell, poor perverted little thing.

"Is that so?" she said softly, and I was ready to see her erupt. Instead, she smiled smugly, and said, "Do tell. Sounds like a fascinating story."

I shook my head. Goddamn, the things I wanted to do to her were obscene. I stepped a little closer, challenging my own self-control as I leaned down and whispered roughly, "I don't tell stories for free, doll."

Her face twitched, jaw clenched. "Yeah? What's your price?"

I grinned. "You, on your knees, begging for my cock down your throat."

There was a brief moment of hesitation before disgust contorted her face, and in that moment, I glimpsed all I needed to. Despite the fact that she shoved away her phone and glared at me with a scoff, I could smell her arousal. "Fuck off. Perv."

"Aww, what, I thought you wanted to hear the story?"

She turned and stomped away, skirt swaying. But the desire was there. The *need*. She didn't have to like me to want me. Hate sex was more fun anyway. The more these poor little humans despised you, the more they hated their desire for you, the more they would break when they finally gave in.

"Hey, asshole, I'm not a tourist either!" she turned back and yelled at me, fists clenched at her sides. "I was born here!"

She left, satisfied with having had the last word. Born here . . . interesting. That was very interesting. She had a greater connection to this damned little town than I'd thought. It didn't make any real difference to me, but again, I was curious why the Hadleigh brats had an interest in her.

Maybe she'd stay away from St. Thaddeus—not that I cared. I shouldn't have even bothered to warn her. If she ended up running headfirst into trouble, that wasn't my business. Humans were only to be played with and nothing more.

6

RAE

STEAM FILLED THE bathroom, the glass shower doors streaked with water droplets streaming through the condensation. I let the water cascade over my face and through my hair, trying to wash away my tense arousal.

It wasn't working.

The walk home from campus after class, in the dark, hadn't been as easy as the morning walk there. The rain had stopped, and the clouds had cleared just enough to let through a little moonlight, but the darkness of the forest at night was impenetrable. The road that took me home was narrow and quiet. I'd kept waiting for a car to go past, hoping for the comforting glow of headlights.

None came.

I'd walked alone, telling myself to remain calm despite the growing sensation of eyes watching the back of my head and the occasional snap of a twig from within the trees. I wasn't one to scare easily, but when the darkness was that deep it was difficult not to feel uneasy.

But by the time I got home, shed my clothes, and climbed into the hot shower, my thoughts had already turned back to Leon. That cocky, perverted asshole.

I'd wanted to slap him for daring to say that shit to me. Then he'd had to go and put those thoughts in my head of getting on my knees for him. Ugh, what an absolute dick. It made me so mad.

And it turned me on.

I squeezed my eyes shut tight, but the darkness of my own mind was not a safe place from these thoughts. Leon was exactly my type, at least from the shallow first-impression side of things. Sarcastic, quick to bite back, with a sardonic smile that made my stomach quiver. I felt like I was in high school again, fawning over some unattainable rock star. I'd glimpsed the colorful lines of tattoos beneath his shirt collar, and he had multiple piercings in the cartilage of his ears and stretched lobes. He gave off a rebellious vibe, maybe even a little artistic.

I sighed, and mentally scolded myself for romanticizing the douchebag's looks. He was absurdly attractive, so what?

If you've never been fucked bent over a pulpit with one man in your ass and another in your mouth . . .

I took a slow breath. I shouldn't have been thinking about him that way, not when I had to see him every day on campus, not when I'd promised myself that I was going to stay away from jumping into bed with assholes after what happened with Rachel.

But it was just a fantasy, and that cold, creepy walk home had me needing a little comfort.

I could imagine his hand stroking up my back, fingers tracing along my spine to the base of my neck and gripping me there. Gripping me like a little doll to be used and maneuvered. *Doll.* He'd seemed to like calling me that.

I swallowed hard, my mouth dry. I couldn't deny that my desires ran on the dark and kinky side.

I sighed, a little whimper coming out with it as I wrapped my hands around my body and my fingers stroked over my hips. In the darkness behind my closed eyes, it was *his* fingers tracing over me.

Something about him wasn't safe; I couldn't put my finger on it, but he set off alarm bells in my brain that told me to run. A rabbit knew instinctively to flee from a wolf. So why, instead of fleeing, was I fantasizing about being caught?

I caressed my fingers down, moving slowly and softly around my navel before I stroked over my abdomen and between my legs. The hot water and my gentle touches sent a shiver up my back, and my arousal swelled. My inner thighs were sensitive, even to my own hands. I leaned against the shower wall, the steam rising around me, and my finger slipped between my labia to stroke over my clit.

My breath caught in my throat. I stroked myself again, merciless to the shuddering it produced in my legs. I'd been rude to him, I knew I had. He easily could have responded to that rudeness by putting me in my place.

I let the fantasy spiral as my fingers continued to play between my legs and my other hand caressed over my throat. I imagined Leon gripping me there, just tight enough to stifle my air, holding me still and helpless as he scolded me.

I used to feel so guilty for fantasizing about being taken advantage of, as if that horrifying reality was something I would ever *actually* want outside the safety of my mind or a consensual role play. But I'd panic-read enough about the psychology of it that it no longer made me feel like a perverted hypocrite. There was something thrilling and cathartic in imagining being helpless. Helpless but pleasured. Helpless but desired.

It wasn't just in horror films and haunted places that I indulged my love for dark things. My fantasies, the ones that made my breath hitch and my heart beat faster, were inky black as well.

"Did you really think I'd let you get away with speaking to me that way?" I imagined his eyes burning into me: bright and vicious, eager once he had me in his hands. *"You should have tried to be a little more respectful."*

My knees weakened as my fingers massaged roughly over my clit, my dripping arousal making me slick. I imagined Leon standing over me, I imagined him laughing at my half-hearted struggles as he pinned me down, and yanked my pants down to my ankles.

"Curiosity will get you in trouble," he snarled. Curiosity . . . yeah, he'd warned me about that. I could hear his scolding voice as surely as if he was there, hot in my ear. *"Just look where it's gotten you. This is what happens to perverted girls who don't want to listen."*

I sunk down to the shower floor, laying back and

letting the water flow over me. I felt pathetically desperate, but I *needed* this.

"Say you're sorry, little Raelynn."

I groaned, arching back, my fingers pressing inside and stroking over my clit as I fingered myself. I could imagine his chuckle, the curve of his cruel smile. I thought of the way his lean muscles had tensed beneath his shirt as I'd snapped back at him. I imagined them tightening in the same way as he bent me over, whispering in my ear, *"I think the belt is what's needed to teach you a lesson. Sometimes little brats just need to be whipped until they cry, don't they?"* I shuddered all over, torn between holding my breath and gasping desperately. *"You should have thought of this before you were bad. Now, apologize, and maybe I'll make you feel good after I—"*

My orgasm gripped me, tensing every muscle until I shook and cried out, mouth agape. The fantasy was too much, it was wrong, it was dangerous. It was twisted to feel such a desire for a stranger to punish me, but I couldn't deny the pleasure. My fingers curled back, unable to bear touching my sensitive clit for even another second.

As the waves of ecstasy receded, I lay there dazed and trembling with the water flowing over me. I got up slowly and leaned against the shower wall, staring at the water as it swirled down the drain. It was raining again, pattering against the fogged-up window above the shower.

I'd really screwed myself now. How the hell was I supposed to see that asshole on campus and not think of this?

RAE

Hey giiiirl, the Main Street Art Fest starts tonight!
Come with??? We're gonna have beers and gan-
jaaaaa!

The text was followed up by a string of wink-face,
leaf, and smoke emojis. It took me a beat to realize the
text was from Victoria; I'd forgotten to save her contact
in my phone. Curled up on the couch with my morning
coffee, I quickly texted her back.

For sure! I'll be there!

It was a relief to already have a new friend willing to
invite me out. Having Inaya had made the entire move

easier, but if I was going to settle down here and get a long-term job, I needed more than just one friend, and Victoria had been nothing but sweet to me so far. I'd worried at first that she wouldn't be, considering she had that Hot-Girl-Instagram-Influencer thing going on. It had only taken years of having people judge me by my appearance to finally start getting it through my head that I shouldn't judge other people by theirs.

An art festival sounded like a danger to my wallet, but I wasn't about to miss it. I could walk to Main Street easily; it was only a little further from home than the university, just in the opposite direction.

I arrived in the late afternoon, bundled up in a cozy jacket, beanie, and comfortable sneakers. Main Street wound between Abelaum's charming brick buildings, lined with cherry trees that shaded glass display windows for numerous cafes, bakeries, antique shops, and clothing boutiques. The street was bustling as Friday university classes ended and more students showed up to participate.

"Rae!" Inaya's voice cut through the crowd. Ahead, I could see her, Victoria, and Jeremiah crowded around the space reserved for the university's art students. Inaya was waving her arms excitedly, and I jogged over to join them.

As I got closer, I realized it wasn't just those three familiar faces watching me arrive. An older man, in his fifties, if I were to guess, watched me approach with the ghost of a smile on his face. He was gray-haired, dressed in a perfectly fitted suit. Something in his face, the set of his eyes, reminded me of Jeremiah.

"I'm so glad you came!" Inaya enfolded me in a hug. Victoria squeezed me after, and made sure to give me a glimpse into her oversized bag so I could see the little bottles of wine tucked within.

"Rae, this is our dad," Jeremiah said, motioning to the gray-haired man who was watching me with a smile. "Dad, Raelynn."

"Miss Raelynn!" Kent's smile was warm, as were his hands as he grasped my outstretched one. He was handsome, carrying a certain sophisticated charm about him. He *looked* like he'd head a historical society, like he was the type to enjoy studying ancient texts by flickering candlelight. "A pleasure to meet you, my dear. I hope you're feeling welcome in Abelaum so far?"

"Very." I smiled. "Victoria and Jeremiah have been wonderful. I'm glad to finally meet you. I've heard you practically own the town, Mr. Hadleigh."

Kent waved his hand dismissively. "Oh, ridiculous! Abelaum is home, full of family and friends. Whatever it needs from me, I'll gladly give. And if you need anything, Miss Raelynn, just let me know . . . and please, you can call me Kent." He paused a moment, as if something had crossed his mind that he wasn't sure he wanted to give voice to. Then he said, "You know, I went to school with your father. High school, and then university. Richard, isn't that right? Richard Lawson?"

I nodded. "Yeah, my dad grew up here. How did you know I'm a Lawson? Family resemblance that strong, huh?"

He chuckled and gave me a wink. "A lucky guess. The

Lawsons lived in Abelaum a long time. It's nice to have one of you back again. Anyway, don't let an old man's rambling keep you. Enjoy yourself! Have a look around."

Victoria seized onto my arm the moment her father's attention dwindled, and with me on one side and Inaya on the other, we wound between the tables to explore. She popped out little pink bottles of rosé, poured them into three empty water bottles and passed them around so we could enjoy the sparkling alcohol as we walked.

"Should we wait for Jeremiah?" I said, noticing he hadn't followed. Victoria just shook her head with a little roll of her eyes.

"He's playing Daddy's Favorite today," she said, and stuck out her tongue in a mock gag. "He always gets all high and mighty about drinking every time a new semester starts, and he's under the soccer coach's eye all the time. Suddenly, he's *devoted* to health and wellness."

We wandered and sipped, until I got distracted with a table of hand-painted tarot decks and couldn't resist stopping. The pretty girl sitting behind the table had long blonde hair, and wore a lacey black dress that reached over her boots. Her pointy, green-colored acrylics were spread over the cover of the book she was reading, a worn-out paperback with a lady swooning in the arms of a shirtless man on the cover.

"Did you paint all these yourself?" I said, looking in awe at the attention to detail on each card in the sample deck. She nodded with a small smile, but before she could respond, Victoria interjected.

"She paints every single one. It's why she's locked in

her room all the time." Victoria sighed heavily, half-sitting on the table. The blonde girl's mouth shut, her smile fading slowly as she put down her book. Victoria went on, "Everly, this Raelynn. Raelynn Lawson."

Everly's bright blue eyes widened slightly. For a moment, she looked at me as if she knew me, as if she was excited, as if—then it was gone. Nothing but a calm, gentle smile remained. "Nice to meet you, Raelynn."

"It's nice to meet you t—"

"You should pull some cards for her, Ev," Victoria said, tossing the sample deck toward her. I glanced over at Inaya, to see if she was getting as peeved about Victoria's suddenly bitchy attitude as I was, but she just shook her head and mouthed, *I'll tell you later.*

Everly didn't look thrilled, but she began to slowly shuffle through the deck. I chewed at my lip, torn between wanting to move on and break whatever tension lay between Everly and Victoria, and staying so as not to be rude. But as I wavered, Everly smiled again and said in her soft voice, "Come a little closer, Raelynn."

I stepped up in front of her. She looked at me as she shuffled the cards, but her eyes were distant. She suddenly didn't look so young anymore. "It's Rae," I said, then quickly clarified, "I mean, my friends call me Rae. You can call me Rae."

"Rae." Her lips curled around my name, like it was something sweet she wanted to eat. "I like that. Somewhere between masculine and feminine." She set her cards face down on the table, took a deep breath, and pulled the first card.

It depicted a stone tower standing tall among a forest, flames licking from its upper window as storm clouds gathered around it. Everly set the card down carefully and paused.

"Change," she said softly. "The life you knew, your strong tower, has been dramatically changed. It is no more." Her lips parted again, only to close without a sound. Whatever she was going to say next, she'd changed her mind.

Well, that felt far more ominous than it should have. I smiled, glancing with a little uncertainty at Victoria, who just shrugged her shoulders and took a long gulp from her "water" bottle.

Everly lay down the next card. It depicted a man lying face down in the snow, his arm outstretched as if he'd been reaching for something. Numerous swords were pierced through his back, pinning him to the ground, blood staining the snow.

Everly said nothing. She wasn't looking at me anymore, but her eyes kept flickering to the side as if she was looking for someone. She pulled the last card, turned it to set it down—

"Excuse me." A woman had sidled up behind me, and I jumped at the sound of her voice. "How much do these cost?"

Everly snatched up the cards, smiling brightly as she answered the woman. Victoria hopped down from the table with another sigh.

"Let's find a bar," she said, finishing off the last of her rosé. "I'm starving."

She led the way as Inaya put her arm around my shoulders and leaned close to whisper in my ear, "Everly is Victoria's half-sister. Kent had an affair right before Victoria and Jeremiah were conceived. They're only a few months apart."

My eyes widened, and I had to resist the urge to glance back. Everly definitely hadn't inherited the Hadleigh family resemblance, but I could at least understand Victoria's derision for her a little better, not that the situation was in any way Everly's fault. Victoria had pulled further ahead, and seemed to have found a bar that was to her liking as she called back to us to hurry up.

But my mind was still on the cards. I didn't know much about tarot, but I think the last card I'd got a glimpse of would have been fairly obvious to anyone: a skeleton in a black cloak, carrying a large scythe as it rode a white horse across a barren field.

Death.

THE BAR WAS bustling with people, but we managed to get a table near the back. Victoria ordered a round of beer and appetizers, insisting she was going to pay for everything. I suddenly got the feeling she had started drinking long before I met up with her that day.

She'd evidently extended an invitation to other friends too, because we'd only been there a few minutes when another group turned up: two women with their boyfriends, and two men who Victoria knew from one of her classes. She quickly clung onto one of them, and before long she was seated on his lap, another round of beers was ordered, and the conversation had grown to such a volume that no one could really tell what was being said, but none of us cared anyway. The bar was filling up, and I was feeling pretty good with two beers warming me and the high energy surrounding me.

I wasn't sure when *he* showed up. Maybe he'd been there the whole time and I just hadn't noticed, but I doubted I could have overlooked him. I glanced across the table, laughing at something Inaya had said, and Leon's gaze slammed into me, sharp and burning, those pale-green eyes holding me captive for only the briefest of moments before snapping away.

Leon was seated in the corner, his back to the wall, leaning back on his barstool with his arms folded and a grin on his face. His arms were bare tonight, allowing me to take a good look at his tattoos. Colorful swaths of ink, like the ceiling of the Sistine Chapel, marked him from his wrists to his shoulders. He wore tight black jeans, Converse, and red T-shirt with jagged lettering emblazoned across the front. He wasn't sitting alone. I could only see his companion's profile, but where Leon's tattoos were bright, the other guy's were dark, shadows and deep details inked across his biceps. Snakebites pierced his lower lip, and a black barbell was studded through his eyebrow above honey-brown eyes.

I considered it an unspoken rule of the universe that more than one absurdly hot person couldn't exist in the same place at the same time, especially not in such close proximity to each other, and to *me*. But these two—muscular, grinning, dark enough to straddle the fine line between intriguing and terrifying—were not only sitting directly within my line of sight, but they kept looking at me.

Leon was really staring, but his companion was stealing glances too, turning just enough to look at me over his shoulder before turning his attention away again. A blush was rising on my face, and for what? Just because they were looking at me? Or because I'd gotten off to the thought of Leon doing awful things to me, and now I had to sit here with his eyes on me and those thoughts prodding at my brain again?

I tried to ignore them. Leon's gaze was hot on my skin, as palpable as fingers stroking my flesh. My foot began to tap against the rung of my barstool, and the mozzarella sticks were suddenly too cloying in my mouth.

I didn't want food. I didn't want more beer. I wanted to satisfy this insatiable curiosity that kept dragging my eyes back to that evil smirking dude in the corner.

Leon and the other man were conversing, and it wasn't easy, but I tried to focus on the noise from their corner instead of the noise surrounding me. There was a brief moment of quiet as Victoria got up to use the bathroom and one of the couples made their way to the bar to order a cocktail. Only then was I able to catch a few brief moments of what they were saying.

". . . finally let me out. Fuck, if that's all he needs me to do, what's a little . . ."

I would have been able to understand more if I had dared to watch Leon's lips move. But I knew that if I raised my eyes in his direction, I'd find him staring back.

"... about you? Hunting again?"

Now, his companion spoke. The man's voice was deep, the kind of voice that balanced firmly on the edge of sarcasm, as if he'd laugh at any moment. "Yeah. I'm getting close ... be fun ... if she doesn't kill me first ..."

I was distracted as Inaya got up to leave and hugged me good-bye. By the time I sat down again, the corner table was empty, and Leon and his friend walked past our table.

His eyes met mine: a challenge, an invitation. There was a pre-roll clutched between his fingers, and his friend had an arm slung over his shoulders. Through the bar's window, I watched the two of them round the corner of the building, likely going to smoke in the alleyway alongside it.

I wasn't the only one who'd watched them pass. Victoria had glared at them the whole way out, and with them gone, our gazes locked with each other instead.

She smirked. "He's hot, right?"

Her boy toy of the night didn't look pleased with her statement, but I couldn't disagree. "Yeah, and a dick."

She shrugged. "Pretty things don't need to be likeable, do they?"

My foot kept tapping against the stool. I slipped my hand into the pocket of my jacket to grip my vape. "I'll be right back." I got up from the table. "Gonna go smoke real quick."

8

RAE

OUTSIDE, THE AIR was crisply cold, my breath forming clouds of condensation as I exhaled. The music from the bar was muted, and the scent of weed was sour and sharp on the breeze. I stood near the corner of the building, the silhouettes of Leon and his friend dark in my peripheral vision down the alleyway. I took a drag on my vape, and the scent of strawberry cream mingled with the odor of weed.

From behind me, the low murmur of the men's voices sent a little chill up my spine. Then Leon's voice called, "Are you just going to stand there and hope we bother you, Raelynn? Or are you going to come get what you want?"

I whirled around, my free hand shoved in my pocket so they wouldn't see my fingers clench. Leon leaned against the side of the building, passing the joint to his friend, who smirked at me before he took a drag. I didn't appreciate him reading into my actions like that.

I didn't appreciate him being right.

"What the hell is that supposed to mean?" I said. Leon shrugged.

"It'll be easier for you to eavesdrop on our conversation if you come closer," his friend said, exhaling smoke with his words.

If I'd actually thought they were a threat to me, I wouldn't have taken another step closer. But that was the weird thing. They should have been frightening, but instead, I felt this bizarre *trust*. This completely unfounded belief that they wouldn't lay a hand on me unless I wanted them to.

And fuck, I did want them to.

I walked closer, standing next to them in the alley's dim light. It was warmer down there—not only because of the building's closeness, but because the two of them emanated heat. It was weird, but it stopped my shivering. Leon nodded at his friend. "That's Zane."

Zane threw up a peace sign, joint at his lips. "Brothers?" I asked.

Leon chuckled dryly. "I don't think most people fuck their brothers."

"Some do," Zane said quickly. "Bros with benefits."

"It's frowned upon."

"As if you give a fuck what's frowned upon." Zane laughed and passed the joint back to him.

Neither of them looked high, and the joint was nearly gone. The only noticeable difference was that Leon's piercing gaze had slightly softened, making it almost bearable as he watched me take another drag from my vape.

"What is that shit?" he said.

"Strawberries and cream." I offered it up for a hit. He shook his head.

"Won't do anything for me."

Leon took a long drag on the joint, the ember at the tip flaring brightly with his inhale. He blew the smoke in my face: piney, sour-sweet. "Better than that sweet vapor, isn't it? That shit you tell yourself is enough . . ." He shook his head. "Just doesn't satisfy."

Zane leaned closer. "You need something harsher, with a little more bite." His teeth clipped together on the final word.

Ignoring Zane, I glared up at Leon's smug face. "You're a dick."

"Oh, Rae." He stepped closer, closing the already small gap between us. My choices were to take a step back—and press my ass up against Zane—or stand my ground. I didn't move, and Leon's hips brushed up against mine. Inches from my face, he took another drag, and the smoke coiled from his lips as he said, "You have no idea just how much of a dick I can be."

I gulped as the smoke caressed over my face. The touch of his body was hot, hard, and utterly tempting. Part of me wanted to grind up against him, really show him that I could be a tease right back. But another part of me wanted to slap him, leave him there in the alley without the satisfaction of knowing just how much he'd gotten in my head.

Without ever knowing how much he'd made me want him.

"Why did you come out here, Rae?" he said casually. But nothing could be casual when he was pressed that close.

"To smoke," I muttered.

"No, no, no. *Why* did you come out *here*?"

Zane was chuckling behind me. I wasn't about to lose my courage. "I was curious." Leon tweaked an eyebrow at me, expecting more, and I managed to get out, "About you. I was curious."

Leon nodded sagely, as if he'd just been told the secret to the universe and realized he'd known it all along.

"Curiosity is dangerous," Zane said softly. His voice was inches from my ear, enough to send a chill up my neck. "I've heard it kills pussies . . . Is that the phrase?"

"Close enough. Tell you what, sweetheart," Leon flicked what remained of the joint down and crushed it under his shoe. "I'll make this game a little easier for you, a little safer. Because I like this game. I like playing with you."

Zane put his arm casually around my shoulders, making me jump. "It's too dangerous to play with Leon without a safety net. I would know." He smirked as if the declaration was a badge of honor. Between the two of them, my mind was a flurry of uncertainty and my body was determined to further betray me with every passing second. There was something ungodly hot about feeling so small between them, skirting the edge of playfulness and danger.

I didn't know what game we were playing exactly. But I was ready.

"Yeah?" My voice squeaked. "How will you make it easier?"

Zane snickered. "Oh, so she *does* want to play!"

"Of course she does," Leon said, his voice smooth as honey. "I knew she'd be good sport."

Not *a* good sport. Sport. *I* was the game, the toy. My heart began to race, my insides tensing with arousal. Fuck, how could this feel so dangerous and yet so sexy?

My breath hitched as Leon's fingers grazed up my neck. I expected him to tip up my chin, but his fingers stopped where my heart beat pulsed, right beneath my jaw.

"Mercy," he whispered. He made that simple word sound beautiful, like poetry, like something tender. "That's all you have to say, and the game will stop immediately. Make sense?"

"You're giving me a safe word," I said softly. "Jesus Christ . . ."

"Christ isn't here." Zane's voice tickled against my ear, the snake's whisper to Eve. "Only the Devil, and he enjoys willing victims."

"Your heart is beating so fast," Leon said softly. "I think you're excited, Raelynn. Do you want to play? Or do you want to leave?"

Zane pulled his arm from my shoulders and stepped aside, bowing as if to permit me an exit from the alleyway. But I didn't move. Holy hell, I was *actually* considering this. My body craved Leon's touch, craved the dangerous game he promised. My fantasies were running wild. But there wasn't much time. The others would wonder where I was soon and start looking for me, if they weren't already.

But the simple, soft touch of Leon's fingers against my throat kept me hooked like a fish on a line.

"You'll stop if I say it?" My voice shook, but it wasn't in fear. I couldn't remember ever being this excited, or this painfully turned on.

"You have my word." Leon's voice was firm, so confident that it left no room for doubt. "And I know we're short on time. I know you have friends inside, good friends who will come looking for you if you're gone much longer. But I don't need long. I only need a few minutes."

"A few minutes for what?"

I could have sworn fire flashed in his eyes when he gave me a wide grin. "To make you come."

I blushed red from head to toe. Zane wagged a finger at me. "Tick-tock, girl. What'll it be?"

"Does it sound like fun?" Leon's eyes hadn't left my face. He was examining me, watching carefully, absorbing my reactions as he waited for my answer.

He wanted a willing victim, and I was goddamn *willing*.

"Yeah, that sounds fun." My voice didn't shake now. All my jitters were inside my stomach as I returned his cocky smile. "But we'll see if you can actually make good on only needing a few minutes."

His fingers, first so soft where they laid against my throat, tightened as he pressed me back to the wall. He was firm, controlled—it stopped my words and took my breath away as he stood over me, so close I could smell him. His scent was warm like a summer bonfire, crisp like cold lemonade. Citrus and smoke.

"Keep watch, Zane," he said, as his free hand caressed down my side. He brought his mouth close to my ear, as his fingers traced the edge of my jeans along my hip, and he whispered, "Making you come won't be a challenge, sweetheart. You're already turned on by your own imagination and the few words I've said to you. So consider what my fingers will do."

Those wicked fingers slipped under the waistline of my jeans. Oh my God, what was I doing? I was about to let a near-stranger finger-fuck me in an alleyway and all I could think was, *Yes, God, yes, please!* His fingers teased along my inner thigh, over my trembling flesh, sending goose bumps down my legs. My breath was shuddering, my hands pressed against the rough bricks behind me. His fingers reached my cotton panties and stroked along the edge.

"Remind me again, Raelynn," he growled, his nose pressed against the hollow behind my ear. His body was so close, melded against mine, hot and heavy. "Remind me again how badly you want me to make you come."

Fucking hell, I'd come from his words alone if he kept talking like that. My tongue seemed to have forgotten how to form words, and it took me a moment to compose myself enough to speak. One long, torturous moment, where his fingers kept teasing so close and his lips brushed against my ear.

"I want you to make me come," I whispered, for if I spoke too loudly it would come out as a moan.

Leon hummed appreciatively, and his fingers began to rub over my panties. "Put your arms around my neck. You're going to need to hold yourself up somehow."

I did as he said, wrapping my arms around his neck and clinging to him. It immediately made the moment feel more intimate, more desperate. I had to reach up to hold onto him, so it meant my face was buried between my arms and nestled close to his chest.

His fingers slipped into my panties. He rubbed over my clit, then over my folds, then he chuckled. "Oh, so wet for me. So soft." His fingers circled my clit, slick with my arousal, moving over the bud until my breath began to come in little gasps. Fuck, he was right—I was already so turned on, my body was *eager* to orgasm. He began to use two fingers to massage me, and a tremor went through my legs.

"Ah . . . Leon . . ." I began to pant, my forehead resting against his chest. From under my upstretched arm, I saw Zane watching us with a sardonically satisfied smile on his face. When our eyes met, he held a finger up to his lips. *Ssshh.*

Then Leon's fingers slipped inside me, and the ability to control my volume was utterly lost.

"Shh, shh, Raelynn," Leon chided me gently, his hand moving from my throat to cover my mouth instead. My moans were muffled against his palm as he cupped between my legs, his two fingers pumping into me as he used the heel of his hand to massage my clit. "Not too loud now. If someone comes along and sees us, I'll have to stop. And you don't want that now, do you?"

I shook my head, eyes fluttering with ecstasy. His fingers were so slick, pumping in and out of me as my pussy clenched greedily around him. My weight rested against him, my arms clinging tighter around him as the pleasure built and my legs began to shake too much to hold me up alone.

"Such a noisy little thing," Leon said. "I love how pretty you moan."

I was in an absolute daze of pleasure. Endorphins made my mind hazy. The maddest thoughts consumed me, thoughts of having his cock inside me, of tasting him, kissing him, and *weeping* from how good it felt. There was no other high in the world like those few precious swelling seconds right before tipping over into orgasm. My nails dug into his back and I cried out against his palm, my body coiled like a spring as every muscle tensed tighter and tighter until—

Release. Fuck. My head went light. I closed my eyes as I shook against him, his fingers pushing me through the waves of pleasure. I felt the briefest touch of his teeth against my neck, as if he wanted to bite, as if he was resisting the urge to hurt me, to consume me.

Leon withdrew his fingers, and I leaned back heavily against the wall in the afterglow. I had no words that would suffice for the rush of that experience: the frantic pleasure, the fear of being caught, the disbelief at what I was doing. Without my noticing, Leon had taken my vape from my pocket, and he held it up to my lips as he also held up his slick fingers to the streetlight's glow. They glistened as I took a slow, light-headed drag from the pen.

"Beautiful," he said softly. He put one finger into his mouth, and sucked it clean as I exhaled. The smoke swirled around his face as Zane came to his side.

"That was fucking gorgeous," he said, slinging an arm around Leon's shoulder and looking me hungrily up and down. Then Leon held up his middle finger, still glistening, and Zane took it slowly into his mouth, licking it clean.

Holy hell, I nearly orgasmed again from that alone.

"Always the middle finger," Zane muttered, straightening his jacket as he licked his lips.

"For you? Always." Leon stepped away, looking me over as I buttoned my jeans with clumsy fingers. He held out my vape. "Thanks for playing. See you on campus, doll." He gave me a two-finger salute, and he and Zane left the alley side by side, chuckling as they went.

LEON

DEMONS HAVE TWO names.

There is the name we are known by: I was Leon, it was how I introduced myself, the name by which I was called. But there was also the name by which I was summoned, a name that could only be written and never uttered. It was the name that commanded my very essence, a mark that was connected intimately to my being. My mark was written in the grimoire, and as such, whoever had that grimoire could summon me at will.

Being summoned felt like fishhooks wrenching my insides out through my navel. It demanded obedience. But merely having my name called by my summoner was only a nudge, a suggestion.

So when I first felt Kent Hadleigh call my name, I ignored it.

He hadn't bothered me since the night I took Marcus's

body up to White Pine, and I was on too much of a high to let him spoil it now. I had my new favorite prey in my sights: little Rae, defiant Rae, *curious* Rae. Fuck, the self-control I'd had to exercise to not make her *scream* in that alley was absolutely unholy. It was going to make me feral if I couldn't have her again. Have all of her. I wanted her blood, sweat, tears, cum. I wanted to taste it all.

Zane just laughed at me. He'd known me for centuries, seen me in my darkest days. He'd been a lover and a friend, when I didn't want to rip his head off. He called me out on my obsession immediately, as if he was one to talk. He hunted souls for fun, always eagerly pursuing the next prize. I'd watched him chase a human for decades just to get them to promise him their soul for eternity.

"No, no, you can't compare the two," he said. "I'm methodical. Concentrated. As for you, well—you fixate. Like a dog with a bone in front of it. I've seen the way your obsessions go, Leon. They don't end well for you."

Which was why I seldom had *obsessions*.

And I wasn't obsessed.

I was . . . interested.

And fucking hell, Kent Hadleigh kept *calling* me.

He'd been at it long enough now that it was a goddamn annoyance. He had to be furious that I wasn't coming, so why hadn't he summoned me? It was his usual method: pull out the grimoire, chalk my mark onto the ground with a few runes, and *demand* I come. I couldn't say no. The use of my mark left me no choice.

The fact that he was going about this so *gently* was odd. So odd it piqued my curiosity enough to obey, if only to see what the hell was going on.

Teleporting was tiring, so I didn't do it often, but I also didn't feel like running all the way to Kent. Light and shadow rushed around me as I dispersed my corporeal form, before assuming physical form again in the living room of the Hadleigh home. Perfectly white carpet, white couches, a shining metal chandelier overhead. The room's main wall was all glass, giving a view of the trees that covered the Hadleigh property's expanse. Everything was so clean and delicate, it just made me want to smash it.

Kent stood in front of me, hands behind his back, his suit looking a bit more wrinkled than usual. His protective iron amulet, carved into the shape of a sword crossed with a wand, wasn't hidden beneath his shirt today, as if he'd put it on hurriedly. The humans wouldn't notice it, but the damn thing made the air smell pungently metallic, so much so that it gave me a headache. His wife, Meredith, was seated on the couch behind him, and she went rigid as I appeared—at least, a little more rigid than her overly Botoxed face already was. Jeremiah was sunk into a chair nearby, his chin resting on his palm as he watched me, looking bored and a little annoyed. At the bar in the kitchen, Everly watched in silence, wringing her hands on her lap.

Something was strange, but I couldn't put my finger on *what* exactly.

"What took you so long?" Kent's voice was snappy, anxious. That was unusual for him indeed.

"Just doing my duty." I shrugged, cracking out the usual tension in my neck that resulted from going in and out of physical form. "Didn't want to leave the campus unprotected. Figured you could wait."

"Slaves don't tell their masters to wait," Jeremiah sneered. "Watch your mouth."

"Or what?" I growled, turning from facing his father to focus on him instead. He immediately straightened up, his jaw working nervously as I stepped closer. "What are you going to do, hm? You want to try me?" He shifted in his seat, his eyes darting back to his father. Typical. "That's better. At least you know when to shut your mouth. You should be scared, boy—"

"Kent, *control* him," Meredith hissed, and Kent cleared his throat.

"Leon, enough!"

I straightened slowly from leaning over a cringing Jeremiah. No pain. No punishment. Kent loved looking for any opportunity to torture me, and he'd just passed up an opportune moment. I looked him over, once more taking in the rumpled suit, the bags around his eyes, the way his hands—

His hands. Empty hands. No grimoire.

No grimoire?

No . . . no, that couldn't be. Kent never let that thing out of his sight.

"I have a job for you, demon. A soul meant for the Deep One has returned to Abelaum. The time has come for the next sacrifice."

I was distracted, trying to determine why the hell

Kent wouldn't have his grimoire with him. The special thing about a demon's second name, about their mark, was that it couldn't be recalled simply from memory, and it could only be permanently recorded in a few specific mediums: if scarred into flesh, or if written by a powerful witch. Without my mark, without the grimoire, Kent couldn't summon me and he couldn't contain me.

It seemed too good to be true.

"Do you want me to kidnap someone," I muttered, "Or do you just want me to babysit Jeremiah while he mangles another sacrifice?"

"Fuck you!" Jeremiah raised his voice, getting a worried glare from his mother. Kent's nostrils flared with the force of his exhale. He reached into his jacket and withdrew two photographs, holding them out for me to see. I got closer to have a look—and cold, clenching fury washed over me.

"Her name is Raelynn Lawson, but Victoria tells me you already know that, don't you?" Kent smirked. He was holding an enlarged student ID photo of her, as well as one of her sitting at a bench between Jeremiah and Victoria. "Bring her to us, and ensure no one sees you. Make sure you leave no signs of a struggle. You are to make it appear as if she left her house of her own accord, drove to the coast, and was in a wreck. Bring her to St. Thaddeus tonight, at midnight: alive, unharmed, and blindfolded."

I didn't take the photos. I simply stared at him. "No."

Kent laughed. "Have you lost your mind? Your summoner has *commanded* you—"

"Make me. Go on, Kenny-boy. *Make. Me.*"

In other circumstances, I knew what would happen. He'd whip open the grimoire, trace over my mark to lend him power over me, and utter some spell from within its pages to cause me pain. Break my bones, crush my lungs, give me the sensation of being burned alive—the punishment spells within that book were wicked, and even I could only endure so much pain. But instead his jaw just tightened, his empty hands clenching.

He'd lost the grimoire. He was powerless.

"She is a Lawson," he said, as if he could persuade me to do what he wanted. "A descendent of the Blessed First Three, one of the God's chosen." Out of the corner of my eye, I could see Everly shifting in her seat. She was the only person in this room with any innate magical abilities, but would she dare turn those against me? "She must go to the Deep One, and you will bring her."

This was why the Hadleigh brats had latched onto Rae so quickly, like goddamn leeches eager to feast on the God's favor. It made sense now: Rae was born here, her family had likely been here since the town was first built. Some unfortunate ancestor of hers had gone down into the mines, and came out with the God's mark on him forever.

"If you hop to it quickly, you'll still have hours with her before midnight," Jeremiah said. "I see you staring at her on campus. Her cunt can be your reward for—"

He didn't even see me move.

One moment he was leaning eagerly forward in his chair, watching the rage spread over my face, and the next I had him by the throat, held aloft over my head as his mother shrieked and his father cursed.

"I should pop your pathetic little skull," I snarled, squeezing his throat until he gurgled and his face began to go purple. His feet twitched, trying to kick at me, as if his pathetic squirming could stop me.

I'd kill them. First Jeremiah, then Meredith, then Victoria, and I'd enjoy every second. The amulet Kent wore, blessed with old magic, prevented me from harming him, but I'd gladly slaughter his whole family and have him watch.

"Leon!" Kent's voice was loud, but even with the protection hanging around his neck, he didn't dare to approach me. Meredith was screaming hysterically. Everly watched from her chair, all the blood drained from her face. I laughed, the sound reverberating around the room as my claws dug into Jeremiah's neck, drawing blood. "Put him down! Obey me! Obey at once!"

"Obey?" I laughed again as I turned to him, holding up Jeremiah with one hand. "Obey or *what*? What will you do? What will you do without your precious grimoire?" Kent looked as if I'd slapped him. "Did you really think I wouldn't figure it out? That I wouldn't notice?" I squeezed a little tighter, and a slow squeak came from Jeremiah's mouth, like air being let out of a balloon. "After all these years, did you really think I'd let you slip up for even a second, Hadleigh? All these years of serving you, risking my life for you as you continue your foolish quest to please a God that will crush you like a bug the first opportunity It gets."

Kent was shaken, but not down. Instead of addressing me, his eyes looked past me, and I felt a brush of magic against my back.

I glanced back. Everly was standing, tears streaming down her face. It was her magic I felt.

Witch magic.

She was young, and untrained, but I still didn't want to deal with fighting a witch.

I looked back at Kent as Jeremiah continued to twitch in my grip. "Dismiss me. Now. And I'll let your son live."

"Dismiss him, Kent!" Meredith shrieked. "Get rid of him!"

Kent hated to lose. Fury contorted his face, his mind likely grasping for another option. But Jeremiah was limp now, and given a few more seconds, I'd squeeze even harder and crush his windpipe.

"You're dismissed, demon." Kent ground out the words. "Leave my presence. Leave this house. Go back to Hell."

God, it felt good to win. Jeremiah dropped to the floor in a limp heap, and I vanished with a grin and two middle fingers up.

RAE

SOMETHING WAS OFF that day, but I couldn't put my finger on what it was.

Maybe it was the feeling of being watched as I walked across campus, the bizarre prickling on the back of my neck that told me eyes were on me, but I couldn't figure out from where. Maybe it was the weird experience of having my Screenwriting professor, Mr. Crouse, remind me—and *only* me—that I could come to his office after class if I needed any help. Maybe it was the fact that Jeremiah hadn't come to school that day, and Victoria couldn't seem to put her vape down during our entire lunch break. I could smell alcohol on her breath again.

"Family problems," Inaya said with a heavy sigh before we parted for our last classes of the day. "I've known Victoria for a few years and she struggles when her parents don't get along. No family is perfect. We just have to try to be there for her."

Inaya was a better friend than I was. She planned to take Victoria out for coffee after class, but the day's weird feelings had formed a solid knot of anxiety in my stomach. Once it started, there was no reasoning with anxiety. I just wanted to get home.

I just needed to *walk* home.

I'd figured those walks home in the dusk would get easier, but no. The sun had sunk beyond the trees, twilight's dusky golden light filtering through the branches. It was beautiful, but the dark was coming. The clouds had been sparse that day, but on the horizon, a mass of dark, purple-gray storm clouds were brewing, moving ever closer. It would probably rain through the night. The thought of curling up in bed with a glass of wine, watching *Scream* for the umpteenth time as the rain pattered outside, made me walk faster.

Since delving into investigating the paranormal, I'd trained myself to consider strange feelings and emotions to be a key part of my investigation process. It was pretty common to encounter feelings of dread, cold chills, and panic in haunted locations. So I tried to give my feeling of anxious discomfort the same consideration I would if I was investigating a haunting; I wasn't going to push the feeling away. It was there for a reason.

I just didn't know what that reason was.

My boots crunched on the gravel as I crossed the road to walk along the dirt near the trees.

"Ugh, gross." I pulled up my shirt to cover my nose.

The wind had shifted, carrying with it the awful stench of a dead animal, sour and rotten. I looked into the trees, expecting to see a dead racoon or maybe a deer.

But there was something *else* standing between the trees.

In the dim light, I thought I was just looking at some bleached, gnarled branches between the maze of trees. The bone-gray limbs were patched with moss and spread out, some high and some low, reminding me of a spider's web. But it was not a web, not a spider. At the conjunction of those strange, branch-like appendages was a rib cage with taut, graying flesh stretched over the bones. There was a spindly, spine-like neck, and a canid skull with the jaw hanging open and a long black tongue lolling out.

I blinked rapidly, my heart pounding. Were my eyes tricking me? It was at least fifty yards away. I pushed up my glasses, leaning down in an attempt to get a clearer view through the branches. It looked like a mutated, rotting dead animal. It wasn't moving. It was even more still than the trees themselves.

It was probably some kind of creepy art installation.

In fact, it *had* to be an art installation. Those long spindly limbs were just wood. The "ribs" were covered with some kind of goopy, painted cloth, or maybe silicone. I shook myself, shuddering as I began to walk away. The Art Festival had only been a few days ago— maybe it was common for sculptures to be set up around town. I would have to find out who was responsible for the piece. It was brilliantly placed and eerily realistic, exactly the kind of creepy shit I liked.

Goose bumps prickled up my back, and I walked a little faster. Something still smelled *awful.*

A twig snapped behind me. I swallowed hard and kept walking. I wasn't about to indulge that prickly, nagging fear.

There was nothing to be afraid of.

Snap.

I wasn't far from my driveway. I could see it up ahead.

I stopped walking.

There had been a sound beside me, something between a bark and ragged cough. And that smell, God. Why was it so strong?

I turned around.

The road was empty. The streetlights had popped on, casting little pools of light leading back toward campus. But there was no one there. Not a single soul. I peered through the trees, through the catacombs of crisscrossed branches, back toward that creepy sculpture.

It was gone.

There was a roaring sound in my ears, like the ocean filling my head in waves of terror. I took a step back, then another. My eyes darted across the road, toward every little growing shadow. I had to be wrong. I had to be. Where the hell—

The glow of headlights suddenly appeared behind me. I turned, to see a small white truck speeding down the road. The tires crunched as they came to a sudden halt beside me, and I narrowed my eyes in the dark as I attempted to make out the driver through the tinted windows.

The passenger door was shoved open from the inside, and from the driver's seat, Leon glared at me.

"Get in."

I was so freaked out I didn't even pause to consider that maybe hopping into his car wasn't the safest idea. It had to be safer than whatever I had just heard in the woods. The moment my door was closed he flipped a U-turn, driving back in the direction of my cabin.

"What are you doing walking in the dark?" His voice was tense, furious. He kept glancing in the rearview mirror. What the hell had I done to make him so mad?

"I'm going home. I always walk."

"You think it's a good idea for a tiny girl like you to be walking through the woods in the dark?" he snapped.

"What the hell is your problem?" I glared at him from across the seat. "If you're just going to yell at me then let me out. It's none of your business where I walk, or when I walk, or how!" His fingers tightened on the steering wheel, his jaw clenched. But he didn't say anything. He just kept glancing in the rearview mirror. What was he doing out here anyway? I hadn't seen him on campus that day and had assumed it was his day off.

Not that I specifically *looked* for him on campus.

"Take me home," I demanded, when seconds had passed and he was still silent. He snorted.

"Yeah, that's what I'm doing." Without any directions from me, he turned onto the narrow dirt drive that led back into the trees toward my house. My eyes widened, my stomach doing a nervous little flip as I gulped.

"How do you know I live here?" That felt like a dangerous question to ask. I really needed to do a better job of thinking these things through. "Have you . . .

have you followed me home? Have you been watching me?"

My cabin appeared out of the trees. I always left the
kitchen light on, so when I got home after dark I could
see the light. It made me feel better somehow, less lonely,
like the house was waiting for me. Leon pulled his truck
up in front of the porch and parked, before leaning back
in his seat and taking a slow breath.

"Leon. How do you know I live here?"

"Don't ask silly questions." He was bouncing his foot
on the floor, and he rubbed his palms over his jeans. It
was like all the energy in the cab of the truck was being
sucked into him, building and building, and he was trying
to keep it all inside without exploding. His eyes suddenly
fixated on my Subaru Outback, parked just beside him.
"Start driving to school. I don't know why the hell you
think it's a good idea to go walking around in the dark,
but you need to cut that shit out."

I laughed. It was a nervous laugh, admittedly, but irritation had a way of making me bold. "I'll do what I
want. Thanks for the ride."

I opened the door, only to have Leon reach across me
and slam it shut again.

My breathing slowed. His face was close to mine,
his arm reached across my body to hold the door shut. I
could feel his heat, warming my skin without even touching it, like being near a blazing fire. His eyes pierced into
mine, pale-green like the lichens that grew on the side of
massive stones—but deep within that color, flecks of gold
glowed like fireflies in the dark.

"Raelynn, I don't want to catch you walking at night again." His tone was vicious but desperate. Almost pleading. "Drive your goddamn car. I don't know what you're used to in California, but no matter how many streetlights come on here, they won't chase away the dark. They'll never illuminate the trees."

The thought of that thing, that sculpture, flashed through my mind. Those teeth, that black tongue, the skeletal face. My fingers plucked at the seat as I imagined it spread among the trees, still as stone in the growing dark. Then—gone. Where had it *gone*?

Leon pushed open the door again. But he kept his arms on either side of me for a moment, pinning me there. "Stay inside at night. Don't go walking around after dark. Understand?"

My first thought was to push back. But squashed beneath him on the seat, with his gaze not letting my eyes go for even a second, all I managed to get out was, "Got it."

He didn't move for a moment, as if he could see the lie in my eyes if he looked hard enough. Then a crooked smirk curled his mouth, and he said softly, "Behave yourself, Raelynn. Or there will be consequences next time."

He straightened up, finally allowing me to hop out of the truck. Dozens of words all shuffled for space on my tongue, some angry, some curious, many confused. But before I could get any of them out, he revved the engine and sped off up the driveway, the glow of his headlights disappearing into the trees.

RAE

THE VIDEO WAS shaky and unfocused. It was aimed at the floor, at first, as the audio came in and out with crackling static. The tiled floor was smeared and spattered with something dark—blood.

The video finally focused. Two young men stood over another, who was lying on his back on the floor in a pool of blood. One of the men had his cell phone to his ear—"Yeah, at the university . . . no, no, he's definitely dead . . . there's blood everywhere . . ."—while the other used his phone to snap photos.

Whoever was filming kept gasping and laughing nervously. "I just can't believe this, man . . . I can't believe this . . ."

He zoomed in on the body. The eyes were open, glassy, and vacant. The jaw hung slack, and at a strange angle. Stab wounds in the victim's chest had created a crater between his ribs. His face was puffy and bruised, the flesh on his arms were cut as if his assailant had been slashing at him wildly. An act of viciousness, of unhinged violence.

The video ended, and I hurriedly clicked away from the webpage, hoping none of the passing students had seen what I was looking at. No wonder they closed Calgary Hall. I was surprised they hadn't closed the entire school, especially considering that whoever had done this hadn't been caught.

Someone capable of doing *that* was still walking around Abelaum.

Maybe that was why Leon had been so furious at finding me walking alone. There was still a criminal out there looking for their next victim, and I may as well have been offering myself up on a silver platter. It was creepy as hell that he knew where I lived, but at the same time, mine was one of the only houses close to the university on that stretch of road. It wouldn't take much effort to guess that if I walked home in that direction, the cabin was probably where I was headed.

Thinking about the terror I'd felt over that creepy statue made me giggle a little now. I'd worked myself up for nothing. Once I'd gotten home, I'd been blushing with embarrassment at my reaction. Blushing at my reaction, and blushing at the heat Leon's gaze had left in me. I felt like I was losing my edge—I couldn't remember the last time I'd gotten that scared.

Which meant it was time to put myself to the test again. I planned to film an investigation in St. Thaddeus, and recommit myself to getting good content uploaded to my channel. *Good* content, if not entirely authentic. I had plans for the next video that were a little less than truthful, but if that's what it took to gain success as a paranormal channel now . . .

Then I'd suck up my pride and do it.

ON SATURDAY, I packed my backpack with the essentials—an electromagnetic field reader, an audio recorder for electronic voice phenomena, my camera, a sheathed knife for protection, and enough snacks to last me through a hike. I packed extra batteries, a small first aid kit, and my secret weapon: the grimoire.

A good play needed the right props. I'd done my best to study the conjuring rituals within the grimoire, but working with online translations was sloppy at best. I'd assembled together bits and pieces until I had a believable string of words. A ritualistic prayer, symbols I would draw on the ground in chalk, and lit candles would provide a perfect creepy atmosphere.

I was going to record a mock summoning in the old church. It was absolute clickbait trash, but I had to generate more views for the channel somehow.

My usual stance was to take investigations seriously and respectfully. If there were actually spirits of the dead present, I wasn't there to disrespect them or anger them. But maybe the magical mockery would be just enough to bring in more views.

I didn't think anything would actually come of it anyway. I'd cobbled together such a hack version of the rituals laid out in the grimoire, any spiritual beings who took notice would surely just roll their eyes. But just to be safe, I was leaving out a key part of the ritual the grimoire had called for: spilling my own blood to complete the summoning. As dramatic as it would be to give myself a little cut and bleed all over the floor, I wasn't *actually* trying to make a demon show up.

St. Thaddeus was nearly an hour's drive away from downtown Abelaum. It wasn't someplace I could simply look up on Google Maps, so I was relying on the directions I'd found on an urban exploration subreddit. Abelaum's quaint business and cozy cabins disappeared as I drove, becoming long rural streets with big family homes set back from the road. The pine trees looked as if they were on the verge of consuming every speck of civilization here; their boughs wrapped around the houses, growing over them as if slowly capturing them in a living cage. The clouds moved overhead, with patchy clearings where I could see spots of blue sky and sunlight shining down. It wasn't raining yet, and I was hoping I could finish my investigation before the downpour started. I wasn't looking forward to hiking in the rain.

I turned the speakers up, blasting "London After Midnight" as I downed my second canned espresso. The anticipation before an investigation had me buzzing, even more than the caffeine. Plenty of people would call me foolish for going to abandoned places by myself—a woman doing *anything* alone was bound to attract disapproval. But I had my knife, and I had pepper spray on my key chain. I wasn't going to let anyone's pearl-clutching about my safety stop me from living.

Admittedly, the only thing that had given me the slightest pause was thinking of Leon's warning the night he'd picked me up from the road. *"Behave yourself, Raelynn. Or there will be consequences next time,"* was something I would have preferred to hear uttered in bed. It didn't scare me; I felt bizarrely thrilled to know going to this old church would probably qualify as misbehaving in his mind.

He could bring on the consequences, if he ever managed to find out what I'd done.

The road narrowed. I hadn't seen a house in at least twenty minutes, and the asphalt was rutted, the yellow paint dividing the two lanes faded into invisibility. The distant bay, my constant companion to the west during the drive thus far, had vanished beyond the trees. My music cut out as my cell lost reception.

Following the directions, I made a quick turn onto a narrow dirt road. The road was clearly unmaintained, the dirt overtaken by grass and rotten leaves. Low hanging branches brushed against the top of my car, and a few stray raindrops dotted my windshield.

The road came to an end at a metal gate. A rusted *NO TRESPASSING* sign dangled from it by one remaining chain, and I pulled the vehicle up alongside it, turning off my engine. According to what I'd read, this was it. I wouldn't be able to drive any further; from here, it was a twenty-minute hike back into the trees.

I gathered my supplies, double-checked the batteries

on my flashlight, and headed out. The path I found through the trees was narrow, and largely overgrown with brush, but I'd expected far worse. The wind rattled the pines overhead, and fallen needles made every step soft. The rain held off, for now; but I still felt the occasional cold drop hit my face.

I spoke to my camera as I walked, recording some backstory for the viewers. "In 1899, forty miners took the lifts down to the lowest level of Abelaum's notorious silver mines—two weeks later, only three of them came out alive." It was the same legend I'd first heard told in elementary school, the story every kid in Abelaum knew. The Tragedy of 1899 changed Abelaum forever, bringing its booming mining industry to a sudden grinding halt. "The mine experienced a massive cave-in, and the lowest levels rapidly flooded, leaving the miners trapped inside. Over the coming days, as they waited for rescue, the men survived in the only way they could: by cannibalizing the dead, and later—killing and eating the living."

I paused as I came to a fork in the path. I knew I had to go to the right; the path sloped slightly downward, and around the sharp bend, I should find a clearing and the cathedral. A tree stood at the center of the trail's fork, and I could see something buried among the twigs and leaves piled around its roots. I grabbed it, and tugged out a wooden sign chipped with age. The ghosts of old painted letters remained on the wood, reading: *White Pine Central Shaft, 1 Mile.*

I held it up to the camera. "After two weeks, rescuers were finally able to clear a way down, right here at

White Pine. Only three men remained alive, including the owner of the mining operation, a man named Morpheus Leighman. The bodies of the others were never recovered."

I turned the camera up the trail to the left. It was almost completely overgrown; twigs, fallen branches, and grass left the path nearly invisible. "Once freed, the men were brought down this very trail. Accounts of the rescue describe them as energetic and strong, despite the days trapped underground. Apparently, cannibalism does a body good. But the rescued men claimed they had experienced something else down in the mines, something otherworldly."

Despite the instructions to head right, I walked a little way up the left path. Something was dangling from a low-hanging tree limb: a small bundle of twigs held together with twine, swinging gently in the breeze. I plucked it down, holding it still for the camera. The twigs were woven into a circlet, and a design had been formed in the middle using more twigs, twine, and . . . *fishbones*.

Just like the strange trinkets Mrs. Kathy used to hang around her porch.

"Even now, the legends of what the miners experienced underground lives on in this small town's local culture. The rescued men claimed they met a monster, a God who had been sleeping deep in the earth. They claimed this God granted them mercy, allowing them to escape in exchange for worship. According to the legends, Morpheus would eventually buy the church located near their rescue site, and dedicated it to the worship of the underground God."

I turned off the camera, satisfied as I headed back toward the other fork in the path. Down the fork and around the bend, the trees cleared. For a moment, the sight of St. Thaddeus took my breath away. The cathedral had three magnificent spires at the front, reaching high into the sky, rivaling the tops of the pines. The wood was blackened with age, covered with patches of moss and fungi. A low stone wall lay in crumbled heaps around the church's dirt courtyard, and it looked as if the steep roof had caved in on one side.

I began to record again, in silence this time, letting the view speak for itself. The church was far larger than I had expected; it was a relic of exquisite Gothic architecture. Beneath the center spire was a large round window of stained glass, although it was so covered with dirt and grime that I couldn't make out what it depicted.

The front doors, still covered in chipping white paint, were chained shut. I wandered around the side of the building, examining the boarded-up windows, filming everything. About halfway down the side of the church was a single door, and this one had already been opened: the chain that once secured it dangled off the handle, the padlock still attached and the links cut.

I'd read online this was the way to get in, but I still held my pepper spray ready. With my weapon in one hand and the camera's flash illuminating my way, I shoved open the door with my foot and the old hinges screeched. Dust cascaded down around the entrance, the shadows thick within. My light cast a sickly yellow beam through the gloom across the nave. A pile of rubble and splintered boards lay beneath the caved-in ceiling, dull light spilling in from above.

The wooden pews still remained, set in long rows up and down the nave. Hymnbooks were tucked into the shelves on the backs of the pews, swollen and moldy with the damp. The air was thick, oppressive in its silence. There was no tingling, no chills, nothing that would have alerted me to lurking paranormal energies.

The church felt dead. Like a void that dispersed all its light, all its energy, leaving only moldering air behind.

But there, at the front of the church, surrounding the pulpit, someone had erected some kind of shrine. I approached carefully, sidestepping splintered beams from the fallen ceiling. Numerous white candles sat around the pulpit, surrounded by their own melted wax. More of those bizarre twig trinkets were scattered around, more fishbones, more twine.

The dust on the ground was disturbed. The footprints were fresh. I hesitated, my camera frozen in my hand as I fixated on those footprints. It wasn't as if this place was unknown to other explorers. I wasn't the first to come here, and I wouldn't be the last. But I didn't particularly like finding such fresh evidence of a visit.

But I'd come here on a mission. I had an investigation to do.

I started with the audio recorder. I wandered around the nave with the camera fixed on me, asking questions to the empty air.

"Is anyone here with me?"

"What's your name?"

"How long have you been here?"

The old building creaked in the wind, and somewhere beyond the pulpit, a little sound made me fall silent. I couldn't even guess what I'd heard. A whisper? The wind? Had something fallen? A footstep, or a knock?

I was used to feeling *something* in these old places. As the minutes dragged by, and the silence stretched on, that began to unnerve me more than anything; it wasn't just that I *wasn't* experiencing chills, or unease—I felt *nothing*. The excited buzz of a new investigation was gone. The awe at the church's architecture had faded. What was left behind was a heaviness that made my thoughts feel slow, as if I was dissociating.

Maybe coming here alone hadn't been a good idea after all.

I needed to wrap things up, but there was one last thing I needed to film. I set up the camera on its tripod facing the pulpit, and cleared a space for myself in front of the mass of candles.

It was time to create some demon-summoning clickbait.

I'd used my translation notes to mark the relevant page in the grimoire, and I turned to it now. The golden eyes of the Killer greeted me. In the dim light, those eyes looked brighter than ever, searing into me with an accusing gaze. I paused, letting my fingers brush over the page. That face was dangerous, sharp, cruel . . . and so goddamn familiar.

With white chalk I'd picked up from the dollar store, I drew two circles on the old boards, one within the other.

Then within the band created by the two circles, I carefully marked the sigils illustrated in the book. The chalk scraped over the old wood, making a sound disturbingly like the scratching of claws. I set around the candles next. Then I used a little oil I'd brought in a water bottle, and poured it into a brass cup I usually reserved for Moscow Mules.

The scene was set.

Blink, blink, blink went the camera's little red light. Recording, watching—the unflinching eye to take in everything I did.

I lay the grimoire open right at the edge of the chalk circle. I lit the candles, and their flickering light danced across its surface, across the illustration of the Killer. Striking gold eyes stared at me in the dark, and goose bumps prickled up my spine.

I'd been careful for years. I'd always been respectful. I'd never brought out Ouija boards, I'd never fucked with things that were said to have the potential to expose me to dark and dangerous shit. Any paranormal investigator worth their salt would have shaken their head at me, called me foolish and ignorant.

"Nothing is going to happen," I said softly. My words felt hollow in the church's dead air. "Just get it over with, Rae."

My notes were composed of cobbled-together sentences I'd translated, bits and pieces taken from various prayers and summoning instructions throughout the book. I'd written them in English, even though I was certain Latin would have sounded more authentic, but

I feared I would stumble over pronunciations and look even sillier than I already did.

It was my last chance to back out. I could stop recording, throw these notes away, and leave. I could cling onto my integrity as an investigator.

But integrity hadn't gotten me very far.

I held my notes to the candle flame's light, took a deep breath, and read, "Powers of the Elder World be beneath my left foot, and within my right hand." My voice shook. I knew I had to sell it, I had to sound as authentic as possible, but this felt *wrong*. "Glory and Eternity touch my shoulders, and guide me on the Path of Victory."

The rain had begun to fall in earnest. It pattered on the roof and dripped down through the hole, trickling into the pools of stagnant water beneath the moldy old boards. The air smelled of dust and wet dirt.

"Spirits of Earth, guide me through the Nether Realm. Great Angels of Eternity, protect me. Voices of the Unending, strengthen me."

I didn't feel so numb anymore. There was a tingling in my fingertips and the tips of my toes. I felt like a block of ice had been set in my stomach. The Killer's eyes still stared.

Watching.

Waiting.

"With this power granted unto me, I issue this command." I made my voice as demanding as possible. With the chalk in my hand, I wrote a final symbol on the old floorboards in the center of the circle, beneath the cup of oil. A symbol which, I could only guess, was a name.

"I call upon this servant of Hell! I demand thee come forth, make of yourself flesh and bone." I traced over the symbol again and again as I spoke, thickening the lines and grating the chalk into every little crevice of the wood. "I demand thee come without aggression, I demand thee bring no harm to your summoner, I demand thee come in obedience and—fuck . . . shit!"

The chalk snapped. The force I'd been applying to it slammed my hand down and scraped my knuckles against the wooden boards, hard enough to cut. Hard enough to bleed.

Wincing, I held up my hand to the camera's light. Blood welled up, and dripped slowly down from my knuckles onto the floor. Damn it. Something told me this place was far from sanitary. I scrambled up, and rummaged around in my backpack. I needed an alcohol wipe from the first aid kit and—

My eyes widened. My breath froze in my lungs.

The blood that had dripped into the chalk circle was *steaming*.

I stared in disbelief. There had to be an explanation. My blood was hot and the air was cold so . . . so it would steam, of course. But it wasn't just steaming, it was *coagulating*. The droplets thickened, they shuddered, they began to run together. They gathered over the symbols I'd written in the circle and sunk into the letters, turning them red.

No . . . no, no, no, this *could not be happening.*

The reddened chalk melted across the boards, spreading like thick, viscous wax. The redness filled the circle completely, stopping right at the edge of the chalk. The steam darkened, becoming thick black smoke that filled the space with the smell of charcoal. My chest tight with panic, I slipped on the straps of my backpack and lingered nervously behind the camera. It was still recording. I was capturing *all* of this . . . this was the evidence I'd been searching for, hoping desperately for.

What the hell had I done?

The camera's flash flickered. The church groaned as if a hurricane was pressing upon it. Adrenaline flooded me, telling me to run. Some deep, primal instinct filled my head with one unending cry: *danger, danger, danger.* This was the lion in the grass, the predator in the dark. My heart beat against my ribs as my legs tingled with the desire to flee.

The camera's flash went out; it audibly burst with the sound of shattering glass. In the candles' flickering orange glow, the smoke began to take shape. It became tall, humanoid . . .

It opened its eyes, and they were gold.

12

LEON

I DID LOVE making a dramatic entrance.

I'd known it was coming. Even as I left Kent that late night, flipping him off as I vanished into the ether, it was with the knowledge that I'd likely be dragged back in front of a summoner sooner rather than later. I couldn't really leave Abelaum yet anyway, now could I? Someone out there had the grimoire, and that meant some little mortal's fingers would be itching to try their hand at the magic contained within. I needed the damn book, I needed my mark in it destroyed. I wasn't the only demon whose name was within it, but with my luck, I'd be the one chosen.

Lucky me.

They'd called me Killer as a warning, but somehow that just made me more appealing, didn't it? Curious mortal minds couldn't resist the danger.

I sent out smoke ahead of me. I brought the wind, I encouraged the rain, I filled the space with the scent of burning. Whoever dared summon me would know they were in over their heads. With luck, they'd make a mistake, they'd flee, they'd step outside their protective circle and when they did—oh, when they did, I'd make them scream. Most mortals weren't so lucky to possess a protective amulet, like Kent had. It was the only reason I hadn't killed him in all the years he'd held me captive, and his father before him, and his grandfather before that.

The room came into focus—a high steepled ceiling and ancient boards. The smell of dust and mold, flesh and blood . . . mint and sage? My gaze pierced through the dark, through the smoke, toward the diminutive figure standing there, wide brown eyes staring at me through her glasses.

No . . . no *fucking* way . . .

She was scrambling, but as I came into being, she raised something above her head. In a fury, I cleared the smoke away, dissipating it with a single breath but letting it linger around my feet—for effect, of course. There stood Raelynn Lawson, holding up a stick as if it were a baseball bat.

"Get back!" she screamed, her voice trembling with fear but vicious nonetheless. "Get—away—from me!" She punctuated every word with a swing of the stick, each swing coming closer.

Of all the people that could have summoned me, of all the goddamned people in this goddamned town, it had to be *her*.

I began to laugh at the absurdity of it all. My laughter was dark and loud, and it filled the room like a roll of thunder. She remained steadfast, stick at the ready, facing me down instead of running for her life. But as my laughter quieted, her face twitched and recognition gleamed in her eyes.

"What the . . ." She lowered the stick, fumbling for her phone. She flicked on her flashlight and shone it in my face, and I was quick to smooth out my disguise. Golden eyes became green, my claws retracted. The urge to disguise myself was an automatic reaction to having a human look at me, but in this case at least, I also couldn't have her completely losing her mind and fleeing.

I didn't know how, but she had the grimoire.

And she was going to hand it over, one way or another.

"Leon?" She gasped, utter disbelief in her voice. I stopped laughing, letting the silence surround us. I dampened the sound just a bit too, so the quiet was smothering, so that it pressed down around her. I wanted her to realize this was a mistake. I wanted her to feel afraid. Just afraid enough to cooperate, not to flee.

Or so I hoped.

I could smell the adrenaline as it rushed through her, savory in its aroma of blood, sweat, and salt. Instead of backing down, she raised the stick again in one hand and kept holding up her phone with the other. What did she think she was doing?

"What the hell?" she yelled. "Is this your idea of a prank, asshole?"

A prank . . . she thought this was a prank. I chuckled,

entirely unamused. "Oh, this would be a good prank, wouldn't it?" I looked around, taking in the familiar pews, the altar behind me, the stench of old burned herbs and below—*far* below—the unnerving smell of seawater. We were in St. Thaddeus. She'd come here, despite my warnings not to, and *summoned* me.

The stubborn, disobedient, foolish little *brat*.

I leveled my eyes on her again, my gaze cold, and the stick shook in her hand, at the ready to strike. "What do you think you're doing, Raelynn? Why are you here?"

"None of your business," she snapped, baring her teeth at me.

"You've *made it* my business," I hissed, taking a step toward her. She swung the stick wildly, ready and willing to try to bash my face if I got too close. She was brave, if nothing else. Foolishly, blindly brave.

God, I wanted to put her over my knee and teach her a lesson. She hadn't even given herself any protection: no herbs, no sigils surrounding her feet, *nothing*. No one with a bit of sense would do something so ridiculously dangerous, and for what? She didn't even seem to realize what she'd done, she thought this was a *prank*—but then I noticed the camera, set up on its tripod.

She'd recorded this.

She'd done this for a *video*.

"You little fool," I said softly. "You hardheaded, insolent, reckless woman."

"Shut up," she said furiously. "Why the hell are you here, you creep? What the hell is wrong with you? Did you follow me out here?"

She truly didn't understand. She thought I was merely here by coincidence. I was honestly stunned into silence at the realization. Never, in all my centuries of existence, had I been summoned by *accident*.

This woman was a walking disaster, a stunning danger to herself, and she didn't even know it.

She threw down her stick and stomped passed me, kneeling to collect an open book from the ground. My heart lurched as I realized it was the grimoire, the urge to rip it from her making my fingers twitch. That book was my ticket to freedom. All I needed was for her to hand it over.

Hand it over *willingly*. The protective spells on the damn thing meant I couldn't take it by force.

"Fucking weirdo," she grumbled, shooting a glare over her shoulder as she collected her camera and tripod. "Who the hell does this shit? You're lucky I'm not calling the cops!"

Oh, what I would have given in that moment to see her expression if I revealed my true form. I wanted to see that righteous indignation melt from her face, I wanted to see her fall to her knees in terror.

"Why don't you?" I taunted. "Call the police, Raelynn, if your phone even has any service. I'd love to see how you manage to explain why you broke onto private property, and into a private building." I chuckled, stepping easily out of the remnants of my poorly drawn summoning circle. She stepped back hurriedly, stuffed her camera into her backpack, and held up her phone. She was recording me; likely a smart move if circumstances had been different.

A smart move if I'd been human.

"Is this the attention you wanted?" She glared up at me as she blasted the phone's flash in my face. "Well, now I have it on video that you're a creep who follows women into the woods. Good luck keeping your job after this!" Her heart was pounding a million miles a minute. I could smell the sweat on her skin.

Her gaze moved toward the door, contemplating an escape. Then she looked down, to the dark stain on the floor where her chalk markings had been. She stared in confusion, her belief that I'd only pranked her not aligning with what she was seeing.

"How . . . how the hell?"

Before she could make a move, I grabbed her wrist and yanked her phone down, taking the annoying light out of my face. I shoved her back until she was pressed against the pulpit, among all the candles and the Libiri's vile trinkets to the Deep One. It was too easy to forget how quick humans would crumble under my strength; reining it in, especially when I was frustrated, took no small amount of willpower. I was certain I felt my disguise slip for a second as I grabbed her—although she couldn't have noticed the flash in my eyes with her light pulled down.

Her eyes were like saucers as she stared up at me, her breath coming in nervous gasps. I leaned down, my face within inches of her, the scent of her flooding me. Fuck, Earthly bodies were far too reactive to stimuli. My heart beat faster, saliva increased around my tongue, and my cock gave an interested twitch as her alluring smell surrounded me.

"I warned you, doll," I snarled. She needed to learn, and if scaring her was the only way to do it, then so be it. "Didn't I tell you to behave? I told you not to come here, not to stick your nose where it doesn't belong. Now you've *really* done it." With one hand still pinning down her wrist, I grasped her chin with the other. My hand fully encompassed her jaw and pressed against her throat; I could feel her thumping heart, pattering like a rabbit's.

"You . . . you can't tell me what to do," she said, all the fierceness gone out of her. I grinned triumphantly to see her shrinking. This was no mere game to be recorded for internet fame.

This was life and death. This was *my* freedom on the line.

"You're messing around with shit you know nothing about." I pulled her forward by the jaw, forcing her to gaze up at me with those defiant eyes. "Curiosity can kill you, Raelynn. What you've started here isn't easily un-done."

Her eyes flickered over my face in shock. "Are you threatening me?"

"I'm *warning* you, Rae." She was pressed right up against me, her legs between mine—a dangerously tempting position. The feral desire to claim her—*all* of her, body and soul—roared up in me. I wanted to see her fall to her knees and beg forgiveness for her mistake. I wanted to feel her soul meld with mine in offering. I wanted to taste her come undone on my tongue.

Something must have shown on my face, because she

began to struggle in my grasp. The wiggle of her body between my thighs made my grip tighten instinctively, a growl rising in me, and her eyes swelled when she felt me restrain her.

But not with fear—with arousal.

Oh. So that's how it was going to be, was it?

I took both her wrists in my grasp—such breakable little bones—and pinned them above her head, right against the carved wooden cross on the pulpit, making her twitching fingers a blasphemous Christ. I traced my finger along her stubborn jaw, pausing where I could feel the eager *ba-bump, ba-bump* of her heart.

"You're very lucky, Raelynn," I said softly, holding her gaze, "that I don't bend you over this pulpit and teach you a real lesson about not fucking with things you don't understand."

A little whimper burst out of her. Somewhere between disbelief and desire, she grit her teeth and growled back, "I'd like to see you fucking try, asshole." She ground her boot down on my foot, as if she could hurt me. I chuckled, as my fingers reached her chin and the tiny, delicate dimple right below her pouting lower lip. She went still as I brushed her mouth, tracing the contours of her lips, her breath shuddering over my skin.

"Don't tempt me," I growled. "Just be a good girl, give me the book, and go."

She had tucked the grimoire into her bag, which was slung over her shoulder and pressed between her back and the pulpit. She'd stopped resisting, so I slowly released my hold on her, and for a moment she didn't move, other than her eyes. Her gaze moved over me slowly, assessing me, contemplating the risk.

Then she dodged away.

It would have been too easy to catch her. I faced her as she began to back toward the exit, her knuckles white as she gripped her phone. If she wanted a game, how could I deny her?

"Raelynn." I smiled, approaching slowly, nonchalantly. "Give me the book. It's for the best, truly it is."

She shook her head. "No. The book is *mine*."

"The book should not *exist*!" There was a petulant, possessive tone that had come into her voice in her desperation to cling to that wretched grimoire, and it stoked my anger again.

"Get away!" She was backing away hurriedly as I advanced. Little fool would rather run than cooperate. She wanted a chase, did she? She wanted a hunt?

Then she'd get a hunt.

I stopped advancing. I watched her retreat with the smile spreading wider over my face.

"Give me the book." My voice was soft in warning. "Otherwise, you're going to be a very sorry girl."

Her jaw tightened. "What are you going to do?" She sneered, bolder now that she had distance between us. "Threaten me more?"

"I don't make idle threats. If you run out of here"—and I knew she would—"then I'm going to hunt you. I'm going to catch you. And when I do—" A thousand possibilities flashed through my head. A thousand sweet tortures. A thousand ways to stoke that arousal inside her until she burst. "—when I do, I'll make you scream."

The little shit *smirked* at me. "Right. More threats." She tugged her bag closer. She was almost out the door. "Don't follow me. Just . . . just stay away."

She turned and ran, and I didn't even bother to give chase. I sauntered after her, pausing when I reached the doorway. The wind howled and rain pattered down, the sun obscured by the thick clouds above.

The smell of blood and magic was in the air, an intoxicating concoction, a sure lure for the Eld. I wasn't the only one that would be on her scent. I watched her figure disappear deeper and deeper into the trees—fleeing blindly, stubbornly, naivety egging her on.

I'd meant what I said. I didn't make idle threats. But I wouldn't even need to hunt this one.

She'd come to me. She wouldn't be able to resist. For now, my only concern was ensuring she made it out of these woods without being eaten alive.

RAE

I SPRINTED THROUGH the pouring rain, stumbling over roots, twigs snapping under my feet. The leaves above rustled in the wind, their boughs groaning like the voices of the damned. Despite my raincoat, my hair and pants were swiftly soaked and I was shivering with the cold.

With every step, I expected to feel Leon grab a hold of me from behind. That absolute *asshole*. How had he done it? How had he managed to sneak into the church and hide without me knowing? How had he known I would be there? How had he made blood congeal, smoke gather, and my chalk circle *disappear*?

Only when I feared my legs would go out did I slow down and dare to glance back. The trees were thick and the shadows even thicker, the world made blurry by the pouring rain. I had to keep going. I was lucky I hadn't lost the trail in my frantic sprint. I checked my phone, hoping I could text someone, anyone, but there was still no service—why hadn't I done that in the first place? Why did I have to be so damn stubborn that I didn't even tell anyone where I was going?

I hadn't told *anyone,* so how the hell had Leon known?

At least I'd gotten him on video, at least I had proof—not only of his prank, but of his threats. I still wasn't sure if he'd been threatening to hurt me, or . . . or do something else. Something that made my brain go hazy and my thighs clench with desire. The moment he'd pinned me against the pulpit and lowered his voice to that dangerous tone, I knew I was done for. Done for mentally and morally, if not physically.

Snap.

I whirled around. That twig hadn't snapped under my own feet, it had come from somewhere else, somewhere behind me. I pushed up my rain-spattered glasses, straining my ears for the sound of footsteps, expecting to see Leon standing there beneath the trees.

But the woods were empty. Utterly empty.

The wind gusted, and when it did, a strange scent prickled my nose. Sickeningly sour and slightly sweet—the stench of rotten meat.

The smell of something dead.

Goose bumps prickled up my back. I'd smelt that before. It was the same sickening odor I'd smelled when I'd seen that strange statue. Unbidden, the memory of its eerie bone face and long black tongue filled my mind.

I forced it away before I truly terrified myself. That wasn't the thing to be thinking of as I walked the woods alone.

But what was that *smell*?

I kept walking, my ears straining for any sounds of being followed. It was just a forest, the same forest I'd walked through earlier without an issue. Creatures died in the forest all the time . . .

Except I hadn't smelled that on the way in. Logical or not, my brain was sounding the alarm. *Move, move, move. Don't stop.* I wanted to run, and I felt the tension up my back and down my legs, adrenaline demanding I sprint. But part of my brain told me otherwise.

When I was little, an overly excited dog had scared me in the park, and when I'd run, its big body had slammed into me from behind, sending me sprawling into the grass. As I'd cried, my mother had told me gently, "Dogs like to chase. Don't run. Don't give them something to chase."

Don't give them something to chase. I didn't know why I remembered it now. I didn't even know if that advice would do me any good. But I forced myself to walk, quickly but as calmly as I could manage. I walked until finally, with a gasp of relief, I saw the gate ahead and my Subaru parked beyond it.

Sitting in the driver's seat, doors locked, gripping the steering wheel, I flipped on my headlights and stared into the trees. I must have sat there for five minutes just staring . . . waiting . . . watching. The rain poured down on the car, and the heater and seat warmers finally began to chase away the chill in my body. I was dripping wet, tired, shaken; I wanted to go home.

I wanted to go home and see what the hell I'd just managed to capture on video.

BACK HOME, THE first thing I did was turn the shower all the way on hot and melt under the scalding water. The heat eased away the cold, soothing the tension in my muscles, and washing away the dried blood on my hand. I let it pour down my back, eyes closed, steam rising around me.

Usually, the unexplained was exactly where I flourished. I *wanted* to see something I had no logical explanation for. But this was different. This wasn't just a disembodied voice, or a vague apparition. This was a living, breathing man of flesh and bone—a man whose very presence seemed to reach deep into my inner darkness and draw out every secret shameful lust.

Why had he been there? *How?*

His eyes were burned into my soul—the way he'd looked at me as his fingers traced over my lips. The vicious gravel tone of his voice still echoed in my ears. He'd threatened to hunt me down, threatened to make me scream. Yet I knew if he caught me—*when* he caught me—it wouldn't be to hurt me.

No, he'd do something far worse.

He'd make me give in.

All those lustful thoughts he brought up in me? He knew they were there. He could *see* them, somehow, as if my skull were made of glass. I had no doubt he'd exploit each and every desire until there was nothing left of me but raw, carnal lust.

He wouldn't even need to take control from me, I'd simply hand it over. Hand him the grimoire. Hand him whatever the hell else he wanted. That wasn't natural. That wasn't *normal*.

I grabbed a bottle of cheap wine from the fridge, poured a large glass, and lay in bed, naked beneath the covers. The rain tapped against the window above my head, the trees outside creaking and swaying in the wind. I put on music to drown out the howling, and lay there until the wine and sheer exhaustion forced me into sleep.

But not for long.

It seemed as if I'd only just shut my eyes, but the playlist I'd put on had ended, and my laptop's screen had gone to sleep. The rain had slowed to only a few little droplets occasionally smacking against the window. I lay there for a while, groggy, trying to figure out why I'd woken up.

What had I heard?

I sat up slowly, frowning. I was still in a dull state of half-sleep, trying to remember if I'd been dreaming. I shuffled out of bed, pulling my blanket with me and tugging it around my shoulders. Regardless of what I'd heard, I needed water. The wine had left me with a headache.

In the kitchen, I filled a glass at the sink and gulped it down, then filled it again to take back to the bedroom. But when I flicked off the kitchen light, I paused.

Someone had been standing in the yard.

I'd only caught a glimpse of them through the kitchen window as I turned off the light. When I looked now, the yard was empty. I blinked rapidly, narrowing my eyes as I stared around my car, and then further, toward the trees.

It was three in the morning.

Why was someone standing in my yard at three in the morning?

Trying to get a better view, I went to the glass doors that led out to the porch and pulled aside the curtain. The clouds had lessened just enough to let some moonlight through, but the silver light was barely able to penetrate the darkness. I flicked on the porchlight, illuminating the deck and just a little way beyond.

There was nothing there.

It had probably just been a deer. It was common enough to see a few of them lingering in the yard in the morning. I was just being paranoid.

I made sure the deadbolt was turned before I went back to bed.

I WOKE ON Sunday morning with my heart pounding. I'd been dreaming, but the memories of it were fading so quickly I could barely grasp them. I'd been wandering in the dark, somewhere pitch black and narrow. But now all that remained was the smell of seawater, briny in my nose as if I'd just taken a dip in the ocean.

Once dressed in some lounge pants and an oversized hoodie, I put on a pot of coffee to brew. The recollection of what had happened yesterday had me jittery, unable to sit still before I'd even downed my morning caffeine. I'd planned to upload all the St. Thaddeus recordings to my computer after breakfast and begin editing, but I also had that video of Leon on my phone. I felt bizarrely nervous to view it.

I went into the gallery, my heart pounding, irrationally scared at what I'd find. What if the video wasn't there, what if it was all static or the file was corrupted?

But it was still there, and it was clear as day.

"Is this the attention you wanted? Well, now I have it on video that you're a creep who follows women into the woods. Good luck keeping your job after this!"

Leon hadn't even glanced at the camera as I shoved it at him. He only looked at me, furious and panting below him, shining that obnoxious flash in his face. I cringed as I listened to myself, wishing that I'd been calmer.

Leon snatched my wrist, forcing the camera down, and the remainder of the video was just a blurry view of the dusty floor, the audio muffled. But I could still make out his voice as he growled, "I warned you, doll. Didn't I tell you to behave? I told you not to come here, not to stick your nose where it doesn't belong."

My stomach fluttered. The viciousness in his voice ignited an immediate, visceral feeling within me. It made no sense to be aroused by that, but there I was.

"What you've started here isn't easily undone."

What had he meant by that? What had I *started*?

"I'm going to catch you. And when I do, I'll make you scream."

My insides quivered. Fucking hell. I'd been threatened by a man who stalked me out into the woods, and my vagina decided to turn on me like this? This was on another level of fucked up.

The longer I listened to his voice, the more I ached to find him again, to—to do what? To jump on his dick? Demand answers? Rage at him for confusing me?

"Give me the book. Otherwise, you're going to be a very sorry girl."

I paused the video. These didn't seem like the words of a man who had just pulled off one of the world's most elaborate pranks. He sounded furious, even desperate. I restarted the video, skipping ahead just a few seconds to the moment right before he grabbed my wrist.

There was a frame, a single frame in the blur of motion when he grabbed me, that looked different. I struggled for several moments to pause it at just the right spot, moving the video backward and forward until . . .

There. A single frame. A frame that should have shown Leon, but it didn't. Instead, it showed a dark figure with Leon's face, with golden eyes and sharp grinning teeth.

One slightly blurred frame that felt like a puzzle piece sliding into place.

RAE

MONDAY MORNING BROUGHT clear skies, cold and pale blue overhead as I walked to campus. I was jumpy, constantly looking over my shoulder, as if Leon would sense I knew his secret and get rid of me before I could let it out. I'd saved a screenshot on my phone of that damning frame from the video. I felt as if I'd already stared at it for hours, trying to glean the truth from that haunting picture.

No one would believe me. They would think I faked the video, photoshopped the image. But after staring at that golden-eyed figure, blurry but undeniable, I knew: Leon wasn't human. The *thing* in that photo wasn't human.

I believed the summoning ritual had worked.

I believed I had summoned a demon.

I believed that demon was Leon.

And I, perhaps every inch the fool he claimed I was, intended to call him out on it.

I kept my cold hands shoved in my jacket pockets so no one would see them shaking. I was riding a bizarre high, somewhere between terror and elation. On the one hand, all my years of seeking the paranormal had come to this; I had video proof of an inhuman, supernatural creature. It was real, it was all *real*.

That was exactly the problem.

I had a very real demon coming after me. Any paranormal investigator worth their shit would say not to mess around with the demonic. In my paranoia, I even began Googling the names of local priests.

What was I supposed to do? Exorcise him? Convince a priest that a campus security guard was, in fact, demonic? They'd laugh in my face.

I, somehow, had to make Leon leave, and not by handing over the grimoire. I didn't know exactly why he wanted it, but that book was likely the only power I had over him. I wasn't just going to hand it over because he asked. I'd stayed up late the night before, translating even more of its passages, trying to figure out if I had any means of defense. I found punishing spells, said to be useful for "taming the unruly servant." And I found instructions for a binding circle said to be able to keep a demon contained within it.

But what made the entire situation so much worse, was part of me didn't want Leon to leave. Part of me was reveling in this, part of me was aching to see what he'd do once he hunted me down. He was playing a game with me, and I knew it. How easily could he have caught me in the church, or in the woods, or as I was sitting alone in my house?

It all made so much more sense—why I was so drawn to him, why I'd been so willing to let him get his hands down my pants, why it seemed like he'd invaded my brain with insatiable lust. He was a *demon*. The literal embodiment of sin and debauchery.

I was a toy to him now, a little doll in his game. But when he came for me, I was determined to be prepared.

I wasn't.

I'd made it through classes, unscathed. The sun was setting, a dull orange glow beyond the black silhouettes of the pines, and the campus was emptying. I'd kept a wary eye on Calgary all day, half-expecting to see Leon standing there in his usual spot, guarding the place. But so far, there had been no sign of him.

It wasn't accurate to say he appeared out of thin air, but it certainly seemed like it. One moment I was walking toward a group of girls headed in the opposite direction, my eyes flickered away for a moment—and Leon was there, walking behind them.

I froze in my tracks. My heart thundered against my ribs, pumping me with adrenaline. *Run, run, run.*

I stood my ground, folded my arms, and waited. If I was going to confront him, this was as good a place as any. What could he do to me with so many witnesses? He was watching me, pale eyes bright. He wasn't dressed in his guard uniform, but instead wore a gray knit beanie and black Converse with his casual jeans-and-hoodie ensemble.

"Well, well, well." He stopped in front of me, smirking, a wicked gleam in his eyes. "Were you looking for me, Raelynn?"

"No," I lied. "I thought you'd take a hint and stay away from me."

"Aw, so mean." He pouted. "I told you what you were in for. I told you I'd hunt you down and make you sorry for defying me. It's been fun watching you looking over your shoulder for the past few hours, but . . ." He shrugged. "It's time to get down to business. Where's the grimoire?"

"Somewhere safe, away from you," I said. "I'm not giving it to you. You need to leave. Begone!"

He snorted, tweaking an eyebrow at me. "*Begone*? Okay, Merlin, are you going to wave your magic wand at me next?" He shook his head, eyes scanning the campus. He was nervous. On the lookout for someone . . . or something. "What are you going to do, Rae? Are you going to run, add a little excitement to the game?" He was already standing close, well within my personal bubble. But then he reached out, nudging my chin teasingly with his knuckle. "Look at you, so big and brave now."

"I know what you are," I hissed. I waited to see a crack in his calm facade, hoping to see him twitch with fear.

Instead he said drily, "Do tell. We'll see if you get it right."

I blinked rapidly, suddenly doubting myself. Did I dare say it, here and now? I pulled out my phone, nervously looking around at the students passing us by. We were in the middle of the sidewalk alongside the quad, in the open. I opened my photos and held up the screenshot to him.

He narrowed his eyes. "What's that?"

"That's you," I said softly. "Why do you have yellow eyes, Leon? And sharp teeth? Claws?" My hand shook, but I clenched my jaw and plowed on. "What the *hell* are you?"

"I thought you said you *know* what I am?" Mischievous sarcasm dripped from his words. "Looks like a good edit to me. I didn't know you had so much time on your hands." His fingers twitched, tapping impatiently where they were folded against his arm. "Your lack of cooperation is disappointing. I thought after a good night's sleep you'd be thinking clearer. But apparently not."

Suddenly, he slung his arm over my shoulder. I yelped, wiggling, but he squeezed me to his side and started walking, leaving me no choice but to stumble along with him. I fit neatly under his arm, squished into the warmth of his chest and surrounded by his intoxicating scent.

"You and I are going to have a problem, Rae," he said softly, "if you don't run home right this instant, get the book, and bring it back to me." His voice was gentle, but a threat lingered in it: a threat that made tension swell in my abdomen, and made me feel small. All the while we kept walking casually, but I could see where he was going.

We were headed toward University Drive—*off* campus.

He cocked his head to look down at me, curiously.

"So tense, Raelynn," he said. "Would it make you feel better to run? You could get all that nervous energy out." He chuckled sadistically, as the thought of running from him made me gulp with trepidation. "I'll catch you again, don't worry. You can't get away."

I took a deep breath, and turned my head to look up at him. He was looking straight ahead, smiling, so damn pleased with himself. I squirmed, trying to remove myself from under his arm. "I'm not giving you shit. I'm not playing your game."

"No?" He stopped abruptly, turning to me as if he were shocked. "Not in the mood to play? Fine then."

I wriggled free of his arm—a lot of good it did. His hand whipped out and gripped my face, squeezing my cheeks as he pulled me close and bent down to look me straight in the eyes. "No more games then. We're going to your house, you're getting the grimoire, and you're going to hand it over before this escalates any further." His eyes were changing. They weren't so pale green any-more, there was a glow of golden light to them. I was unable to look away, frozen in his gaze. His touch dug into my skin.

"More threats," I said. We were right at the edge of campus, if I could just get away . . . "You don't scare me, Leon. You're not going to trick me into giving you the grimoire."

He chuckled, bringing his face close to mine. He ex-amined me, his eyes stroking over me. It was as if his gaze was peeling back my skin, laying bare my bones and all my wicked thoughts. "You don't even know what tricks I have in store for you yet, Rae," he said. His free hand tucked my hair back behind my ear, his fingers tracing down over the piercings in my cartilage and making me shiver despite myself. When his fingers reached that tender spot right below my ear, my eyelids fluttered as the overstimulating sensation prickled all the way down my spine.

"Mm, Raelynn . . . it's going to be fun breaking that stubborn mask of yours. You have no idea . . ." Another shudder went over me at the caress of his breath on my ear. ". . . what absolutely *filthy* things I'm going to do to you."

My body was betraying me, but I still had *some* self-preservation left. I jerked from his grasp, pulling away so hard that I stumbled over my own feet and landed hard on my ass. He looked down at me curiously, a sardonic smile making him bare his teeth.

"I thought you said you didn't want to play?" he said.

Panting, I scrambled to my feet and ran.

15

LEON

RAELYNN RAN. SHE ran and every muscle in me went tense as a coiled spring. The intoxicating draught of adrenaline flooding her only made it worse. I had to pause for a moment just to calm myself down, otherwise I'd catch her too quickly and the fun would end.

Humans were, and always had been, our prey. It had been far too long since I'd had the opportunity to hunt.

I strolled after her, following her scent after she disappeared from my sight. She'd walked to campus that day: I swear the woman had no sense of survival at all. The Eld had been swarming for days and yet she insisted on making an easy target of herself. The sooner the grimoire and I were away from her, the better.

She was my summoner, but she'd already, technically, dismissed me. The moment the grimoire was in my hands, I'd be gone from this awful little town and her life would go on as usual. Well, that wasn't entirely true. There was no guarantee the monsters would lose interest in her. And the Hadleighs weren't just going to leave her alone either.

I frowned as I walked, irritation making me quicken my pace. With or without me, the Hadleighs would have Raelynn as their sacrifice, just another victim lost to Abelaum's notorious bad luck. She'd disappear, her body never to be found. Her friends and family would search, they'd create campaigns and give interviews and weep on live television. But Raelynn would be gone, her soul consumed by a God.

That bothered me.

Whatever. I'd never met a human who wouldn't leave me for dead and kick me while I was down for good measure. It wasn't my business what went on in the human world once I was gone. Rae was amusing, but not worth the trouble of risking my life to stay. I'd already wasted time keeping the Eld away from her.

She'd have to fend for herself, and so far, she was doing a terrible job of it.

She was still running, but not toward home, and I was confused until I turned onto a side street and saw a flash of her disappearing—inside the thick oak doors of the Westchurch Cemetery chapel.

Of course she'd run to a church. Typical.

The sun had set, and the moon was a mere sliver. I breathed deeply from the cold wind that rushed around me as I reached the chapel steps.

Death was in the air. I had to be quick. In the night, the Eld were hunting.

The hinges creaked as I stepped inside. The chapel smelt of dried flowers and embalming fluid, the kind of place that felt sterile and cold. I let the door slam ominously behind me and meandered between the pews.

"Oh, Raaaelyn," I called. "Come out, come out . . . I told you I wouldn't let you get away—oh, *fuck*—"

My skull rang, courtesy of something heavy and wooden slamming against it. I turned, rubbing the back of my head, to find Rae standing there with a large wooden crucifix.

"Begone, demon!" she yelled, thrusting the cross forward. She'd really put her strength into that strike. She would have laid out a human unconscious. Impressive.

I snorted. "Oh, stop. Your obsession with trying to bludgeon me to death is getting old."

She wavered, but I was firmly blocking her exit, and her resolve hardened. "Do you deny it?" she demanded. "You're a demon, aren't you?"

I rolled my eyes. "Yes, doll. Congratulations, you've done it!" I clapped my hands, making her jump. "You've caught the big, bad demon. What a marvelous investigator you are." I snatched the crucifix from her hands, snapped it in two, and tossed it aside. "What now, hm? You look like you're in a bit of danger, Rae. You're looking a bit helpless." I advanced, and she dodged around the next pew. I vaulted over it easily, startling her so badly she yelped and tripped back onto the seat.

I planted my hands on either side of her, leaning over her. She gulped, her legs squeezed together, her eyes wide, her lips parted as she stared at me—fury, defiance, and barely suppressed desire on her face.

I'd always found it strange how desperately humans tried to hide their own lust, as if it was something to be ashamed of.

"You're . . . you're really . . ." Her voice cracked and she gulped. It was honestly cute how frazzled she was.

"A demon? In the flesh, darling. Now, I think I won fair and square. You have nowhere else to run. So, are you ready to go fetch the grimoire, or do you need a little more convincing?" I paused, enjoying how small she looked there on the pew: just an innocent little church girl accosted by evil. "You're so cute when you're irritated. Even your freckles are red."

She growled. She was fighting with herself, squirming between my arms. The scent of her arousal made me want to rip off her clothes, bite her flesh, *take* her—

"Convincing?" she scoffed, but her voice shook and the laugh she forced out was nervous. "What convincing? You're just trying to play nice, as if that will . . . make me . . ."

I was toying with the top button on her sweater. Her heart was pounding beneath my fingertips. It had been a long time since I'd looked at a mortal and felt that much desire—and it was only made worse by her unshakeable defiance. She was determined to challenge me at every turn, where any other human would have had the good sense to keep retreating.

"Demons don't play nice, doll," I said. "We play tricks."

A spark lit up in her eyes. I'd given her an opportunity; I was allowing her the chance to give in without surrendering too much of her pride. It was awfully generous of me, but hell, I wasn't entirely evil.

"Tricks?" Her voice had shrunk to a whisper. "What tricks?"

I'd shown her my eyes, so I decided to give one more taste of what I was. I brought my lips close to hers, so close our breath mingled. I licked my tongue over my lips, its forked sides spreading to start from opposite sides of my mouth until they slid down to meet in the middle.

Her eyes were the size of saucers. She seemed to have forgotten how to breathe. The possibilities of a split tongue tended to have that effect, but I'll admit it was *particularly* pleasing to see her shaken. She was squirming again, but this time, it wasn't in hopes of escape.

"Oh, shit," she whispered. Thoughts of what this tongue could do would be running rampant through her head. Her defiance was wavering, her desire overpowering her.

I grinned, and brought my face down to whisper against her neck, "So, shall I show you my tricks?"

Bang!

Raelynn leapt up from her seat, crushing herself against me at the sound. The chapel doors had swung open so hard they slammed against the columns behind them. The wind howled inside, carrying with it yellow leaves and a pungent, sour smell.

"What is that?" Rae's voice choked up as she peered around me. "What . . . oh my God . . ."

I sighed heavily. The click and scrape of nails across the chapel stones sounded its arrival, as did the low, rumbling growl in the Eld's throat.

"The game is on pause, doll," I said, pushing her further behind me. "Don't think I'm done with you yet."

RAE

THE MONSTER THAT walked through the chapel doors was straight out of my nightmares. I'd thought the bizarre, canine-skulled thing in the woods had been an art piece—but seeing it move, seeing it sway low to the ground and gurgle as its long black tongue dripped thick saliva across the floor, absolutely shattered my belief.

It shouldn't be real.

It *couldn't* be real.

But it *was*. Snarling, white eyes shot through with reddened veins rolling about in its head, it stalked into the church and rose up on its thin, deer-like back limbs. Its teeth clicked eagerly, a sound like the chattering of a cat chasing a bug emitting from its bare bone jaws.

"Leon." My voice was a hiss, tense and desperate. My hands were knotted up in his shirt. "Leon . . . do something . . ."

"Do something?" He shot me a narrow-eyed glare, and said mockingly, "*Oh Leon, do something! Save me, please, oh please!* What happened to *Begone, demon?* What happened to trying to bash my head in with a crucifix?"

The creature snarled at the sound of his voice. It was swaying in its stance, sizing up an attack. The smell rushed in my nose again and I nearly gagged. In the church's dim light, I could see the beast's body in all its wretched horror: skin that was gray and moldering, the bones pockmarked with little holes of decay, the teeth blackened, sharp, and jagged.

"What is it?" I whimpered, too terrified to be angry at Leon's sass. "What the *hell* is that thing?"

Leon cracked his knuckles and rolled back his shoulders. "One of the Eld. They're ancient creatures born of the blood and misery of dark places." He glanced back at me over his shoulder. "They're the kind of things that come skulking around when you cling to dangerous magical artifacts you have no business keeping."

Before I could retort, before I could be furious he chose now of all times to keep pushing about the damned grimoire, the creature threw back its head and *howled.* Not like a dog, but like a man. Like a man in agony, like a man unleashing years upon years of pain and fury into one gut-wrenching cry. Then it leapt and, somewhere between what my eyes could see and my brain could process, Leon collided with it.

They slammed into the seats, sending wood splintering and screeching across the floor, and I had to leap back to avoid having a pew slam into my gut. I shrunk back against the wall, unable to tell which beast was winning in all the chaos. Their movements were too fast, too unnatural. I blinked rapidly as my vision blurred, but it was only because their speed was too much for my eyes to follow.

I'd seen large dogs fight before—the snarling, screeching, and yelping had haunted me for days. But this was so much worse. The sound of them was ungodly. It rumbled through the chapel's stone floors, echoed from the corners. It was the sounds of something living being torn apart, the sounds of a monster bearing down on its prey.

Suddenly Leon rose up, the monster's skeletal head gripped between his hands, and crushed its skull like an egg bursting open.

"Oh my God . . . oh my God . . ." My mouth hung open. The long-limbed, rotten monster lay destroyed in the rubble of the pews. The stone floor had been deeply scratched. The smell of death hung thicker in the air than ever. And Leon . . .

Leon didn't look human anymore.

His hoodie had been torn apart in the struggle, laying his chest bare. His myriad of colorful tattoos couldn't cover the long, deep scars etched into his skin. The veins in his arms had gone black, like inky roots snaking their tendrils up from his clawed fingertips. He hung his head back, catching his breath, his teeth all elongated and sharp. He ran a gory hand through his hair, streaking the blond with the dull red of the monster's blood. His eyes, when he turned them on me, were as bright and golden as the sun.

"Now," he said, drawing in a heavy breath. "Where were we?"

"What the fuck," I clutched my head in my hands, inching around the toppled pews. Blood and gore were spattered across the floor, and the creature's body was *melting*. It had become a goopy, blackened consistency that squirmed with living worms. I clapped a hand over my mouth. I was going to be sick—

"More will come for you, Rae," Leon said, discarding the shredded remnants of his jacket. He walked over to the bénitier near the front of the chapel and dipped his hands in the holy water, scrubbing off the blood and tinting the water pink. "I told you what you started isn't easy to undo. This beast is the *least* of what may come hunting you." He splashed water on his face, droplets streaking down onto his chest.

As he stood there, stained with the blood of a monster—fanged, clawed, a monster in his own right—I thought he was simultaneously the sexiest and most terrifying thing I'd ever seen.

Dazed, in utter disbelief, I turned and wandered out the church's open doors. The cemetery seemed peaceful now that the shrieks and cries had been silenced, and only the chirping of the crickets remained. The night air was cool, crisp and clean; the smell of death was fading as the monster's body dissolved.

This couldn't be real. This had to be a dream or . . . or a nightmare. I rubbed my hands over my face. Here I'd thought I only had a demon to deal with, but this was so much worse.

"We were in the middle of something, Raelynn."

I whirled back around. Leon stood in the light at the bottom of the chapel steps, hair damp, dark bloody stains on his jeans. I remembered suddenly—just before that monster burst in, I had been about to allow myself to do the unthinkable.

I had been about to give in. I had been about to beg him to shove that unholy split tongue down my throat. After what I'd just seen, I should have been entirely turned off, horrified, disgusted. I should have been running.

But instead, I wanted him to wrap those bloodstained hands around my throat. I wanted him to manhandle me with even a fraction of the strength he'd just used to rip that thing limb from limb. I was staring down what was very likely the most dangerous man in Abelaum, and I wanted him to rip my clothes off right there in that graveyard.

"Thank you," I said tightly. "I . . . I might've . . . if you weren't here . . ."

"You would be dismembered, but alive, being dragged deep into the forest where they could consume your body slowly." He smiled. "And I prefer thanks in actions, rather than words. Give me the grimoire."

I backed away until my thighs bumped against a headstone behind me. Leon advanced, impatience in every step until he stood right before me. The rise and fall of his chest, his breathing heavy, was hypnotizing. His body was slim but his muscles had swelled. I wanted to caress my hands over the tattoos—saints and angels and snarling wolves—and over the scars beneath them.

"Why do you want the grimoire so badly?" I said, stalling.

"It contains my mark, my sigil," he said. "It's the last physical record of it remaining on Earth, and having my mark means being able to summon me. Once I have it, I'm destroying it." His eyes lit up. "And I'll never return to this godforsaken town."

"If I give it to you," I said slowly, "will those things go away? Will they stop coming after me?"

He winced, and gave a little shrug. "Maybe."

"*Maybe?* What the hell am I supposed to do then?"

"Try offering me your soul." His tone was cocky, but clipped, as if he'd allowed the words out only begrudgingly. "Offer me your soul in exchange for protection."

I stared at him, stunned, until I began to slowly shake my head. "No. No way. I'm not offering you my soul."

He shrugged again. "Good luck then. Now . . ." He leaned over me, those damned tempting full lips curled into a saucy smirk. "How long are you going to ignore that little problem of yours?"

I frowned, self-consciously squeezing my legs together. "What problem?"

His smirk widened. "You are *dripping* at the sight of me."

Blood flooded my cheeks, and heat flooded between my legs. I sputtered, looking away—but I couldn't deny him. I couldn't lie.

"Fuck you," I muttered.

"You're welcome to."

"Why don't you just do it?" I blurted out, throwing up my hands. "You keep threatening and teasing and . . . and . . . *looming* over me." I glared up at him, my fists clenching when I found him laughing.

"Just do it?" He chuckled. "Just bend you over and ravage you here and now? Just do it, so you don't have to give in? No, no, no." He clasped his hands behind his back. "That would be too easy. I want to see you squirm, I want to see you *beg*. If you're going to be damned, you need to go willingly."

The tension inside me was going to explode. My clit felt swollen, my panties were damp. The sight of him shirtless and bloodied, having just unleashed his true hellish self to save my life, was unreasonably arousing.

"Please, just—"

"Aw, *please*." He pouted, mocking me again. "Please? Please, what? Use that pretty mouth of yours, come on. *Speak*."

I clenched my teeth, a petulant whimper squeaking out. I was damned, just as he'd said.

"Do you want to set up your camera first?" he said. "This would make for great clickbait, wouldn't it? *Fucked by a Demon in a Cemetery*?" He chuckled to himself. "I'd watch that."

"You're an asshole," I whispered.

"You are what you eat."

"Fucking hell," I gasped, my hands clinging for the headstone behind me as if that would somehow keep me grounded. I hadn't felt this unbearably, irrationally horny since I'd taken Ecstasy at my eighteenth birthday party. I lowered my voice, as if the dead themselves could hear me and clutch their pearls at what I was going to do. "Fuck me. Please."

He shook his head and brought his face down closer, motioning to his ear. "Can't hear you. A little louder please. Fuck you where?"

"Goddamn it, Leon—"

"I just ripped a living thing to shreds, doll. I'm in a *very* sadistic mood and will gladly let you stand there and stumble through humiliating yourself all night. Or, you can just say what you *really* want, and I'll bend you over this headstone, eat your little cunt until you drip down your thighs, and fuck you until you forget your own name. What'll it be?"

I gulped. I'd never been very religious, but it only felt right to cross myself before I dared to say, "Bend me over and . . . and fuck me . . . fuck my cunt . . . please—"

RAE

HE GRASPED AT my sweater and *tore* it, sending the buttons flying into the grass. He gripped my waist, claws digging into my skin as my mouth opened for him and his forked tongue caressed over mine. His taste was the sweetest poison, tingling in my mouth as I groaned into him with abandon. My noise only encouraged him, the feral growl he gave in response deepening as he wrapped a clawed hand around my throat and squeezed—squeezed until I whimpered and it came out as little more than a pitiful squeak.

He grinned at me, all wicked teeth and a wolf's hunger. "Aw, sweet little mortal. So fucking *breakable*." He squeezed tighter, gripping the sides of my throat until my head swam and euphoria washed over me, and his claws dug into my skin with the sweetest sting. It was the kind of pain that gave me goose bumps, that had me shivering for more. He nipped at my pouting lower lip, chuckling as he hovered close and whispered into my mouth, "Say please if you want to breathe."

"Please . . . please—"

He released my throat, only to lift me and sit my butt on the headstone. He pushed my legs apart with his hips, the stone cold through my skirt. He breathed against the hollow between my collarbones, and trailed his tongue along them until he reached my neck and bit. His fingers tangled in my hair so he could pull my head back and bite me again, lingering where my veins pulsed so dangerously close to the surface. He was going to leave marks all over me.

I'd given into my lust for a demon—I wanted his body so badly it terrified me. My hands clawed up his back, digging in eagerly between his shoulder blades as he snarled in enthusiasm. He released my hair and dropped to his knees, his hands moving to possessively grip my hips.

Those bright golden eyes staring up at me from between my legs made my breath stop. He bit at the thin fabric of my leggings, catching it in his teeth and leaving a small tear. When he looked up at me again, there was a wildness in his eyes, a hunger that made adrenaline pump through me as if my body was trying to tell me to run.

"All this clothing in my fucking way," he growled, and he ripped a hole in the leggings with his claws, leaving my thigh almost entirely bare. Then he did the same to the other side and kept going—ripping, tearing at them as if their presence was a personal insult. I clung to the headstone to hold myself up, my legs beginning to shake. When nothing was left of my leggings but torn rags, he lowered his head and ran his forked tongue up my thigh until my entire body quivered.

"So sensitive," he murmured. He lingered at the highest point on my thigh, nipping my skin. "The way you shiver, fuck, I love to see you shake." His hands traced up the outside of my thighs, under my skirt, where he found the lacey edges of my panties through what little remained of my leggings.

Those panties were his next victim. He ripped the fabric and tossed them aside, but not before he pressed them to his nose and inhaled deeply. His pupils swelled, and he looked at me like he was starving. His black claws pricked into my sensitive skin, leaving behind beads of blood. He licked up each little red droplet, and grinned as my mouth gaped open in shock.

"You think I won't consume every last bit of you?" he said, his voice so deep and dark that it seemed to slither up my spine and wrap around the back of my skull. "I'll fucking eat you alive, Raelynn." His claws dug in, and this time I couldn't hold back a cry of pain. He held me there, his eyes alight as he watched a thin trickle of blood well from my skin and streak down my thigh—only to be caught by his tongue.

"I won't be satisfied with merely your blood, Raelynn." I was shaking on my perch as his mouth came nearer. His eyes lingered between my legs, bright and inhumanly golden. "Your blood, piss, sweat, cum—I want it all. *Mine.* Abandon your inhibitions now. You won't have a use for them anymore."

His tongue snaked out, its forked sides flicking the air. I'd seen a split tongue as a body modification, but his was strikingly long. It was monstrous. It filled me with such mixed feels of excitement and fear that when I first tried to open my mouth, all I managed to get out was a gasp.

"I want to feel it," I whispered. "Please . . ."

He stood, and lifted me easily from the headstone. My head swam as he turned me with my back to his chest and my head dangling toward the ground, completely upside-down in his arms. My glasses slipped off my nose and into the grass. The world became a blur, but I couldn't keep my eyes open long anyway.

My pussy was right beneath his face, exposed, my skirt useless to cover me in this position. I panted desperately—embarrassed, eager, completely discombobulated. Then—oh *fuck*—his tongue slid over me, between every fold, lapping up my arousal and, *God,* swirling over my clit. I shuddered, jerking involuntarily, and his grip tightened on me. His claws were digging into my sides where he held me, but the pain only made it better. He took my labia in his mouth, sucking as if it were a meal, then he went in with his tongue again, moving it with focused precision over every inch of sensitive flesh.

My head felt heavy from the angle, but the rush of blood to my skull only served to heighten my dizzyingly growing pleasure. It was overwhelming, almost unbearable. I was moaning with every merciless touch of his mouth as my legs wrapped around his neck.

"You taste so good." The hunger in his voice made me shake, reigniting some instinctual urge to flee, to struggle despite how good it felt. I squirmed in his grasp, trying vainly to escape his mouth. He laughed at me, and switched effortlessly to hold me up with only one arm around my waist, so he could move the other between my legs and massage my clit with his fingers.

"No escape, doll. You know what your safe word is." Then his mouth went to work again. Soon enough, voluntary movement was impossible. His fingers worked my clit and his tongue—unnaturally thick, unnaturally long—pushed inside me. I gasped, wiggling as he caressed inside me, a stimulation I had not thought possible.

"Leon . . . Leon, *please* . . ." My words were choked with panting, and he rubbed me faster. I moaned, and he withdrew his tongue only to plunge it in again. My entire body began to tense, then trembled.

"I'm going to make you come, Rae," he growled. "And I want you to keep begging as I do."

My orgasm was imminent, rushing toward me at an unstoppable speed. I clapped my hands over my mouth, muffling my cries of "Please, please, please" as my pleasure became torture under his sadistic tongue.

My clit throbbed under his fingers, and his tongue went so deep that my spasming pussy tightened around him. My toes curled in my boots, my cries choked up in my throat and all I could do was try to breathe and somehow keep my soul from leaving my body.

"What a good girl." He lowered me, and I lay dizzied on the grass, my eyes unfocused. In a blur I saw him pick something up, and he leaned forward to tuck my glasses back onto my face. He wiped drips of my cum from his chin and licked his fingers clean.

Then he stood over me, unbuttoning his jeans and sliding down his zipper. He took down his black briefs, and *fuck*—if there could have been any remaining doubt in my mind that he wasn't human, the sight of his hard cock dispersed all doubts. His thick head had two additional ridges behind it, and a swell on the underside, making his girth terrifying. He gripped it in his hand, spat on the shaft and stroked as he bared his teeth at me.

With a dark chuckle, he whispered, "Try to run."

I loved a struggle. He was unleashing my darkest desires one by one. I felt slow and drugged with pleasure, but I still tried to scramble up, as if I could actually get away. I crawled no more than a few inches before he seized me and pinned me.

"Pathetic." His teeth nipped at my ear as he whispered. He pressed my head against the cool grass, his palm hot on my cheek, and with his other hand jerked up my hips so my ass was raised, ready for him.

"Do you want it, Raelynn?" His voice was a caress, as dark and dangerous as the touch of a snake's scales. His cock moved over me, slick with my arousal. "Do you want me to wreck your little cunt?"

"Yes," my answer was a groan, tight with anticipation and shaking. "Yes, please—"

His ridged head pressed against my entrance, then inside, every inch stretching me tightly around him. He hunched over me and dragged his claws up my back as he began to thrust. When he'd said he would wreck me, fuck, he'd meant it. The ache and stretch as he fucked into me would have had me struggling to maintain my position if he hadn't been holding me in place.

Bent over, face against the grass, hips held in place by strong hands from which I knew there was no escape—I was absolutely dripping for it.

I'd never had a problem being vocal but, God, I sounded pathetic. Whimpering with every thrust, somewhere between words and animalistic cries. He'd fucked anything human out of me and left me just a shaking, needy toy for him to use.

"How does it feel, doll?" His fingers tangled in my hair, claws scratching along my scalp. "Use your voice, come on now. Or can you even speak at all anymore?"

"So good, fuck, hurts so good." My tongue stumbled over those words. Language was just too hard. My mind was sinking fast into a space of hot, smothering darkness, but I was perfectly happy to suffocate there, happy to drown in ecstasy. I arched my back, leaning into him despite the ache. The feeling of his cock was unlike anything I'd ever experienced, ridged and swollen where no man's could be, so that every thrust was shocking.

"This could be the fate of your soul." He laughed sadistically. "All it takes is a simple bargain, and you're mine. Mine to use and pleasure however I wish. Mine to mark, mine to hurt." He pressed into me hard, so hard my moan was nearly a sob. Fuck, the pain made the pleasure so much sweeter. "It's alright if you're not ready to give up your soul yet, but you will, doll. You've already given in."

He drove into me with long, steady strokes. I wanted nothing more than to have his cum inside me, filling me.

"Leon . . . give . . . give me . . ." I couldn't get the words out. It felt too good. He pulled me up, so I was on all fours, grasped my face and squeezed my cheeks.

"What was that?" he growled. "Speak up, Rae, I can't hear you."

"I want . . . your cum . . ."

He squeezed tighter, forcing my mouth open. He slid two fingers inside, claws dangerously sharp across my tongue. My mouth was forced to stay open, salivating as he pressed down on my tongue. He'd made a mess of me in every way, and I could only cry out as his pace quickened and suddenly, I felt his cock throb inside me.

"Say it again," he said, low over my back. His voice in my ear seemed to reverberate within my head and sing within my very blood. "Beg for it. Beg for what you want."

I couldn't form words with his fingers in my mouth, but that didn't prevent me from trying. And that was when I realized—as I knelt there babbling uselessly, drool running down my chin, practically sobbing with the pleasure of it—he was absolutely right. I had already given in. I'd said I wouldn't give him my soul, but I'd practically given it to him already.

I'd given myself up to a demon and there was no going back.

"Please . . . please . . . please," was all I could manage. The more I begged, the more my pussy tightened and began to clench around his girth. My last orgasm had rocked me, but this one got its grip into me and wouldn't let go. I sobbed from the force of it, and he hooked his fingers a little deeper into my mouth so that I couldn't muffle my sounds. I was certain I was loud enough to wake the dead.

My pleasure brought him to his peak, and his already thick cock swelled even thicker. He bit down on my shoulder as he throbbed, spilling inside me. He took his fingers from my mouth and pulled my hips back, pressing deeply into me as he came, filling me until I could feel him dripping down my thighs.

18

LEON

THE MOMENT SHE'D looked at me with those wide, defiant brown eyes and told me to do it, I knew I was fucked for this woman. Foolishly, madly *fucked*. When she made herself my willing victim, I wanted to steal her away back to Hell right then and there.

I hadn't planned to offer her a deal. Some demons loved nothing more than collecting human souls to raise their status in Hell, but I honestly couldn't be bothered. I *shouldn't* have bothered. But now I couldn't get the idea out of my head: she was mine. I needed her soul. Fucking her, claiming her body, listening to those cute little whimpers as she shook with pleasure—that could become a quick addiction. The kind of thing I wanted guaranteed to me for eternity.

I'd offered a damn good bargain too. Considering the

circumstances, my protection should have come at a far heavier price than just her soul.

What else was I supposed to do? Stick around, risk my life, and protect her out of sympathy? Out of *kindness*? I'd been trampled over by enough humans to know better. She'd pay up or I'd be gone. I'd take the grimoire and be on my way.

The taste of her lingered on my tongue, the sweet scent of her in my nose. I leaned back against a nearby headstone, holding her against me, my eyes half-lidded as I surveyed the dark, empty graveyard. Her orgasms had shattered her, but we couldn't linger there for long. More Eld would come.

Rae sighed, and for a moment, I thought she was asleep. I'd left dark-red marks across her neck and shoulder from my bites, marks that would be purple bruises by morning. I'd be gone, but my marks would linger on her for days.

Mine. My human, my doll, my tender flesh, *mine*.

Maybe I'd give her more time to think on my deal. Maybe a few more days on Earth wouldn't kill me . . . or maybe it would, and I was getting disastrously obsessed over a human plaything.

She stirred, and suddenly stiffened. Slowly, as if she were trying not to startle a wild animal, she squirmed out from my arms and stood. She brushed the blades of grass from her skirt and plucked at the leaves and twigs in her hair, a little tremble in her hands. It occurred to me that she'd be cold without her leggings—the leggings I had completely destroyed.

"I'm escorting you home," I said, not bothering to get up yet. The cold headstone felt good against my back. "You'll give me the grimoire, and I'll be gone."

I waited for her protest, looking forward to more sassy defiance. But instead, with her back turned to me, she said, "Why were you in Abelaum? Before I summoned you?"

"I was in service to my previous summoner."

"And that was?"

"Kent Hadleigh."

She turned, her expression tight and desperate. "You mean to tell me that Kent Hadleigh is . . . a wizard?"

"Magician." I shrugged. "Even the most non-gifted mortal can use the words written in the grimoire. But once they no longer have the book, it's impossible to remember what was written in it. Attempts to copy the text will rapidly fade and become illegible. Once I destroy the grimoire, no one will be summoning me ever again." I grinned proudly at the thought. My freedom had been a long time coming.

I rose, stretching my arms over my head. The night air was cool and the sky was clear, sparkling with stars and the faint glow of the sickle moon. The singing of the crickets and the sound of the breeze rattling the pine needles made me want to run through those woods one last time. I felt good for the first time in a long time.

Rae was watching me suspiciously, eyes narrowed. I could practically hear the gears turning in her head.

"Well?" I nodded my head toward the cemetery gate. "Would you like to lead the way home?"

She folded her arms. "Why did Kent summon you?"

I sighed heavily. So nosy, this one. Endless questions. "For the same reason his father and his grandfather summoned me. They needed protection from the Eld."

She gulped. She shot a nervous glance over her shoulder, toward the chapel, where the body of the beast lay.

"How can something like that exist?" she said softly. "It seems like they'd be killing people all the time, that they'd be seen."

"People go missing all the time in the woods." I stood beside her, and she looked over. Her eyes drifted down my body, lingered over my chest, and very pointedly avoided looking between my legs, despite that I'd already buttoned up my jeans again. I grinned. "The Eld are attracted to magic. Unless a human is unlucky enough to come across one deep in the forest, it's unlikely the average mortal would ever encounter one. Eld won't bother to come hunting in human cities unless they have a good reason."

"Then what's their reason?" she said. "They're coming after me because I have the grimoire, I get that." She didn't *get that,* but whatever. "But were they only coming after Kent because he had the grimoire before?"

"Start walking, and I'll keep talking," I said, giving her a nudge in the direction of the gate. "The sooner we get the grimoire out of your hands, the better."

She pouted, but she was obedient for once. The buttons on her sweater were ripped off, so she tugged it tightly over her chest and folded her arms to keep it closed. We left through the gate together, not a single car in sight as we made our way up the road toward her home.

"I need to know how to protect myself from those things," she said suddenly. "You said they might not stop hunting me, so . . ."

"Move away from Abelaum," I said. "That's the best thing you can do. They'll hunt you wherever you go now that magic has touched you, but living in Abelaum is like sticking your hand straight in a beehive and wondering why you're getting stung."

She looked at me in alarm, but I was just trying to be honest. There was no point in lying to her that things would somehow get better once the grimoire was gone. She'd be slightly less attractive to the Eld, but the Hadleighs were a whole other problem.

"I can't just move," she said. "I don't . . . I don't have the money yet . . ."

"Then stay in at night. Board up your windows. Burn rosemary and sage from sundown to sunrise, Eld hate the smell of it. And stay away from the goddamn Hadleighs."

She frowned. "Why? If Kent is a magician, maybe he can help me!"

I scoffed. "Not a single member of that family is interested in *helping* anyone but themselves."

Her frown deepened into a glare. "They've been kind to me. You're just saying that so I'll feel like I have no choice but to accept your *bargain*."

"Do you want to know what Kent *really* does?" I stopped walking, hot with frustration. "Do you want to know what his *Historical Society*"—I put massive air quotes around the fabricated title—"really is about? There are far worse things in Abelaum than monsters. You know the legends. You've been to the church. The Hadleigh family isn't interested in helping you. They're interested in furthering their own power."

She bit her lip, arms still folded. I couldn't fault her suspicions—she knew I was a demon, of course she'd believe I was a liar. But it didn't matter if she believed me. As long as she heard me. As long as I could reassure myself I *tried* to warn her.

Guilt wasn't an emotion that was natural to demons. We simply had no room to learn it. If a young demon fucked up in Hell, they'd likely find themselves dead, slaughtered by someone more powerful than them, or executed by a Reaper if they *really* pissed someone off. There was no room for *guilt*. Get away with it, or get it right the first time.

Feeling that annoying, needling, uncomfortable *press* of guiltiness now, only served to show I'd been on Earth far too long.

I didn't owe this woman a damn thing, but it sure as hell felt like I did.

She'd stopped walking. She was staring at me, a little way ahead of me on the road, arms clasped around her drooping sweater, shivering in the cold. It made me want to hold her, wrap her up, warm her. Fucking hell, I'd gone soft.

"What do the legends and the church have to do with the Hadleighs?" she said softly.

"Morpheus Leighman owned Abelaum's silver mines,"
I said. "His son, Benjamin, changed his surname to
Hadleigh, after his father's cult nearly got the family run
out of town."

Morpheus: the first summoner in centuries that I
hadn't been able to kill. He'd been careful, obsessively
so. A smart man. Trapped underground with his miners
when the shaft collapsed, he discovered many things in
those long-forgotten underground caverns. He'd found
the remnants of an old religion, centered around the
weakened God that spoke to him in the dark; he'd found
the grimoire, written long ago by a powerful witch . . .
and by extension, he'd found my name. He'd found the
iron amulet the witch had made, offering him additional
protection from me.

As much as I'd wanted to, I couldn't kill him, nor
could I kill his son Benjamin when Morpheus passed the
grimoire and the amulet on to him. I had remained captive, over a century in service to the same family as they
grew in power, largely thanks to me.

"His family's cult," Rae murmured, her eyes wide
in the dark. "You're talking about the God, right? The
monster in the mine?" She shook her head. "That's a stupid story told to scare children. The only cult members in
Abelaum are edgy teenagers who want to hang around in
St. Thaddeus and pretend they're communing with some
Old God while they trip on acid." She scoffed. "Come
on. I literally research this stuff for fun. I'm not scared by
Abelaum's personal creepypasta."

I laughed. "Fine. Don't believe it. Kent is obsessed with

keeping that church from being torn down and the mine shafts from being sealed because he's just *really invested* in the town's history. Victoria and Jeremiah want to be friends with you so badly because they're just such good, kind people." I brushed past her, walking on toward her house. I could feel her glare on the back of my head.

"What exactly are you even trying to say?" she snapped, jogging to keep up with me. "If Kent believes there's a God in the mine, so what? Is he planning to make all of Abelaum drink the Kool-Aid? Is he going to try to recruit me to the cause?"

"Not recruit you," I said. "Sacrifice you."

She laughed, but she sounded nervous now. "Right, okay. The Hadleighs are all members of a cult that practices human sacrifice and I'm their next victim. Oh, *please.*" She would have sounded more determined if her voice wasn't shaking with cold. "Your ploy for my soul won't work. I'll survive without your deal just fine, thank you very much."

"Says the girl who was just fucked by a demon."

"You don't get to hold that over my head." She tossed back her hair, chin up proudly. "A woman should never be ashamed of wanting sexual pleasure for herself."

"No, she shouldn't be." We had turned onto the dirt road that led toward her cabin. The crickets were unnervingly quiet, setting me on edge. "But a woman should consider her best options when she's flung herself down a rabbit hole of magic and monsters."

"I *am* considering my options," she said, her voice so drenched in confidence I knew she was faking. "Selling my soul isn't one of them. You can get your grimoire, leave, and I'll figure this out *alone.*"

The cabin was just ahead, the windows warmly lit from within. I wondered if she left lights on because she was forgetful, or because she liked seeing the glow when she came home in the dark. She was silent for a few moments, then said softly, "So, do I need to take a Plan B or something? You know . . ." She motioned at her skirt. It reminded me that her panties were still lying back there in the graveyard, and I suddenly, *desperately* wanted to lift her up and consume her again until she screamed.

I resisted.

"Unless you're a full-blooded witch, you have nothing to fear," I said. "I could come inside you again and again without consequences."

Her face reddened, and a little saunter came back into my step as we came up to the cabin's front porch. I frowned as her motion-activated light flicked on, illuminating a white and orange cat sitting just above the steps.

The crickets were so quiet.

The night was so still.

Something wasn't right.

"Cheesecake?" The confusion is her voice was evident as she scooped up the cat from the porch. The feline mewled, and rubbed his head against her chin before giving me a slow blink. "What are you doing outside, buddy?"

Alarm had already set in for me, and it took only a few more seconds for her. With the light on, she could

now see that her front door was ajar, the curtain billow-
ing softly in the breeze.

"I locked that," she said softly, clutching the cat to
her chest. "I closed it, I know I did."

I was in front of her before she could blink, putting
my body between her and the open door. I peered into
the house, sniffing the air, listening. If whoever had broken in was still there, I'd rip them to pieces before they
touched her.

She pressed a little closer behind me, peering around
me. Her scent was all over this place, mingled with the
smell of the forest creatures that had passed through the
yard, and the cat in her arms. But there was something
else, too: something soft but deeply sweet, rich as caramel.

A witch. A witch had been here.

And there was only one witch I knew of in Abelaum:
Everly.

I straightened slowly, the tension going out of me.

"What is it?" Rae said, her voice cracking in alarm.
"What happened? Is someone in there?"

"Not anymore," I said, stepping aside from the door.
"A human was here, but they're gone now."

"What the hell?" She brushed past me, moving cautiously as she put her cat down on the kitchen table and
continued on into the living room beyond. The cat,
however, had no interest in staying inside. He bounded
back out onto the porch and sat again, staring curiously
into the woods with his tail twitching. "Someone went
through my things! There's papers everywhere, they even
opened my boxes!"

Worry began to knot inside my chest. Why the hell had the witch been here? What did she want? Everly wasn't like her father. From what I'd observed, she was as much his captive as I had been. Her mother had been the same: bound to Kent by love and the shared blood in their child. Kent protected Everly with the same possessive obsession one would protect a prized weapon, and without the grimoire, she was his *greatest* weapon now. The fact that she had come here alone was strange.

"Shit! Goddamn it, no!"

Her pained, furious cry sent me instantly to her side. She was crouched in front of a low bookshelf, tearing volumes down, searching.

"What happened?" My voice was harsh with alarm but it didn't faze her. She looked up, red-faced, jaw clenched with fury and fear.

"They took the grimoire," she whispered. "It's gone."

It felt like cold water being dumped over my head. "Are you sure?"

"It's *gone!*" She threw up her hands, clutching her head. She sounded on the verge of tears. "*Goddamn* it, it's gone, it's fucking *gone,* what the fuck!"

Gone . . . the grimoire was gone, *again.* Had Everly taken it back to Kent? Was I about to be forced back to him?

Or had she kept it? That grimoire was written by the founding witch of her mother's coven. It was her birthright; it was all the knowledge of the witches that had come before her. Everly's power was still feral, untamed in her blood. But if she were to harness it, if she were to escape Kent and train herself to command her magic . . .

I shivered, but it had nothing to do with the cold night air whispering through the open door. Witches were not to be trifled with.

"We have to get it back!" Rae got to her feet, fists clenched, her glasses slipping down her nose. "We have to find out who the *hell* took it—"

I grabbed her suddenly, clapping my hand over her mouth and muffling her furious cursing. She struggled, but only for a moment.

Then she smelled it too.

Death. Pungent and sour on the air. Rae jolted against me, her heart fluttering like a bird. Through the open door, we could both see her cat standing on the porch, back arched, tail puffed. A low, angry growl came from the little animal's throat, fixated on something in the trees.

The house creaked, as if it were tensing in preparation. *Scritch, scritch, scritch.* Rae's head jerked toward the sound, as something scratched at the side of the house. It was coming closer, making its way toward the deck and the open door.

And the cat.

Something wet touched my hand, and I realized she was weeping. I uncovered her mouth, only to hear her whisper desperately, "Cheesecake . . . here kitty, kitty . . . come back inside . . . come back inside, *please* . . ."

The trees groaned. The smell grew sharper. The brave little cat twitched his white tail and yowled as if he were the biggest, fiercest beast in those woods.

I'd always liked cats. The fact that this one belonged to Raelynn, well, perhaps that made me a bit more determined to not see it die. I didn't think I could bear to see her heart break like that. And hell, the little creature was fierce. What else so small would face down the Eld with a puffed tail and some tiny claws?

"Don't leave the house, Rae," I whispered firmly. "Whatever you see—whatever you hear—don't you dare leave this house." Her breathing was quickening, fear rising as she realized I was going to leave. It made me want to grip her tighter, keep her closer, drag her along with me—

But she was safer here.

There was a rustle, a rapid snapping of twigs—and the cat was snatched from the porch.

19

RAE

IN THE SAME moment Cheesecake disappeared, Leon did too. One moment, his arms were wrapped around me tight; safe, warm, possessive, a barrier against the night. A barrier against the thing that lurked outside, that made my hair stand on end and twisted my stomach.

Then, in a blink, he was gone.

The door slammed shut. I was alone, and the night was utterly, deathly silent other than the sobs that choked up in my throat.

Not Cheesecake. Not my sweet chubby kitty. No. No, no, no.

Leon had told me to stay inside, but there was no threat outside that door that was going to keep me from going after my cat. The mama bear came out and regardless of self-preservation or even regular old common sense, I wasn't just going to stand there. I wasn't about to abandon Cheesecake to those things. No way in hell.

I kept a baseball bat near the front door, and it was the only thing I grabbed before I flung the door open and sprinted off the porch. My mind was racing with confusion and fury, I was flushed with adrenaline and yet the world seemed to move slowly around me. I kept expecting to hear the awful cries of my cat fighting for his life, but the night was so silent. So cold. My tears felt icy on my cheeks.

I stalked toward the trees near the side of the porch, closest to where Cheesecake was snatched. I held the bat up, at the ready. I'd seen Leon crush the skull of that Eld beast *thing*. I knew they could be killed. If I bashed its head hard enough, I'd get my cat back.

I took a step into the trees. Then another. Another. My shoes crunched on pine needles and fallen twigs. It was impossible to move silently. I was an easy target. I couldn't see more than a few feet in front of me, and even then, everything was just dark shapes against a darker background. The vile smell of death was strong, stinging my nose and turning my stomach.

"Cheesecake?" I whispered. "Here, kitty . . . kitty, kitty . . ." My voice shook. My terror was rising. I felt like I was walking through a nightmare.

Snap. I whirled to my left. That footstep hadn't been mine. I tightened my sweating hands on the bat, arms trembling, ready to strike. I suddenly felt so weak, as if no matter how hard I tried, the strength would go out of my arms the moment I swung. But I had to try. I had to.

Meow?

For a moment, I thought my heart would burst. Hearing Cheesecake's uncertain little call in the darkness—alive, not in pain—made me run toward the sound. But I halted abruptly when I noticed a dark figure leaning against a tree, my cat cradled in his arms.

Leon.

It was almost too dark to see, but as he held out my wide-eyed, disheveled kitty, I was certain I could see something dark marring his shoulder, and running in rivulets down his arm.

I grasped Cheesecake close, gasping with relief. Leon was breathing raggedly. There was a distinct scent of iron in the air.

"Goddamn it, woman," he hissed. "I told you—*I told you*—to stay inside."

I gulped, beginning to back away toward the house. There was another sound in the darkness, beyond Leon, something like a low, growling purr.

"Get *back* inside. Don't you dare come out until sunrise." Leon pushed off the tree, his golden eyes bright even in the dark. "Cinnamon, rosemary, and sage if you have it. Burn it outside your door. Keep your windows covered and your lights on—they hate the light. Don't make yourself an easy target."

I nodded rapidly. With my cat clutched tightly in one arm and my bat in the other hand, I sprinted back for the house. I rummaged through my spice cabinet, tossing jars of herbs across my countertop until I managed to find rosemary and powdered cinnamon. With shaking hands,

I poured them both into a stone mortar, and used my lighter to burn them. They smoldered, but wouldn't hold a flame. It would have to be enough. I didn't know what the hell I was doing.

I put the jar of burnt herbs outside my front door. I covered every window, I turned on every light. I took the largest knife from the block in the kitchen and sat on the couch, heart pounding, trying to catch my breath as Cheesecake stared nervously at the door.

Eventually, I heard the crickets start up their song again. The tightness seemed to go out of the air, whatever pressure had been squeezing my lungs was gone. Cheesecake curled up on the couch beside me and began to groom, pulling twigs from his fur. I was light-headed with exhaustion and sick with worry, but if Cheesecake didn't sense danger anymore, then I assumed Leon must have chased the monsters off at last.

This was all too dangerously real. All these years of seeking the paranormal, and suddenly I was in the thick of it. Suddenly there were demons, monsters, and magical books, and *I* was witnessing it.

Not just witnessing it, I was getting intimate with it.

Closing my eyes, I could feel Leon's tongue on me again. It was so wrong that it felt right. I'd fucked an in-human being, a *monster*. I'd looked at him with his claws and sharp teeth, I'd seen the blood smeared across his body, and I'd wanted him. I'd *begged* him for it.

As I curled up on the couch, my knife close at hand, I kept hoping I'd hear Leon call my name outside. He was an asshole, but I felt safer with him near me. Even though he'd told me protection came at a price, he'd already pro-tected me, for nothing. He'd even protected my pet. I had a hard time believing someone willing to risk injury to save an animal could be evil.

But I couldn't accept his bargain. Stories throughout history warned of the dangers of giving in to a demon's temptation, and selling my soul for protection would surely come with a catastrophic price. I may have fucked up my integrity as a paranormal investigator, but at least I knew better than to sell my soul.

How much of what Leon had told me was I supposed to believe? He claimed there were Gods, he claimed Kent Hadleigh was a magician leading some kind of human-sacrifice cult. Magic, murder, and monsters—all this, hidden in quiet, charming Abelaum?

The Abelaum of my childhood had felt like a fairy kingdom. But the Abelaum I'd returned to felt like the fairy kingdom had been taken over by Maleficent, filling it with thorns and darkness.

I lay down on the couch, hugging a pillow for com-fort. I doubted I would get much sleep, but my eyes were aching and my body felt heavy. I had to try to rest. Whatever nightmares I had couldn't get any weirder than reality.

RAE

I WOKE UP late.

I jolted up from the couch, my heart pounding as memories of the previous night returned. Leon, the monsters, Cheesecake, the grimoire—I rubbed a hand over my face, dreading that I had to try to make it through classes that day.

I had to get a shower; my legs were sticky, my panties abandoned somewhere back in the cemetery. I realized how achingly sore I was as I washed. I had hickeys across my throat and shoulders, even my thighs. Then there were the scratches, the little cuts from his claws. They were tender under my fingers, but I couldn't stop touching them. The memories of his cock throbbing inside me as he came got me so distracted that by the time I got out of the shower, there was no way I wasn't going to be late to my first class.

Luckily, Cheesecake seemed no worse off from his ordeal. He rubbed around my feet, mewling hungrily until I put some kibble in his bowl.

"No crisis of reality for you, huh?" I said, pouring my coffee into a to-go mug. "No surprise to you at all that the woods are infested with monsters?"

I finally took Leon's advice that day and drove to campus. Finding and then paying for parking made me even later, and I got a glare and shake of the head from my professor when I crept into my first class. I set my laptop to record the lecture, because there was no way I was going to absorb any of the information. I was too distracted trying to wrap my mind around the fact that the woods were swarming with monsters, I'd been offered a bargain with a demon, and supposedly that old legend about the God in the mine was real.

It *wasn't* real, of course. Leon was obviously lying to try to scare me into giving him my soul. The Hadleighs weren't some creepy cult family, there was no underground God. But the monsters were real, I couldn't deny that. I had to figure out a way to deal with them.

I'd brought my camera's memory card with all the footage from St. Thaddeus. Instead of joining up with Inaya and Victoria for lunch, I grabbed a sandwich from the cafeteria and headed to the library. The murmur of students speaking in hushed voices, the soft sounds of turning pages and scratching pens eased a little of my anxiety. Libraries somehow always managed to feel safe.

Long wooden tables were set up between the rows of bookshelves on the first floor, but I needed somewhere more private. The study rooms on the third floor would be perfect, so I took the elevator up. I found a space in a far corner, with some plush chairs and a table set up between two large windows looking out on the quad. I put on my headphones, waiting as my footage loaded in. I had several hours from the whole adventure, plenty for a two-part video series.

No one would believe what I'd recorded. It would be entertaining, sure, and the ad revenue might be nice, but things had gotten a hell of a lot more serious. I wasn't very interested in making the latest viral video anymore.

I was going to upload the footage, but it would be a cry for help. Monsters were stalking me and my best defense was a baseball bat. Surely, someone out there knew more about this than I did. Maybe, if I could get this footage in front of enough eyes, someone would reach out.

Watching it back, even having been there to witness it in person, I could hardly believe what I was seeing. The smoke around the summoning circle, the congealing blood—then everything cut off in static once Leon appeared. But I had the footage of him on my phone, which I could use to fill in the blanks. I'd have to try to get a recording of one of the monster, the Eld; if I set up some cameras on the porch, I could record them if they came in the yard again.

I began to edit, lost in my music, until I noticed a subtle pressure on the back of my neck growing harder . . . then *tighter* . . .

I whipped off my headphones, resisting the urge to leap up from my seat as I looked over my shoulder. Leon was there, leaning against the back of my chair, his head bobbing slightly to the beat of the music playing from his earbuds. It seemed way too casually human for a demon to be listening to music on Bluetooth, and he wasn't even bothering to hide his monstrous looks. His sharp claws tapped on my chair, and his golden eyes met mine as he gave me a wicked grin.

"Trying to make us go viral, doll? I'd advise against that."

I snapped my laptop shut. "Why? Scared of your secret getting out? Afraid the church will come after you?"

He chuckled, tugging out an earbud and shoving it into the pocket of his gray sweatpants. Wearing those was just *mean*: his dick-print in them was obscene. He flopped down in the chair across from me, legs spread, his smile widening as I did my best to maintain direct eye contact.

Don't look down, Rae. Don't you dare look at that thick hunk of meat that *still* has your pussy throbbing.

He spread his legs just a little wider. "If the church came after me, they'd exorcise you first. But it's not some overzealous priests you need to worry about. If you start making a fuss about me to the masses, Hell will come for you first."

I glared. Eye contact, maintain fucking eye contact. "I'm guessing a video of a demon going viral would piss off Hell's PR department?"

"Something like that." He shrugged, wincing briefly

at the movement. I suddenly remembered the blood on his arm last night.

"You're hurt."

He waved his hand at the words. "Don't change the subject. You seem a little calmer today. You didn't try to bash my head in on sight, so that's a step in the right direction." His claws stroked over his chin, just as I could imagine them stroking between my— "Have you reconsidered my deal?"

"No," I said flatly, folding my arms. "No deal."

"Aw, what's the little doll so afraid of? You're sitting here worried over a smart bargain when you should be worrying about the *other* monsters at your door." He grinned. "If *they* consume you, it won't be nearly as fun as our little games."

I gulped. His lips had parted slightly, and between his sharp teeth I could see his red forked tongue. The touch of it between my legs was seared into me, as if my clit could remember the slow strokes.

I swear the damned demon could read my mind. "You'll get a lot more of that if you take my deal," he said, his voice low as he got up from his seat. He came at me slow, resting his hands on the arms of my chair, and leaned over me. "Tell me, Rae, what is it you're afraid of? Do you think Hell is all fire and brimstone? Hell is like Earth: beautiful in some ways, dangerous in many, but I'd keep you safe. I take good care of my toys."

This asshole, insisting I was his toy. Luckily, he couldn't see my toes curl in my shoes. "Why do you want my soul so badly anyway? What do you get out of it?"

"Status," he said. "Power, too, when the energy that

makes you a physical being is bonded to me. And, of course, a new possession." He winked. "We demons have a thing for possession, if you haven't heard."

"Well, I'm not your possession," I said sharply. "And I don't want your deal. So fuck off."

A crack appeared in his cocky exterior: a flicker of irritation that jerked the corner of his mouth. His nails had sunk into the soft fabric of the chair I was sitting in. I smiled, and he narrowed his eyes even further.

"Just how do you think you're going to survive without my help?" he said.

"I'll figure something out." I shrugged. My general outlook was that every problem had a solution. I just had to approach it from the right angle. There was *always* a way. "The internet has plenty of resources. And I'm sure Kent Hadleigh would be glad to help."

That got to him, just like I knew it would. He growled, bringing his face even closer to mine. "Have you not heard a single thing I've told you? Kent is not your friend. The Hadleighs will gladly make you disappear the first chance they get."

"Yeah, yeah, the God in the mine, the cult . . ." I waved my hand. "If Kent is so evil, and you hate him so much, why didn't you kill him? The grimoire called you *the Killer,* after all. Was that meant literally, or just to refer to you being a total buzzkill?"

He scoffed, pushing away from the chair. I settled in a little more comfortably. I was playing with fire here, but it was admittedly thrilling to be pushing a demon's buttons like this.

"Kent is well protected," he said, pacing slowly around my chair. "The magical artifacts he's collected are powerful, and he carries a trinket to protect him from demon kind. I gladly would have killed him long ago if I could have. I would have killed his grandfather, and ended the whole bloody family line."

"But you didn't," I said, resisting the urge to watch him as he disappeared behind the chair. Not being able to see him made the hairs on the back of my neck stand up. "Some killer you are."

"Oh, doll." His voice was a purr, and suddenly his hand came over the back of my chair to wrap around my throat. His claws lay sharp against my skin, a shiver of fear going up my back. "I earned that name. Before the Hadleighs, there was not a single magician who summoned me that I didn't slaughter. Killing those who would bind me against my will is my single greatest joy. A demon can't just kill indiscriminately, but if we have the opportunity, killing those who would enslave us is a right, if not a duty."

His hand tightened, pressing my head back so I was forced to look up at him. He was leaning over the back of the chair, watching me curiously, like a cat that had caught a particularly interesting mouse.

"I couldn't kill Kent," he murmured. "And I didn't kill you."

"Why?" My voice was squeakier than I'd hoped, but I couldn't really be blamed when there was a demonic claw pressing into my throat.

He frowned. "I don't know. Perhaps I should reconsider my decision." Another squeeze, and the breath I tried to take was stifled. I gripped the chair cushion beneath me, watching as his irises swelled with pleasure at my squirming.

"What a funny fear response you have, doll. When I frighten you, I can smell your arousal. I wonder why that is?" He let go, disappearing for a moment only to pop up at the side of my chair. I tried to snatch my hand away, but I wasn't fast enough. He seized my wrist, and then the other, and held them pinned. "Could it be that you find the stimulation of fear to be pleasurable? I already know you enjoy pain."

He pulled my wrists toward him, pausing for a moment when a whimper escaped me. Slowly, he brought my hands to his lips, and kissed the back of my fingers one by one. His touch was mesmerizing, his hands so warm around my wrists and his lips so soft. He took my fingertip in his mouth, closed his lips around it, and I felt the two forked sides of his tongue wrap around my skin. My breath caught, and he smiled as he pulled my finger from his mouth.

"You can't hide it from me." He leaned over the arm of the chair, pinning me there again. I had no way to escape—and I didn't want one either. "Increased perspiration, rapid heart rate, that sweet scent of your pussy already slick for me . . ." He ran his tongue over his teeth, and I almost melted into the chair. "If I told you to bend over right here, in the middle of the library, and stay quiet while I finger that dripping cunt until you come, you'd do it."

I couldn't even come up with a retort. He was right. He was right, and God, I wished he would.

"Or maybe, I shouldn't be rewarding you for being so goddamn argumentative." His tone darkened. "Maybe I should put you over that table and spank your ass until it's a nice, bright, cherry red. Maybe I should make you hold your own panties in your mouth while I do, to keep you quiet. Maybe . . ." He was so close, his lips brushed my ear, his voice a whisper that slithered into my head and wrapped around my brain. "I should make you spread your legs while I spank you, so I can see just how wet you get every time I leave another mark on your skin."

I could hardly breathe. I was a goddamn waterfall at that point. He'd released my wrists and I'd hardly even noticed. Our eyes met, his gaze an inferno. "Spread your legs, doll. I know you want to."

I obeyed without a second of hesitation. My nerves were tingling with the anticipation of his touch. I was shaking, I wanted it so bad. My brain had gone completely lust-drunk: no thoughts, just need.

His eyes flickered down to my spread legs, then back up to my face. He was shaking his head. "Oh, Rae. Poor pathetic little human. Are you going to beg me?"

"Please . . ." God, I did sound pathetic. I didn't care. He'd wound me up like a little clockwork doll, and I couldn't stop. "Leon, please."

He laughed, and pushed away from the chair. It was as if he snatched the air from my lungs at the same time, a cold slap in the face as he put distance between us. "It really is too bad for you that I enjoy seeing you suffer. But frankly, thinking of you having to get through your next class with your panties soaked and your pussy still begging to be filled just gives me the warm fuzzies." He smiled happily, and turned away with a little wave of his fingers. "*Au revoir, petit jouet.* I'm sure you'll suffer beautifully for me."

He left me like that, hot and shaking in my chair. God, I hated him. *I hated him.*

Deal or no deal, I knew he wasn't done with me yet.

RAE

IT WAS NOTHING short of torture to get through the rest of the day. I already hadn't been in the headspace to concentrate, but Leon had shattered my brain into pieces and I likely looked like a zombie through my next two classes. I kept expecting him to pop up again and make good on those filthy threats, but when I left campus and he still hadn't made an appearance, I had to accept that he'd meant it.

He wanted me to suffer. He was probably watching me from somewhere, laughing and jacking off like the absolute pervy dick that he was. He'd even managed to stop me from getting my video ready to be uploaded, which was probably his plan all along.

But his dirty-talk distraction wasn't going to convince me to go along with his little bargain.

Pulling up in front of my house in the dark brought

a sobering dose of reality. I parked close to the porch, but I still sat there for a minute, the engine turned off, staring into the shadows under the trees. My porch light had popped on from the movement of my car, but the light didn't go far. If a monster was lurking in those trees, waiting, I had no way of knowing.

I exited the car and pressed the door closed as softly as I could. My body said *Run,* my brain said *No sudden moves.* My keys jangled as I pulled them out at the door, my heart pounding so hard it hurt. The night air was cold. In the corner of my eye, the darkness pressed close as the trees slowly creaked.

I didn't realize I was holding my breath until I was inside. I locked the deadbolt, staring out through the glass door at the yard as Cheesecake mewled hungrily around my feet. Never in my life had I been scared of the dark, but now the thought of what could hide within it almost made me feel sick. At least tonight, as I slowly scanned the yard, nothing was there.

Until my eyes reached the porch, and there, just off the side, beneath the railing, a skeletal canine head with a gaping mouth stared back at me.

I flung the curtain closed so fast that Cheesecake sprinted away in alarm. I backed away from the door, hands pressed over my mouth to hold back the scream that desperately wanted to come out. The porch creaked, and there came the slow scratch of claws on the wood.

The morbid stench of rot seeped into the house. It was sniffing at the door, its breathing rough. I was backed into the living room, torn between running into the kitchen for a knife or barricading myself in the bathroom.

I'd seen one of those things fight. If it wanted to break through the glass, it could do it easily.

A sharp cry, like a fox screaming, made me jump and nearly trip backward onto the couch. It was so loud, but somewhat muffled, as if its mouth was pressed right up against the door. Softer, as if it was distant, a longer cry answered.

Then another.

And another . . .

Until it was a cacophony of howling screams in the night.

My limbs were locked up with fear. It was calling the others. It knew I was in here. They all *knew*.

I had to call the cops. I had to get a weapon. I had to—

There was a hoarse growl, a bang, and rapid shuffling. Then . . . silence. Utter silence.

A minute passed, and then came the slow *thump, thump, thump* of footsteps across the deck. They creaked on the top step, then came the crunch of dirt.

The footsteps were gone. The night was silent. After another minute, I heard the crickets begin to chirp again.

Leon had been watching after all.

I SLEPT HORRIBLE that night. I used up the rest of my cinnamon and rosemary, leaving it to smolder in a bowl just inside the door because I was too terrified to unlock it. At least it made the house smell good. In the morning, I chugged down two ibuprofens with my coffee and got to work, editing my footage. Leon had arrived just in time the night before, but I couldn't depend on a demon to keep saving me. I had to get this evidence out to people who could help me, and fast.

I got a text from Victoria just after my second cup of coffee, inviting me over for a study session. I had homework due on Monday, but I honestly couldn't find it in me to care. I'd probably end up doing everything Sunday night in a frantic attempt to finish on time. I turned her down, and almost immediately got another text, this time from a number I hadn't saved.

> I know you turned down V, but maybe you'll study with me instead? ;)

I had an idea, but I asked anyway: Who is this?

> Jeremiah
> Sorry, lol
> Might've snagged your number when you gave it to my sister.

I rolled my eyes. I knew it. It's not like I'd told him he *couldn't* have my number, but this felt like he was pushing to see where my boundaries were. Why did he even know I'd turned down Victoria's invitation?

Despite my determination not to believe Leon's wild stories about the Hadleighs being members of some cult, a little red flag of suspicion was waving in my mind. They weren't cult members (as if!) but Jeremiah was still giving me some weird vibes.

Well, like I told Victoria, I already have plans today

His response was a sad face. Aww, plans without me? I want an invite next time!

I put down my phone. I didn't have time to deal with another cocky boy, I had monsters to worry about. I started another pot of coffee, then jogged upstairs to change out of my pajamas.

I had just slipped into some loungewear when I heard something bang against the side of the house. Cold dread washed over me, and Cheesecake scrambled up to hide under my bed. The sounds were coming from the wall near the firewood pile; it sounded as if something was rummaging through the logs.

Leon had made it sound as if those things only came out at night. I had no more herbs to burn. I didn't think there was anywhere in the house I could barricade myself that a monster wouldn't be able to break into.

Maybe they were weaker during the day. Maybe I shouldn't hide this time.

I grabbed my knife, and then my baseball bat from where I had it stashed near the front door. Between stabbing and bashing, I figured I could take down one of those monsters. It had been about five years since I'd last played softball, but my swing was still in good shape.

No hiding in fear this time. I wasn't helpless. These

monsters needed to learn not to fuck with Raelynn
Lawson.

I crept out of the house. The day was cool and gray,
birds singing in the trees. There were deep scratches in
the wood just outside my door, and I remembered the
huge claws on the monster in the chapel. I'd have to
move fast, bash it to a pulp before it could slash me.

I held the bat high as I neared the corner of the house,
gripping the handle of the knife in my teeth so I could use
both hands to swing. My heart was in my throat. This
was madness. I should have stayed inside. Who the hell
did I think I was, Van Helsing? I was a paranormal investigator, not a monster hunter!

As I stepped around the corner, the monster was coming the opposite direction. I flailed as it loomed in front
of me, swinging the bat down with a scream.

The bat made contact, but it didn't hit a monster.

Instead, it was caught and gripped solidly in one of
Leon's massive hands.

"Oh . . . oh my God . . ." The knife fell to the ground
as my mouth hung open in horror. Leon was stone-faced,
staring at the baseball bat gripped in his fingers, inches
from his head. He'd dropped several long pieces of wood
in order to catch it. Mouth twisting sourly, he glanced
down at the dropped knife, then back to the bat, then
to me.

And he began to chuckle, the laughter of a man who'd
just caught someone doing something very, *very* naughty.

"You are the maddest woman I've ever met." He
jerked the bat out of my grasp and tossed it down among

the wood pile beside him, but he'd dropped something from his opposite hand as he did so. I looked down at the thump, and nearly screamed again.

"What the hell, Leon?" I backed away from the pile of heads he'd dropped to the ground. *Heads*—the severed, skeletal heads of three Eld beasts rolled in the dirt. I backed away in disgust as he glared.

"Fucking hell, you need all the help you can get. A knife. A fucking baseball bat." He snorted, grumbling to himself as I tentatively bent down and snatched up the knife. He collected the heads from the ground, holding them by the bits of scraggly fur and long hair clumped on them, and the pieces of wood he'd collected as well. He brushed past me, toward the front yard, a slight limp in his right leg.

I trotted after him.

"What are you doing?" He'd gone to the edge of the trees near my front driveway, dropped the heads again, and was lining up one of the long pieces of wood he carried with the ground. He was dressed in a black T-shirt and tight jeans, and his hair was disheveled and sported faint streaks of darkened blood. "What happened last night? Did you kill all of them?"

The questions tumbled out of me. The relief I'd felt when seeing him—a monster that wanted to fuck me, not a monster that wanted to kill me—had brought all my energy back.

"Did you kill all of them?" he mocked, and I folded my arms in irritation at how high-pitched he made my voice. "*No,* I didn't kill all of them. I led them away,

Raelynn, and killed what I could. You expect me to kill every bloody Eld in Abelaum?" He snorted again. "Kill *this* for me, Leon—kill *that* for me, Leon—do you have any idea how goddamn tired I am of you humans expecting me to just *kill* everything for you?"

He was in a far worse mood than the last time I'd seen him. Probably something to do with that limp, if I had to guess. I shrunk at his irritation, but gave a little shrug. "You snap bones with your bare hands. You're the strongest person, er, strongest . . ." He gave me a slow, exasperated look. "You're the strongest being I've ever met, okay? I figured you could kill anything."

"Almost," he said softly. With a sudden violent jolt, he jammed the wood into the ground with his bare hands, the narrower end sinking into the damp earth and standing upright. He picked up one of the severed heads and speared it down on top of the wood. I stared at it in horror as black goop oozed down the stake.

"Leon, what . . . what are you doing?"

"Warning off the other Eld," he muttered. He collected the other two heads and stalked off again, moving along the trees until he found the next spot he approved of and lined up another stake. I followed tenderly, my feet bare since I hadn't had the sense to put on shoes before I went outside to fight monsters. I lingered beside him, trying not to stare at the heads.

"Their skulls are the only part of them that don't rapidly decay," he said, spearing the ground again. "Keeping them around can make the others a little less eager to come into yard."

I winced in disgust as he mounted the next skull on the stake. The once-white eyes in the skeletal sockets had shriveled and blackened like old grapes. Absolutely disgusting.

"I can't just keep severed heads around my yard," I said.

"Oh, *I'm* sorry." Leon turned to face me. "Do they not fit your aesthetic? Would *death* suit your aesthetic better?" He paused, giving me a long look up and down. His eyes lingered on my neck, on the numerous hickeys he'd left there, and he grinned sadistically. "Red and purple suits you well."

My cheeks heated as I rubbed my neck. Every day since our tryst in the graveyard, I'd felt giddy pleasure at the sight of those marks. They represented the ecstasy of the pain I'd endured. They were a scarlet letter, branding me as wicked, lustful girl.

"I should turn your ass the same colors for all the trouble you've caused me," Leon grumbled, and I sputtered in protest. "Losing the goddamn grimoire . . . you should have given it back to me to begin with, in St. Thaddeus. Now I have to run all over the Pacific Northwest to track the thing down."

"God, you're an even bigger asshole than usual today." I folded my arms. Like clockwork, my raging horniness at his threats flared up again. If spanking me would make him feel better, damn, he could go for it.

As I've said: self-preservation, I have none.

As I kept following him, I began to realize just how tired he looked. His hands were filthy, there was a tear in the back of his shirt, dirt smudged along his neck and in his disheveled bloodstained hair, and there was a faint, dirty, red gash peeking over the top of his T-shirt from his shoulder. I gulped, remembering the oozing blood from a couple nights past. "Are you hungry? Do you need a snack or something? Will that calm you down?"

He only grunted as he chose the next spot to display my morbid protection charm.

"Why did you come back here, Leon?" I said, as he mounted the last head and ran his filthy hand through his hair. "I don't have the grimoire—and I'm *not* giving you my soul." His eyes flashed as he glared at me. "So why did you bother to come?"

". . . wasting time," he muttered. He shoved his hands in his pockets, looking at me as if he wanted to say more, his lips pressed into a thin, hard line.

I stepped closer, closing the gap between us. He didn't smell sweaty, like I would expect from a man who'd been running through the forest all night. Instead, he still smelled faintly of wood smoke and lemon, the kind of comforting smells that made me want to get close and close my eyes.

I reached for the neckline of his shirt, and he didn't move a muscle. I pulled it down, carefully, revealing the rest of the red, angry mark I could see on his throat. But it was so much worse than merely a mark. A jagged, open wound ran down his chest. The skin was torn open, the wound deep, ripped through his tattoos. It was darkened with dirt, reddened, and puffy. My eyes widened as I stared.

"Leon . . ."

"It will heal," he said firmly. "The beasts cut deep. I was trying to be careful . . ." His voice lowered, almost imperceptible as he said, "Didn't . . . didn't want to hurt the cat."

"And you're limping." I frowned. "You're *hurt,* Leon."

He cleared his throat and took a step back, tugging my hand from his shirt. "It's nothing. I've had worse."

But it wasn't nothing. It was a wound he'd sustained while trying to protect me, while trying to protect Cheesecake. He'd let himself get hurt rather than risk injuring the animal I loved. He could have let Cheesecake die, and abandoned me to the same fate.

But he hadn't.

Why the hell did this demon care if I died?

"It's filthy," I said. "It'll get infected . . ."

"Demons heal far better than humans do. It's fine."

"Come inside." I motioned toward the house. "Let me clean it."

He blinked rapidly. It was subtle, but as he looked between me and the cabin, he actually looked confused. "Inside?"

"Yes. Come inside. Get a shower. Let me clean it at least." I motioned to him, trying to urge him to follow me like a lost dog. "Just . . . come. Please. Let me help you."

LEON

THE SOAP SMELLED exactly like her: peppermint and sage, tinged with the natural smell of her from all the times it had been rubbed over her skin. Her scent was everywhere in the house—obviously, she lived here, but being surrounded by it for a prolonged length of time was making my cock strain.

It had hardly been two days since I'd fucked her, but it felt like ages. Leaving her needy and desperate on campus yesterday hadn't been as easy as I'd thought it would be. I'd worked myself up too much teasing her, and had gotten so restless that I'd gone back to the cemetery and found her panties in the grass.

They were still in my pocket, my personal trophy.

I'd left my marks on her neck, but scrubbing myself down with her soap was going to mark me too. How the hell was I supposed to handle that without craving her? She'd infested my mind. She had me desperate to possess her.

That was what we demons wanted, in the end. To possess, to own. We liked to leave our marks: some temporary, some more permanent. The silver hoop with the green jewel in my left ear had been pierced and threaded through by Zane, and I'd put a needle through his tongue in return. A mark was a bond, a claim. Even demons that hadn't been lovers in years kept each other's marks.

But bonds were weaknesses, they were vulnerabilities. As I could already painfully feel, they only led to one getting hurt, particularly when it came to humans. The very nature of human delicacy made them appealing: it wasn't easy to keep them. They died, they broke, they faded away. Trying to keep a human alive could drive one mad.

I shook my head, growling in the water. Rae refused to listen to my warnings, the petulant brat. She'd thought she'd fight off the Eld with a kitchen knife and baseball bat—it was shocking she hadn't brought her camera along too, to record the evidence of her encounter. She was going to get herself killed, running into trouble like that.

I'd left the bathroom door open as I showered. I couldn't see her through the fogged glass of the sliding door, but I could sense her eyes on me. She was seated out there somewhere, in the living room likely, pretending to be disinterested.

If she was going to tempt me, then I was going to tempt her too. Tempt her until she broke again.

The drive to claim her, protect her, *keep* her, was so deeply rooted in my mind that there was no shaking it.

Here I was slaying monsters for a human. Worrying over a human. Risking life and limb for a human.

I still needed to find the grimoire. I didn't know what the hell Everly planned to use it for, or even where she was, but if she decided she wanted to summon me herself, there would be nothing I could do. I'd go back into servitude once more.

I turned off the water, and stepped out of the shower just in time to catch Rae quickly turn back around, head down as she sat on the couch. I grinned at the back of her head, and the floor creaked under my feet as I approached.

"Should I sit?"

She glanced over at me, then quickly looked away again, a blush rising on her cheeks. There was no point in putting back on my clothes if she wanted to tend to my wounds, and seeing her try desperately not to stare made it even better. She got up abruptly from the couch, motioning to it.

"Yeah, uh . . . sit. Sit down." Her attempts to avert her eyes from my cock was cute, and ultimately futile. Funny how she could still blush when she already knew what it felt like inside her. But then the sight of my injuries, oozing blood again from the shower, distracted her. "Jesus, Leon! You need stitches!"

"Not necessary." I settled on the couch, stretching my arms over the back of it, and its firm softness immediately awakened an odd pang of nostalgia. I did have a home back in Hell—I hadn't set foot in it in over a century, but it was still there, waiting for me. There were some comforts one could only associate with home, with a place that was familiar and safe.

Fuck, what did safety feel like?

Rae threw up her hands, walking away as she grumbled, "So your magical super demon powers grant you the ability to fight off gangrene? Or create new skin? Your shoulder is infected!" She returned, arms full with a bag of cotton balls, a bottle of hydrogen peroxide, and a damp washcloth. Her eyes fell on the gash running from my thigh down across my knee, and she winced as she set her supplies down.

"God, what the hell would you do without me?" she said it playfully, but there was a note of real concern in her voice. It made me frown, and I shrugged.

"Likely go to Zane's place and sleep it off," I said. "A few days of solid sleep can heal almost anything. Although, under Kent's control, I'd just *hope* for a few days of sleep when I was injured. He never quite grasped that even demons need time to heal."

She frowned now as she knelt with the cloth and carefully dabbed at the edges of the wound. She still didn't believe me about Kent—or didn't want to. But I liked how she looked on her knees.

"Zane is a demon too, isn't he?" she said. I nodded. "Are there others? In Abelaum?"

"Could be. I haven't met them. But everywhere there are humans, there are demons. We're drawn to the brightness: human lives burn so brightly but so briefly. An explosion, a roaring fire in the night. We demons . . . are more like smoldering coals. Burning on and on.

Dulling and flaring. We're always seeking more. We're driven toward that light, to take it, own it."

"Why?"

I chuckled at her curiosity. "Why do humans breathe air or drink water? It's necessary. It's irresistible."

I don't think my answer satisfied her, but she quieted for a bit.

"You and Zane," she said slowly. "You're lovers?"

I snorted. "Once upon a time. We're companions who share similar pleasurable tastes."

She laughed, dabbing a cotton ball soaked in hydrogen peroxide along my leg. "*Companions,* right, okay. Way to not give an inch on any emotions there." She shook her head. "Are all demons like you?"

"Bisexual? Yes, but we don't have a need to label our attractions like you humans do."

She laughed again. "No, that's—that's not what I meant. I meant, like, are all of you so . . . closed up. You just replace emotions with anger or sarcasm. Are you all like that?"

I glared down at her. "Years of torture and solitude will have you learn that anger is the safest emotion. It's the strongest. It's a fire that will keep you going in the dark."

The playful smile on her face fell, and she went on cleaning my leg in silence. The gentle touch of her fingers over my skin nearly made me flinch—not from pain, for pain I could endure, but simply from being *touched.* Soft hands weren't something I typically encountered.

A happy little chirp announced the arrival of Rae-lynn's cat, sauntering down sleepy-eyed from the stairs.

He came straight for me, hopped up on the couch, and curled his chubby orange-and-white body against my side, purring as he kneaded the cushions with his claws.

Raelynn paused as she watched me stroke the cat's head, using my claws to give him proper chin scratches.

"He rarely comes down to visit people," she said. "He's usually too shy."

"Cats and demons tend to get along well," I said. "They're the only animal that can be found both on Earth, and in Hell."

"Figures." She laughed, but then her face grew somber. "Thank you for saving him. Really. He means a lot to me."

"You would have gone after him yourself if I hadn't. And then we would have had a dead cat and a dead woman. I was trying to minimize damage."

Her eyes were moving over my face; searching, wondering. It was as if she could tell I was lying; the last thing I'd ever tried to do in my existence was *minimize* damage. I was a killer. A destroyer. Saving things wasn't a path I usually chose.

She rose up from her knees. "Okay, time to take a look at that shoulder."

She leaned over me, pushed up her glasses, and her nose wrinkled as she examined the gash. It wasn't pretty: ragged torn flesh and still bleeding. She was right about it being infected, but putting so much thought and care into one's wounds was a human thing. Forget about it and sleep it off was my usual plan. If an injury posed a greater risk to me, I'd know, likely because I'd be in pieces.

She picked up another cotton ball and doused it. "Are you, uh . . . going to put on pants?"

I grinned, settling in a little more comfortably. "No."

She rolled her eyes, but a blush rose on her cheeks. The way the blood filled in the spaces between her freckles was adorable. It made me want to hold her face in my hands and feel the heat beneath my fingers.

She shooed the cat aside and, for the sake of easy access, straddled my lap. Her crotch pressed against my cock, and her eyes flickered up to mine as it twitched at her closeness, the cotton ball paused in mid-air.

I widened my eyes teasingly. "Is that comfortable?"

She bit her lip in silence, bending forward to clean the wound, moving slowly around the tender flesh. I kept the grin on my face, her thighs twitching slightly against mine, the scent of arousal flooding her. Her eyes were focused on her work but her mind was elsewhere.

"You said Hell is like Earth," she said, staring at the wound, as if she could force her arousal away if she focused on gore. "Is it really?"

"It's bigger," I said. "So big that only the oldest of demons have ever seen the ends of it. There's wide empty plains, forests so deep and filled with monsters that only our strongest dare to go in." I stared at the ceiling as I recalled it. I'd been on Earth for over a hundred years. I wasn't all that old, for a demon. Nearly a quarter of my life had been spent here in captivity. "There are oceans as clear as glass and as black as ink. Trees bigger than Earth's tallest mountains. The cities . . . they're art. Metal, glass, and stone, carvings of marble and wood."

Her eyes had grown wide. She was seated on me fully now, too enamored with my words to try to hover over my lap. It had been a long time since I'd spoken of home. Zane had been polite enough not to bring it up, and he preferred to spend most of his time on Earth anyway since he found humans so entertaining.

But I ached for Hell.

"What do you do there?" she said. "Do demons . . . have jobs?"

"Most do. It keeps us occupied to do something fulfilling. But we come and go as we please. Resources aren't limited. Money and economies are nonexistent. Precious metals are as common there as dirt. We do whatever pleases us."

"Sounds more like Heaven than Hell."

"Heaven is overrated. Too many rules."

She looked down when she laughed that time. Something about the shy aversion of her eyes and the sound of her laugh was making me . . . feel . . . something. But my brain kept confusing whatever overwhelming feeling this was with a desire to squish her, as if I could find an outlet for this annoying emotion by just taking her face in my hands and squeezing.

I managed to resist.

"What did you do there?" Her question snapped me out of my fantasies of affectionately crushing her. "For fun?"

She wasn't cleaning my wounds anymore. She was listening with rapt attention, waiting eagerly for what I would say. "There's plenty to do. There's—"

"No, no, what did *you* like to do?"

I hesitated. Talking about Hell was strange; talking about myself was even stranger.

"I . . . I liked to . . ." Fuck, it had been so long. "I liked to explore. To wander. I wanted to see the edge of Hell, see all the places even others of my kind wouldn't go to."

Wandering into the unknown, with hardly any plan and no expectations, was the wildest I'd ever felt. To lay in a dark woodland where no demon had set foot for millennia, or find some ruin of a city the Old Gods built, was my freedom.

"You miss it," she said softly.

"Every day."

Our eyes locked. There was something about those wide brown eyes that felt as warm as her hand, as bright as the sun, as deep as the forest. Eyes that were searching my face for answers, for insight, as if she could crawl inside my head and nest there like a little bird.

"That damned curiosity of yours," I said softly. "I was like that once. I think I envy you, to still look at the world with such fascination."

"You can still," she said, frowning. "Why not?"

"If you live in the dark long enough, you'll forget what the light feels like."

She looked like she wanted to argue, and she tossed the cotton ball aside, back on the coffee table. When she turned back, she laid her hand against my chest again.

"It will heal better now," she said. "Just . . . keep an eye on it."

"I have more important things to keep an eye on. It'll be fine."

"You can drop the tough guy act—you have a bloody open wound on your chest that's likely infected," she pursed her lips irritably. "I don't know if demons can die, but it would probably be better if you didn't."

"It'll take more than a few beasts to kill me." I cracked my neck, and winced when the movement sent sharp pain from the wound down through my arm. "We can die, sure, but I'd have to be ripped to pieces—unable to heal fast enough to keep up with blood loss and shock. It would heal faster with rest but . . . I have to find the grimoire."

"You can sleep here," she said. "The couch is pretty comfortable."

I tweaked an eyebrow at her. "Trying to tempt me to stay? You'll have to offer more than a couch."

She glared. Her hair had fallen forward, the soft black strands partially obscuring her face. I tucked it back behind her ear, my fingers brushing over the multiple studs and rings pierced through her cartilage. The sight of them made my cock twitch.

"Indulge me, doll," I said. "Convince me to stay. Tell me your deepest, darkest desire."

RAE

MY DARKEST DESIRES were tucked away in the back of my mind, the kind of things I'd only hinted at to my previous partners yet hoped they'd somehow figure out. They weren't the kind of things I had any experience in speaking out loud, and his request made me protectively shove those wickedly secret things even deeper.

"I don't know." It was a lame answer, and by his expression, he knew I was lying, immediately.

He rolled his eyes, and a bizarre pressure squeezed the back of my neck. "Oh, come now, Raelynn. Don't play coy with me."

"Stop doing that."

"What?" His crooked smile was anything but innocent.

"That little mind game . . . trick . . . thing." I shuddered at the sensation of fingers running over my scalp. "I know that's you. It's . . . weird." Weirdly pleasurable, in a way that made my mind feel void of anything but lust.

"Does it scare you?" His eyes widened. He was a sight to behold like this: entirely naked, fresh from the shower, so close that I could trace the lines of his tattoos under my fingertips. "I think you've made it clear you like it when I scare you, doll."

I gulped, as the mere sensation of a touch around my throat was replaced with his actual hand—not squeezing, just holding. He gripped close beneath my jaw so I couldn't lower my head, so I couldn't avoid his eyes. "Go on," he whispered. "Tell me your sins, wicked girl. Tell me what you think about when you're alone, and your mind wanders. Tell me what makes touching yourself irresistible."

I wasn't ashamed of my desires—or at least I tried not to be, which wasn't the easiest thing in the world when kinky sadomasochistic interests still resided firmly in the realm of taboo. It wasn't as if I thought a demon was going to judge me; I knew he'd embrace whatever I told him. That was the scary part. Trusting him with those intimate pieces of me that I knew he'd be eager to indulge.

I took a deep breath and since I couldn't look away, I closed my eyes. "I think about you hurting me, making me suffer, and rubbing it in my face how much I like it."

Well, shit, there it was. Masochist Rae had come out of her cage.

When I opened my eyes again, he was smiling, his eyes reaching right into my soul and pulling out the rest of my raw words. "I think of you making me bleed, making me scream, making me come so hard I can't think straight. I think of how easily you could kill me, but you don't. You keep me alive to use me like . . . like . . ."

"Like a doll," he said, and there was such wicked hunger in his voice that I shuddered. His cock twitched against me and I almost moaned, barely choking down the sound. "How cute. Do you want me to treat you that way? Like my little toy?"

"Yes," I whispered, my legs beginning to shake in anticipation. I had fantasies of being desired so intensely that nothing could stop that need—consensually hurt and ravaged, allowed to revel in sensations that were beyond dark. But that had never been something I'd trusted another human to know.

Yet here I was, trusting a monster with it.

A monster who'd already saved my life more than once.

Leon gripped my ass with one hand, the back of my neck with the other, and brought our mouths together in a voracious kiss.

I closed my eyes and allowed myself to drown in him. He smacked my ass as he kissed me and I yelped into his mouth, shuddering at the sting as his sharp teeth bit my lip. I tasted iron, and he broke the kiss to lick the blood from me, forked tongue playing over my skin. I moved my hips back and forth, grinding down against him, the smack of his palm encouraging me. Every impact shot tingles up my spine and over my skull, until I was gasping and he pulled my mouth to his again, stealing away what little breath I had.

It was more than pain. It was more than pleasure. It made my body come alive. It made me ravenous. I wanted him to consume me, to take and use all of me, and to consume him in return.

His big hand squeezed around my throat, encompassing it easily. His tongue stroked over mine, tasting my mouth as the air left my lungs and only a faint feeling of floating remained. How could I drown in pleasure? How could ecstasy replace the very oxygen inside me?

He stood, lifting me with him—one hand around my throat the other looped under my ass to hold me up as my legs wrapped around his hips. The veins in his arms had turned as black as the ink of his tattoos. His irises had enlarged until the gold in his eyes was a slim ring, an eclipse of the sun in his gaze.

"Beg me to use you, Rae," he growled, allowing me only enough air to stay conscious, only enough to smile in a daze and nod. He gave me a vicious little shake. "*Words,* girl. Beg me."

"Use me . . . please . . ." My words were weak, a pitiful whimper barely squeezed out of my throat.

"You're Hell's little whore, aren't you?" he said. "So eager for all the wicked things to crawl out of the dark and take you. Wicked things aren't gentle, Raelynn." He brought his mouth close to my ear, his words soft. "All the time you've spent playing in the dark—is this what you were waiting for? For some evil thing to come take you?"

He lay me down on the coffee table, the surface cool and hard beneath me as he pinned me against the wood.

"I'm going to break you in every conceivable way." He chuckled, then laughed, as if the thought of what he was going to do sparked some feral energy in him that couldn't be contained. "I'll make you scream for more pain. I'll make you weep for your own destruction."

I was scared—of course I was scared. I'd always chased fear, so I could experience it on my own terms, in exactly the ways I wanted. In fear, I found desire. In fear lived all the ancient sensations that demanded I know I was *alive* and *struggling* and *feeling*.

He yanked off my pants and sweatshirt, smirking when he saw I wasn't wearing a bra and my nipples were perky as the air hit them. He straddled me, so I was sprawled beneath him on the wide table, and took my breasts in his hands, squeezing them, his claws pricking at my skin.

"Does it hurt, little doll?" He pinched my nipples beneath his fingers, rolling them just slightly. I began to pant, as every tug and squeeze sent trembles down through my abdomen. "Why did you never pierce these, hmm? You've had needles through your ears, your nose— did these frighten you too much?"

Watching my face, he closed his mouth over my erect nipple, flicking his tongue over the tip. My hips bucked up, pressing against him, but his free hand seized my waist and pushed me back down. He administered the same torturous stimulation to my other nipple, until I was groaning helplessly, shaking under him. His tongue swirled circles around my breast before closing over me, sucking until I squealed.

If this was sin, I'd gladly purchase my one-way ticket to Hell.

He was probing my mind again, using whatever dark power it was that allowed him to make me feel touches that weren't there and impulses beyond my own subconscious. He was pressing me down, as if bands were slowly tightening around my wrists, ankles, and abdomen, strapping me to the table. I couldn't see them, but my mind was certain the bounds were there. Soon I could only squirm. I couldn't lift my arms or close my spread legs.

"What are you doing?" My voice was a whisper, heavy with lust, shaking with the nerves bubbling up in me. He raised his head, his mouth parting from its merciless torture of my nipple.

"Only what you so desperately want," he said, and his claws traced over my cheek. "You could resist the restraints, if you wanted. It would be easy. How funny . . ." He hovered over me, sharp teeth close. "You're not even trying to get away."

His claws moved down my throat, over the tender pulse of blood in my veins, down my chest, down, down, until he came to the edge of my panties.

"You really should just stop wearing these," he said. "I'm only going to keep ruining them."

The panties ripped easily in his hands. My heart fluttered in my chest as a single claw circled my clit, a threat and a promise wrapped up into one cruel motion.

"Remember, little doll," he growled, his head lowering slowly between my legs. "Say *mercy* if you want our play to end. But beg for me to stop and plead for your life if you want to continue."

Every word was pushing me deeper into the cavernous bond between our imaginations, deeper into the fantasy of fear and captivity he was weaving. The fantasy that I was helpless, his fighting prey.

But that fantasy wasn't true, even as I allowed myself to indulge in it. He was watching every breath I took, watching my pupils swell. He could smell every chemical change that went through me, he could hear my heart speed up and slow down. He knew my every reaction on an even more primal level than I did.

He'd stop at my word. I knew that. I trusted him in that.

But an ending was far from what I wanted.

Telling me to beg for my life? It aroused that deep desire for fear, my hunger for danger. "Let me go," I whimpered. "Please . . . please let me go . . . don't—"

"Shut the fuck up," he gripped my face, his tone vicious. "Open your fucking mouth, now."

I was giddy as I obeyed. When he spit on my waiting tongue and followed it up with his thick cock, I groaned to feel it press all the way to the back of my throat. It was so thick, and from the angle of him above me, he couldn't even get all of it in. He gripped my hair, moving my head over him, laughing when I gagged on a deep thrust.

"Aw, is that too much, little doll? But dolls take whatever their master wants, don't they?" He held me down a moment longer, letting me gag again before he let me go and I lay my head back, gasping.

He gripped my hips and flipped me onto my stomach. Those invisible ties tightened over me again, keeping my legs spread. He squeezed my ass, spreading me open even more. "Is your pussy still sore?"

Two fingers pressed inside me and I cried out, squirming as he mercilessly fingered me. "Still sore," I gasped, but I still moaned as he moved inside me. It felt good despite the pain; the sting only made it better.

"Well then, it would be mean of me to use your pussy again, wouldn't it? I guess I'll have to break in another hole instead."

My body flushed cold at the thought of him squeezing that thick cock inside my ass—*impossible*—but then his tongue was between my cheeks and all other thoughts vanished from my head. The forked sides probed, licking my puckered hole with such hunger that I wasn't left even a moment to feel embarrassed to have his face down there. It felt too good, and his fingers were still working my pussy.

"So wet," he murmured. "Such a good little fuck doll. So eager to be destroyed."

Waves of pleasure reverberated through me with every thrust of his fingers, with every swirl of his tongue. My eyes rolled back, and the invisible ties drew tighter. I was so close, and right as my orgasm gripped me, he pulled his mouth away and pressed a finger inside my ass, mingling the sudden stretch with the already overwhelming pleasure.

I cried out as my body throbbed, two fingers in my pussy and one in my ass moving in unison to draw out my peak to such an impossible degree that I was shaking, unable to squirm away, mouth hung open as every last rational thought left my brain.

"Fuck, there's my good little whore," he said, bent over my back, breath hot against my neck. His tongue stroked over my skin, over the marks he'd left across me, a chuckle rumbling in his chest as I fell apart on his fingers. "You look so good with my marks on you. All mine, just as you should be. Your soul is next, Raelynn. One word and you're mine for eternity."

Between the pleasure, the pain, the mind-blowing endorphins making me high, I almost could have given him my soul. *Almost.*

"Do you have lube, little doll?"

In my daze, I somehow managed to acknowledge that he'd asked a question. "Bedroom . . . upstairs . . . uh, nightstand drawer . . ."

He was gone only a few seconds, and then he was leaning over me again. I gasped as I felt a cold drop of lube near my puckered entrance, but his fingers warmed it quickly as he began to rub it between my cheeks. He pressed a finger inside, deep and slow, working me up again as I shuddered with the aftershocks of my last orgasm.

Then he pressed a second finger inside my ass, and I whimpered at the stretch. He bit down on my shoulder, growling gutturally as his hips moved eagerly against me. "Leon, please . . . please . . . fuck . . ." My begging was aimless; they were the only words I felt capable of forming. I nudged my hips back against him, encouraging his fingers deeper. The digits spread, tight as they worked to relax me.

"Oh, does my toy want more? A little more pain?" He pressed deeper and I groaned, his fingers slowly pulling in and out of me. "Little humans like you want to play rough but it's so easy to break you. You tell me if it's too much, understand?"

"Yes," I managed to gasp. "Yes, please—"

Suddenly he lifted me up onto my hands and knees. He gripped my hair as he probed me again, pressing into my ass far easier than he had the first time.

"Your ass is mine from now on, Raelynn," he said. "*Mine*. I'm going to fill that tight little hole up with my cum, you hear me?"

"Fuck . . . yes," I groaned again as his fingers left, to be replaced with the thick, terrifying head of his cock up against my entrance. I began to gasp, the sheer anticipation making me shake. He eased me up, holding me tight, so I was on my knees leaning back against him with his cock poised to enter me.

He kissed my neck, and whispered, "Shh, shh, little doll. Catch your breath. Are you ready?"

I took several long, slow breaths. My hands were shaking at my sides, my legs were trembling, my body a flooded mess of endorphins. He left more kisses up my neck, across my jaw, and turned my face to take my mouth. I wanted to cry—not from pain but from the intensity, from the rush of it all—and a few tears made their escape as our mouths parted.

"I'm ready," I whispered.

He took his time entering me, and damn did I need it. I'd played with small anal plugs before; they were nothing in comparison to him. He barely got the first ridge of his head in before I was tapping his leg, squirming. He held me there, soothing me, a gentle monster despite all the viciousness.

Deeper—tighter—slowly he filled me completely. He curled his body over mine, arms tight around me, one hand holding my face in a grip that was half tender and half brutal. He tipped my head back, so it rested against his shoulder, and my back arched.

"All mine, fuck doll," he whispered, moving inside me. My eyes fluttered shut, and his hand caressed down my body, tucked between my legs and massaged my clit. "All mine."

He fucked into me slowly but deep. The touch of his hand wound me tighter, the pleasure clenching my muscles until I squeezed around him, and his pace grew rougher. I was stunned I could fit him, stunned I could take it—and he was going to make me come again from fucking my ass.

"Come on my cock, doll," he commanded. "Come for me."

My orgasm wasn't an explosion but a massacre—it shattered inside me and had me crying, breathless, shaking as my arousal dripped down my legs. He held me so tight I couldn't move an inch. I could only kneel there, bound up in his arms, my body overwhelming me.

Fuck doll. *His* fuck doll. It was the only thought left. I was floating in darkness, swaddled in sin, vibrating with the wicked culmination of my fantasies coming to life. He was rough now, my muscles loosened enough to take it. When his cock began to throb in my ass, I could feel every pulsation.

The way he moaned before he came inside me was easily the hottest thing I'd ever heard. I melted into him as he swelled hot inside me. I reached back with a shaking hand, finding the hair at the nape of his neck and gripping, as if I'd never let go, as if I could keep him there forever.

24

RAE

LEON LAID ME out on the couch and left me there, but I could hear him moving somewhere in the house. Cabinets softly closing, the creak of floorboards, a burbling sound like boiling water. In high school, there had been a brief period of time where I'd thought I would get into track and field, but even then, even after my most intense training, I hadn't been so utterly drained. Every last ounce of energy in me had been leached away, my limbs were limp and capable of nothing more than the occasional twitch.

He'd meant it when he said he'd destroy me. He'd done exactly that. I was sore, high on the afterglow, eyes half-lidded as I lay there and stared at the coffee table. I'd never be able to look at that thing the same way again.

It was my sacrificial altar, the shrine on which I'd offered up my sins to a demon to eat.

"Raelynn."

I jumped halfway into a sitting position, only to groan at the head rush it gave me. I hadn't even heard him approach. He'd dressed, and as I leaned back on the couch, he held out a plate and a steaming mug.

"Tea and cookies?" I took it as he offered them, blinking rapidly in shock. He'd made my favorite mint tea—not that he could have possibly known it was my favorite—and stacked three chocolate chip cookies on the plate.

He sunk down on the opposite side of the couch, looking wearier than I'd ever seen him. Our fuckfest must have taken the last of his strength; even the golden glow of his eyes was dulled. "You've lost a lot of calories, sweated out vital nutrients. You may experience minor shock symptoms from the adrenaline." He sighed heavily, waving his hand as if it should have been obvious. "If I'd known you hadn't eaten anything yet today . . ."

I frowned around a mouthful of cookie. He was absolutely right, of course. I was shaky, and my stomach was churning with hunger pains. "How do you know I haven't eaten?"

I didn't get an answer. When I glanced up at him again, his head had nodded down to his chest and he was fast asleep, breathing slowly.

Damn. I guess I'd destroyed him too.

LEON NEVER WOULD have admitted it, but it was obvious to me—he'd pushed himself to his limit. I didn't know how many of those Eld beasts were out there, but he'd killed three and fought off even more. His mysterious demon powers didn't heal wounds instantly, and his injuries were alarming, to say the least. Running around with wounds like that wasn't healthy, demon or not.

But now I had a *demon* sleeping on my couch. It was either a paranormal investigator's wet dream or worst nightmare. After I eased him down onto a pillow and threw a blanket over him, I did what any proper investigator would: I got out my camera. I snapped photos of his claws, the black veins still barely visible in his arms, the slight point to his ears that I hadn't noticed before beneath his hair.

He was softer in his sleep. The monstrous energy with which he carried himself was calm. Despite the claws, he somehow seemed more human than ever. Quiet. Vulnerable.

Vulnerable. Ha. As if he actually was. I couldn't let myself underestimate him: not even weakened, not even sleeping.

I had no doubt my invasive recording would have pissed him off. But I was literally dealing with an entirely unknown humanoid species in my living room. Could I really be blamed?

Out in the yard, I zoomed in on the disgusting heads Leon had speared around the perimeter. Good God, I could only hope Inaya didn't decide to stop by unannounced. It may have been the beginning of October, but even under the guise of Halloween decor, the skeletal heads were alarming. Their smell bizarrely wasn't as bad as when they were alive, but a moldy, rotten aroma still lingered around them.

Who could I possibly show these videos to? A priest? A demonologist? Cryptozoologist? I knew fellow Youtubers who would be fascinated by them, but I didn't need to inspire fascination. I needed help that didn't require selling my soul.

Once again, my thoughts went back to the Hadleighs.

Was Leon really lying when he told me they were my enemies? I kept trying to remind myself not to underestimate him, that surely a demon would be out for himself above all else, but that was getting harder to keep believing. He'd played to every masochistic fantasy I had, but not once had I felt unsafe. I trusted him—but I somehow still doubted him.

After all, his bargain was still the barrier between me and being guaranteed his protection. At the end of the day, he was pursuing me for his own ends.

The Hadleighs were my only other possible link to help.

LEON SLEPT THROUGH the rest of the day and into the night, not stirring even when I cooked dinner and put on the TV. He remained curled up under the blanket, still as stone except for his occasional slow breaths. Cheesecake, despite my best efforts to stop him, hopped up on the couch and promptly made himself comfortable against his new demon best friend, kneading the blanket with loud purrs before he curled up against Leon's side.

Having him down there made me feel safer as I climbed into bed, but I still spent a few minutes staring out the bedroom window through the curtains, watching the trees. The crickets were singing, the night was empty. Maybe those heads really would keep the Eld away.

I lay in bed with my music playing softly until sleep finally took over. The darkness behind my eyelids deepened until consciousness was right on the cusp of slipping away . . .

"Lawson."

The voice was deep, masculine—unfamiliar. I paused, unsure what I'd even been doing that required me to stop and listen. It was cold. Almost completely dark. The smell of damp earth was heavy in the air, the strong mineral aroma of wet rocks making it difficult to breathe.

Where was I?

"Lawson. This way."

I turned. I was staring down a long, narrow tunnel. The ceiling was low, and a series of wood and metal tracks were laid out on the ground—as if for a cart of some kind.

Far at the end of the tunnel, a little light glowed. It seemed to float in the air as the voice called again, "Move it, Lawson. Boss says we're heading down to the new level."

Dread knotted up in my stomach, but I couldn't be sure why. I trudged forward, my body feeling heavy and clumsy, unfamiliar. I looked down—leather boots, stiff jeans, some kind of thick overalls—

I wasn't me . . . this wasn't me . . . this wasn't my body.

I followed the light, bouncing slowly ahead of me. I could just barely see the outline of the man who held it: big, bearded, a pickaxe looped through his belt and tapping at his leg as he walked.

"Ya know that level ain't stable." My tongue moved, my voice produced that sound but—it wasn't my voice. It was gruff, deep, and unfamiliar. "Smells down there too. Like dead fish."

"Leighman don't care about that now, does he?" The voice ahead chuckled. "He'll be down there today. Thinks the boys found a new vein. All hands on it."

The tunnel was coming to an end. A structure of bare wooden boards was suspended over a deep, dark shaft, and the man I was following stepped onto it, the wood groaning under his weight. I couldn't stop my own feet; I was merely along for the ride as I stepped onto the platform beside him. My stomach sank at the knowledge of what lay below—nothing but deep, endless darkness.

The ancient elevator jolted as my companion yanked back a lever. "Down we go."

Down . . . down . . . down. In my peripheral, the man stood silently. I desperately wanted to see his face, but it was too deep in shadow. "Ain't got a good feeling about today, Kynes."

He nodded. "Aye. I'm with ye'."

He lifted his lantern a little higher, and finally, my head turned. But instead of a face, the man who stood beside me in the lift was utterly blank. No eyes.

No mouth. No nose. Nothing. As if his flesh was clay, smoothed over and forgotten.

I wanted to scream. I wasn't supposed to be here. This was all wrong. Dreaming . . . yes, of course, I had to be dreaming, I had to be—

Something cold hit my face, and I looked up. Water . . . water was dripping from above . . . and the smell of brine, of stagnant seawater, of fish lying beached in the sun—

I awoke with a jolt, gasping, trying to gulp down enough air to fight off the sensation of drowning. I was lying in bed, the pale light of day spilling in the gap in my curtains. I got up shakily to push the curtains back, my bare feet cold on the floor as I looked out on a rainy morning.

It was just a dream. It had only been a dream.

Then why had it felt like a memory?

25

RAE

I AGREED TO meet up with Inaya and Victoria for lunch over the weekend. Leon was still sleeping like the dead, and it felt odd to leave him alone at home. I wasn't sure if it was normal for a demon to sleep for so long, but I wasn't going to try waking him up. Victoria was running late, so Inaya and I got a table at a little cafe serving Sunday brunch, a corner seat near the window where we could watch the rain.

"We should watch *Midsommar*," Inaya said, as we sipped mimosas and planned our next movie night. "Or maybe we should start with some classics and go for *The Exorcist.*"

"You know I'm always down for Friedkin's genius," I said. The mimosas here were bottomless: lucky for me, because I'd already entirely downed one. I was restless, and a little desperate, and I'd hoped getting out of the house would help, but it hadn't done much yet. "We could get wine-drunk and watch *Hocus Pocus* after."

"Oooh, yes, girl, I'll bring this new pinot I tried. It's so good. It's honestly a crime I haven't come over for a visit yet. I'm so sorry."

"Don't you dare apologize," I laughed. "The place has been a mess anyway." A mess . . . besieged by monsters, currently hosting a sleeping demon . . . yeah, it wasn't fit for visitors. I was still contemplating if I should insist on having the movie night at her apartment—considering I had no idea when Leon would wake up. Or leave. Or . . .

If I even wanted him to leave.

She was scrolling through a list of horror films on her phone, trying to come up with one that I hadn't already seen. I let my eyes relax, staring off into the hazy rain outside. I envied Leon for being able to sleep for days straight; *I* needed to sleep for that long. People ran by, hoods up, shoes sloshing in the growing puddles. I loved watching the rain, but the gray day made me sleepier than ever.

The clouds above were thick and dark, as if a thunderstorm was brewing. They were moving rapidly, swirling and coiling like steam pouring off dry ice.

Inaya was speaking again, but her voice was fading in and out. There was something strange about the clouds. I'd never seen clouds move like that. They were so dark, almost black. The pale glow of lightning flashed behind them, but in the illumination, I realized those dark-gray coils weren't clouds at all.

They were tentacles: massive, thick tentacles moving through the clouds.

Suddenly, it was as if my head was being squeezed. Every beat of my heart felt too hard, too slow. I wanted to look away. I wanted to close my eyes. The sensation of drowning was burning through my lungs, as if my dream from last night was trying to yank me back in. The smell of damp earth, salty brine, rot—panic tightened in my chest.

Beyond the clouds, beyond the dark tentacles, the vague silhouette of something truly, incomprehensibly massive was moving.

"Hey! Raelynn!"

I gasped, and Inaya jerked back in surprise. She'd grabbed my arm across the table, and it had snapped me out of my weird hallucinations. The sky looked normal. No tentacles. No silhouette. Nothing but the sound of the rain and dark, thick cloud cover.

Inaya was staring at me with a wide, worried gaze.

"What the hell just happened?" She reached across the table for my forehead, her hand cool against my skin. "Are you sick? You were shaking and your eyes were twitching."

"I'm fine," I said softly, pulling off my glasses and rubbing my eyes as if I could somehow push the memory from my head. That massive shape . . . it made me feel sick to remember, as if my body was rejecting the idea of something so *wrong* existing on Earth. "I just, uhm . . ."

"Helloooo, ladies!" Victoria walked up to the table. "Sorry I was so late, ugh, more family drama." She sat next to me, giving me a quick hug. She tucked her pink Coach bag onto the seat between us, and slid a Tupperware container onto the table. "Did you order yet? Oooh my God, mimosas, yes! I need a whole tub of that shit." She began to wave her hand for the waiter, snapping her fingers as she urged him over.

I'd never hallucinated before. I'd never experienced terror that felt so consuming. Perhaps it had been a panic attack, or a waking nightmare. Maybe the stress of all this was getting to me more than I thought.

Or maybe Leon hadn't been lying. Maybe there really was a God in the mine. Because that horror, that thing I'd seen in the clouds, was the closest thing to a God I could imagine.

"Rae," Inaya was still staring at me, her voice seemingly the only solid lifeline I had to reality.

Victoria looked between us curiously. "What's wrong? What did I miss?"

"It's nothing," I said softly. "Hungry, I think. I zoned out. I'm fine."

The expression on Inaya's face made it obvious she didn't believe me.

"Well, let's get some food in you then, girl! Here, you two can be my critics." Victoria pulled the lid off her Tupperware, revealing chocolate cupcakes within. Each one was beautifully decorated, with sparkles of purple edible glitter and little candy ghosts. "I'm going to make a bunch for the Halloween party, but I wanted to try out the recipe first. Are they boozy enough? They're bourbon chocolate maple."

It was hands down one of the best cupcakes I'd ever eaten. I knew it was a ridiculous judgment of character, but I didn't feel like a death cult member would be baking delicious cupcakes for her friends. Was I really supposed to believe that Victoria worshipped some ancient God? Or Jeremiah? Or even Mr. Hadleigh?

My vision of an evil cult just didn't mesh with this family.

"These are so good," Inaya gushed. "And there will be plenty of booze at the party, girl; you don't need to get anyone drunk off cupcakes too."

"Rae, consider this your formal invitation if I haven't invited you already." Victoria smiled brightly. "I honestly can't remember who I've invited and who I haven't. Like, half the campus will be there."

A Halloween party . . . that was perfect.

"Wouldn't miss it!" I gave her a thumbs-up, just in case my words were too muffled by the cake in my mouth. Leon had mentioned Kent having artifacts, and some kind of protective charm—if I could use the cover of the party to do a little snooping, maybe I could find something to protect me. It was risky, but if anything Leon had told me about the Hadleighs was true, then *asking* them for help was out of the question.

We ate and chatted, and for a couple hours, I almost forgot about the monsters in the woods and the demon on my couch. But when we got up to leave, Victoria said suddenly, "Oh, by the way, if you could give me or Jeremiah a call if you see Everly, that would great."

"If we see her?" I said. "Why? Is something wrong?"

Victoria rolled her eyes. "She . . . left. It's been a while now and Daddy is . . . concerned." She smiled tightly. "She's not right in the head, you know? Who knows what kind of trouble she could get into? Keep an eye out for her. We're just worried sick."

We parted ways, and as I walked back to my car, my food churned in my stomach. Something told me Victoria wasn't worried about Everly.

Something told me that if Everly had left home, she had a damn good reason.

THERE WAS NO sign that Leon had stirred at all while I'd been gone. I dared to nudge down his shirt for a peek at his injury, and was shocked to find that nothing remained of it but a splotchy scar gashed through his tattoos. Not even my touch woke him; he gave a little sigh at the brush of my fingers, but nothing more.

I wouldn't have expected demons to be such deep sleepers, but I wasn't complaining. If he was there, I was safe. My touch may not have woken him, but I had a feeling a monster would.

But once he woke up, I didn't think he'd be sticking around. I hadn't taken his deal, and he was still fixated on finding the grimoire. I planned to hunt for something to protect myself with at the Hadleighs', but the party was weeks away. I needed just a little more time with him here.

A few minutes of intensely browsing the internet offered a solution.

The website I'd stumbled across looked sketchy, haphazardly thrown together by someone whose knowledge of coding had stopped in the late '90s, but the information was good. *How to Bind and Command a Demon to Your Will* looked like something straight off the cover of the *National Enquirer*, but at this point I wasn't going to turn up my nose at anything.

Speak clearly and boldly.

Make your commands as straightforward and detailed as possible.

Keep the demon confined to a binding circle, whereby it can only leave at your explicit command.

A binding circle. I could remember reading about that in the grimoire. *That* was what I needed.

I'd somehow managed to conjure up enough magic with some old markings and strange words to make a demon appear at my command. So why couldn't I make him do other things at my command? Like stay and protect me, for a start.

The sketchy website, luckily, provided instructions for drawing a binding circle. With my laptop in one hand and some white chalk in the other, I crept downstairs to confine my demon.

I wasn't about to let myself consider how furious he'd be. This was a matter of life and death, and I had to survive. I nudged the rug out of the way, and painstakingly drew a circle on the floorboards around the couch. I marked down the runes, checking and rechecking every part until I was confident I'd replicated it perfectly.

All that was left to do now was wait. If he woke up

and couldn't leave, then the ball was back in my court. I could command him to protect me until I could either get away from Abelaum or until the monsters lost interest.

If the binding circle *didn't* work, well, it would be fairly obvious what I'd tried to do. Leon's prior threats to spank me would likely seem meek in comparison to whatever vengeance he'd think up for daring to try to trap him.

I had other problems to deal with until my captive demon awakened, namely, disguising the garish severed heads I had staked around my yard.

It was a fifteen-minute drive to the nearest Target. I headed straight for their Halloween section, snatching up strands of black lights, faux headstones, a couple plastic skeletons, and some boxes of fake cobwebs. I figured the best course of action would be to hide the monster heads in plain sight. No one would think twice that they weren't just part of the decor.

It was this, or avoid having anyone come near my house for the indefinite future. I was still trying to live a normal life despite being hunted by deranged monsters, damn it.

It was evening by the time I got home, and Leon was still asleep. But he'd changed position, so that at least told me he was beginning to move. Nervousness coiled in my stomach at the thought of him waking, and I rechecked my work on the circle for what was likely the dozenth time.

It would work. It had to work. He'd be trapped and he'd have no choice but to obey.

He'd be *pissed*.

I wasn't pleased about doing it. But I was going to survive this.

While I still had daylight, I coiled the strands of blacklights around the stakes holding the severed heads to make them look a little more festive. I'd have to get some pumpkins and carve them, but that part could wait a few days. As I tested out posing my plastic skeletons around the yard in various provocative positions, I decided it was time to call the one person I knew besides the Hadleighs who might have the slightest inkling about all the weird shit happening in Abelaum.

My dad.

"Hey, sweet pea," he answered, using the nickname he'd given me as a baby. It occurred to me that it was probably a lot later in Spain than I had considered, but Dad had always been a night owl. "Decide to come join us yet?"

Dad hadn't been particularly fond of me choosing to move back to the town he'd grown up in rather than go with them to Spain, and I was beginning to suspect he had a damn good reason for that. But I couldn't exactly just blurt out to him that I was being hunted by monsters and was trying my hand at mastering a demon.

"The offer is tempting, but I think I've got it under control here," I said, smiling despite the fact that it was an utter lie. I didn't have it under control. Not in the least. "Just wanted to give you a call, see how it's going. How's the weather over there?"

Dad loved to talk once he got going; he told me all about their house, promising me that Mom would email me photos of the place soon. Their drives into town consisted of exploring the coastline, trying tiny cafes, and falling in love with Spanish coffee houses. I continued decorating as he talked, letting him ramble despite the growing anxiety in my stomach. His voice was a comfort—a tiny piece of home, of normalcy.

But nothing was normal anymore.

"Made any new friends up there?" I finally was given the space to get a word in, but I still stuttered for a moment before I answered.

"Uh . . . I, uhm . . . yeah. Yeah, everyone is really friendly up here."

Dad chuckled. "Those small towns can either be real friendly, or real off-putting. Folks gotta welcome you in."

"They've been really welcoming," I stood back, surveying the skeletons' newest position, with one bent over in front of the other over a log. It made me snicker, so I decided to keep it. "Actually, I met someone who says they went to high school with you. Kent. Kent Hadleigh? Sound familiar?"

There was a long pause. For a second, I thought the line had gotten disconnected.

"Hadleigh," Dad said slowly. "Yes. Yes, I remember Kent. Wealthy family. Big house . . . up off of uh . . ." I heard him snapping his fingers in thought. "Off Water Crest Drive. How'd you run into him?"

"Art festival in town. I went with his kids, they've been really cool to me." Why did it make me so nervous to ask this? What was I so afraid of hearing? "Did you know Kent very well? Were you friends?"

He chuckled. "I wouldn't say we were friends, no. We ran with different crowds. His family was, uh, well . . . bit of an odd bunch, the Hadleighs."

"Really? How's that?" Odd, like, eccentric? Or odd, like, *I run an evil death cult*?

"It's just those small towns," Dad muttered, and I could practically hear him shake his head. "Gossip goes around, people get all kinds of strange ideas. Superstitions and such, you know. The kind of stuff you like, I guess, but they really take it seriously. The Hadleighs have lived in Abelaum a long time. One of the founding families, as I recall."

"Our family was up here a long time too, weren't they?"

"Oh yes, your great-great-grandfather, Titus Lawson, moved over there when it was still just the mining operation. There was always a Lawson in Abelaum, up until us and your grandmother moved." He paused. "And, well, now there's a Lawson there again. I suppose that place just draws us back, eh?"

"I guess so." I felt a bizarre mixture of relief and disappointment. Relief, because my father hadn't immediately reacted in horror to the Hadleigh name. But now I had even more questions than answers. "How is Grams, anyway? What is she—"

"RAELYNN!"

The voice boomed from the house like thunder, making me shriek and nearly drop my phone. Birds took flight from the trees, flocking away in terror. Something prickled up my back, like nails frantically grasping, trying and failing to get a hold on me.

"Rae? Raelynn? What in hell was that?" Dad sounded alarmed, and I hurriedly tried to calm him.

"Oh, uh, it's nothing. Everything is fine, Dad. I turned on the TV and it was uh . . . really loud—"

"WHAT THE FUCK, RAELYNN!"

Shit. Shit, shit, *shit*.

"I've gotta go, Dad, sorry, my uh, my friend just got here."

Hanging up the phone felt like setting the first nail in my own coffin. I tucked it into my pocket, my fingers suddenly painfully cold, and turned back toward the house.

Leon was awake.

26

LEON

I WASN'T GOING to kill her.

I wasn't going to kill her, *goddamn it*.

But, oh, I was going to make her *fucking regret this*.

I should have known. I should have stuck to my instincts. Humans weren't to be trusted. Humans were selfish, advantageous, conniving things that would take advantage of you the moment they had the chance. Her sweet touches, her absolutely irresistible body and tempting wickedness—it had gone to my head and I'd let my guard down. I'd been so eager for a safe place to sleep, to just finally have a moment to rest.

I'd never considered Raelynn would pull off a binding circle after the absolute mess she made of summoning me in St. Thaddeus. I'd been foolish. I'd been weak. Lesson fucking learned.

The cat was staring at me with his ears plastered

against his head in alarm and his tail puffed. I paced the circle, which encompassed the couch and coffee table, looking for the slightest error, for even a single missed mark or break in the lines, but no luck. It was constructed perfectly. Impenetrable. A boundary of primitive magic, simple but effective.

What the bloody hell she thought she was going to get out of this, I couldn't even guess. She'd trapped me, but controlling me was another matter entirely. Unless she'd figured out a way to magically inflict pain, she'd have to keep me in that circle until I rotted, because she couldn't make me obey.

Stubborn girl. Foolish girl.

There was a soft step and I whirled around, to find that she'd crept in the front door. Her hair was disheveled from the breeze, the round tip of her nose was pink with cold, and her freckled cheeks were flushed. She pushed her glass up her nose, nervous fingers twitching before she shoved them into the pockets of her jacket in an effort to look tough.

I jabbed my finger at the floor. "What the fucking hell is this?"

She gulped. Her heart rate sped up. Her fear tasted sweet on the air, but it would be even sweeter when I had her pinned underneath me for a proper punishment. She fidgeted, withdrawing her hands from her pockets again, and said, "A binding circle. If you want to leave it, you have to do what I say."

If I'd widened my eyes any further, my eyebrows would have flown off my head and speared through the ceiling. "Oh, is *that* what it is? Oh *my*, thank you *ever* so much for explaining, I've certainly *never* encountered a goddamn BINDING CIRCLE."

The house creaked as my voice rose, and Rae shuddered but her jaw tightened, and her brown eyes hardened as she looked at me. "I didn't want to, Leon. But I need your help and—"

"I OFFERED YOU MY GODDAMN HELP!" I was certain I heard one of the windows crack. The cat was looking perpetually more alarmed, and Rae was coiling up like a spring, steeling herself against my fury. "Your soul in exchange for protection. It's an easy bargain, Raelynn."

She was shaking her head. "That's not *easy,* Leon. That's eternity. I can't . . . I can't just . . ."

I scoffed, pacing again, barely able to rein in my anger to even talk properly. I wanted to rip up the goddamn floorboards. I wanted to yell until every window cracked and the foundations shook. That crushing, sickening, smothering entrapment was bearing down on me. I thought of Kent's concrete prison, the hours alone in the dark, the years of choosing between pain and obedience.

No. Not *ever* again. Not even for her.

"I just need you to protect me," Raelynn babbled on, as if she thought her words would calm me. "Just for a little while, not forever. Just until I—"

"Until you *what*?" I sneered. "Until you manage to move away from here? Until you run far enough away that maybe the monsters won't track you down again?" I laughed bitterly. "Goddamn it, Rae, don't you get it? It's you. They're after *you*. They'll keep coming. *I told you.*"

She frowned. "What . . . what do you—"

"I told you the real reason the Hadleighs are so god-damn friendly to you," I snapped. "They'll keep coming after you no matter how far you go from this town." I let her tension build. I wanted it to seethe. I wanted her terrified, as she should be. "You're meant for their God, Raelynn. You're their sacrifice."

Her hands were clenched at her sides. "Why me?"

"Three survivors of the disaster in 1899." I held up three fingers. "Three who ate the flesh of their fellow men. Three who were chosen by the Deep One. Three lives spared, but the God does not spare for nothing. In return, someday, those lives must be given back."

She had gone pale. She was shaking her head. I stuck in the knife a little deeper, and twisted it.

"Some old relative of yours survived that mine, Raelynn," I said, my toes pressed right up against the boundary of the circle. "The God *let* him survive. In ex-change, It demands a life back: yours."

She looked as if she'd seen a ghost. Her voice shook. "No. You're a liar. You're just trying to get me to—"

"I haven't told you a single goddamn lie, Raelynn! Not one!" I growled so loudly that she stumbled back a pace and clutched onto the kitchen counter. I knew I was looking truly beastly at that point. Every muscle was taut, my claws fully distended, my teeth sharp enough that I couldn't fully close my mouth. "Fuck, I've been more hon-est with you than any human I've crossed paths with in four hundred years! And I've been more kind, more merci-ful, than I have with *anyone* who has dared summon me."

I wanted to hold her pinned against that countertop. I

wanted to run my claws along her neck and sink my teeth into her and make her scream—but hell, even now, even *now*, I didn't want to harm her. The thought of causing her unwilling agony was vile.

I hated it. I just absolutely hated it.

"Why do you think they call me the Killer, Rae?" I hissed. "Did you think it was because I'm a guardian, killing the enemies of my master? Because I'm a fucking guard dog who only bites those who trespass?" She looked like she wanted to run—but where could she go? If she wanted to keep me trapped here, I wasn't about to make it easy for her. "I've killed every single summoner who's ever called me. Every single one, and I was glad to do it. You humans think you can just *use* whatever you want for your own gain. As if I'm a tool to be maneuvered and locked away and worked until I break. *Fuck* that. Any summoner who calls up my name has been made an example to those who would dare consider it after. Look it up. Paris, 1848. London in '41. Istanbul the year before. Want a real pretty picture of my work? Cairo, 1771. They still tell legends of it. My *best* kill, honestly."

She looked sickened, as if she'd finally realized exactly what she'd gotten herself into. It was difficult to do it from a binding circle, but I still managed to nudge a little something into her mind: an image of that kill I was so proud of, of the three summoners I'd ripped to shreds after they dared try to make me obey.

"Stop!" She clutched her head, casting off my influence easier than shooing away a fly. "I get it, you're pissed! I just . . . I don't know what to do . . . I . . ."

"Erase the circle, Rae," I said. "Now."

She frantically shook her head. "No. No way. I can't let you go. Not yet. Just . . . just give me some time . . ."

"Raelynn. Now."

More headshaking. More clenched fists. Fucking brat. Then my eyes fell on Cheesecake, that chubby, far-too-curious cat.

Of course. A cat was far easier to influence than a human.

I nudged his mind, and he came meandering over. He'd gotten right to the edge of the circle when Raelynn realized some hint of what was happening, and began desperately clicking her tongue and hissing, "Oh, no, no, no . . . kitty, here kitty, kitty . . ."

Cheesecake flopped down and began to roll. He rolled his fluffy fur all over the chalk, and I felt the magic binding me shudder, then drip away like water through a leak. The cat kept rolling, enthusiastically rubbing his face along the chalk and catching it up onto his fur.

Raelynn's hands covered her mouth in horror. Poor little thing, watching her plans fall to ruin—ha! I clasped my hands behind my back, smiled, and stepped over the cat and out of the trap she'd set for me.

"Oh, Rae. You just couldn't resist finding out what happens when you piss off a demon, could you?"

RAE

THE LAST THING I saw before the house plunged into darkness was Leon's wide, sharp smile and golden eyes blazing with righteous fury. I'd fucked up. I'd really fucked up. Why did I ever think I could control a demon? Why did I think I could make that work? Some chalk and a Google search didn't make me a magician—but it sure as hell might make me a corpse.

The house had gone completely dark. Not dark like the night—dark like a void, as if all light had been sucked up. I couldn't see my hands in front of my face. I couldn't see the floor beneath me. But I could feel the cold, creeping up around me like frosty hands settling on my back. I heard a little *pat, pat, pat* and the jingle of a bell as Cheesecake fled up the stairs. He had the right idea.

Run.

I tried to find the stairs, but my foot struck something

hard and I swore, stumbling in the dark. Laughter sounded, echoing darkly from all around me. The sound of scratching claws came from somewhere above me, dragging eerily along the ceiling like something out of a horror film.

"Stop it, Leon!" Fear dug in deep between my lungs. I held out my hands, trying to feel for something, *anything,* in the dark. "I get it, okay? You're pissed! And I probably deserve that." A breath against my ear made me whirl around, striking at nothing. More laughter. I whirled again, furious, goose bumps prickling over every inch of me.

"Leon! Come *out!* Stop playing with me like this! If you want to punish me, just fucking do it!" Silence followed. Complete and utter silence, so heavy that I wanted to hold my breath because it sounded too loud. I gulped, and whispered, "Leon, please . . . please come out . . ."

Suddenly, across the room, two golden eyes blazed into my sight. Just eyes, no form, no face. Staring at me, staring into me. If looks could kill, his would have set me on fire.

"I've been in Abelaum since 1902." Despite his gaze across the room, his voice whispered directly in my ear. "Over a hundred years, Raelynn. A hundred years of servitude. Coming and going only when summoned. Killing when ordered. Fighting when commanded. No sleep. No safety. Months and months in the dark, in *confinement.*"

His eyes vanished. I shuffled around, my hands outstretched, trying to find the stairs, the couch, a wall, anything to center myself. "Leon, I'm sorry, okay? I get it, I do, I shouldn't have tried to trap you."

"I offered you a deal." His voice was above me now, sounding even deeper and more inhuman than ever. "A damn good deal. And I'm being very generous, because that deal still stands. I'll tell you a secret, Raelynn."

A little light returned: gray and cold, just enough to see my breath form clouds in front of my face.

His hands grabbed me from behind, one around my waist and the other around my throat, hugging me tight against him as his tongue licked my ear and he hissed, "I really fucking want your soul, Raelynn. I want it so goddamn badly it makes me sick. I want to *own you,* from now until eternity."

His teeth nipped at my skin and his tongue played, teasing that sensitive spot just behind my ear until I was twitching.

"You deserve to be punished," he said. I managed to nod as his hand gripped my jaw.

"I know."

His hand around my waist moved lower, gripping my hip so hard his claws pierced through my jeans. "What did I *fucking* tell you about wearing panties?"

He shoved me forward, and I stumbled but caught myself. I immediately stripped out of my jacket, pulled off my shirt, and began to peel my tight jeans down my legs, stumbling from foot to foot. I could see only his silhouette in the dark, watching me, eyes bright.

"Trying to be a good girl now, are we? Suddenly so cooperative. Do you think taking your punishment so eagerly is going to make me go easy on you?"

With my jeans around my ankles, he seized me again

and pushed me against the wall, his body pressed close to mine. Some bizarre mixture of fear and need made me moan as his thigh pressed up between my legs. Hearing him speak about his captivity had been like needles slowly stabbing into my heart. The guilt was eating away at me. I'd acted out of desperation, but I'd tried to take advantage of him in the process.

Demon or not, he didn't deserve that. He didn't deserve to have felt trapped where he'd thought he was safe.

I deserved whatever punishment he decided to mete out. I needed it to make this awful guilt go away.

"The little doll wanted to play at being master." One claw traced down my cheek as he shook his head. "How did that work out for you?"

I gave a frantic shake of my head. "It-it didn't . . . didn't work—"

"No, it didn't work at all." There was a rumble to his voice that shivered through my belly. He leaned over me, pressed his forehead to mine, and asked softly, "Mercy?"

I knew what I'd done. I knew what I absolutely deserved.

"No. No mercy."

He chuckled darkly as he stepped back, giving me a little room to breathe. "Good answer." He unbuckled his belt, the metal clinking, the leather making a smooth sound as he slid it out of his jeans. He ran it through his hands as he doubled it over, and snapped the two sides together. "No mercy."

I watched wide-eyed as he raised his hand and curled his finger at me. "Come here. Now."

I obeyed with slow, shuffling steps. I dreaded it. I wanted it. I needed it. I knew exactly what he was going to do, what I was going to let him do. I stood before him, naked except for the panties he'd scolded me for wearing, and my bra. He paced around me slowly, taking his time, snapping the belt intermittently and chuckling when I jumped.

"You're looking a little nervous, doll." He stood in front of me again, and tapped the belt up under my chin, tipping my face up toward him. "Tell me, do you know what is about to happen?"

I gulped. "You're . . . you're going to spank me."

He grinned. "I'm going to whip you, Rae, until your ass is red and you're begging me to stop. Then I'm going to put you down on your knees, and you're going to gag on my cock until you prove just how sorry you are."

My body was on fire. Guilt, humiliation, and desire made for a truly heady cocktail. I nodded. "I understand."

"Bend over."

A whimper escaped me as I obeyed. I felt so much more vulnerable like that: bent at the waist, reaching toward my ankles, nearly naked. His arm looped around my waist, pinning me close to his side, and the smooth leather belt trailed lightly over my skin.

"This is a very important lesson, doll," he said, and the belt drew back from touching me. "Don't piss off a demon."

The belt smacked down, cracking across my skin with a bite that made me yelp. I didn't try to stand up nor did I struggle. A second lash came, landing right where the first had left me tender. My cry was louder that time, and I bit my lip.

"Naughty girl. Do you think you don't deserve this?"

Another lash, another cry. It stung like fire across my skin. Resisting the instinct to struggle away from it was nearly impossible. I sucked in my breath and said, "I—I know . . . I know I . . . deserve it—"

The belt fell again, and again, the burn building up until I screamed, and he paused. My legs were shaking, every breath trembled, and my eyes had welled up with tears I knew I wouldn't be able to hold back much longer.

"How are we, doll?" he said conversationally, and even the sudden, soft touch of the belt teasing over my skin made me flinch. "I don't think you've learned your lesson quite yet, but God, you sound so *pitiful*. Are you sorry?"

"Yes," I whimpered. I knew he wasn't done. "I'm sorry."

Just as I'd suspected, the belt lashed down again. I shrieked, my bare toes curling, and I found myself clinging to the leg of his jeans just to hold onto something. Those tears I'd been holding back escaped, but they weren't miserable—they were cathartic.

It felt good to cry. It felt good to endure the pain. It tempered the guilt inside me, and stoked the roaring inferno of my desire. The belt stroked slowly over me again, tingling across my stinging skin.

"If we were in Hell, I'd do this in public," he said. "Demons do love to see a good whipping. There's just something about that exquisite *suffering*." The belt cracked down, and I would have dropped to my knees if he hadn't been holding me up. "It really is beautiful to see."

"I'm sorry!" I cried. "Leon, I'm . . . I'm sorry—"

"*Are* you sorry? Or are you just a horny, pathetic little mortal who wants to get off?"

I gasped as he stroked two fingers over my panties. But it wasn't enough for him to feel the damp through my underwear; he shoved them aside, and his fingers pressed inside me. I was so slick he slid in easily, clicking his tongue as if in disapproval as he pumped carelessly in and out of me.

"So the belt makes you wet. Poor perverted little thing."

He kept fingering me, pausing only to whip the belt down before pressing his fingers inside me again. My cries had turned to moans. My eyes practically rolled back every time he pushed his fingers into me. It hurt so good. The sting was going to linger on my ass for days, yet another mark he'd given me.

Another sign that no matter how much I resisted giving him my soul, I was his.

I was left gasping after three rapid lashes. As I tried to catch my breath, he said again, "Are you sorry, doll?"

"Yes." My voice choked with a little sob, but it was heavy with lust. "I'm sorry, Leon, I'm sorry, I am, I promise, I'm so sorry."

There was a clatter as he tossed the belt to the floor. He pulled me up, and I was dizzy for a moment while I adjusted to standing upright. He held me there, one hand in my hair and the other gripping my jaw. There was no anger on his face. There was only desire, and some desperate, almost *pained* emotion that I couldn't name.

"Prove it," he said softly, and I nodded my head as I dropped to my knees.

I had to open wide for his cock, and he couldn't fit it all in before he hit the back of my throat and brought a gag out of me. He didn't keep his hold on me; he let me work, he let me grip his hips with my hands and look up at him as I moved my tongue up and down his length. Seeing his face twitch with pleasure, his lips parting slightly as I moved my mouth over him, was almost as pleasurable as having his fingers inside me.

"Good girl. Taking it so well for me."

My insides clenched, and I couldn't resist touching myself as I continued to suck him. One hand on my clit, the other wrapped around his cock to stroke him as I pressed him into my throat. He exhaled sharply, and pulsed in my mouth, salty precum dripping onto my tongue.

"Just like that, fuck. Are you going to swallow every drop for me?"

I nodded eagerly, watching the pleasure on his face as he laid a hand against the back of my head and thrust into me. His girth made me gag, but I could take it. He moaned, deep and guttural, and the sound tipped me over the edge. I shuddered on my knees, my fingers rubbing me to orgasm, my mouth slack as he used it for his pleasure.

His cock throbbed against my tongue, spurting his

cum into my throat. His taste was hot and salty, sweetly bitter. I swallowed it all, sucking every last drop from his shaft before I popped him from my mouth and smiled up at him, light-headed and weak with pleasure.

"There's my good little doll."

I couldn't get up, so he came down to me, wrapping me up in his arms where I finally went limp.

Calm fell over us, punctuated by the fire on my skin. I stared up at him, my breathing slowing, then stopping completely when he leaned down and kissed my lips.

I didn't expect to feel tenderness from that wicked mouth.

28

RAE

THE EVENING LIGHT was dim beneath the trees, almost dusk. The scent of the pines, the rattle of the aspen leaves in the wind, and the smell of rich damp earth all took me straight back to my childhood. Running through these woods. Digging my hands into the dirt. Watching squirrels scamper up the trees.

"I've missed coming out at night," I said softly. Leon was nearby, behind me, leaning against a trunk. He'd walked with me into the trees, arm around my shoulders, silent now that he'd gotten all of his anger out of his system. There was a spot on the property back behind the cabin, where a massive pine had fallen years before I was born, and the carcass still laid there, covered in moss and lichens. I was perched up on it, my booted feet knocking against the wood as I swung my legs. I heard the flick of a lighter, and the sour scent of pot wafted through the air.

Were all demons such stoners? It wasn't as if Leon *acted* high. If anything, his moods went from a dangerously quiet calm to raging impending apocalypse.

"So you *have* been listening to me," he said. "You're safe to go out after dark, as long as I'm here. Unless the Eld beasts get particularly bold, they won't come back around with me near you. They've learned I'm dangerous."

I stared into the trees as my feet swung, as if my eyes could permeate the dark. How did humans ever survive before electricity, before fire? How did we ever make it out of the dark?

Probably by having far better survival instincts than me. I'd been running blindly into the dark for years, screaming into it, waiting for an answer.

"I used to go walking at night all the time in California," I said. "We lived close enough to the beach that I could walk down a few blocks and listen to the waves. When the moon was full and the fog rolled in, I'd sit out at the pier for hours."

I glanced back at him. The cherry-red tip of the joint in his mouth flared in the dark, casting an orange glow across his face. "Where is your family now?" he said. "You moved here alone."

"Spain. My dad finally retired and my mom's side of the family lives there. They have a house in some gorgeous coastal city now." I laughed, a little bitterly. "I could have gone with them. They wanted me to. But I had to be *independent*." I air-quoted around the last word. "What a different time that would have been."

Something that could have been a frown flickered across his face, then disappeared just as quickly. "Then your father's family is from here?"

"I was born here. Stayed here until I was seven, then we moved down to California. My grandparents moved around the same time we did. Now my Grams lives in Colville after Papa passed."

"You should visit her. I'm sure she misses you."

"You're trying to get me to leave town."

"Absolutely."

My fingers plucked continually at a stubborn bit of moss on the trunk beneath me. The temperature had dropped rapidly as the sun set, and the chill made me shiver.

Leon motioned to me, curling his finger. "Come here."

I hopped off the tree and went to his side, where he pulled me close against him and offered me the joint. His heat warmed me almost immediately, and he held the joint to my lips as I took a drag. "Did you like this place? As a child?"

"I thought Abelaum was magical as a kid," I said. "I convinced myself that fairies lived in the forest. Right there." I pointed at the fallen log, which was riddled with cracks and crevices, and little gaps beneath it where the moss made a curtain. "I used to come out here with cookie crumbs and little bottle caps full of honey, and I'd leave it for the fairies."

"I'm sure they appreciated it."

I looked up at him, eyes wide. "Fairies are real?"

"They are. But they're not very nice. And you're un-likely to ever see one unless you really piss them off." He stiffened. "Don't you fucking dare try to piss them off for a video." I laughed, and his arm around my shoulders curled up, nudging up beneath my chin and tightening across my throat. He brought his mouth close to my ear, and said, "I mean it, Rae. Do *not* piss off the fae."

"I won't," I choked out, still smiling because how the hell could I resist smiling with his muscles tightening around my throat? He relaxed his hold, leaning back a little more comfortably against the tree. A few minutes passed in silence as we smoked together, the high relaxing me against him.

After several minutes, I said, "So . . . how old are you?"

"I'm not sure," he flicked down the stub of the joint, crushing it beneath his shoe. "I don't have any memories beyond the 1700s. My kind don't give much attention to age."

"You're immortal then?"

He shrugged. "Old age and disease won't take me. I could grow bored and fade away as some of my kind do. Or I could be ripped apart—that would kill me. Crush my skull and I probably wouldn't be able to heal. I'm immortal if I'm careful, and if I wish to be." He smirked. "I'm not very careful. Living forever isn't so terribly im-portant."

"What's important then?"

"Freedom," he said softly. Crickets had begun to chirp, and a few stray raindrops made their way through the trees to splatter against my face. The darkness had moved in close now, like a cold blanket wrapping around us. From inside the cabin, the darkness seemed sinister in the way it filled the windows and was barely beaten back by the porchlight. But standing in it, calm and quiet, wasn't sinister at all.

The dark was peaceful.

"Leon," I said, after several more minutes passed in silence. "You said the God demands a life in return for my ancestor's. What . . . what does that . . ." I didn't know how to finish the question. I knew what I needed to ask, but I didn't *want* to ask it.

He understood. "Three survivors, three sacrifices. The Deep One promised power to those who fulfilled Its demands. It's been asleep a long time, It's weak. But with three souls, It will be free, and the human world will come under the rule of an ancient God once again."

It sounded so fantastical, so *impossible*. But I'd heard that voice calling in my dreams. I'd seen things, felt things.

"The Hadleighs already sent me after you," he said, and my stomach twisted into a knot. "That was Kent's last command: bring you to him, alive. Make your disappearance look like an accident. Leave no evidence that you'd been taken to be murdered. Your family would have had a funeral without a body."

He said it so calmly, but there was something like anger in his tone. It didn't take much to imagine how truly horrifying it would be to be hunted by Leon, *truly* hunted.

I never would have escaped.

"Why didn't you do it?"

"Kent had lost the grimoire. I didn't have to do the shit he said anymore."

"But if he'd had it . . . would you have come after me?"

He stiffened a little, and was silent. Then, finally, he said roughly, "Kent tried and failed to sacrifice a girl before. Juniper Kynes. He got Jeremiah and Victoria to lure her into the woods. Drug her. When she ran, he sent me after her." His teeth clipped together, again and again: a slow, irritated click. "I lost her in the woods. There were consequences for failing to fulfill Kent's orders, so I did everything I could to hunt her down. But she escaped me."

I couldn't imagine being able to escape him. It seemed impossible. "She got away? Did she live?"

"That's what I've heard," he said. "I'm shocked she managed to fight off the Eld all these years. Kent considered her a loss, and they went after her brother instead. That one was successful. Marcus is sleeping with the God now."

I shoved out from under his arm, staring at him in horror. "Marcus? The boy that got stabbed on campus?"

He nodded. "The first sacrifice. Two more to come."

"Did you kill him?" I whispered, the knot in my stomach pulling tighter and tighter.

"No." His voice was firm, his eyes bright in the dark as he shoved his hands in his pockets. "Kent would never allow a demon to perform a sacrifice. One of his own little cult, his *Libiri,* need to wield the knife. Prove themselves to their God. It would be a waste of the God's favor if I did the killing."

My breath came out shaky but relieved. He'd already admitted to killing people—numerous people, probably dozens—but somehow it still mattered whether or not he'd killed an innocent like Marcus.

He was staring at me. Watching me. Consuming me with the fire in his eyes. "Does that make me less monstrous?" he said, his voice quiet in the dark. "Does it somehow make me redeemable, that I didn't wield the knife? That I only dug up his corpse? That I only did the grunt work?" He didn't really expect me to answer; he just kept going. "Do the atrocities I've committed get a pass in your mind because I had to choose between obedience and torture? Would you have forgiven me for taking you, if you knew it was to avoid pain?"

I gulped. His voice was tight, as if he was still in pain, as if whatever tortures Kent had inflicted to force his obedience were still lingering. "You wouldn't have taken me."

He scoffed. "What the hell makes you so certain of that?"

"You wouldn't have," I whispered. I didn't know why I was so certain. Perhaps it was just that flawed survival instinct again, imagining I was somehow too special to die.

Or perhaps it was because I could so vividly remember him picking me up in his truck as I was walking home in the dark. Perhaps it was because I could still hear the fury in his voice when he'd said, *I don't know*

*why the hell you think it's a good idea to go walking
around in the dark, but you need to cut that shit out.*

"Why did you protect me, Leon?"

He looked appalled at my question. He shook his
head, but I insisted. "Why are you protecting me? Why?
What makes me any different than the last girl?"

He was really scowling now; his hands were working
inside his jacket, as if he was clenching and unclenching
his fists. His jaw, too, was tensing. But I let the question
hang. I wanted an answer. There was a hell of a lot going
on that I didn't understand, but him? Us? Whatever the
hell that meant? I wanted to know.

"I decided I wanted you," he said simply, but the
words barely made their way out from between his teeth.
"I saw you, and . . . and I felt . . ." He winced, as if the
word stung. *Felt.* What did a demon feel? "Not anger.
Not hatred or fury. You . . ." He turned his face away,
staring back into the trees. "You're a light in the dark,
and I've been in the dark a very long time."

His words were like fists beating against my heart. It
hurt, somehow, to hear something so genuine from him.
And it terrified me, to feel it tug at me, to feel those beating fists press into my heart and *pull.*

He looked at me again, and I forgot how to breathe.
"I want you. Irrevocably. But I can't settle for less than
all of you. Body and soul, Raelynn. We demons, when we
see something we like, we need to possess it. It's in our
nature."

He took a step toward me, and I took a step back.
He smirked at that, his sharp teeth so white in the dark.

"Does it frighten you, to be so desired? To know I want you regardless of time or distance? To know I want you as mine, wholly possessed without question?"

How could I be frightened of the very thing I'd wanted? I couldn't imagine being desired so determinedly that eternity wasn't a question, but a demand. It was not only a promise of protection, of safety. It was a promise of ownership. Desire. Bondage. A reassurance of forever.

"I can't settle for less." He circled me, slowly, shoes crunching on the twigs and leaves, his voice deepening to a growl as he said, "It's enough to drive me to madness, Rae, wanting you so *fucking* badly. But I've lingered on Earth for too long now." He laughed humorlessly, and I felt the familiar caress of him getting inside my head, the subtle influence that made my spine tingle like fingers brushing over my skin. "I want to have you, but I can't unless you agree. That's the curse of it all. I can't—" He cut himself off, wrestled with the words, then, "I can't linger here and watch you die."

I blinked rapidly, as if he'd slapped me. "I'm . . . I'm not going to die."

"Oh, but you will. You will, as all humans do. That light will go out and death will *take you* from me." It was so dark, I couldn't see his face now. Only his eyes, preternaturally bright. "But with your soul, death can't touch you. The God can't touch you. Nothing, *nothing* will take you from me."

My chest felt tight. The weight of his words was suffocating, and perhaps it was the lack of oxygen that made my face feel so hot.

"You used to come out here and feed your fairies," he said. "You believed in something you couldn't see, something you couldn't grasp. I did too, once. Boulevard du Temple, Paris. 1755. There was a young man with a violin and fire in his heart. I believed, with such certainty, he would be mine. And I was young. So much imagination." He shook his head. "Humans grow old so quickly. Your lives are the blink of an eye when you see all eternity stretched out before you. Yet I kept bringing honey to something I couldn't hold, I couldn't possess. He died." He nodded, as if to remind himself that it was true. "His fire was gone. So *easily*. And then my name was called by strangers, to Cairo. By the time I'd freed myself, and went back to France . . ." He fluttered his hand. "I never found his grave. I searched. I haunted the cemeteries so long they began to tell stories of me. Zane found me there." He shook his head. "He dragged me back to Hell. Told me I was mad. Mad for a human whose soul I could never possess."

"Leon . . ." I didn't know what to say. It had been centuries, but his voice was still rough with pain. So many years, and a single human death haunted him.

Ironic that a killer would be tortured by a death.

"I've spent enough time haunting graveyards," he said. "If you gave me your soul, neither Gods nor men could take you from me. And that frightens you."

"Of course it does." I was surprised to hear my voice break. It was frightening because it didn't feel real. It felt impossible.

Breakups were easy, too easy. Because they needed space, because it just wasn't working, because I was moving, because I was too much. But commitment? To belong? To be really and truly wanted? That was hard.

Humans weren't good at forever. We weren't built for forever.

"Raelynn. Come here."

I went to him without hesitation, and I stood in front of him feeling so small, somewhere between frightened and hopeful, as if there was anything he could possibly say that would make all this make sense.

His fingers brushed over my face, and I leaned into his palm. For a moment, the whole world was the touch of his hand. The warmth in him. The citrus-smoke smell of him. For a moment, I thought of eternity.

"I'm leaving."

I opened my eyes. "What?"

"I need to find the grimoire. Then my time on Earth is done. I've been here long enough."

It felt like cold water dripping down my ribs. I didn't want to hear him say that, but I couldn't prevent it. I couldn't say the words that would make him stay. I couldn't say anything at all. I could only let the decisions I couldn't bear to make form a stranglehold around my lungs and squeeze until it hurt.

Maybe he thought I would say something. The silence stretched out between us, and he pulled his hand away from my face. It was cold. So cold. He leaned his face down, the gap between our mouths so small, but somehow it was a chasm.

"Go inside," he said softly. Such a simple dismissal. He'd taken all that passion, all that desperation, folded it up and tucked it away as neatly as if it was never there. My stomach twisted, tighter and tighter. My lungs squeezed, smaller and smaller.

"I don't want you to go," I said. He frowned.

"Then make me stay. Properly. Not with petty magic tricks."

Give up your soul.

Terrifying, alluring. Everything I wanted and was terrified of having. A weight so heavy it crushed the words inside me.

Leon smirked.

"Go inside, doll. For tonight, I'll watch. In the morning, I'll go."

"That's not fair." My voice sounded petulant. Desperate.

He shook his head. "No. It's not. I've yet to find fairness anywhere on Earth."

I had to walk away. Had to. So I turned and trudged back through the trees, refusing to look back. Why look to see if he was following or if he'd vanished already? Why pretend he was some mortal man whom I could convince to stay for *just a little longer,* until things got too serious and everything was too stifling and I wasn't worth the effort?

Why pretend he hadn't offered exactly what I wanted, and I'd refused it?

RAE

THE DAYS RAPIDLY grew colder as Halloween approached. One day it started raining, and simply didn't stop. The downpour went on for hours, and even when it lessened, heavy droplets still tapped against the windows and created a tiny river system across campus. Inaya and I would eat lunch together indoors, huddled close on the wooden benches in the big dining hall, laughing and sipping hot coffee to warm our hands.

Victoria and Jeremiah frequently joined us.

I'd been able to make friends in my classes, and Inaya had introduced me to more of her own group, so I tried to make a point of inviting other people, but the Hadleighs turned up even when I least wanted them there. It was almost like they knew I was trying to get some distance from them, so they were drawing closer than ever.

Their presence made me anxious, Leon's warnings about them echoing in my head. Sometimes, knowing they'd be there in the dining hall was just too much, so I'd find a place to eat outside so I could avoid them. I wanted to warn Inaya about them, but I didn't know what I could tell her. The things I was worried about would sound ridiculous to anyone who hadn't seen the things I'd seen.

It would sound ridiculous to anyone who hadn't learned to trust the words of a demon.

There was a courtyard behind the library where I'd sometimes eat, seated at a bench tucked into a little alcove against the building. It was cold, and my fingers felt numb as I ate my sandwich, but I was determined to tough it out. Victoria had been texting me all day. The number of events she'd invited me to over the past week was absurd. Every time I turned one down, she'd come up with another one.

It would have seemed so innocently friendly, but I believed Leon's warning. I wasn't safe with the Hadleighs.

"There you are."

I nearly dropped my sandwich. Jeremiah stood there, his hood pulled up, smiling. The rain was dripping from his coat, and I scooted over quickly as he took a seat on the bench beside me. I knew his last class was all the way on the other side of campus. There was no reason for him to be back here—unless he'd been looking for me.

"Aren't you cold?" He looked at my shivering hands, and before I could say a word, he enfolded my hands in his. I tensed up, instinctually wanting to pull away. His fingertips were cold, and he blew on my hands to warm them.

I tried not to shudder. "It gets too stuffy inside," I said. "Sometimes it's nice to just be alone, with my thoughts."

He paused, his eyes locked onto mine. "Alone with your thoughts . . . yeah. I get that." He smiled, but it didn't reach his eyes. "Victoria was worried you didn't text her back. So I figured I'd look for you."

I'd felt my phone buzz. I hadn't even bothered to look. "Oh. Well. Here I am. Totally fine. My phone died earlier, so . . ." I shrugged. Please go away. Go away, go away.

He chuckled, shaking his head. He still hadn't let go of my hands. "I have an extra charger. You can borrow it when we go back inside."

"Well, I have to get to my next class in just a few minutes, so—"

"Do you? Your next class? Already?" He glanced at his watch. "You still have thirty minutes, don't you?"

I pulled my hands back. There was no one else back here. No one came to this courtyard, especially not in the pouring rain. "I'm trying to get there earlier to talk to the professor."

He nodded slowly. "Right, right. Okay. You're funny, Rae." I didn't think this was funny. Frankly, he didn't sound very amused either. "Have you been talking to Everly?"

"Everly? No, I . . . I thought she was missing. I haven't seen her."

He smiled widely. "Oh, she's not missing. There's no need to use a word like that. Might get people alarmed. She just left home. She'd get these crazy ideas in her head, and end up scaring herself."

I began to collect my things. "I really do need to go—" He grabbed my arm, hard. I stared at his hand, then back up at his face, and said, "If you don't fucking let go, I'm going to start screaming."

He waited a beat before he released me. "Sorry. Sorry, Rae. It's just . . . I was worried that maybe Everly had started a rumor, and you'd heard it."

I narrowed my eyes. "What kind of rumor?"

"She'd come up with really *sick* stuff, Rae," he said, leaning close. His breath smelled weird, like fish. "She had this wild idea that me and Victoria were trying to kill her." He laughed. "Crazy, see? Who would come up with an idea like that about their own family?"

I nodded. Anything to get him to let me leave. "Yeah, crazy."

"I just wanted to make sure you didn't believe something like that," he said softly. "We're not like that. We just want you to feel welcome." His hand, leaning against the bench, had moved closer. His knuckles were touching my thigh. "I just want you to feel at home."

I got up abruptly, hugging my bag to my chest, my sandwich still sitting on the bench. "Well, I haven't talked to her, and I'll let you know if I see her."

He leaned back on the bench. He wasn't smiling. He was just staring at me, his eyes moving over me slowly. "Alright. I'll see you at the Halloween party, right?"

I did my best to smile. "Yeah, of course. Wouldn't miss it."

"Good girl." I shuddered from head to toe. That wasn't something I ever wanted to hear out of his mouth. "I'll be seeing you then. Wouldn't want you to be late to that little meeting with your professor."

THE CABIN WAS so quiet, especially with the rain pouring for days on end. Quiet and lonely. I enjoyed some alone time, and Cheesecake was an affectionate companion, but there was a void he couldn't fill. I tried to stay occupied with homework. I tried to ignore my growing anxiety about the Halloween party.

I tried not to think of Leon. I tried not to remember how good his arms felt around me.

But when I wasn't having nightmares of my name being called from long, dark tunnels, I was dreaming of him. Dreaming of his voice, of his lips on mine, of his strong hands holding me. I dreamed of his words, again and again.

Make me stay. It's enough to drive me to madness, Rae, wanting you so fucking badly.

It may have just been a result of the rain, but the woods around my house were getting quieter. No crickets. No birdsong. No deer in the yard in the early mornings. Just the endless patter of rain, and the trees groaning in the wind.

I was probably just being paranoid, but when I'd go out to my car to leave for class, my neck would prickle as if eyes were on me. But no matter how many times I scanned the trees, there was nothing there.

Nothing I could see.

The severed heads Leon had brought were beginning to fall apart, crumbling and rotting as they fell from their stakes and became one with the soil. With them gone, how long would I be safe? How long would the Eld stay away? I bought more cinnamon and rosemary, and found a shop in town that sold bundles of sage. I called my grandma, and of course she was ecstatic to have me over for fall break. But that was nearly a month away.

I spent hours after sundown staring out the window into the yard, watching. Waiting, my camera in my hands. I'd play back the footage of Leon sleeping, comforted by the sight of his face. I'd recorded it in hopes of sending it to somebody who could help me, but now I felt strangely protective of it. The closest I got to reaching out to anyone was an email to a local pastor, but all I managed was to write *Dear Father Patterson* in the body of an email before I deleted it. A priest couldn't fight monsters.

I wasn't getting nearly enough sleep. My nightmares were getting worse. The rain just kept pouring, but I was still waiting on the storm.

Something was coming. Something was watching.

The weekend before Halloween, I jumped at the chance to spend a Saturday at Inaya's apartment, just the two of us. I tucked a bottle of wine in my bag, bundled up in my coziest sweats and hoodie, and was hurriedly trying to lock my door as the rain poured around me when something on the porch railing caught my eye.

Dangling from a length of twine tied around the rail, was an X, formed of twigs and thin white bones tied together. Something round and lumpy was pinned with a needle in the center of the X.

I gave the lumpy thing a poke with my finger, and my stomach curled in revulsion.

It was an *eye*. A fish's eyeball, pinned in the center of the twigs and bones.

It dropped from my hands, swinging back and forth on its length of twine as cold dread flooded me. I looked frantically around the yard. Who the hell had left this here? It hadn't been there the day before, which meant someone had to have come through the night, come into my yard, and tied this hideous thing outside my door. Nauseous, I ran back in the house, grabbed a pair of scissors, and cut the thing loose from the porch. I went to the edge of the trees, and with as much strength as I could muster, I hurled it into the forest.

As I stood there, shaking, I heard a twig snap.

I froze, staring at the kaleidoscope of shrubs and branches. The sound of the rain was like static in my ears, dripping off my hood and pooling in the mud around my feet. Something had moved. Somewhere out there, in the shadows, something was watching.

Too scared to leave him alone, I put Cheesecake in his harness and packed him into the car with me. He'd gone on enough car rides to be calm, and he stared curiously out the window as I drove to Inaya's apartment.

I wanted to keep driving and driving until I was out of this town, this state. I'd keep going until I was back in California, or hell, I'd pack up and join my parents in Spain.

I didn't understand what it meant, but finding a trinket with a fish eyeball tied to my porch couldn't possibly be anything good.

"Hey, girl—oh, oh my God, are you okay?" Inaya's face fell the moment she saw me.

"I'm fine, I'm good, just a little . . . uh . . ." I gulped, shaking as I stomped the rain from my boots. "I brought Cheesecake, sorry, I just, uh . . ."

I was scared. I was so goddamn scared.

"Woah, woah, yeah, you should sit down." I let Cheesecake hop to the floor and Inaya led me to the couch and got me to sit. For a few minutes, all I could do was take deep breaths to fend off the panic as she rubbed my back. Cheesecake, eager for attention, hopped up next to her and began head-butting her side in hopes of chin scratches.

When I raised my head to see Inaya with one hand rubbing my back and the other petting my cat, I nearly sobbed. "I'm sorry. I'm so sorry to come over such a mess."

"Rae, please, stop apologizing," Inaya said gently. "You know you could come over here with a body in your trunk and I'd go grab a shovel." She gave me a little smirk and side-eye. "But I do hope that's not what's wrong."

I giggled, snorting grossly as I wiped tears from my

face. "No bodies in the trunk this time, babe. Just some creeps leaving *Blair Witch* shit in my yard."

I told her about the trinket, the feeling of being watched, even my trip out to St. Thaddeus and my fears that it may have attracted some attention to me—although I didn't specify attention from *what*. She listened quietly, Cheesecake happily curled up on her pink sweatpants as she stroked him. When I finally took a breath after describing the horror of the fish eyeball, she said, "Well, that's weird as hell. Rae, seriously, you need to stop going to those creepy places alone. What if someone had snatched you? What if you'd gotten hurt? What—"

"Yes, yes, Mom, okay, next time I'll drag you with me!" We both giggled as she rubbed her face in exasperation.

"Look, we both know how weird people can be around here," she said. "Honestly, someone probably saw you go to the church and wanted to freak you out. Or maybe Mrs. Kathy thought she was being neighborly." She rolled her eyes. "Or, if you really think about it, it's *October*. It was probably someone pulling a Halloween prank."

"Yeah, you're . . . you're probably right . . ."

"Stay here a few nights," she said. "Trent is in San Francisco for the week; we'll go pack a bag for you tomorrow, and we'll just hang out. It'll be good for you to get out of the woods for a while."

My shoulders sagged with relief. Getting some time away from the cabin was desperately needed. The longer I stayed there, the more trapped I felt: netted in by trees, wrapped up in darkness, the rain and fog making it seem as if I was alone in a gray, wet world.

I GOT BETTER sleep that night at Inaya's than I had in weeks. Cuddled on the couch with Cheesecake, I didn't even stir until I began to hear the soft sounds of her moving around in the kitchen in the morning, putting on the kettle for tea.

No weird dreams. No fears of what lurked in the night. Just sleep.

Of course, Cheesecake simply didn't understand why I didn't have his breakfast immediately ready for him. I decided to head back to the cabin and get what I'd need for the week before he started screaming in protest of his imminent starvation.

I was feeling lighter. Happier. Despite the gloomy skies and the clouds rumbling with thunder, I felt like I had some hope.

I could survive this. I'd find a way.

Inaya's apartment was near the bay, a five-minute drive from my house. Abelaum's downtown streets glowed warmly, even in the rain. By evening, the bars would be full of students eager to start celebrating their Halloween weekend. I couldn't help wondering if Leon would be among them, mingling among the unsuspecting, hunting for another soul.

My hands tightened on the steering wheel. He'd spoke of feeling *something f*or me, something that made him want my soul for eternity. Yet he left. He *left*.

I sighed heavily. He didn't owe me protection. After all he'd been through, why would I expect him to stay? He'd been a captive here so long, why would he choose to spend his freedom chasing after one disastrous human girl?

He was probably long gone. He'd probably found the grimoire and gone straight back to Hell where he belonged. Good riddance. I didn't *need*—

I slammed on the brakes as something darted in front of my car. My head was thrown forward and my entire upper body tensed with the effort not to bang my head against the steering wheel. Panting, I raised my head and pushed my glasses up my nose. My headlights lit the wet road before me, pools of yellow light that glistened with the soft, drizzling rain.

What the hell had I just seen?

The road was empty, but I could have sworn I'd seen something. Something pale as moonlight, humanoid but naked. Long, too long in all the wrong places. Horned— horned like a stag.

But there was nothing there.

I eased off the brake, driving slower now. It must have just been a deer. The illusion that it had a human form was just that: an illusion, my paranoid brain making up frightening things in the woods. Maybe I needed to see a doctor and start taking something for this anxiety. I'd already seen it start to affect my grades—

I stopped again. Something was on the road. Not just one *something*, but three.

Three tall, pale-white figures.

Their necks were too long. Their shoulders drooped and their arms—too long, too thin—hung slack. I couldn't be sure if they were draped in rags, or if their skin was drooping and wrinkled. Their long legs ended in bizarre, two-pronged hooves, as if they were wearing massive heeled shoes *backward* on their feet. They stood in the middle of the road, scattered, as if they'd been wandering and my approach had made them pause.

They were all staring at me with milky white eyes, their massive sets of pale antlers strewn with strange, dark, leafy plants—seaweed?

With trembling fingers, I managed to find the button to lock my doors and click it. The sound made them twitch, but otherwise they were completely still. They didn't sway. Their chests didn't move with their breath. They could have been stone, if it weren't for those eyes, staring into my soul.

I couldn't drive forward without hitting them. They were spread out across the road so I couldn't pass. I kept hoping to see headlights behind me, or ahead, but the road was empty except for us. My logical brain demanded that I consider them to be just early Halloween revelers, dressed up in really good costumes. Not real. They couldn't possibly be real.

Then, the one closest to the car moved.

It came slowly, every movement accompanied by a crackling of its joints that I could hear even with my windows rolled up. My knuckles turned white on the wheel. If I didn't move, maybe I wouldn't incite it. If I didn't move, maybe those milky white eyes wouldn't see me.

It stood right outside my driver door. I stared straight ahead, eyes stinging, whimpers coming with every breath.

What the hell was I supposed to *do*?

The creature leaned forward, and placed its boney, pale hand against my window. Wetness seeped around its thin fingers, as if it was waterlogged, weeping down the window pane.

Then, from behind the stag skull, it spoke in a harsh whisper that hissed right through the glass, "It waits for you, Raelynn. It waits in the deep, dark place."

I slammed on the gas. I didn't care if I crunched their boney bodies under my tires, but as my car sped toward them, they leapt out of the way, their speed nothing like the slow, hobbling gait I'd witnessed from the first one. I was swerving, the steering wheel wobbling as my tires struggled with my speed and the wet road. The car bottomed out as I hit the dirt driveway toward the cabin, jostling me as I sped over the bumps and potholes.

I didn't say a word to Inaya about it when I got back. I explained away my trembling hands with continual complaints of how cold it was. I claimed I was just celebrating the weekend when I poured myself another glass of wine before noon. I wanted to cry. I wanted to hide.

But I had to figure out how to fight.

I wasn't going to die a sacrifice. I wasn't going to disappear, forgotten into these godforsaken woods.

LEON

I COULDN'T LEAVE her. I'd resigned myself to it.

By day, I searched for the grimoire and the witch who'd stolen it. But I returned at night, watching Rae's cabin in the dark, to make sure the beasts didn't get too close. They were hungry. So damn hungry, they were crawling out of the ground like maggots the colder and wetter it got. The radio began to crackle with reports of missing hikers, and I knew the beasts were feeding but it wouldn't keep them occupied for long.

Things were getting worse.

The Gollums had woken up. The whole forest smelled like their rot. Mushrooms were sprouting up like mad. If the God's human servants weren't giving It what It wanted, then It would send the Gollums to do it instead: pale-white beings that stalked the forest in silence, their intelligence far beyond that of the Eld.

I could only hope they didn't find her.

I'd park my truck at the road and stand back in the darkness of the trees. I'd watch her shadow move past the lit windows, I'd listen to her hum as she cooked dinner and the way her socked feet shuffled across the wooden floor when she danced.

I knew better than to fall for a human. Humans were meant to be toys, not treasures. But it ached. Fuck, it *ached*.

Not even monsters could convince her to accept eternity. Perhaps I was simply too inhuman to understand the terror of forever, the dread that gripped mankind when faced with making decisions for the afterlife.

Demons swore bonds to each other at a mere glance sometimes, yet she couldn't just . . .

She couldn't. There was no use in dwelling on it. She couldn't, and I would have been wise to stay away from her.

But I couldn't.

Just a fucking fantastic predicament all around.

The skulls I'd placed to scare the Eld had rotted away, so I left the only other thing I knew of that could deter them: one of the vile little trinkets the Libiri so loved. Sticks, bones, string, and a fish eye—symbolizing the eye of the Deep One—would usually get the Eld spooked.

It spooked Raelynn too, but at least it made her vacate the house for a few days. With her hidden away at an apartment in town, she'd be harder to find. Safer, at least for a little while. Which meant I could hunt for the witch in earnest.

Everly was proving hard to find. She wasn't with the Hadleighs anymore, having somehow managed to escape Kent's careful watch over her. Every whiff I'd get of her would blow away as quickly as the wind, and I'd never been very good at the slow, steady art of tracking. I'd never had the patience, and now that I needed it, I simply didn't have the skill.

But I knew someone who did.

It was near one in the morning when I met Zane by the bay. The rain had slowed to a misty drizzle, like static through the fog slowly rolling in off the water. The world was soft and pale, and the cherry on Zane's joint flared in the dark.

"I'm surprised you're still here." Zane let the smoke curl from his lips as he spoke. "I thought you'd bail out the moment you got the grimoire."

"I'd planned to. Problem is, I don't have the damn thing. It was stolen from her, from Raelynn." Zane glanced over at me, wide-eyed. He knew how important that wretched book was, how all my freedom hinged on destroying my name from its pages. "But I know who's got it, and I'm hoping you can help me find her. Something is hiding her scent." I frowned. I didn't like to admit I wasn't the best hunter, but Zane already knew it. It wasn't shame that made me avoid placing all the blame on myself.

Something *was* hiding the witch's scent, making her harder to track, throwing it in all directions so I'd never know if it was east or west.

Zane shrugged, passing me the joint. "I'll do what I can. Who has it? You got a name?"

"Everly Hadleigh. The young witch."

"Aaahh." Zane gave a slow groan. "The damn witch? No shit?"

"No shit." I took a drag, wishing once again that the weed they had on Earth was anywhere close to the herb in Hell. Their stock had gotten better in recent years, but it was still nothing in comparison. And damn, I needed the high.

I was getting frustrated. And when I was frustrated, I got reckless.

I couldn't afford to be reckless now. Not with the grimoire, and not with Rae.

Zane was shaking his head. "Leave it alone, Leon. Forget the grimoire, go back to Hell." I could hardly believe what I was hearing. *Zane,* telling me to give up? "The witch won't summon you, trust me."

I frowned. "And why wouldn't she? Why should I risk it?"

"She won't," he insisted, taking back the joint. "She's already got an Archdemon."

I nearly choked on the last of my exhale. Goose bumps prickled all the way down my arms and left my fingers cold. "How the hell do you know that?"

"Because he almost killed my girl," Zane said grimly. "That's how."

I paused. "An Archdemon almost killed your . . . have you made a deal with a human?"

"Yeah." Zane grinned proudly, but the expression soured. "And this woman has got one damn big bone to pick." He gave me a quick look up and down. "I'll do my best not to let her see you."

"Why is that?"

"Because she'll remember you." He tapped a finger against the side of his head. "She can really hold a grudge." Seeing the question on my face, he leaned over and said softly, "Juniper Kynes. Can't say the whole situation of nearly being a sacrifice left her feeling very *forgiving*."

"Ah, shit."

"She's out for the blood of anyone who's wronged her. It's been a fun ride but *fuck*." He flicked away the joint, and it disappeared into the waters of the bay. "She might get me killed."

"Juniper," I murmured. There were few things I'd done for Kent that I could attach any kind of moralistic regret to. But the night Juniper had fled through the woods, high on acid and covered with sacrificial runes, counted among things I wished I hadn't been involved in. "Of all the humans for you to take a fascination with, it had to be her. She gave you her soul?"

"She offered it," he said. "I was already hunting her, but the deal was her idea."

I wasn't about to admit how jealous I was. "So now she's *your girl*, eh? What happened to not falling for humans?"

"Never said I fell for her." Zane frowned, shifting his stance. He was such an obvious liar. "But of course she's mine. I claimed her."

I chuckled, although I was a fucking hypocrite to taunt him for it while I was still pining over an absolutely hopeless situation.

"So, Everly," I said. "You know where she is? And this Archdemon of hers, how strong is he?"

Zane sighed heavily. "In a fight to the death, the two of us together, against him . . ." He shrugged. "We'd hold out for a few minutes. Maybe."

"Fuck."

"I'm telling you not to go after her, Leon."

"Noted. Where is she?"

"Goddamn stubborn bastard," Zane scowled, hands shoved in his pockets. "There's an old coven house, northwest of here. I'll text you the coordinates, as close as I can estimate them. Juni and I went there looking for—"

"*Juni?*" I snorted. "Fucking hell."

"Oh, shut up." He shoved me, and reached into his jacket for another joint. "I think we both know you're a goddamn bleeding romantic, Leon, so don't taunt me for it." He put the joint to his lips and lit up, the sour smell wafting around us. "Anyway. We were looking for the elder witch, Heidi. Didn't find her."

"I could've told you she died years ago." Zane tweaked an eyebrow at me, and I shook my head. "Suicide. I didn't do it, though Kent likely would have set me on her sooner or later."

"Ah, well . . . we got another nasty surprise instead. I thought he was going to rip us to shreds before Everly gentled him like a lamb. We were lucky the witch was willing to talk with us. If she hadn't been, well . . ." He shuddered. "I wouldn't be standing here right now. That Archdemon would have killed us both."

"You get a name?"

"Callum." Zane flicked his ash to the wind. "Never heard of him. He's ancient. He's been out of Hell a long time, if I had to guess."

"Perhaps the coven summoned him a long time ago, and made a deal with him."

"Maybe. Hell, I'd stick around for a witch's soul." He glanced over at me pointedly. "Have to make the trouble worth it."

"Yeah? All that trouble with Juniper worth it?"

He exhaled sharply. "She's a little monster. Vicious as hell, body like a fucking succubus. It's worth it."

The night grew colder as we stood there, passing the joint in silence. It always felt the same with Zane: always steady, the one constant through my few centuries of life. We could part for decades like it was nothing, then spend decades more in each other's company.

A howl pierced the night, and Zane and I glanced toward the trees at the far side of the shore. Dark, long-legged shapes scuttled through the shadows, like massive spiders on the prowl.

Zane spat in the sand. "Fucking Eld. Been centuries since I've seen so many in one place."

"They've been hunting Raelynn," I said grimly. "Stalking her house. They're forming packs. I nearly lost my arm to them." I rolled my shoulder, where the tenderness still lingered deep, near the bone. It would heal eventually.

"They've been coming for Juniper too, but she holds her own well enough. They dug up her brother from the yard though."

"Marcus?"

He nodded. "She buried him in the yard up at her cabin and the beasts dug him up."

I shook my head. "She went down into the mine and got his body out?"

"Yeah. I went with her. Wouldn't recommend it. Awful place."

I had to laugh. I'd been feeling sorry for myself, but at least Raelynn wasn't dragging me right onto the God's doorstep. "She's mad."

"Completely. She's going after the Hadleighs next." He grinned at me. "Don't think I'll be able to convince her to save the old bastard for you to kill."

"Dead is dead." I shrugged. "Tell her to hurry up. It's hard enough keeping Raelynn alive. Damn woman's sense of self-preservation is broken."

"If she's spending time with you? Clearly."

"Asshole." I shoved my knuckles against his shoulder as I turned to go, and he caught my wrist, holding it captive.

"Hey. Don't get yourself killed," he said softly.

I scoffed. "I'll be fine."

"You'll be *reckless*."

"Hasn't killed me yet—"

His fingers moved from my wrist to my throat, squeezed, yanked me forward so we were face to face. "Don't. Get. Yourself. Killed." Each word punctuated by a squeeze. The bar in his tongue flashed silver as he spoke, the mark I'd put there ages ago. "Got it, kid?"

I scowled. "I fucking hate that."

"I know." He let me go with a shove, and took another long drag from the joint. "Call me if you need me."

"And you'd better do the same."

I stalked away up the beach toward the road, where the truck was parked beneath a flickering streetlamp. Just before I reached it, I turned and yelled, "Hey! I'll be fucking pissed if you die!"

He laughed. "Well, I'm not trying to piss you off, Leon. I've seen what happens to the poor bastards who do."

I love you too, asshole.

31

LEON

THE COORDINATES ZANE gave me sent me deep into the northwestern forests. Perpetually wet and vibrant green, the air thick with the smells of the dirt and natural rot, I soon picked up the scent I'd been searching for: softly sweet and sharp, like berries crushed in pine needles. Witch's magic permeated the air as surely as the rain. Inescapable and unmistakable.

The grimoire was her inheritance by any human right: but my name, my sigil, and my freedom that hinged on it, was mine. And I'd have it back one way or another.

I found the coven house in the early morning hours. The light permeated the trees in pale, wet shafts and illuminated a manor covered in creeping vines and tiny, budding white flowers. It looked like a cathedral overtaken by the woodland: its three spire-like towers rose up among the trees, their boughs grown lovingly around it, their roots curled close around the foundations, as if to guard it in a nest of hemlock and spruce, moss and ferns.

I kept my distance at first, stalking in a wide berth through the trees, surveilling the windows, the doors, trying to get any hint of what lay beyond those walls. I had limited experience with Hell's terrifying royals, but for nearly an hour I was certain that Zane must have been wrong: there couldn't be an Archdemon in that house.

I couldn't smell one, feel one, I saw no hint of one. It was only the witch's power that drenched this place.

So I got bolder.

Excessively, recklessly bolder.

I couldn't simply walk through the front doors—especially considering the house's large red double doors were wrapped in lengths of black thread, intricately braided and knotted, forming powerful wards of protection around the entry. I found the windows similarly protected. But at the very back of the house, almost entirely hidden beneath a mound of dirt, leaves, and moss, I found a small wooden door set into the foundation of the house.

A cellar.

The rusting hinges were impossible to open without noise, but I took my time to ease them open and slipped down into the dank space. Bunches of herbs hung from the ceiling alongside shelves of canned goods and old, locked crates. I found wooden stairs at the far end of the room, and climbed up to find myself in a large, disconcertingly old-fashioned kitchen that smelt strongly of cinnamon, cloves, and oranges.

I was feeling pretty damn confident. I'd happened upon the place when the little witch's Archdemon wasn't even at home. A piano was playing softly from above as I crept out into the entry hall and, strangely, I could hear birdsong. Despite the dreary light outside, the house was as well lit as a spring day.

I was making my way toward the large staircase to the upper floor when something seized my throat, squeezed with a vice grip, and hurled me backward to fly through the air until I hit the far wall so hard, I swear my being slipped back into Hell for a moment.

But only a moment.

Then I was on my feet, muscles tensed, claws distended, ready to—

Seized again, my arm was jolted from its socket as I was flung in the opposite direction and landed hard on the stone floor, skidding across its smooth surface. The movement was so fast I saw nothing more than a dark blur, nothing more than—

Grabbed again, thrown, and this time my skull hit the banister and I tumbled down the stairs to lie limply at the foot of them. I could take a beating, but fucking hell, all the air had been forced out of my lungs, my arm was dislocated, and my body was heating drastically as it attempted to repair what was almost certainly several fractures in my skull. I didn't even make an attempt to move as footsteps pounded slowly across the floor toward me, and the sole of a boot pressed down on the top of my head.

Pressing—crushing me against the stone—harder—my vision flashed—

"Fucking fuck, stop . . . stop!" My voice broke, but what did it matter when my skull was about to be cracked like an egg? I scrambled on the floor, but that foot resting on me may as well have been the weight of an elephant.

"Going to beg for mercy already? You're no fun." The voice that spoke was all gravel, deep as night, dark as the furthest depths of Hell. The piano had stopped, as had the birdsong. I shuddered from head to foot and stopped struggling, and instead licked my bleeding lips and focused all my energy on healing as rapidly as possible.

"Callum," I said quickly. "It's Callum, isn't it?"

There was a pause, then the boot left my head, and fingers knotted in my hair, hauling me up until I dangled on the tips of my toes—and faced the Archdemon I'd been so certain wasn't here.

"Do I know you, hellion?" It was impossible to tell where his solidly black eyes were looking, but I tried to keep a stoic face; showing pain was exactly what he'd want, exactly what would spur him on. He was taller than me, but slimmer. Dark-haired, with a slim mouth and rigid jaw. How the hell I hadn't smelled him, I couldn't fathom; he reeked of blood and wood smoke, and the energy within his presence was palpable. My closeness to him was almost unbearable, like having my head pounded with soundless bass.

But when he hauled me up, he left his throat exposed. Leaving me an opening to—

All it took was the slightest twitch of my hand, and my face got bashed against the far wall again. Dazed, I raised my head from the floor, spitting blood onto the stones. The Archdemon paced along the hall, snapping his fingers as if to some invisible beat.

I hated him. I really, desperately wanted to rip him to shreds.

He didn't bother to throw me again. Instead, he drop-kicked the heel of his boot into my face and I felt something snap in my jaw.

"Alright!" I held up a hand—felt him grasp it—the bastard snapped my wrist back, breaking it like a twig. I snatched it back, cradling it to my chest as I screamed furiously, "Fucking hell, stop! I'll go, I'll fucking go, god-*damn* it . . ."

"Go?" He laughed, or at least I guessed that he did. The sound was just deep rumbles in my aching head. "You're really not fun at all. Why don't you try to squirm for the door?" He squatted down near me, still snapping his fucking fingers. "I'll let you reach it, I promise. I won't let you get *beyond* it, but won't it feel good to—"

This time, my claws made contact with his face, and he leapt back to the foot of the stairway.

"Fuck you," I snarled, jerking up to my feet, blood pouring from my nose, my jaw making some truly bizarre popping sounds as it knitted itself back together. Callum curiously touched along his face, where I'd laid open his cheek straight through to his teeth, and regarded the blood on his fingers with an all-too-calm curiosity.

"Clever," he murmured. "And here I thought you couldn't take the pain."

"I've spent the last century in pain," I spat onto the

floor again, cracking my stiffening neck. There were some very unhappy vertebrae at the base of my skull. "I'm not here to cause any trouble for you or your witch, I only want—"

Slammed onto my back again, the air rushed out of my lungs, and Callum crouched over me with an expression of clinical indifference. With his face already knitting back together, he sunk his claws into my cheek and began to tear. "I don't care what you want, hellion, any more than a spider cares for the wants of a fly."

I tried not to scream, but fuck, it *hurt*. For the first time, I began to think I wasn't going to get out of this alive.

"What pretty teeth you have, hellion—"

"Callum, stop!"

The Archdemon went stiff as stone, his claws still sunk into my face. There, at the top of the stairway, Everly Hadleigh stood in a pale-green dress, her long hair coiled up and pinned in a messy pile atop her head. She came slowly down the stairs, her expression grim but wide-eyed, her gaze fixed on my face.

I gave her a very bloody grin.

"Hello again, Everly."

She came close, just beyond my reach, and looked down at me as if I was an unpleasant specimen she had to study. She looked healthy, her eyes bright, her steps light. Breaking free of Kent's stranglehold would do anyone a world of good.

"Leon," she spoke softly, almost disappointed. "Did Kent send you after me?"

"Fuck no." Callum's claws clicked against my teeth unpleasantly, and I snapped at him in retaliation, hoping I'd at least catch a finger. No such luck, but Callum didn't try to hurt me in return. So obedient to the witch's orders. "I'd sooner rip out my own intestines than obey Kent again. I came for my sigil. On my own."

She looked confused for a moment, then her eyes widened in realization. "Oh . . . the grimoire, of course . . ." She laid her hand against a large pocket in the skirt of her dress—a pocket I could see was burdened with something very grimoire-shaped. "You've already paid a visit to Raelynn then. Is . . . is she still . . ."

"Alive?" I offered. "Absolutely. I've seen to that."

Everly smiled. "Have you really? I never would have expected that from you." She was silent for a moment, chewing on her thumbnail as she thought. "Raelynn was never supposed to end up with the grimoire. I made a reckless decision to steal it from Kent, but with the way he always watched me, I couldn't keep it hidden on my person. I shoved it in a box. I thought I could go back for it later, but . . ." She sighed heavily. "Fate is merciless sometimes."

So it had been her doing all along. I should have known. Kent never would have lost the grimoire himself; it was too precious to him. No one could have taken the book except Everly, who's magic would override the grimoire's need to only be passed willingly between owners.

"When Kent told me that Raelynn was the next sacrifice, I couldn't bear it. I couldn't let him make me a murderer, or make me *help* with a murder." She scowled, her hand tapping nervously against her side. "Kent

wanted Jeremiah to do it, and I was to help. I was supposed to guide him through the sacrifice, so he wouldn't
make such a mess like he did last time." She sounded
nauseated, and swallowed hard. "All my life I'd seen
you as a monster for always obeying him. Kent warned
me that demons were cruel, that they were wicked. But
that day you left . . . you protected her." She clasped her
hands behind her back, suddenly stern. "Why did you
protect her? Why did you defy Kent for her?"

It was difficult to shrug in my position, but I tried it
anyway. "Just didn't feel like obeying the old bastard
anymore."

She laughed softly as Callum's claws jerked in my
face. "I need a real answer, Leon. Answer me honestly, or
you're not leaving this place alive."

I'd only ever known Everly to be meek and quiet. But
the coldness in her tone told me there was a whole other
side to her I'd never known was there. I wasn't left with
much of a choice. Tell the truth, or let Callum slowly rip
me to pieces.

But fuck, what even was the truth?

Why did I protect her?

Why had I been risking my life for her?

I knew the truth—but knowing it and accepting it
were two different things.

Callum jabbed his knee into me. "My lady asked you
a question, hellion."

My lady. Gag. This fucking guy. Neither of them realized just how damn difficult it was to describe feelings I
didn't truly have words for, but fuck it, I'd try.

"I care about her. I want to protect her. I want to keep her alive, because . . ." Because I want her soul? Because I want the pleasure of her body?

"Because?" Everly's voice was patient. "*Why*, Leon?"

I winced, and for a brief moment I struggled against Callum's hold as if it would do me any good. He didn't budge an inch.

"It's because I feel something for her, okay?" I snapped. "Is that enough for you?"

She frowned. She looked truly confused. "What do you feel?

God, this was torture. Give me pain and torment any day over this shit. "It's . . . it's . . . fuck, God fucking dammit . . . I think I love her, alright? I can't bear the thought of losing her. Every goddamn second that I'm here, wasting time with you two trying to get my sigil back, is a second that she's left unprotected, and if anything happens to her, I'll be holding you both personally responsible for wasting my time!"

My voice echoed in the wide hall. Callum blinked slowly, and glanced up at Everly. "Enough?"

She nodded. "Enough."

He got off me and stood back, just beside Everly. I crawled to my feet, hissing at the unpleasantness of movement, still not trusting that the Archdemon wasn't going to toss me across the room again.

"That's one hell of a security system," I grumbled.

"I'd hoped you would keep her alive," Everly said, her long fingers plucking at her dress. "I never thought I'd see a demon want to protect a human." She glanced at Callum, who was still regarding me like a bug he'd really rather squash. "When I realized you were defying Kent for her, it changed everything."

"Then help me," I said. I wasn't going to get through a barrier like Callum. I'd end up as a bloody pulp on the floor. I needed the witch to cooperate. "My sigil is all I need. And you'll never be bothered with me again."

She frowned, and her hand went protectively to her pocket again. Her expression hardened as she said, "I'm willing to give you your sigil, Leon. But you need to promise me something."

"Demons don't make promises." Not technically true, but I wasn't about to jump into making promises to a witch. "Unless you're trying to make a deal?"

Callum growled at my suggestion, an angry dog worried over his bone. It was a silly thing to suggest anyway: Everly had clearly already given him her soul. Souls weren't able to be offered in parcels, it was all or nothing.

Everly wrapped her hand around his arm, and his growling stopped. The softness of her touch made me remember Rae sitting on my lap, and how gentle her hands were while she cleaned my wounds, and something bizarrely warm seemed to leak through my stomach.

Was she safe? Had I been gone too long? What if she—

"I need you to keep Raelynn alive," the witch said. The demand was so unexpected, my confusion must have shown on my face because she said quickly, "Time is running out. The Deep One is restless, and my father knows it. If he gets Raelynn, then I . . ." She took a deep breath. "I might not be able to kill the God."

I barked out a laugh. "You—what? You're trying to kill the God?" Surely, she was joking. It was a terrible joke, but still. "You can't be—"

"She means it," Callum said roughly. "I've been alive long enough to see Gods die, hellion. They're not above death."

"I'm going to put an end to all this." Everly reached into her pocket, and at last, she drew out the damned little book. "The Deep One never should have been awoken, and It never should be freed." She flipped through the pages, her fingers moving rapidly as if she already knew exactly where to turn. She tore out my page, my sigil emblazoned across it, and held it up. "You say you *think* you love her, but it's clear that you do. It was clear the moment Kent told you to take her."

Love. What an awful, beautiful, terrifying word.

There were only a few beings I'd ever dared grant it to. The one human I'd dared utter it to, before Raelynn, well—I'd regretted it. I'd learned just how much it hurt to lose a *loved* thing. I'd promised myself I'd never experience that again. I wouldn't bother. It wasn't worth it.

Yet here I was, so goddamn certain that in every way, she was worth it.

"I'll do what I can," I said, when what I wanted to say was that I'd kill anything that tried to hurt her, and if keeping her safe meant stalking her every damn day to make sure she didn't fall into trouble, then I'd do it. "But I'm not a guard dog."

I expected Everly to insist, but instead it was Callum who smirked and said, "You don't hide your feelings for the human woman very well." He turned and wrapped his arms around Everly so that she was tucked up under his chin, and muttered, "He'll protect her. Send him off. I want to continue our game."

Her cheeks flushed red, and as she extended her hand to give me the sigil, I noticed for the first time the imprint of braided rope around her wrists.

Fuck. I'd want to hurry back to that game too.

Taking that sigil into my hands felt surreal. I almost expected it to crumble into ash the moment my fingers touched it. The last record of my name on Earth, my last tie to this place. My freedom.

I could leave. I could never look back. There was nothing to keep me here anymore. Nothing.

Except . . .

I folded the paper up and tucked it into my pocket, and turned for the door without a word. It was no concern of mine if the witch killed the God, or if all of Abelaum burned, or if humanity itself was wiped out under the heel of a sadistic God.

But Raelynn? She was mine. I wasn't about to give up what was mine.

32

RAE

"DAMN, IS THIS a house or a modern art museum?"

Inaya chuckled at me, my nose pressed to her car window as she drove up the winding driveway to the Hadleigh's house—estate, mansion, literal museum perhaps. The place was massive, tucked back among the trees of their sprawling, stone-walled property. "Girl, I told you it's excessive. You've never been to a party like a Hadleigh party. Their place is unreal."

Unreal was accurate. The house had been constructed in such a way that the upper floor was larger than the first, like it was floating above the ground. It was all hard edges, steel, concrete, wooden beams, and massive glass walls. I could see the crowds gathered on the upper floor through the glass, dancing to the thumping bass that I didn't even need to exit the car to hear.

A knot of anxiety had been growing tighter in my

stomach with every day leading up to October 31st, and this legendary Halloween party that half the university campus suddenly seemed to be talking about. I guess I was now regarded as having some kind of "in" with the Hadleighs, because I'd gotten approached more than once by people on campus that I didn't even know, asking if they could get an invite or if the party was, "just, like, open to everyone?"

Stepping out of the car, dressed in an orange sweater, short skirt, and knee socks as Velma from *Scooby-Doo*, only solidified that anxious knot inside me. I didn't feel safe here. In fact, I was certain I *wasn't* safe here, but what the hell could the Hadleighs do with so many people around? Sacrifice me in the middle of the crowd like some kind of morbid Halloween stunt?

Not only that, but the sun was setting. Twilight's pale golden light streamed through the trees, but the shadows lay thick beneath them. In that darkness, I knew what was lurking. I knew the monsters would follow me here, watching, waiting for the opportunity to grab me.

Their gross severed heads had seemed to do their job to keep them away from my yard, but those things were nearly rotted now. I'd kept sleeping over at Inaya's, since Trent was away on a business trip she enjoyed the company. But I'd started hearing the howls again at night, even from her apartment. Inaya thought it was foxes screaming, but I knew better. I knew what hid in the dark.

I wasn't here to get drunk, but I was certain I'd need the liquid courage anyway. Somewhere in this house, there had to be something that could help me. A weapon, or maybe some clues to make the monsters leave me alone. Maybe some kind of spell to make the God lose interest in me.

I didn't have the slightest idea what I was looking for, I just knew I had to find *something*.

Or I could have just taken Leon's deal, but noooo. I had to go and ruin it.

I bit my lip as I looked up at the house. My hopes of Leon coming back were dwindling by the day, and now, I figured it was better to just pretend he'd never existed—as if my pussy would ever let me forget him, the traitorous ho. The demon had probably gone back to Hell and taken the grimoire with him.

I didn't have time for regrets. I had to survive.

The front of the house was lined with cars. The moment we opened the front door, the blasting music reverberated through my body. Despite the cold outside, the crush of bodies inside the house made the air hot, the smell of marijuana and alcohol in every breath I took, the constant murmur of loud conversation making it impossible to hear what Inaya said as she turned to me with a smile and motioned somewhere deeper in the house. I followed her into the crowd, but we'd only made it a few steps when I heard my name called out with a shriek.

"Rae! Oh my God, I'm so glad you made it!" Arms wrapped around me from behind, and the familiar scent of Victoria's vanilla body spray wafted around me. She planted a big kiss on my cheek before she similarly greeted Inaya. She was wearing a tight black bodysuit, red heels, and a leather rabbit mask over her eyes, her long brown hair pulled back into a high ponytail. She looped her arm through mine, and then through Inaya's, weaving with us through the crowd. "Let's get you some drinks, ladies! Love the thigh-highs, Rae, so cute!"

Her words were slurring, and Inaya and I exchanged a quick amused look. She led us through the massive living room, where the music was playing from a large sound system against the far wall. A long white bar, lit from beneath with pale-blue LEDs separated the living room from the kitchen, and was lined with numerous bottles of liquor, mixers, garnishes . . . and Jeremiah.

He was standing on the counter, pouring tequila straight from the bottle into the open mouths of two women crowded against the counter. They sputtered on the alcohol, seizing lime wedges to bury the taste as Jeremiah laughed.

"Who's next?" he yelled, laughing as he turned around on the bar. He caught sight of us entering, and called, "Hey! Raelynn! Your turn!"

"Noooo, thank you!" I said quickly as Victoria began to pluck various bottles from the bar, like a witch selecting her potions and poisons.

Poisons . . . my stomach turned a little. But she wouldn't . . . would she?

Wondering if my friend was going to kill me was a truly bizarre experience. As if one part of my mind hadn't yet caught up with the other, there was still that little voice in my head waving her hand dismissively, saying, *Victoria isn't going to kill you, silly.*

Inaya shook her head as Jeremiah hopped down from the bar and sauntered over between us, leaning against the counter and giving me a mischievous smile. He was shirtless, wearing white trousers and suspenders with a bowler hat, his face painted to look like a mime. I'd never seen him with his shirt off; soccer kept him slim, but he was muscular, his abs rigidly defined and his biceps tightening as he raised the bottle of tequila toward me.

"Come ooonnn," he teased. "One little shot."

"As if you even know the definition of a *little* shot." Inaya scoffed.

My eyes must have drifted a little too much, because Jeremiah's smile widened, and he said softly, "See something else you like?"

For a moment, I couldn't breathe. Phantom fingers tightened around my throat, gave one tight, possessive squeeze, and were gone. I gasped softly, my eyes darting around the room, surveying the crowd—

And fucking Jeremiah thought I'd gasped for *him.*

"Relax, Rae." He pushed away from the counter, and the way his eyes slid over me made me feel slimy. "Tonight is gonna get crazy. Let yourself lower your inhibitions a little." He winked, and luckily turned away before I scowled. He had no idea just how low my inhibitions could get; but it wasn't him I was looking to lower them for.

The pressure that remained on the back of my neck disappeared as Jeremiah left the room, but my heart was still pounding. I knew that feeling, those bizarre phantom sensations.

But what was Leon doing *here?*

"To the fucking wildest night of the year!" Victoria cheered as she pressed a red Solo cup into my hands, and another into Inaya's, before she tipped her cup back and chugged whatever concoction she'd whipped up for us. Despite the anxiety shooting off alarm bells in my head, I gulped down a mouthful: sweet, refreshingly cold, a little bitter, only barely betraying just how much alcohol was in it. Warmth spread as it went down and settled in my stomach. If Victoria was going to be pouring drinks this heavy, I'd really have to be careful.

I needed to find an opportunity to sneak off and explore, but I couldn't do that with Victoria clinging around us. The party was raging, but people weren't nearly drunk enough. I'd give it an hour, maybe two, before I figured it would be safe enough to sneak away.

"Where are your parents for all this?" I shouted over the music as Victoria swayed to the beat. It had been ten minutes, and she'd already finished the drink she'd made and started another.

"Vacation house," she said. "They have a beachside place up near the Sound. They stay there for a week or so sometimes to *rekindle the flame.*" She rolled her eyes, but at least now I knew that I wouldn't have to worry about running into her parents during my snooping. She looked at me, eyes half-lidded and hazy. "Where are your parents?"

"Spain," I said, almost certain I'd told her this before. "They retired there. I could have gone with them, but uh, I dunno . . . had to seize my independence or something." I laughed, but her expression remained blank.

"You probably should have gone with them," she said, her blue eyes locking straight onto mine with a sharpness I didn't expect from her drunken state.

But then her expression soured, and she said hurriedly, "Mm . . . I'll be right back . . ." She scurried away, one hand covering her mouth, still determinedly clinging to her drink. Despite the alcohol, I felt way too cold. I chugged down the rest of my drink and headed back to the bar for another.

I couldn't lose my nerve now.

As I mingled in the crowd, I began to think I'd only imagined Leon's possessive phantom touch. Maybe I'd only wished it was there; it was just my brain reacting to an uncomfortable interaction by imagining that the demon was close, watching me, protecting me.

I took a long sip of my drink and winced. I'd put way too much alcohol in it and not enough mixer, and was about to turn back to the bar to try to fix it when Jeremiah popped up beside me.

He had two cups in his hands.

"You don't really look like you're enjoying that," he said, motioning to my poorly made cocktail. He didn't wait for my confirmation before he slipped the drink from my hands, and handed over one of his instead. "Try it."

I sipped—of course it was better than mine. Refreshing, limey, sparkling. I nodded. "Yeah, that's way better."

"Just come to me if you want another," he said, bowing as he headed back to the kitchen, likely to throw away the mess of alcohol I'd made. They were good hosts, even if they were secretly plotting to kill me.

I stayed at the edge of the crowd, swaying with my drink, watching couples grind up on each other to the pounding beat. Inaya had wandered off, and I was still trying to work up the courage to sneak away when I noticed a couple at the far side of the room eyeing me.

They were dressed in identical black suits and bowties, their faces painted to look like skulls. The woman's long, wavy black hair was pulled into a ponytail, and the man's hair was dark and slicked back. They were both tall, colorful tattoos peeking out from the wrists and necklines of their jackets. They were the type of couple that looked far too absurdly attractive—it was almost irritating to have that much sex appeal taken up by two people.

They kept staring at me for so long it was beginning to make me blush. There was something vaguely familiar about the guy, as if I'd seen him around campus . . . maybe I had a class with him. It was the woman who made the first move, making her way slowly across the living room to stand beside me along the wall. Despite the suit, she was wearing steel-toed boots and *towered* over me.

When she smiled at me, I was suddenly certain that she could literally step on me and I'd say thank you.

"Hey." Her voice was husky. "Having a good time?"

I nodded, flustered as fuck to have a beautiful girl talk to me without prompting. "Yeah, it's pretty wild. Definitely the biggest party I've been to."

"I'm Sam." She held out her hand, the slightest stutter in her voice as she said her name. Her fingers were warm and rough, as if she worked with her hands a lot. "Would you . . ." She nodded back toward her partner, who winked at me as I glanced over. So familiar. Where the hell did I know him from? ". . . would you wanna dance?"

I was more likely to trip over my own feet than actually dance with them. But her hand was so warm on mine, and across the room her partner was flipping through the music on the TV and selected a song called "Distance" by Apashe.

I smiled and nodded, and she tugged me by the hand across the room, her dark-brown eyes on my face as she brought me closer to her man. Then she was in front of me, arms around my neck, and he was behind me, hands on my waist, and our bodies swayed to the dark, swelling rhythm. It didn't even matter that I couldn't dance, because between the two of them I was moved however they wanted me, pressed close between them.

Sam's body moved closer, her thigh edged up between my legs, and her fingers caressed down my neck as her head leaned down—her lips brushed against my ear as she whispered, "You need to stop drinking that, babe."

But the thing was, I didn't want to stop drinking. Whatever Jeremiah had made me was good, and the alcohol was finally easing away that vicious knot of anxiety in my stomach. Not just easing it away—destroying it entirely. I felt great. I felt warm. I felt like laughing. And

God, I was turned on. The touch of her fingers was vibrant, tingling over my skin, and I raised the cup to my lips again.

She pulled me forward, and then she was leading me again through the crowd. Her man had his hand on my arm, and I was really damn confused as to why we weren't dancing anymore, until we were in the bathroom, and he'd closed the door, and she—

"I told you to stop drinking it," she hissed, gripping me by the back of the neck as he took the cup from my hands. "Sorry, babe, it's for your own good."

Right as I opened my mouth to ask what the hell she was going on about, she tugged me forward, bent me over the toilet, and shoved her fingers into my throat.

It had been hours since I'd ingested anything but sugary alcoholic drinks, and I vomited up most of the liquid into the toilet. I tried to shove her off, but she was shockingly strong, and shoved me down harder and pressed her fingers back again—more gagging, more vomit. Her man was watching, standing in front of the door like a guard. Only when I gagged and nothing came up did she let me go, to sink down dazedly against the wall as she flushed the toilet and tossed the remainder of my drink in after it.

"What . . . what the fuck is wrong with you?" I gasped, clutching my stomach, my throat sore from her fingers, my entire back tense with the effort of trying to fight her off. She sighed heavily as she rinsed my cup in the sink and filled it from the tap, then offered it to me as she knelt down.

"You're gonna need to get a hell of a lot smarter if you're gonna live, Raelynn," she said, and I realized I'd never given her my name. "Don't you ever, *ever* consume anything Jeremiah Hadleigh gives you."

I sipped the water cautiously, my eyes darting between her and the man—and that was when I realized: his eyes were golden.

"Zane," I whispered, and he gave me a cheery salute.

"Took you long enough to recognize me." He pouted mockingly. "Fucking hell, Leon wasn't lying about you being a chore to keep alive. Sucking down roofies like you don't have a care in the world."

"Roofies?" My voice shot up an octave in alarm. "What—"

"Your drink was drugged, babe." The woman sighed heavily. "The Hadleighs don't intend for you to leave this party, let me make that perfectly clear. And I've got shit to do, so keep drinking that water, get your head straight—I need you to get it together and leave."

My mind was spinning, not just from the vomiting and drugs lingering in my bloodstream. Zane reached down, offering me a mint to ease the gross taste of bile from my mouth. Zane was here . . . so did that mean . . .

"Is Leon here?" I choked out. Zane just shrugged.

"He's around," he said. "Not watching you closely enough, that's for certain."

Sam hauled me to my feet, her fingers like a vise on my upper arm. "Look, we're gonna call you an Uber and you're gonna go the hell home. Or get the fuck out of town, preferably. I'm not about to have everything ruined because the Hadleighs' next sacrifice is ready to just lay herself at the altar."

She nodded to Zane, who shook his head at me and opened the door—

Only to find our way blocked by a man dressed in black.

RAE

DAZED WITH THE remnants of the roofie in my system, for a moment I thought I was staring down an assassin who was about to kill me. The man glared at me, his gaze furious from the eyeholes of the balaclava obscuring his face. But that glare was as golden as the sun, and the moment realization dawned on me, I yanked myself out of Sam's grasp and flung my arms around him.

Leon's scent enveloped me, soft citrus and smoke. Comfort. Safety. I never would have imagined feeling a demon's arms tighten around me would provide that feeling, but I could have cried from relief at seeing him again. He was dressed entirely in black: cargo pants, boots, and some kind of tight military jacket. The perfect costume to completely obscure his identity.

"I was beginning to think you'd forgotten me, doll," he growled, holding me close with his hand gripping tight on the nape of my neck. "It was a cute little show you put on grinding between these two, but it gave me a feeling you've forgotten who you belong to."

Zane chuckled, but Sam was glaring. "Maybe if you'd paid a little bit closer attention, it wouldn't have been necessary."

Leon cocked his head curiously, his fingers toying with my hair, tugging at it lightly as if he was resisting the urge to pull. The only parts of his face that could be seen were his eyes and his mouth, which was twisted into a smirk. "Juniper Kynes . . . so grown up now."

I gasped at her name. Juniper—the last sacrifice. The *failed* sacrifice.

She remained grim-faced. "I'm not a scared little girl anymore. I'm much better armed than I was at fifteen."

"So glad you remember me." Leon glanced cautiously down the hall. He was no longer holding me against his chest, but he kept his arm around my shoulders as I stood beside him. "Hold on to that anger. It keeps you strong."

I'd never seen a person move so fast. Juniper whipped out a knife she'd had tucked beneath her jacket and pressed the blade up against Leon's mouth. Zane groaned, and I felt Leon stiffen just slightly as I sucked in my breath.

"You're lucky Zane has any affection for you," she hissed. "Because you were first on my list."

My fingers tightened on Leon's jacket, my hand balling into a fist. If this bitch thought she could threaten *my*—

"Easy, girl." I wasn't sure if Leon was referring to me, her, or both. The tension went out of him. "Don't threaten me with a good time."

When she didn't immediately move the knife away, Leon ran his forked tongue along the blade. Blood welled up as he tasted the knife's edge, and dripped over his lips, staining his teeth as he gave her smile.

"Enjoy the party," he said, gave Zane a quick wink, and kept me close as he walked away.

But he didn't walk me back toward the party. He headed the opposite direction, further down the hall, where the house was quieter and the music was a subtle beat that rumbled the floor. The wall to our right was all glass, giving a view over the lawn toward the trees. He didn't say a word, but I felt his tension building up again, heat and hardness under his skin. We turned a corner, near a stairway leading to the upper floor, and in a move so quick it left me dizzy, he yanked me from his side and pinned me to the wall.

His kiss tasted of iron as his hand wrapped around my throat, the tightness of his grip barely restrained as his bleeding tongue played over mine. He'd asked if I'd forgotten him, but my body would never forget. His kiss was like firecrackers going off in my head, an instant hot rush that tingled all the way down to my toes. His blood stained my mouth like a wicked offering, my belly tightening up as his body pressed to me, and I felt the hardness of his cock against my hip.

His taste was violence, his blood the sweetest sin I'd ever consumed.

He squeezed my throat, urging a whimper out of me as our mouths parted for a brief moment and he gave me a bloody grin.

"Fuck," My voice cracked as I gasped. He extended his forked tongue, blood still slowly welling from the cut across it, and I couldn't resist. I tasted his tongue with mine, caught it between my lips and sucked until our mouths met again: bloody and vile, perverted as hell.

"What the hell do you think you're doing here, Rae?" His voice was rough, exasperated. "Already trying to hop on the next demonic dick you encounter?"

"We were just dancing," I muttered. "I—"

"Oh, don't worry, doll." His fingers caressed my cheek, and he used his thumb to wipe his blood from around my mouth as he kept his grip on my throat. "I'm not jealous. It's cute how desperate you are. But I think you know that no one else will fuck you like I can."

I gulped, looking up at him as he loomed over me. "You left," I said softly. "You left me."

He shrugged. "You didn't make me stay."

"I've been so fucking scared, Leon."

His hold softened, a wince flickering over his face. He didn't give me any distance, as if he was afraid I might slip away. "Fucking hell, Rae. Why the hell did you come here?"

"I didn't exactly have a choice," I said, frowning despite my arousal. "I need a way to protect myself and I thought maybe I'd find something here."

Leon's eyes flickered back down the hall, pausing at whatever noise he'd heard, before turning his skeptical gaze back on me. "So you're here to sneak around in Kent Hadleigh's own house? To search for a weapon?"

"Yes," I said, folding my arms—although the motion didn't have as much petulant impact when I was pinned by my throat to the wall. "Are you going to help me or not?"

"Help you—" He gave a single, hard laugh. "I'll help you over my knee is what I'll do."

His hold tightened again, and another whimper squeaked out of me, this one sharp in anticipation. His free hand moved down, settled near my hip then gripped my ass, before giving it a sharp spank.

His grip choked my sharp intake of breath at the sting. "I knew I should have marked you," he growled. "I'm not a jealous being, Rae, but I don't like to see you play without being marked as mine before anyone else." His eyes flickered down, then his head lowered too. He pushed up my sweater, kissing slowly, tenderly along my breasts above my bra, before biting my flesh hard enough to make me yelp.

"I told you I wanted to pierce these," he said. "You'd look so good with my metal in you."

How much that idea scared me only made it hotter. Imagining him piercing my nipples to "mark" me was making me wet, and without even realizing what I was doing, I ground my hips up against him. The stimulation was just enough to make me shudder before he shoved me back against the wall again.

"Was that *Yes, please do it*?" he said. "Or am I just imagining how goddamn eager you are?"

Fuck, I wanted him—*needed* him, right here, right now. These weeks without him had felt like an eternity. But I couldn't forget where we were, and I couldn't forget what I'd come here for.

"If you help me find my way around the house, you can mark me," I said softly. His eyes narrowed, his jaw hardening as he considered my offer.

"Mm, that's a very naughty offering, Rae." He was so close I could barely breathe—it took all my self-control not to wrap my arms around his neck and kiss him again, taste him again. "I don't want you in this house."

"We'll be quick," I said.

"Why do you think there's anything at all in this house that's worth risking your life for?"

"You said Kent had magical artifacts. If he has a charm to protect him from you, maybe he has something to protect me from the God." His eyes had narrowed. He didn't like it, but I wasn't wrong. "Help me find it. Because if I'm not going to enroll in your Demonic Protection Plan, I need *something* to defend myself."

He didn't look happy as he glared from behind his mask, but finally his expression softened. "So I help you find Kent's stash and I get to pierce those cute little nipples, yeah? That's the deal?"

I gulped, but I still had enough alcohol in my system to sound completely confident as I said, "Yeah. That's the deal."

"Alright then. Stay quiet, and stay close."

We crept up the stairway, emerging onto the upper floor near some kind of secondary living room with a covered pool table and large, thickly cushioned white chairs. It was a good thing the party had managed to stay contained to the front of the house. There was no way we could have managed this if the guests had spread out. But the upper floor was dark, all the lights off and the doors closed.

A clear indication that no one was meant to be up here.

I was itching to open every door, but Leon knew where he was going. The hall ended at a cross, and Leon headed to the right, taking us along another glass-walled hall with a view out over the dark yard. The house was so big that the thump of the music seemed vastly distant now. I kept expecting to feel my phone buzz in my pocket; Inaya would start wondering where I was soon. Hopefully she was distracted enough—drunk enough—to forget about me for a little longer.

The hall ended at a set of gray double doors. Leon held a finger to his mouth in warning before he took a long and careful look at the doorknobs, then at the crack between the doors.

"What are you looking for?" I whispered, only to have him wave his hand at me yet again to be quiet. Slowly, he opened the door, cracking it just an inch before the tension went out of his shoulders and he pushed it open the rest of the way.

"Checking for any protective magic," he said. "Would really be a stupid way to go if you escaped the God only to be killed instantly for touching a doorknob."

The knowledge that there were spells that could kill with just a touch had me stepping much more cautiously through the doorway. The bedroom was spacious, with gleaming wood floors and a large white rug. Everything was in monochromatic tones, from the gray sheets to the white pillows and the black curtains pulled back on the far glass wall.

Leon quietly shut the door behind us, glaring around the room as if it personally offended him. "Never thought I'd find myself creeping back in here again. Hate this room."

"Were you in here often?"

"Once or twice, and that was too many. Kent had a thing for administering punishments while he was lounging around in here. I suppose it was a relaxing pastime for him to magically break a few of my bones when I fucked up his orders."

It was grim to imagine such a luxurious space being used for something so sinister. It was even harder to imagine Leon under someone else's command: he had so much power, so much overwhelming strength that the thought of him being ordered around by a mere human sounded ludicrous.

But even a powerful demon could be broken with pain.

Everything in here looked expensive: the modern glass and steel chandelier overhead, the black marble fireplace beneath the massive flatscreen, the huge painting in a gilded frame above the bed. It depicted a woman standing in the midst of a stormy sea, her arm outstretched with a dagger pointed toward the sky. Black tentacles were coiled around her arm, as if to grasp the knife with her. It looked like it could have been painted in the Renaissance, beautiful and dramatic. But it wasn't a weapon.

Nothing in here looked like a weapon.

The open window showed only our reflections until I passed by it, and a floodlight flickered on below, illuminating a large section of the lawn. Motion caught my attention, and as I stared, I saw something dark and skeletal creep back among the trees.

They'd followed me here. Of course they had. I couldn't shake these monsters no matter where I went.

Leon's arms wrapped around me from behind, and his teeth nipped at my ear as he whispered, "Why are you afraid of them lurking around, when you know the most dangerous thing in this house is me?" He turned me in his arms, nudging up my chin with his fingers. "And I'm on your side, lucky for you."

Goose bumps crept up my spine with my back turned to the window. I hated knowing they were out there. I hated this constant feeling of being hunted. "Are you?"

He frowned. "Excuse me?"

"Are you on my side? Really?"

His expression grew serious, almost angry. His playful smirk was gone. "What the hell gave you the idea that I wasn't, Rae?"

I bit my lip, shaking my head. "You plan on leaving again, don't you? I don't know what I'm supposed to do if I don't find something here to protect myself. Those things won't leave me alone." I tried to look back out the window, but Leon caught my face and wouldn't let me look.

"I came back," he said. "Doesn't that count for something?"

"It's temporary," I said, trying to keep my voice steady. But I was scared, and I'd been keeping all my fears and frustrations quiet because who the hell was I supposed to talk to about it?

Who would understand, besides him?

"I don't do *temporary*." His voice was a snarl as he tucked his hands behind his back. It felt like a warning now, when he did that. His hands were clasped away, but that didn't mean he didn't want to touch me. It was an indicator of his self-control, an effort not to do too much before I was begging for it. "You *have* forgotten—you're mine, Rae. Frankly I should punish you for daring to suggest otherwise."

My mouth had gone dry, but my pussy hadn't. It was heating quickly at his words, swelling in anticipation. I ran my tongue over my lips, realizing just how foolish I'd sounded. These weeks of loneliness and fear had gotten to me, and I'd missed his attention more than I could ever say. I'd missed his fire, his brutality, his absolutely immoveable certainty that I belonged to him.

I needed that assurance now, desperately.

"You won't punish me here," I said. "In Kent's own bedroom, you wouldn't dare—"

"You think I wouldn't?" His voice had dropped dangerously low. He stalked around me as I stood there, heart pounding with the rush of pushing him. I wanted a reaction, and if challenging him would get it, then that's what I'd do.

"What if you'd caught me in here a few months ago, Leon?" I said, resisting the urge to turn as he stalked behind me. He'd managed to wipe from my mind the fear of the monster lurking outside, turning all my attention to him and what he was doing.

What he *planned* on doing.

"What if," he murmured, then chuckled. "What if, indeed? Are you trying to suggest, that if I'd caught you in here while I was still in Kent's service, I would have caused you harm?" He brushed his fingers across the back of my neck, stroking through my hair, his claws sharp as they scratched lightly over my skin. "You underestimate me, Rae. Kent never even would have had to know I'd caught you here. But I still would have had to punish you, if only to teach you a lesson about sneaking into places you shouldn't."

I gulped. His hands slipped around my waist, claws digging through the fabric of my sweater to prick against my hips. His lips brushed against my neck, then caressed beneath my ear, and I closed my eyes as my breath shuddered.

"So nervous," he said softly. "What do you need, doll?"

"A distraction," I whispered. "I need to feel safe. I need . . . I need you."

I felt his lips curl into a smile against my skin. "A distraction? Shall I distract you with the thought that even if Kent still commanded me, I wouldn't hurt you?"

He came around to stand in front of me again, his claws tracing along my jaw until they pressed into the tender skin right under my chin. "Even as I punish you, as cruelly and brutally as I please, I'm still going to protect you. Is that the distraction you need?"

"Yes. Please."

"*Please.*" He chuckled. "It sounds so pretty when you say it. Are you going to submit willingly, or do I need to force you to accept what you want?"

I took a slow step back, then another. I was restless, my limbs trembling, tingling with adrenaline and the need to fight, to run.

"Ah, so by force it is." He came after me, every step just as slow and measured as mine. My face was hot, and he inhaled deeply before his eyes flashed gold, and he gave me a wide, sharp grin. "I can smell that. Your dripping arousal, so fucking eager for me."

I shook my head, but inside I was screaming *yes*. The fantasy of being taken by Leon—forcibly, as punishment—made my pussy throb. Very real terror lurked outside, but in here, I was safe in his hands. Safe, even as he played my fear like a violin.

Dangerous fantasies felt cathartic when there were so many real things to be afraid of.

"You shouldn't have been wandering in forbidden places, doll. See what happens when you do?"

He lunged for me, and I catapulted across the bed to make a run for the door. I knew I wouldn't reach it. I had no desire to get away. But my heart still leapt into my throat when he grabbed hold of me and yanked me back, throwing me down on the mattress. His strength was irresistible; he threw me around like a ragdoll, flipping me over so that I lay on my back with him straddling me.

It felt good to throw my fists at him, to kick and buck and wiggle. I knew it was all useless, that I wouldn't get away. But struggling released my tension, it eased that jittery energy in me. When he snatched my wrists and pinned them to the bed with one big hand, and used his other hand to grip around my throat, arousal burned through me like wildfire.

I panted beneath him as he leaned close, laughing wickedly. "Tell me you remember, Rae. What makes the game stop?"

"Mercy," I whispered.

"Good girl." His grip tightened roughly, his claws digging into my neck. He looked terrifying and unknown with the mask on, and I could imagine he truly was a stranger, a demon I'd never met who'd caught me snooping where I shouldn't be.

"Better keep quiet," he growled. "You don't want my employer to find out about this now, do you? It'll only be worse for you if he does." He chuckled as I turned my head away from him defiantly, and he ran his tongue up the side of my face. I shuddered at the sensation, and a whimper escaped me as he bit my ear.

"Let me go," I squeaked around the pressure of his hand, squirming uselessly. My thighs tightened with need as his forked tongue flicked at me from between his parted lips, taunting me. "Please, let me go."

"Not a chance." He dragged me back to the edge of the mattress. He stood behind the bed, yanked me over the edge, and held me down on my stomach so that I was bent over the side of the mattress. His hand slipped beneath my skirt, his nails ripping the thin fabric of my black stockings. "No matter how much you squeal and beg, you don't fool me; you're going to love every second of what I'm about to do to you. I'm going to fucking ruin you."

"Fuck, Leon . . ." His hand rubbed between my legs, rough and careless. I found myself grinding myself down against him, eager for more stimulation, desperate for the feeling of his fingers over my clit. He pulled his hand away, pressed my face down against the mattress with a hand on the back of my head, and smacked my ass three times in quick succession.

"Filthy little slut." He reached between my legs again, ripping my stockings and tugging my panties to the side to plunge two fingers into me. I cried out as he mercilessly pumped his fingers, gripping at the sleek sheets beneath me, the pleasure taking brutal hold.

"Aw, so wet," Leon withdrew his fingers, leaving me gasping, and held them up in front of my face. My arousal glistened on his skin, webbing between his fingers as he spread them. He laughed darkly, giving my head a rough shake. "Filthy girl. You love being thrown around, hm? Open your mouth."

He pushed his fingers past my lips, the taste of my own arousal making me moan. I sucked on his fingers, my tongue slipping between them and over the tip— he'd mercifully sheathed his claws to finger-fuck me. He smacked my ass again, and I yelped, but went right back to licking up every last drop of myself from him.

"Such a naughty little thing," he growled. "Let's put that mouth of yours to better use, shall we?"

He manhandled me to the floor, controlling me with a hand on my neck and another on my arm. I struggled against him, just to experience that euphoric feeling of denying something I desperately wanted and knowing it would come anyway.

I wanted to fight, and get what I wanted anyway.

He forced me to my knees and unbuckled his belt. The clink of the buckle and the familiar sound of his zipper sliding down had my stomach twisting with need. My mouth was watering. I knew what was coming. I watched eagerly as he pulled out his rigid cock, thickly veined and monstrous, and held it in front of my face.

"Open."

I glared up at him with a defiant smile. "No."

His eyes flashed, and he rolled back his shoulders, shaking his head. He tugged me up higher on my knees, leaning down until our faces were inches apart. "Don't. You. *Dare*. Say *no*. To *me*. Or I'll slap that cheeky smile off your face."

I grinned wider. "Hurt me, Leon," I whispered. "Hurt me."

The veins in his arms seemed to thicken with the effort of holding back. "Brave girl," he said softly. "Are you sure about that? You're asking a demon to hurt you; I'm used to playing with those who can bleed and not die, who can be thrown and not break."

"You won't break me," I said. "Fucking *hurt* me, asshole."

His palm slapped across my face, heavy and stinging—but perfectly controlled. His strength was tempered. He gave just enough to make it sting, softened the impact with his other hand to prevent my head from whipping to the side. For a moment my mouth hung open in shock, my cheek stinging and my eyes beginning to water. He paused with me, waited with me, and I knew his eyes were on me, gauging my reaction.

I raised my gaze again, petulant, and spat, "You don't scare me."

"No?" He tugged my hair, and the viciousness of those sharp teeth through the dark mask made goose bumps go up my spine. "You want to be scared, little brat?" Something was changing. His teeth had grown longer. His irises had swollen, leaving only a thin ring of gold. His tongue, when it snaked out to flick teasingly at my face, was *black*. "I'll give you something to be scared of."

He slapped me again, then again. My head was buzzing with the concoction of dopamine and adrenaline that this stinging pain was pumping through me. His slaps were heavy, leaving biting tingles across my face. I didn't just enjoy the pain—I reveled in the endurance, in resisting his orders for as long as I could bear it. When I raised my watering eyes up to him again, he truly did look like a monster, something out of my nightmares that had me helpless in his hands.

"Scared now, girl?"

Scared—enamored—overwhelmed—needy as hell. This wicked stretch of my imagination that allowed me to exist as both frightened and calm at the same time, this dangerous game, was exactly where I wanted to be.

I shook my head defiantly, flinching when his fingers stroked over the skin he'd just slapped. "I'm not. I'm not scared of you."

"So brave," he said, and pouted his lip out mockingly. "And so fucking foolish. Pathetic little mortal. Defying a demon feels good, doesn't it?" He squeezed my cheeks between one hand, and pushed the fingers of his opposite hand to my lips, forcing my jaws open. "Let me see that pretty little mouth. So perfect for my cock." His fingers pressed against my tongue. I almost gagged, and tears leaked from my eyes with the effort not to. I could feel my pussy dripping, clenching with desire.

He looked at me like I was nothing more than a toy, but when he lowered his voice and spoke again, there was reverence in his words. "Your mouth is perfect. Your body is perfect. Your mind, that damned curious mind, is perfect." His hold on me wasn't gentle, but the kiss he laid on my forehead was. "You're mine, even if you don't believe it. And I treasure what's mine. Now, open your fucking mouth."

This time, I obeyed.

He pressed his cock past my lips. The taste of his flesh on my tongue was intoxicating, and my eyes fluttered shut as he thrust into me. He fucked my mouth mercilessly, punishing me—rewarding me. Only when a gag finally jolted through me did he slow his pace, holding my head in place as he used my mouth for his pleasure.

"Fuck, you take my cock so well." The roughness in his voice made me moan. I could hear the pleasure in his words, barely controlled, and I moved my tongue along his shaft, eager to feel him throb. "Ah . . . *fuck,* baby girl . . ."

The pet name stirred something in me, something light, fluttery, and warm in my belly. He'd never called me that before. His pet names had always carried a teasing tone, but this one—this one was tight with his pleasure, this one dropped from his lips as if he hadn't even thought about it, as if it had come out in a moment of vulnerability.

It made the intense arousal flooding me blaze even hotter. I gripped his hips as I began to move my head in rhythm with his thrusts. I dug my fingers into him, then reached around and clawed at his back. I wanted to leave my marks on him. I wanted to draw blood. I didn't know if I could possibly even make this monster feel pain, but I wanted to try.

His thrusts became harder, and he laid his palm against my stinging cheek, encouraging me to look up at him. "You're going to swallow every drop, aren't you?" he growled, and I managed to nod my head around his girth. I longed for the taste of him, I wanted it so badly that I groaned. He held my head in place, thrusting deep as his cock throbbed against my tongue, then flooded my mouth with his cum.

I gulped down every drop of him. I clung to him, holding him deep in my throat so I wouldn't miss a drop. Every time my mouth tightened as I swallowed around him, his hips twitched forward, shudders going up his back.

He pulled away from my mouth, gripped my chin, and with my lips still wet with him, he kissed me with a hunger that wanted to crawl inside of me, that wanted to swallow me whole. I bit at his lip and he bit back, then his tongue was in my mouth and I found myself limp in his grip, all the tastes of him an intoxicating cocktail in my mouth.

"You're fucking filthy," he whispered, parting from me just enough to speak. I smiled—tear-stained face, cum down my chin, mascara running.

"Make me filthier."

He spit on my lips, and as he watched me lick it off, I thought he might truly lose control. The viciousness in his eyes, the hunger there, was nothing short of terrifying. Terrifying, and yet I'd never wanted someone so badly. Every nerve in my body was on fire, sensitive to the touch. I held back a shriek as he lifted me from the floor and threw me back on the bed, where I landed on the sleek sheets and soft pillows. I scrambled, another useless attempt to struggle, but he pinned me down on my back and yanked down my skirt.

"You're still hard?" I gasped, as if I couldn't see what was obvious. It was as if he hadn't even orgasmed: his cock was still rigidly hard, a pearly bead of precum sliding from the tip as he pushed my legs apart.

"Remember what I am, baby girl," he growled. "I'm hard as long as I want to be." He leaned closer, a whisper against my skin. "And I promised to ruin you."

I was dripping wet, but the stretch of him entering me still made me cry out. He covered my mouth with his hand, stifling my noise as he filled me deeply. "Remember," he hissed harshly, biting at my neck as he spoke. "Three taps if you want out." The reminder of the signal grounded me for a moment, reminding me of reality, before I floated right back into that delicious, dark fantasy.

Watching him over me, his face masked, his eyes bright, bloodied marks from my teeth on his lips, brought me to the edge of orgasm almost immediately. The stretch of his cock inside me, and his fingers rubbing my clit shoved me off the precipice and sent me tumbling into ecstasy.

I clenched around him, screaming against his hand as he fucked me into oblivion. He slowed his pace, drawing out every second of pleasure. But then, even as the waves receded and I managed to catch my breath, my head light, he whispered, "You're not done yet. I want to see you come again. Scream for me again."

He lifted my legs, holding them up so he could reach an even deeper angle. My shuddering pussy clenched again, every touch on my overly sensitive, swollen clit making me twitch. I was crying, "Please, please, please," against his hand, my mind spiraling into thoughtless bliss. He bit against my neck, his lips curving into a smile on my skin as I arched up against him, hardly able to draw breath as my tension wound tighter and tighter.

I sounded like an animal as I cried out against his hand, shaking under him, the flood of endorphins making

me sob. I barely realized I was crying until his hands
were wiping away my tears, kissing my face, murmuring, "Easy, baby girl. You did so good, you're so fucking
beautiful."

I turned my head, to press my face against his chest as
he lay down beside me. I felt silly for crying: I wasn't sad,
I wasn't scared, I wasn't hurt. But it had been so good,
so wildly consuming, that crying against his chest for another minute felt like catharsis.

"Sorry." I giggled as I sniffled, just an absolute mess
all around. "Sorry about the crying—"

He pressed a finger to my lips, shushing me. "Don't
you dare apologize. Come down however you need to.
I'm here with you."

We lay there in silence, listening to the distant thump
of the music. As I calmed, I realized that the knot of anxiety that had been tormenting me for days was gone.
He'd unraveled it, with his fingers, his tongue, his wicked
words. Nothing that lurked outside was as dangerous
as him.

And I was his. He treasured what was his.

"Enough of a distraction for you?" He smirked at me,
and I pulled up the mask he wore because I wanted to
see his face. It hadn't been all that long since I'd last seen
him, but it still took my breath away. His beauty was
dangerous, it was alluring. Like those brightly colored
poisonous frogs, with looks that begged to be touched
but would kill you with one brush of your fingertips. But
I touched him anyway, caressing my fingers over his face.

"It was a good distraction," I said.

"Hopefully I've fucked those anxious thoughts out of your head. Don't waste that sweet fear on vile beasts, not when I'm here."

But how long will you be here?

We couldn't lay there forever. He told me not to be afraid, but I knew he was still on alert: he was still listening for footsteps, his eyes still darted toward the window, the door. He was anxious, so I didn't have to be. But for another minute, it felt good just to lay there, just to breathe, just to feel his fingers play in my hair.

"I'm surprised a demon would use a safeword," I murmured, staring at the chandelier overhead. The bed was absurdly comfortable, but the painting of the woman behind me was giving me the illusion of eyes looking down at me.

He sniffed, shaking his head. "We demons value free will above all else. We may play with the illusion of being forced, but what fun is it if your victim doesn't desperately want you? We don't call it that in Hell, a *safeword*. We all know to call mercy if the play needs to end. It's a more polite, and rather more intimate, way of saying, *Stop or I'll make you stop*." He shrugged, then after a moment, shoved himself up off the bed with a grin.

"I've always wanted to desecrate this bed," he said, holding his hand out to me to help me up. "Finally got to make it properly filthy."

"Kent may have to burn it," I said, as he wrapped me up in his arms and held me close again. His lips pressed against the top of my head, and I whispered. "I missed you."

I meant it, but it set my heart pounding to say it out loud. He tensed, his grip on me tightening slightly. "Why?"

Because you make me feel safe, warm, wanted, and you have a monster dick that gives me the best orgasms of my life.

I wasn't quite able to meet his gaze. "I like having you around."

When I did finally look up, his brows had drawn together as if my words were confusing. He let me go to rub the back of his head, ruffling his hair. "Well, you're certainly one of the first humans to say that." He awkwardly cleared his throat. "We've spent enough time here. Let's get down below."

LEON

I'D NEVER SEEN Kent open the way down to the basement; given that my binding circle was down there, I could simply teleport to it at Kent's command. I could only leave the circle with his permission, and he'd usually phrased his commands in such a way that I had to immediately return to it when my tasks were done. The basement was a place I'd never wanted to step foot in again, never wanted to see nor smell nor come close to.

But here I was.

I knew the entrance was somewhere in his master bedroom, and I suspected it had something to do with the massive bookshelf against the far wall, with a strange gap at the bottom as if there was a track underneath. That was what I inspected first.

Playing with Rae, taking out my nervous energy on her as she did the same to me, had calmed some of my unease at being in this damned house. But it still lingered, a prickling of anxiety on the back of my skull. I hated this room. I hated the smell of it. I hated the perfectly clean carpets and white walls, and that there was still a faint smell in the air of those cigars Kent loved to smoke. I didn't want to stay here for a moment longer than I had to, hearing Jeremiah and Victoria distantly in the house as they got drunker and louder. The temptation to go out there and slaughter them was strong, but Hell's royals-in-charge frowned upon demons making spectacles of themselves in front of humans.

Slaughtering the Hadleigh siblings in front of a crowd of drunk college students sounded fun, but wasn't worth the ensuing fall out from Hell.

"I take it you didn't find the grimoire?" Rae asked from behind me, watching me as I felt along the underside of the shelves.

Oh, yes, I found the grimoire. But I'm too obsessed with you to leave you, so here I am, still risking life and limb to be near you, still driven absolutely mad by your voice and smell and eyes—

"No, didn't find it yet," I looked back over my shoulder and gave her a wink. "Lucky for you."

The more I reminded her how "lucky" she was that I was still here, the more I felt like a complete asshole. Implying that the grimoire was the only thing keeping me from leaving was a vile lie, one she couldn't possibly believe for much longer. I'd gladly admit I was generally a dick, but Rae made me want to be . . . nice . . . to her.

Only to her. Everyone else could get fucked.

In a far corner of the shelf, my fingers grazed over a cold metal plate set into the wood. I pressed it, stepped back, and the bookshelf moved silently across the track, slipping into the wall and revealing a stairway leading down into the dark. Rae gasped, stepping forward eagerly as if she was ready to run straight down into the dark. I pressed my hand against her chest, stilling her as fluorescent lights flickered on and illuminated the cold, concrete stairwell.

"Are there cameras down there?" she whispered, as if the stairs themselves might hear and tattle. "Or motion sensors?"

I shrugged. "Don't know. There's only one room down there I've been in. We need to be quick."

She nodded determinedly. There was a flush to her face, and her heartbeat had sped up again. She was excited—of course she was. Facing down a dangerous adventure? Better than a walk in the park apparently.

There was something so painfully hot about this tiny woman's foolhardy bravery.

She went ahead and I followed, pressing another metal plate on the inner wall to close the bookshelf behind us. We went down two flights of stairs, and more lights flickered on overhead.

"Wow." Rae's eyes widened as she peered around the space. "This looks like a supervillain's headquarters."

"It may as well be." I was getting a creeping, nasty feeling up my back being in here. The black-painted concrete walls and wooden floors couldn't disguise the claustrophobic crushing weight of this place. Demons weren't meant to be underground, yet that was where the Hadleighs had always kept me.

"Is this his evil conference table?" Rae said, smiling at her own joke as she circled the long, shining wood table set up in the middle of the room, lined with chairs. She'd taken her phone out of her pocket, and as she wandered around, she held it up to record. I didn't have much faith in human justice systems, but if the Hadleighs wanted to make my girl disappear, it would only be harder for them the more records that remained of her whereabouts. Recording her exploration here was probably a good idea.

"I'd hear them talking sometimes," I said. "His closest members of the Libiri would meet with him here."

"And behind all these doors?" She looked up and down the room, at the thick metal doors secured with keypads. "How can we get in?"

"Electrical locks are easy enough to influence," I said. "Take your pick. I don't know what's behind any of them, except the one at the end."

She looked toward the far end of the room and the nondescript metal door there. When I was under Kent's command, the only way in and out of that room was with his permission. Now? I was far from eager to step foot in it again.

"What's in there?" Rae said, and I sighed, extending my energy across the room to influence the electricity in the door's lock and pop it open.

"See for yourself."

The creak of the door's hinges was familiar. I could swear it was the only door in the entirety of this house that Kent allowed to squeak. And the smell inside—stagnant, damp, dust, mold. I turned away from the open door, just so I wouldn't see the familiar flicker of its pale fluorescent bulb.

I used to break that bulb every day until Kent figured out what I was doing. Then he broke my fingers in return.

I didn't want to be in here. I didn't want to smell the cold damp concrete, the metallic iron. I didn't want to hear the hum of the air filtration system through the vents. The walls were solid concrete except for those vents that blew in cold, sterile air. Air that smelled like nothing, air that was as oppressive and stifling as the walls.

"It's empty," she said. "It's just an empty concrete room. It's cold."

"Look down."

I suppose she did, to judge by her sharp intake of breath. I distracted myself with unlocking the other doors, until she called back, with a tremble in her voice, "Leon, did . . . did he keep you in here?"

I didn't answer. She wanted a weapon besides me, so I'd damn well find her one. I wrenched open the first door once its lock was disabled, only to find a simple study within: desk, bookshelf, chair. Unhelpful. I turned for the next door—

And found her standing there, blocking my way.

"Leon." Her voice sounded hurt. Pained. I hated it. I didn't want her to sound that way. "Did Kent keep you in that room? That's a binding circle on the ground, isn't it?"

"So you really can learn magic from Google," I muttered. It sounded mean, perhaps it *was* mean. I'd never given a fuck how I sounded until it came to her, until it came to seeing the emotion in those big brown eyes behind her glasses. I tried to step around her, but she got in front of me again.

"Yes, I was kept in there," I said, sharper than I intended, but sharpness was the better option to pain—to fear. "On and off for a hundred years or so. This was the basement of the old house, before Kent rebuilt it with his fancy block of glass and concrete up there. I used to watch the roots grow through the dirt walls, until Kent poured more concrete and sealed the door, and there was no light, no warmth, nothing." I glared over her head, back toward that room. I'd spent hours, days, weeks in there when the various generations of Hadleighs had no use for me. Just a tool, tucked away in the dark before they thought of a task for me again. Stuck in that damned tiny room, in that damned tiny circle, staring at the walls until my mind went numb.

It made me sick. It made me want to—

Her arms were around me. She wrapped them tight around my middle, her head against my chest. She sniffed, and squeezed a little tighter.

"I'm sorry," she whispered. "I'm so sorry."

My first instinct was to pull away. I didn't need comfort, I didn't need her apologies, I didn't need her feeling sorry for me. I hated pity. And her apologies were empty because it wasn't *she* who had locked me down here. For centuries, humans had imprisoned my kind when they could, and run from us when they couldn't. In return we'd tempted them, hunted them, used them. Humans were selfish and fickle, short-lived opportunists. They were not to be trusted, only good for pleasure.

But her arms were still tight, shaking around me as she sniffled again. Why the hell did this hurt her? Why did she give a damn what had happened to me?

Putting my arms around her in return felt . . . strange. Warmer than it should have. Softer. The longer she held on, the more I realized I didn't really want her to let go. My greater instincts were still struggling, pushing, setting off every alarm bell to tell me that allowing myself to linger in this moment was weak and useless.

But this anger, this fury that kept me going, wasn't for her. None of it was meant for her. I'd built up my walls to protect myself, not to shut her out.

"We don't have much time." My voice came out harsh, if only to keep it from being soft. She pulled back from me a little, and hurriedly wiped her eyes. I didn't truly understand why she'd cry for me, but humans did strange things when they empathized with another.

Odd, to have a human think of my pain.

But it had been her gentle hands that had cleaned my wounds, too.

"Right." She raised her chin, jaw set tight and determined. "Let's find something to fuck these bastards up."

I wanted to hold her again. I didn't want her to have to fight. I wanted her safe, protected, *mine*. Instead I watched her open the next door, and her eyes lit up when the light flickered on within.

"Jackpot," she said, and when I peered in over her shoulder, I quickly saw why.

The black walls within were lined with shelves, covered in artifacts that reeked of age and magic. More shelves were clustered in the center of the room, and there were water-stained crates with dead barnacles accumulated across them, stacked in the corners. Rae's eyes were wide as she entered and gazed around.

"It smells like the ocean," she said softly. I nodded.

"These all must have come up from the mine." I ran my fingers along the cracking spines of several books piled upon one of the shelves. "I remember some of these things. After the mine flooded, and Kent's grandfather, Morpheus, summoned me, one of the first tasks he gave me was going down into the mine and bringing up whatever I could."

Back then, I'd had no idea what I had been brought into. It was the first time I'd been summoned in over fifty years, and unlike most of my summoners, Morpheus didn't make any mistakes. He was careful, calm, calculated. He made every order clear. By all accounts, at first, he'd treated me fine.

Until the God got Its tentacles deeper into his head. Whispered in his ear. Turned his mind from simple curiosity to greed.

"The tunnels are all flooded down there," I moved along the shelves, covered in so many trinkets I could recall bringing up. "I spent weeks swimming through them, finding this shit, bringing it up. And the longer you're down there, the louder the God becomes. The more interest It gets. It tries to get in your head."

Bowls, tools, candles. Books, statues, jewelry. Anything and everything I could get my hands on was kept here from the deepest inner chambers, the ones the miners had broken into by accident. Other people had worshipped the Deep One too, long ago, and it was their artifacts that Morpheus had wanted.

It was these artifacts that I'd feared Kent would figure out how to use, and turn against me.

We reached the far end of the room, where a glass display case held a series of black daggers. Their handles were intricately carved, wrapped in knotted red string, and the closer I got to them, the more certain I was that I couldn't touch them. They vibrated with an energy powerful enough to turn my stomach, some old magic that had fermented with the years, growing stronger and more vicious until just the sight of those blades sent a shudder up my back.

"Those," Rae said, "I need one of those."

The case was locked with a good old-fashioned metal padlock, so it required an old-fashioned method of getting in. I slammed my elbow against the glass, shattering it, and Rae yelped in surprise.

"Jesus *Christ*, Leon," she hissed. "You could have warned me!"

I chuckled, stepping back quickly from the case so I wouldn't have to be near that unpleasant magical humming. "Take your pick, doll. And don't call on Christ as if the bastard is going to come anywhere near me."

She rolled her eyes at me, stared curiously into the shattered case for a moment, then carefully selected a knife from among the glass shards. She pulled it from its sheath, revealing a straight blade black as ink, the same color as the rope wound around its handle. She brandished it toward me playfully, and looked shocked when I jolted back. To her eyes, it would have looked as if I teleported six feet back.

"Woah." She stared at the knife, then back at me. "Does this . . . does this actually scare you?"

"It's unpleasant," I grumbled. "There's old, feral magic in it. Don't get any ideas—if that thing cut me, it wouldn't heal quickly. But it would be the same for the Eld." I grinned. "Keep it close, but away from me. It smells bad."

"I don't smell anything." She frowned in confusion, sniffing at the knife as if her human nostrils could somehow pick up that magical smell. I gave her a tap on the arm.

"*Away,* Rae. Tuck it away, shit." She quickly tucked it into the band of her skirt, under her sweater. "We need to get out of here. The Hadleighs can't possibly be happy that you've been out of their sight for so long."

She nodded enthusiastically, as pleased as a kid who'd been given a piece of candy. She'd gotten what she wanted, but I didn't feel any better. I didn't want her to have to use some old knife, I didn't want this small human fending off monsters. I was more than capable of protecting her myself.

Except I'd locked up my protection behind stipulations and deals, and she was determined to DIY her safety.

"I'd like to see the Eld come for me now," she said, as we made our way back up the stairwell. I could hear the music pounding, drunk humans laughing and shouting. Too much noise to isolate out any individual conversation, which made me nervous. Even down here, the scent of cigars was strong. Perhaps even stronger than it had been in the bedroom. I hoped that knife was worth it, because lingering here was a risk we really shouldn't have taken.

Rae reached the door first, and pushed the metal plate to slide the bookshelf open. "I'd like to see them try to get their claws in me and get a face full of—oh."

Her *oh* dropped like a stone in my stomach.

Kent Hadleigh sat there, a cigar in his mouth, waiting for us.

RAE

KENT DIDN'T LOOK angry; he didn't even look surprised. He sat in a thickly cushioned leather chair, puffing his cigar, the vanilla-mahogany scent of it wafting around the room. His pale gray suit was unbuttoned, as if he'd just settled in for a relaxing evening.

He wasn't even supposed to be here. The smile he gave me was like ice sliding down my spine. My heart began to thump painfully hard. I glanced back, just to reassure myself of where Leon was: close, just to my side, still as stone.

The ice running down my spine settled solidly in my stomach. My palms began to sweat. The knife I'd stolen was digging into my hip and I was certain the guilt would show all over my face.

"Miss Raelynn, my, my, what a curious little lamb you are," Kent mused, carefully ashing his cigar in a small stone tray on the table beside him. He must have cameras in here. He must have been watching the whole thing. "And you . . . pull the mask up, boy."

Leon didn't move. His tension was palpable, a physical force emanating from beside me. Kent *tsk*ed in disapproval, and spread his hands innocently. "No one's in trouble here. But considering you both snuck into my private quarters, it's only polite that I know who you are. Now . . ." There was a glint, a flash of steel—and Kent had a pistol in his hand. My pounding heart stilled completely, aching in my chest. "The mask, boy. I'm not playing games."

This time, Leon moved. I didn't need to look at him to know he'd uncovered his face: Kent's expression told me everything. For the first time, he did look surprised.

Then angry. So angry that his finger twitched on the gun, and a sound somewhere between a sob and choked gasp was wrenched out of me.

"Demon," he nodded slowly. "And here I thought you would have left Earth after you nearly killed my son, but no. Still here, still meddling in my affairs." Leon had tried to kill Jeremiah? For a brief moment, my curiosity tried to override my fear, only for the ominous click of the gun's hammer cocking back to slam my terror back into place.

"It won't kill me," Leon said quickly. My head felt light, and I desperately wanted to lean up against something so I wouldn't fall. But I felt certain that one wrong move would result in a bullet through my brain. "How many bullets do you have, Kenny-boy? Five? Six? Enough to slow me down before I rip you apart?"

Kent's expression was immoveable, frozen solidly in a state of distaste. Then the gun moved imperceptibly, to be aimed at me.

"Fuck, Mr. Hadleigh, wait—" I held up my hands, flushing hot then cold. I couldn't die like this. Not here. But Kent wasn't even looking at me.

"The girl will die from a single bullet," he said calmly. "Not the most ideal way to make the sacrifice, but dead is dead."

"Sacrifice," the word slipped past my lips like a prayer, disbelief and pleading wrapping themselves around it. "I'm . . . I'm not . . . not a sacrifice . . . I'm not . . ."

"You care for her, don't you?" Kent chuckled, shaking his head. He was still focused on Leon, and whatever he saw in him seemed to amuse him greatly. "How funny. To think, the demon doesn't want his toy broken. Had I known you could be controlled so easily, I never would have bothered with all the effort of punishing you with magic. But of course, the toy you want is the one you can't keep." He sighed, as if dealing with petulant children, and slowly, his eyes slid back to me. "I understand the inevitable can be shocking, Miss Raelynn. It can be horrifying. And no doubt this demon has been feeding you lies about us. About our God, our purpose. Corrupting you."

"He's been protecting me," I gasp, and dare to step closer to Leon. His arm wrapped around me immediately, pushing me firmly behind him.

"If you kill her," he growled. "You seal your own death."

Kent smiled slowly. "Then we are at an impasse. What a twist of fate. The Killer becomes the Protector. Why?" He chuckled, puffing the cigar as if it was all just a grand game. "Is her cunt so enjoyable? You could still use it once she's dead. What a thought: you, down there in the mine, rutting against her corpse like a rabid dog."

I felt sick. Leon's claws were distending, and the heat rolling off him was almost too much to bear. The door was so close, only a few steps away.

A few steps and a gun.

"All in due time," Kent said, still chuckling at his own little inside joke. "Today, I'm afraid, is not the day you die, Miss Raelynn, although my children *did* think they would be successful." He tapped at the cigar. "Impatient, those two. Always competing. A healthy coping mechanism, in my opinion. They are facing the inevitable too, you know. Three lives once spared is now three souls that must be given. Our God is clear. A Lawson, a Kynes, a Hadleigh. Three lives, three souls."

"You're going to sacrifice one of your own children," I whispered, realization dawning. Kent solemnly nodded and took another puff on his cigar. As if it was nothing. As if it was normal.

"My father prepared me for such an eventuality," he said. "I'm sorry yours didn't do the same for you. Your father, paranoid as he was, always preferred to keep his beliefs firmly planted in logic. Never allowed himself to think there was a bigger picture. But there are things that defy logic. Things that defy all human knowledge, all science." He stubbed out his cigar, and stood without lowering the pistol. Leon jerked me to the side, closer to the door, and Kent held up his hand. "I'm not through here. We may be at an impasse, demon, but I still have something to say to Miss Raelynn. Something she deserves to hear."

"She doesn't deserve your lying words," Leon snarled. But the gun was still cocked, still aimed, and not even a demon could stop a bullet.

"My children tell me you have an interest in the occult," Kent said. "A fascination for it. So I knew—I *knew*—you would see the wisdom your father refused."

"What wisdom?" My voice felt so hollow, my body like a shell. As if I could vacate it and leave this nightmare, go back to a world where things were so much less dangerous and made so much more sense. My father would have laughed at all of this, shaken his head, called it nonsense. He would have come up with a perfectly logical explanation for everything.

Except there were no logical explanations here. Logic had flown out the fucking window, crashed into a telephone pole, and gone down in a flaming blaze.

"These sacrifices are not in greed, Miss Raelynn," Kent said. "They are merely a necessity. It is natural for humans to resist their own death, to fixate upon survival, but this is much bigger than merely three lives. The Deep One is waking up."

Raelynn.

I jumped. It was as if the name had been whispered right in my ear, as if the syllables slid over the interior of my skull and nestled against my brain. Kent was nodding.

"You hear Its call. All those meant for It do. For years my children have dreamed of It. They understand that, when one of them is eventually chosen, their fate will help procure mercy for all of humanity."

"Bullshit," Leon hissed, but Kent was unperturbed.

"The God will wake whether we help It or not. And when It does, when It reclaims dominion over Earth, It will know that we humans keep our promises. That we are good servants. That we are worthy of mercy."

"Ask any Archdemon what it was like to live in a world ruled by the Old Gods," Leon snapped. "Every one of them will tell you they are not beings capable of *mercy*."

"The demon lies. How typical." Finally, slowly, Kent was lowering the gun. "You will not go to the Deep One tonight, Raelynn. But soon. Soon you will, and I ask only that you consider my words: your sacrifice secures mercy for all people. The world is changing. The great awakening is about to occur. And there will be pain, and bloodshed, but in the end . . . there will be peace. Peace through your sacrifice. So when you come to die, Miss Raelynn, know that you were meant for it."

The gun was lowered, the hammer relaxed, and without another word, Leon snatched me up and rushed me out the door.

36

RAE

WE FOUND A back way out, a glass door that led to a deck. Leon carefully lowered me over the side before jumping down himself. Then into the trees that nestled close around the house, he dragged me breathless through the dark, my chest aching with panic and the cold air, until finally I had to beg him to stop.

"We have to move quickly," he insisted, pacing as I doubled over, kneeling on the ground, unsure if I was about to vomit or pass out or both. "You need to get out of Abelaum, Raelynn. Somewhere he won't look, somewhere they can't find you." Still pacing, fists clenching and unclenching, teeth clicking together furiously, he muttered, "He thinks he can take you from me. I'll rip off his hands before I ever let him—"

"Leon . . ." I swayed to my feet, panic still clenched

so tightly around my heart that it hurt. "Don't leave me again . . . please . . . please don't . . . I . . . I can't . . ."

"I'm not *fucking* leaving." He grabbed me, half gentle, half vicious—as if he could force what he was saying to be believed, the tighter he gripped my arms. The whites of his eyes were darkening, the gold in them like fire in the night sky, and even the veins on his forearms were running black now. "Nothing is going to take you from me. *Nothing.*"

"But-but my soul, you said . . . you said—"

He pressed his hand over my mouth. "Shh, shh, stop. *Stop.*" His hand was shaking. His claws were pressing into my cheek, little pinpricks of pain. "Don't you fucking doubt that I'll have your soul. I'm not letting you get away. I'm not letting anything"—he grasped me so hard, so tight, that I could hardly breathe, his heat rushing over me in waves—"*anything* take you from me. I'll rip Heaven and Hell and this goddamn Earth apart before I let them steal you from me."

He'd claimed I was his before but always with the caveat that my soul was a requirement. Now? It was as if the very idea that I might be taken was repulsive, *insulting.* Maybe that should have scared me too, but the ache in my chest calmed, even with my heart still pounding. For a few seconds, the only sound between us was our breathing: hard, heavy.

No oxygen in the world was enough when this fear, this longing, this inevitable desire wanted to steal every breath from my lungs.

Slowly, Leon uncovered my mouth, but he still gripped

my cheeks between his fingers. He held his head high, his jaw locked. "Not a goddamn thing is taking you from me, baby girl. No man, and no God. I'll kill them all."

Snap.

I nearly got whiplash from how quickly he wrenched me back, his body between me and whatever had just taken a step in the darkness. For the first time, I noticed how silent the woods were. How oppressively empty they seemed. No crickets, no rustling of the little creatures moving through the underbrush. Even the wind was still.

But there was a smell. Like a damp cellar. Like mold.

A figure—tall, lean, pale as bone—stood about a hundred yards away among the trees. I might have thought it was the trunk of a broken aspen at first glance. But another second meant seeing the white antlers on its head, tendrils of seaweed clinging to their prongs—the long, knobby limbs—the hooves on its too-long bent-backward legs.

The eyes.

Large milky white eyes, staring.

"Leon." My voice shook. My hands were knotted into fists against his shirt. Slowly, careful not to make any sudden moves, he pulled the mask from his face and dropped it to the ground.

When the mask dropped, the creature jolted; it moved—rapidly like still frames from a movie, jerking, unnatural—every motion accompanied by a click as if its bones were popping.

In the blink of an eye, it was fifty yards closer.

"What the fuck is it?" I whispered, panic tightening my throat.

"A Gollum," he said. His hand was frozen, outstretched where he'd dropped the mask, as if he didn't dare move it again. "A creature of rotten earth. They serve the God. Its will is their will, they're an extension of Its influence. Listen to me. Carefully." His head twitched in my direction and the Gollum twitched too. Then it was utterly still, save for a slight twitching in its long, boney fingers. "When I move, pull out the knife. Keep it ready."

My hands felt too cold, too numb, to do anything with that goddamn knife. "Can you kill it?"

He tweaked his eyebrow up, glancing back at me, a smirk on his mouth. "For you, baby girl, I can kill anything."

The Gollum lurched forward, and Leon met it before it could cross even half the distance that remained between us. In the dark, the only way I could track their movements was by the sudden flashes of the Gollum's pale white form. The sound was like thunder, like columns of wood smacking together. The Gollum was shrieking, terrible screams that echoed through the woods, but it wasn't going down. It just kept fighting, matching Leon's strength and speed.

I tugged the knife from under my sweater, holding it in front of me as I backed away, until I was pressed against trunk of a pine. My heart pounded in my ears, adrenaline demanding I run while the little sense I still had in my brain anchored me to the spot. I'd seen these things before. I knew there was more than one. If this one was here . . .

Then where were the others?

There was a massive crack, and Leon hurled a long tree limb like a baseball bat, striking the Gollum so hard that its body crumpled like a spider. But it was only for a moment. The creature jolted up again, clicking as it did, and its twitchy head fixated in my direction.

It opened its mouth, a horrid groaning gurgle spewing out of it as it jolted rapidly toward me.

Leon seized its arm and ripped it back. The Gollum slashed at him before leaping onto his back, wrapping its long limbs around him and *squeezing*. Leon ripped at it with his claws, his teeth, thrashing himself backward to slam the monster against any surface he could find. He ripped into its arm and blood sprayed across my sweater, or at least, I thought it was blood at first. As it dripped down my shirt, and I touched it in horror, I realized it felt like thick mud.

The monster wasn't letting go. It was gripping tighter despite the gashes Leon was opening in its limbs. Leon gripped the hands around his neck, snarling ferociously, and *snap*—the long fingers crunched in his hands and the monster shrieked again, finally falling off of him.

But the moment it let go of him, it came for me.

I couldn't get away with the tree at my back. By the time my brain processed that the twitchy creature was on top of me, its broken fingers were wrapping around my skull, and the moment it squeezed, everything went dark.

Dark . . . but there was hard, damp earth beneath my hands.

Dark, but there was a smell of dust in the air, of wet earth.

Dark, but somewhere ahead of me, water was dripping.

I pushed myself up slowly from the ground, reaching out blindly. I felt a dirt wall to my left . . . and to my right. Nothing in front of me. Nothing behind.

What the hell had happened? Where was I? This wasn't the forest.

My heart drummed against my ribs, my lungs felt tight. Where was Leon?

Where was the monster?

Raelynn.

I scrambled to my feet, pressing myself against the wall, trying not to hyperventilate, trying not to be too loud. It was the voice from my dreams. The voice I'd heard calling to me in my nightmares.

The God's voice.

My knife was gone. No matter how many times I blinked, no matter which way I looked, there was nothing but darkness. Panic was sinking its claws in deep. The water, dripping somewhere nearby, was trickling faster now. It wasn't just a drip. It was a stream.

I took a step, and my foot splashed into water.

My vision jolted, like static cutting through my eyes, and for a split second I saw the monster again, clinging to me, white eyes staring down into mine as Leon's hands wrapped it into a chokehold from behind—

Back into the dark. There was water at my ankles now. The trickling stream sounded like a rushing river.

A flood . . . the tunnel was flooding.

Raelynn. Come to me. Let me help you.

I stumbled forward. I knew the voice was dangerous,

but I couldn't stand here and wait to drown. The water was rising rapidly. It would be up to my knees in a moment. I had to follow the voice. I had to find it. Maybe, somehow, it could help me . . .

The night sky burst into my vision, and I gasped for air as if I'd been drowning. I was lying on my back, my head was burning, I was so dazed that I couldn't move. I could only stare through the ragged limbs of the pines, their needles piercing the starry night sky as the clouds swept over the moon.

There were footsteps behind me . . . closer . . . closer . . .

Leon stood over me. Something was smeared on his face: blood or mud, I couldn't be sure. Slowly he crouched down, scooped me up into his arms, and cradled me against his chest.

His shirt was wet, stained. As he began to walk, it was with a stiffness that hadn't been there before.

I tried to talk, tried to ask what the hell had happened and if we were safe. But my tongue felt like it was made of cotton, and I realized that my hand was still clenched in a viselike grip around the knife.

"Just sleep, baby girl," he muttered, even as my exhaustion swooped in as the adrenaline subsided, and I found myself barely able to keep my aching eyes open. "I told you I'd kill it. You're okay. You'll be okay."

37

RAE

THE BEDCOVERS WERE pulled up over my head, my breath creating a warm cocoon as I lay nestled on soft pillows. My groggy brain knew it wasn't my bed, but it also knew that something bad had happened last night, and pushing down the covers to see where I was seemed pretty frightening.

There was a shower running somewhere. The sheets smelled freshly cleaned and were crisp, like hotel sheets. I wasn't wearing my costume from the party, but an over-sized sweater that smelled distinctly of smoke and citrusy pine. Leon's smell.

I pushed back the covers, blinking slowly. The curtains had been thrown back to a gray day over a sea of snow-dappled pine trees clustered around the roofs of a small town. The room was undoubtedly a master suite, and on an uppermost floor judging by the view. The bed was massive, the walls made of stained wood and the decor like the interior of a modern log cabin.

I sat up, rubbing my eyes before I noticed my glasses, and my knife, sitting on the bedside table. Suddenly, it all came back in a rush that twisted up my stomach—the roofie in my drink, Juniper and Zane, Kent, the Gollum in the woods. My body still thought there was danger, and I could vividly remember what it felt like when the Gollum touched me.

The mine . . . those cold, flooded tunnels . . .

I jumped as the bathroom door opened, and Leon sauntered out naked, water dripping down the inked art-work on his chest as he rubbed a towel over his hair. He spotted me awake, smirked, and paused with the towel around his shoulders.

"Finally awake," he said. The mirror behind him gave a drool-worthy view of his tattooed back and his ass—men's asses were too rarely given the appreciation they deserved. I just nodded, hoping that the blush creep-ing up my face wasn't visible. Trying not to stare at the monster-dick between his legs was proving impossible, no matter how many times I'd seen it before.

"And how do you feel?" He came up to the edge of the bed. I wanted to lick the water off his chest.

"Like I haven't eaten in five years," I said, honestly. My stomach was about to ingest itself. Horrifying events probably should have killed my appetite, but I desper-ately wanted a big breakfast.

If Leon was part of that breakfast, even better.

"Good, I already ordered room service. Should be

here shortly." He tossed aside the towel and crawled up on the bed, and my heart stuttered. "You're the first course, doll."

My makeup from the previous night was likely smeared all over my face and I hadn't brushed my teeth, but he genuinely didn't care. He pushed me back on the pillows and shoved my oversized shirt up, sucking first one nipple and then the other as he pressed my legs apart. "Don't forget our deal," he murmured in between lapping his tongue over my now-hard nipples. "I get to pierce these sweet little buds. Soon—today, in fact."

I'd forgotten, but the moment he reminded me my head rushed with heat. He gripped my hips, tugging me into position so I was held up just slightly off the bed, my back arched, and began to eat me like it was his last fucking meal.

I gasped sharply, my clit swelling between the lapping of his tongue and suction of his mouth. My fingers tangled in his hair, gripping tightly as he forced a trembling moan out of me.

He chuckled, a brief break as my legs shook around his head. "Keep pulling my hair like that, baby girl. I like pain too."

I liked that new pet name he had for me; it made my belly warm, but so did his admission. I tightened my grip on his hair, even though I doubted anything I did could truly hurt him. But as I tugged, he moaned against me. He lowered my hips, but only so he could free up a hand and press two fingers inside me as he continued to lick at my clit.

"Fuck, I'm gonna come . . ." Ecstasy was washing over me hard and fast, drowning me. He pumped his fingers faster, pressed my thigh down so my trembling legs couldn't close, and swirled his tongue over me mercilessly until I gushed over his fingers, gasping as I soaked the sheets.

And he didn't stop.

"Again, baby girl," he growled, his fingers still working me, smiling sadistically as I wiggled beneath him, the stimulation almost too much, almost painful, but so damn good.

"I can't . . . can't!"

With one hand still fingering me, he gripped my throat with the other—not squeezing, just holding me pinned to the pillows—and said, "You can, and you will. You don't have a choice."

He was right. With his tongue and his fingers working their magic, my eyes rolled back in my head when I orgasmed again. I couldn't even catch my breath, let alone speak as he slowly raised his head and licked his fingers clean.

"Fucking delicious," he murmured. "And just in time for the main course."

There was a knock at the door as room service arrived, and I promptly hid my shaking form back under the covers as Leon answered the door with the towel around his waist. The waiter sounded particularly flustered as he asked if Leon would be needing anything else.

The overly laden tray was left on the small table, and I ate as Leon dressed and lounged on the bed. He'd ordered just about everything on the breakfast menu, so I started with the eggs benedict and strawberry pancakes.

"Where are we?" I asked in between bites.

He shrugged. "Northeast of Abelaum. I just kept walking until I found a place to stop."

I frowned. "Toss me my phone, would you?"

As I suspected, I had about a dozen missed calls from Inaya and frantic voicemails. Guilt gnawed at me, even though I hadn't really had a choice but to leave her last night. It was nearly eleven in the morning, so I called her back.

"Holy fuck, Raelynn, I thought you'd gotten kidnapped!" I winced at her greeting. "Girl, where *are* you? I was about to file a missing person report—"

"I'm okay, I'm okay, I'm so sorry," I said quickly. I glanced over at Leon, who narrowed his eyes in question. "I . . . I had to leave early last night. Someone, um . . . someone drugged my drink."

There was a beat of total silence on the line. "Oh my God . . . oh my God, are you . . . ?"

"I'm okay, I promise. I'm sorry I didn't call you or anything, I was just—"

"Don't apologize, oh God, I'm just glad you're okay!" The relief in her voice made me feel even guiltier. I wasn't exactly lying, but I couldn't tell her the whole truth. "Do you need me to bring you anything?"

"That's okay, I'm good. Can you just take care of Cheesecake for a few days? I'll come pick him up soon, I promise."

"Of course!" The sound of Cheesecake's little meow

in the background made my heart hurt. "He can stay with Auntie Inaya as long as he needs to." Another pause. "Do you . . . do you know who drugged you? Did they try anything? I'll kick their fucking ass, Rae."

I took a deep breath. "The only person to hand me a drink was Jeremiah. It didn't leave my hand all night." I couldn't tell her the whole truth, but I wasn't about to pretend she could trust the Hadleighs.

More silence. Anxiety twisted my stomach. *Please believe me, Inaya, please.* It wasn't a blatant accusation, but my point was clear. I knew they were her friends, but she didn't *know* them. She didn't know what they were capable of.

"Then he's not coming near us again," she said, and I wished I could reach through the phone and hug her. "Fuck him. Do you want me to tell Victoria?"

"No," I said. "No, I . . . I don't know if she'll . . . if she'll believe . . ."

"Fuck her too if she doesn't!" She sighed heavily, her mama bear slowly calming. "But I get it. I get it. This will stay between us unless you're ready to tell anyone else. I'm just glad you're okay."

We chatted for a few more minutes before I hung up. The relief of having Inaya know that Jeremiah couldn't be trusted—even if she only knew a small part of *why*—lifted a massive weight off my back. I ate a little more enthusiastically once I was off the phone, shoveling forkfuls of crispy hash browns into my mouth.

Finally satiated, I hobbled back to the bed, crawled up onto the mattress, and pressed myself against Leon's bare chest. With my face buried against him, I let myself melt into his heat for a moment before I said, "What are we going to do?"

We. I wouldn't have even dared to think of it a few days ago. Even now, with him having snatched me away and hidden me . . . somewhere . . . I still felt a pang of anxiety to dare say *we.* What even were we in all this? Just a possessive protector and his pet? Friends or . . . or lovers?

A summoner and her demon?

"I can tell you what I'm going to do, and what you're going to do," he said, his arm around my shoulders so I was held against him. "I'm going to keep you safe. And you're going to listen to me, so that I can protect you properly."

I raised my head, grinning mischievously. "I'll listen. Doesn't mean I'll obey."

He snorted, squeezing my arm. "Henceforth, the consequences for endangering your life will be severe, Rae. Think twice before you decide to be a brat."

"*Henceforth?*" I giggled. "Your seventeenth century came out there a bit."

"Back in my day . . ." He put on a gravelly old man voice, and easily rolled me onto my back, following after me so that he straddled me as I lay there. "Humans had a much more proper fear of demons than to be teasing them, baby girl." He snapped his teeth, all sharp and wicked, and said softly. "Still feel like teasing?"

The playfulness in his eyes made my heart skip. I traced my fingers along his chest, finding the smooth pale lines of his scars and following them. Torture scars, battle scars, stories of pain that lingered on this absurdly strong, immortal body. He watched my fingers move, suddenly still as stone, and I wondered if it was because he was trying not to flinch away, like he had the first time I'd touched him gently.

"Are we safe here?" I whispered. Strong as he was, I didn't want to see him fight again. I didn't want to see him have to turn into an animal to survive or to ensure *I* survived.

"For now. We'll stay here for a while . . . then move on if the Hadleighs or any of the beasts get wind of where you are."

"I can't hide forever."

"I know. And you won't. Just until it's safe."

"I know there are other Gollums, besides the one last night." I gulped. "I saw them."

He frowned. "When?"

"When you were gone."

His frown intensified, and he stood up from the bed. I sat up, hands knotting nervously in the blankets as he picked up a black long-sleeved shirt from the floor and pulled it on. "You should get dressed," he said. "There's some clothes in the bags near the door. I need to do some scouting today, make sure no one's on our trail. And I need you occupied while I'm gone so you don't go wandering off."

I was about to remind him that I wasn't a puppy who would go running off without a leash, but stopped myself before I lied. I was a wanderer, and he was absolutely right to worry what I'd do if I got bored. *I* worried what I'd do if I was bored. The plastic bags near the door had an assortment of clothing in them, mostly in black, brown, and dark blue.

"How do you know my size?" I said, holding up a long blue plaid skirt to my waist in front of the mirror. "And my style . . . this is cute . . ."

"I've been observing you for months," he said, lacing up his boots. "How could I *not* know those things?"

He'd even gotten the right size in a pair of chunky boots. With a black turtleneck and gray denim jacket atop the skirt, I turned away from the mirror and found him watching me, hands stuffed into the pockets of his joggers.

My ex had once said that my style was like *if Janis Joplin had a lovechild with Sisters of Mercy.* It was more weird than sexy, which wasn't something I thought about most of the time—except when a supernaturally sexy demon was staring me down like he was considering eating me again.

"Why are you blushing?" He took my face in his hands, which made my blush far worse, considering I couldn't look away from him. "I thought I'd fucked all the shame out of you already?" He kissed my forehead, and wrapped his arm around my shoulders. "Apparently I need to corrupt you a bit more, baby girl."

RAE

I DIDN'T KNOW what to expect when Leon said he was going to keep me "occupied"—but leaving me at the hotel's spa for several hours hadn't even been on my radar as a possibility. Getting my nails done and my back massaged after soaking in a mud bath was a bizarre contrast to the past few weeks; it felt too normal, too *safe*.

Not that it had ever been exactly normal for me to have a spa day. That wasn't something that typically fit in my college-student broke-vlogger budget.

I couldn't fathom where Leon had gotten the money for this, either. Did demons have money? Did they have credit cards?

"You're carrying a lot of tension in your shoulders." The woman massaging my back was blonde, pretty, a few years older than me, with a voice so soft she probably could make a fortune off recording ASMR videos. "Slow, deep breath . . . I'm going to work out the knots here."

They'd given me wine, and after a glass I found it pretty funny that she probably thought all that tension was from stress at work or school, rather than being hunted by monsters and a death cult.

Funny. Just hilarious.

She did her job though. I hadn't felt so relaxed in months. As I walked back up to the room that evening with my body feeling like jelly, I realized that I couldn't wait to move out of Abelaum. I couldn't wait to leave that goddamn town behind.

Fuck reconnecting with the magic of my childhood. Once I'd graduated and gotten to see Inaya's wedding, I was moving as far away from this place as I was able to. Money was an issue, but I'd rent out an unfinished basement on the East Coast if I had to.

And Leon . . .

It had become too easy to imagine him going with me. Living with me. *Staying* with me. But as I got back up to the room and ordered room service again for dinner, I knew that was a dangerous train of thought to go down. Dangerous because that wasn't something I should get my hopes up about.

Leon was a demon. An immortal. A monster. He wanted my soul. He wasn't about to be domesticated— and I didn't want him to be. I didn't want a demonic variation on the white-picket-fence nuclear-family ideal. I just didn't want him to leave.

His absence would be a void I couldn't fill, which seemed so silly considering the lifetime I'd been through since moving here had really only been a few months. But it was like the first time I'd seen a ghost; it had been so brief but so stark, and the moment I'd realized what had happened I'd known I could never let that go. It's weird that one brief moment can change the course of your whole life.

I finished dinner, and the sun set, but Leon still hadn't returned. I streamed YouTube on the TV, putting on some deep dive into an unsolved mystery from the 1970s to keep myself distracted. Nothing like watching the story of a woman disappearing without a trace to soothe my brain.

Tap, tap, tap.

I paused the video, looking around the room with a frown. I'd thought it was the sound of raindrops hitting the window, at first, but the sound was too steady, too purposeful. I waited, listening for it again to figure out where the hell it was coming from.

Tap, tap.

I got up slowly from the bed. It sounded like a finger tapping on wood, but it made no sense—it sounded like it was coming from the far corner, near the sliding door out onto the balcony. The only thing on the other side of that corner was the bathroom on the inside, and the balcony outside. I stared at the wall, at the shining, roughly polished wood, my heart beginning to pound.

Why did it sound like it was coming from *inside* the wall?

By the time I saw the movement behind me reflected in the window, Leon had already clapped his hand over my mouth, and wrapped the other around my throat.

"Fear smells good on you, baby girl," he murmured, and twisted me around so I faced him, one hand still over my mouth and the other wrapped tight around my back. He flashed sharp teeth at me, his eyes bright. "I missed you today. It's torturous, spending hours thinking about what I'd get to do to you when I got back."

He uncovered my mouth. I smiled up at him breathlessly, my pounding heart beginning to slow. "Are we safe? No one's after us?"

"We're safe," he said, still not giving me an inch of wiggle room as he held me close. He frowned a bit. "I couldn't find the Hadleighs. They're up to something, or . . ." He shook his head. "They haven't managed to track us. So, on to better topics."

He nudged a black paper bag on the floor with his foot, and I picked it up curiously. My mouth gaped open as I pulled out the plastic packaging inside.

"Holy shit, Leon, you . . . you think it will *fit*—"

"If I can fit, the toy can fit," he said, as I stared wide-eyed at the dildo I'd pulled from the bag. It was absurdly thick, around his same size, and molded of purple silicone with a suction cup at the base.

"I didn't know you were into toys," I said.

"I'm into whatever I can use to make you scream." He grinned as I rummaged a little further in the bag, and pulled out another box containing a blue and white vibrator. "I suspected our playtime tonight might be too intense without some distractions."

I was excited for anything he had in mind that involved toys like these, but he caught my curiosity. "Intense? What . . . what do you mean?"

He used his claws to slit open the packages, and handed the toys back to me when he was done. "Go clean them, and try to remember: what did I tell you I'd be doing today?"

It only took me a minute to remember, and fear's cold fingers slid up my back again. Fear and hot arousal coiled inside me like a snake—just as dangerous, and just as terrifying. Music began to play from the TV as I cleaned the toys, and I recognized the haunting, gravel tone as "Anti-Social Masochistic Rage" by Ghostemane. And I'd always thought *my* music taste was creepy.

When I emerged from the bathroom, he was sitting at the edge of the bed, running a cotton ball along a thick steel needle, a bottle of isopropyl alcohol at his feet.

I froze at the sight of that needle. Shit. *Shit.*

"I've never pierced a human before," he mused. "When I pierced Zane's tongue I didn't have to worry about any infections." He glanced over at me and winked. "Don't worry. I did my research. I wouldn't want to break my little doll."

I wanted to run for the door. I wanted to scream. I wanted . . . I wanted him to do it. My hands were already shaking. My heart was a fluttering bird trapped in the cage of my ribs. My head was light as a balloon.

Leon curled his clawed finger at me. "Come here, baby girl."

I stood in front of him, the toys nearly forgotten despite how tightly I was gripping them. He set the needle aside on a towel he'd laid on the bed, beside a pair of metal forceps and two small stainless steel bars with balls at either end, and took the vibrator from my hands. "Put down the toy. Position it so you can kneel on it."

My mouth was suddenly dry, but my pussy certainly wasn't. I positioned the dildo on the floor, suctioning it to the shining wood at his feet, giving myself enough room to kneel over it. He switched on the vibrator curiously, the buzzing sound igniting some instinctual arousal. I loved the vibrator I had at home, but damn, that thing could take me from zero to one hundred painfully quickly.

He laughed darkly as he switched it back off. "Oh, Rae . . . I'm gonna make you scream."

I laughed, sort of. The sound was a little too tinged with hysteria to be purely laughter. The anticipation was an adrenaline high, absolutely merciless, as it made every muscle in my body twitch and my clit swell with warmth. He reached out and dragged a single claw slowly across my cheek. "What's your safeword?"

"Mercy," I whispered.

"Good girl. Undress."

I stripped off my shirt, tugged down my skirt, and goose bumps prickled over my skin. He didn't touch me as I unhooked my bra, then slid down my panties. He just watched, golden eyes taking in every inch of me with the slow, calculated gaze of a hungry wolf. Planning where to bite first.

"I can smell your wet cunt." He chuckled. "Touch yourself. I want you to feel how wet you are."

I obeyed, sliding my fingers down. I was slick, and the sensation of my fingers sliding over my clit made me shudder. I tried not to gasp, but my eyes fluttered and I couldn't bite back my whimper.

"Put your fingers in my mouth."

Again, I obeyed. His forked tongue slid between my two fingers and swirled over them before he sucked them clean. He closed his eyes, savoring the taste and licking it from his lips.

"Kneel. Press the toy inside yourself."

I dropped down to my knees on the cool, smooth wood. He held out a bottle of lube and squirted it into my hand so I could rub the slick concoction over the dildo beneath me. Wet as I was, a toy that thick wasn't going to go in easily. I gulped as I positioned it at my entrance, watching his eyes as he watched me in return.

"Impale yourself for me, baby girl."

I groaned as I lowered myself onto the toy, the thickness stretching me until it ached, until I had to pause halfway down, panting. He leaned down, caressed his hand over my face and gripped the hair at the back of my head. "Deeper."

I pressed down, whimpering at the stretch of it inside me. Finally I was kneeling all the way down, resting on my heels as my legs shook. He tipped my head up, using my hair as leverage, and kissed my mouth slow, taking his time as his tongue played with mine.

As he kissed me, he turned on the vibrator. With my eyes closed, I had no idea what he was doing until the vibrations pressed to my clit and I cried out into his mouth. He kissed me harder, muffling those cries of pleasure as he held the toy against me, sending tremors through my legs. Only when I was at the edge of orgasm did he pull back, grinning wickedly at my desperate gasps.

"Ride that cock, baby girl. Slow and deep."

I did as he said, even though my legs were shaking and weak. The fullness of the dildo inside me had me moaning, my pussy clenching around it as I lowered myself down again. As I did, Leon wet another cotton ball with isopropyl alcohol and took my breast in his hand.

"Keep riding, nice and slow, just like that."

He disinfected one nipple, then the other, the damp cotton cold against those hardened buds. Then he took the forceps, clicking them together ominously. "All the way down, Rae. Fill yourself up. Now, hold this against your clit." He handed over the vibrator, which I held between my legs with shaking hands. He took up the needle. "Hold as still as you can for me."

"Fuck," I gasped, shaking, terrified, so turned on that I knew I was only seconds from coming. But he was only seconds from piercing that needle into me, and by the way my belly was tightening, my body was eager for that pain. I craved this intimate, gentle violence.

He pinched the forceps around my nipple, holding it

tightly as I stared down at it with wide eyes, anticipation stealing my breath away. "Look up at me, baby girl."

I looked up, and he gave me that sharp, demonic grin. "Are you scared?"

"Fuck yes."

"Do you want this mark?"

I nodded quickly, my entire body shaking with the waves of pleasure the vibrator was forcing through me. "Yes. I want it. I want your mark, please."

The needle pierced through my skin; my vision flashed and my head went light. The pain was sharp and pinching, but not unfamiliar. I'd gotten piercings before, just not *there*. But the meeting of that pain with my pleasure, the pinnacle of anticipation finally reached, shattered me like thin glass. I screamed, not from the pain but from the release, from the exquisitely perfect cocktail of sensations.

I came as that needle pierced into me. The pinching, merciless pain tipped me over the edge. I shook, moaning as Leon fit the jewelry in.

"That's my girl," he murmured, and held my head in his hands. "You took it so well, fuck, look at you." His eyes moved over me—my face, my chest, down to my shaking legs. "Beautiful girl." He kissed my forehead, my cheek, the breast he'd just pierced, while I floated in ecstasy, the aftershocks trembling through me. "One more, baby girl. One more. Ride that cock again."

I didn't know where I found the energy to obey. I'd sunk so deep into that blissful headspace of submission, of pleasure, of willing helplessness. It was a dimension without fear, without the dread that had hung over me those past few months. It was safe, it was beautiful, it felt so good. My pussy stretched and pulsed around that thick toy as he unwrapped another needle from its clear plastic seal and cleaned it.

"Hold still for me. Turn the vibrator back on."

My clit was so sensitive that just barely touching the humming head of the vibrator against it made me groan. Holding still was so much harder now. I couldn't stop shaking, as if my body couldn't contain the multitude of sensations flooding it. I kept my eyes on his face as he positioned the forceps, and smiled when I saw the barely tethered excitement flash in his eyes as he held up the needle.

He was *monstrous*, but he was *mine*. And I was his, as surely as if he'd already claimed my soul.

I'd spent so many years chasing darkness, reaching out for it, calling to it, and now I'd sunk into it. It had embraced me and I didn't want it any other way. The darkness was sharp but, God, it was warm. It was terrifying, but it was safe.

The darkness was a demon leaning over me with fire in his eyes, whispering, "You're mine, baby girl."

The second needle hurt worse, but it shattered me just the same. My head tipped back, eyes closed, groaning at that brutal sharpness and the tingling, fiery pleasure that flowed through my veins, from my core all the way to the tips of my toes. I dropped the vibrator, the stimulation far more than I could bear. My head was so light, I was sinking so deep.

Leon didn't let me fall. He was on his knees beside me, arms around me, cradling me against his chest as he lay kisses over my face and whispered, "There's my girl. Ssh, easy. Easy. Deep breaths, baby girl."

I realized the music had changed. I recognized it . . . Cigarettes After Sex . . . "Nothing's Gonna Hurt You Baby." I floated there, eyes closed, shattered and warm, protected in his arms. I could forget all the danger outside these walls, and let darkness be my shelter here. I could let wickedness be my sanctuary, perversion my therapy, and a monster be my lover.

39

LEON

"I CAN CLEAN them myself, you know . . . doesn't that gross you out?"

I narrowed my eyes at her as I carefully nudged the cotton swab along the bar through her nipple. "I've done things for pleasure so disgusting it would make most humans vomit. Cleaning the marks *I* gave you is far from gross, Rae."

She smirked as I moved to clean the other bar. I had her sitting at the edge of the large tub, her shirt off, a pair of oversized pajamas on her lower half. "Disgusting things, huh? Like what?" Her dark eyes glittered in that mischievous way that set my brain on fire. That playful curiosity drove me wild, just like it had the first time she'd ever snapped back at me.

I was fucked for this girl. Well and truly fucked.

I knew what that feeling was when she'd slept against

me last night, limp and exhausted—the ache in my chest, the pain of it so bitterly sweet as I held her. I couldn't say many things terrified me, but that did. The way I felt when I saw my metal in her, shining on those luxuriously soft, irresistible breasts, terrified me so deeply it almost stopped my breath.

I wasn't supposed to *feel* anything for a human. But here I was, willing to risk life and limb for this little hellfire of a woman.

I set aside the saltwater solution and cotton swabs and kissed her left breast, then the right; then her neck, warm and pulsing with blood; then her face, soft and blushing as she giggled. Her laughter made me growl, it ignited an immediate desire to pin her down and play with her until her giggles turned to screams of pleasure.

"Ah, careful, they're sore!"

It took every scrap of self-control I had to let her up from the edge of the bathtub, then watch her finish undressing and step into the shower. "Keep the curtain open," I said, leaning back against the sink. "I want to see you."

My self-control didn't hold on much longer. I stripped down, and while the soap was still slick on her skin I fucked her against the wall until she breathlessly cried my name, and damn, my name sounded so good when it came from her mouth. She was bent over with her hands against the tile wall, and I reached around to squeeze her face and demanded, "Say my name again, baby girl. Cry for me."

She did, and fuck, that was heaven.

I ordered her too much food again, but I liked the way her face lit up when she saw all the breakfast plates delivered. She was midway through a plate of thick Belgian waffles piled with peaches when her phone rang, and her eyes narrowed in concern as she looked at the screen.

She glanced up at me, uncertainty on her face. "It's Victoria."

I got up from the bed, glaring at her phone as if I could ascertain the Hadleigh woman's intentions just by looking at it. It rang until it went to voicemail, paused . . . then began ringing again.

"See what she wants," I said softly. I wasn't entirely sure what technologies the Hadleighs had at their disposal—like if they could ascertain our location from a phone call—but it was time to be moving our location anyway. Better to know what lies they were going to attempt to spin now, than to remain in the dark.

Rae managed to put on a shockingly friendly tone as she answered, "Hey, girl! What's—"

Her face paled, and I could hear Victoria's voice clearly on the line. "Daddy is dead. It's done, okay? It's fucking done."

"Victoria, what are talking about?" Rae's eyes were wide as she looked up at me, mouthing, *What the fuck?* My mind was spinning. Of all the stories I'd expected to hear, this wasn't it.

"My dad is *dead,* Raelynn!" Victoria's voice was choked, breathless—frightened. Why was she frightened? "God, and I'm not even sad about it. What kind of fucking daughter am I?" Then, softly, "What kind of father would kill his child?" A sob, then a bitter laugh. By her cadence and rapid breath, she was walking quickly, nearly running. "It doesn't matter. None of it fucking matters anymore. I'm not even sorry, Rae, I did what I had to do. We both did." There was a pause. She was holding her breath.

She was *hiding*.

"Victoria, I'm so sorry about your dad—"

"Don't play stupid." The emotion had gone out of her voice. "You're not sorry. Neither am I. But it's done. You and that demon did what you had to do too, didn't you? Maybe I should thank you." Another bitter laugh. "Bye, Rae. Honestly, congrats. You survived."

She hung up. Raelynn stared at the phone in her hand, blinking slowly, processing. What the hell had just happened? By her tone, Victoria wasn't lying. She wasn't faking. She was terrified.

"Kent Hadleigh is dead." Raelynn stared up at me, something like a smile daring to pull at her lips. "He's . . . he's *dead*. Oh my God. Did you . . . was it you?"

"I goddamn wish it was." I began to pace as I thought. Kent was dead. The Libiri would be in chaos, scrambling for a leader. Vulnerable. And to judge by her words, Victoria thought I was the killer too. They were in the dark; they didn't even know who was attacking them. "I told you, Kent kept himself protected. It would be difficult for any demon to cause him harm. But Juniper . . . Juniper could have killed him."

"Of course! She was at the party." She grinned, suddenly bouncing out of her chair. "It's fucking *done*,

Leon! He's *dead*!" She threw her arms around me and I flinched, but so did she when her enthusiasm caused her to press her tender piercings against me. Even that didn't dissuade her. She was smiling, moving her shoulders in that silly dance she did when she was excited.

I wished I could share her enthusiasm.

"I can go back!" She stretched her arms above her head, sighing all the tension out. "I've only missed a day of class, I can actually get through this semester and pass!"

But this seemed too easy, too . . . convenient. I did believe Kent was dead, but I *didn't* believe this ended with him.

This wasn't over. But I didn't know what was coming next. I didn't know where the danger lay now.

Who was going to take Kent's place?

"I'll call Inaya and tell her I'll pick up Cheesecake to-night," Rae said excitedly. I didn't stop her as she made the call, but taking her back to Abelaum felt too dangerous. It felt too soon. The Libiri couldn't possibly give up this easily. The Hadleighs were just one family, but they weren't the only family who put their loyalty in the Deep One.

Or maybe I really didn't like the idea of Rae no longer needing my protection from them. Maybe I didn't like the idea of going back to that town that held so many bad memories for me. Maybe I just wanted to take my girl anywhere else in the world but there, and watch her hunt ghosts to her heart's content, and never have to think about the Libiri again.

Yeah. That was probably fucking it.

"Leon?"

She'd hung up the phone, and was sitting in front of her half-eaten waffles looking suddenly sobered. "Is it . . . I mean . . . do you think it's safe to go back?"

I rubbed a hand over my face. I knew why she wanted to go back. I knew humans got attached to places and things, and that leaving all the sights and smells that had grown comfortable for her was hard. I knew she thought finishing school was important, and I knew she loved that cat. I knew humans did best when they had some semblance of normalcy. Of home. Of safety.

I knew whisking her away and forcing her to leave everything behind wouldn't work, or that perpetually moving her from hotel to hotel was going to stress her out.

"I don't know." That was the most honest answer I could give. "I don't know what the Libiri will do now that Kent is gone. And with or without the Libiri, the God still wants you." Fear flickered over her face, and was swallowed down with a heavy gulp. "Its servants will still come after you. The monsters will still stalk you."

The way her face fell and the way all that tense hope went out of her, felt similar to a hammer crashing against my ribs. I sat down at the edge of the bed, motioning her over. She stood in front of me, the new metal in her nipples pressed against her shirt, her fingers fiddling with her pajama pants. I brushed my fingers over her lips, her cheek, through the soft strands of her hair. I wasn't good at being gentle; it made my fingers twitchy. But it was worth the self-restraint to feel her lean her face against my hand.

"Do you want to go back?"

She nodded. "I'm not really any safer here, am I? The monsters don't care about city limits. It's not like I can go out after dark here, or walk around by myself." She sighed. "I mean, I . . . I still . . . I need you with me."

"You're mine," I said simply. "I'm not leaving."

"I think about it every day, you know." She bit her lip, eyes staring off so she wouldn't have to meet mine. "The deal you offered. I think about it. It's just . . ." She tried to turn away, but I kept a grip on the nape of her neck. I wanted to see her face, her eyes. I didn't want her hiding her fears from me. "It's a big decision, Leon."

The way I ached for her soul was nearly unbearable. It was a constant pressure on the back of my mind, an itch I couldn't reach. The need to possess her, wholly. We demons had the power to take nearly anything we wanted, but a human soul?

That had to be given willingly.

It was fucking torture.

I got up from the bed, kissing her forehead as I tugged her head back to look up at me. "I know. I'm waiting, Rae. I'm not going anywhere. You'll give it to me eventually." I smirked, and shrugged, as nonplussed as I could manage to fake. "Pack up, baby girl. Let's get you home."

RAE

EVEN AT MIDDAY, thick fog obscured Abelaum. The streetlights were still on, glowing pale yellow, and cars drove slowly along the narrow suburban streets. The town lay blanketed in the damp, as if it had gathered the fog close and held it there, like a cloak to hide its secrets.

I'd hoped to feel some kind of weight lift, but my unease was growing;,partially because Leon was clearly on high alert. He was rigid in his seat as he drove the truck down Main Street, his eyes flickering along the sidewalks, watching every passerby, narrowing at every car.

Kent's death didn't hit the state news, but it got a spread in the town's tiny newspaper. *HEAD OF LOCAL HISTORICAL SOCIETY DEAD IN APPARENT SUICIDE* was the headline on their website. *Suicide.*

"No," Leon said firmly, when I read the headline

aloud. "That man was too self-righteous to ever end it himself. His killers just knew how to cover their tracks."

We stopped at Inaya's apartment first to pick up Cheesecake. He purred in my arms, rubbing against my chin as Inaya leaned against her doorframe and said worriedly, "I haven't been able to get a hold of Victoria at all. Jeremiah said she went to stay with her grandparents, and I know I should just give her time, but . . ." She chewed at a pink-polished nail. "It's just so awful, Rae. I never thought Kent was struggling like that. His poor family."

My natural inclination was to agree with her. But Kent being dead meant he wasn't trying to kill me. So while I put on a sympathetic face as I hugged her good-bye, all I could really think was, *Thank God he's dead—thank whatever God is on my side.*

The cabin was cold when we walked in. After just a few days without a human inhabiting it, the place already felt a little less friendly. It was strange, after spending so much time in old abandoned places, I knew the feel of them, the scent of them, the way the air felt stiller in them. It hadn't taken long at all for the cabin to start feeling like that.

I turned on all the lights, despite the gloomy daylight outside, lit a few candles, and watered my window of neglected succulent plants. Leon sat on the couch with Cheesecake—who couldn't seem to leave him alone—scratching the kitty's head as his brows knit tighter and tighter with some unspoken question growing in his mind.

"It still doesn't feel right, does it?" I said, having run out of useless tasks to keep me occupied.

He shook his head. "The danger isn't over, Rae. Kent was an obvious threat, but the God still lives. It still has its servants. This isn't over."

My hands knotted at the edge of my sweater, my nails digging into my palms even through the fabric. "Let's go to the store. I need stress snacks."

THE GROCERY MARKET was just off Main Street, its flickering neon *Food Mart* sign dwarfed by the pines around it. Leon parked near the door and gripped my arm before I could hop out of the truck, taking a long, slow look around the parking lot. Satisfied, he released his grip and said, "I'll keep an eye on the door. You'll be safe."

His protectiveness made the fear knotted in my gut begin to unravel. I leaned across the seat, tangling my fingers into his blond hair as I kissed him—his lips first soft with surprise, then vicious as he dragged me over to him, his tongue pressing into my mouth with possessive hunger. The tender piercings he'd given me pressed against his chest and I whimpered into his mouth, his grip tightening and his claws digging into me at my noise.

"Don't tempt me to bend you over the truck bed and fuck you," he growled, smirking at me as I caught my breath.

"I'm already tempting you," I said, a chill of excitement going up my back when his eyes flashed gold.

"You'd better get your ass in there," he growled. "Or the only snack you're getting is my cum down your throat."

As much as I wanted that, I did really want snacks too. He smacked my ass as I crawled over him and out of the truck, and I was still smiling as I walked inside, the bells on the glass door jingling behind me.

"Welcome to Food Mart," the checker called, boredom on his face as he glanced up briefly from his phone. I think I shared a class with him, but I probably shared a class with most twenty-somethings in this town. I grabbed a basket and headed straight for the chip aisle, grabbing Fritos and a can of bean dip before heading to the cookies. Chocolate chip or peanut butter . . . chocolate chip or . . .

In my peripheral vision, I could see that someone was standing at the far end of the aisle. Not walking closer, not talking with anyone, just . . . standing there.

I glanced up, right as he finally walked away. A young guy, yet another person I probably shared class with. Our eyes met as he headed to the next aisle, but his phone was in his hand and he'd probably just been standing there to answer a text.

I was way too paranoid. Leon was right outside in the truck. I didn't have anything to fear. I grabbed the peanut butter cookies, then headed back toward the freezers for ice cream. So many options, how the hell was I supposed to choose? I opened the freezer door, the glass fogging immediately.

It was only after a minute of standing there with the cold air blasting me, that I realized someone was standing on the other side of the fogged glass door.

I glanced down, my hand tightening on the freezer

handle. I could see clean white sneakers beneath the door, standing close, facing me.

I let the door close, taking a quick step back. Jeremiah stood there, hands in the pockets of his letterman jacket, smiling.

"Hey, Rae." He smiled cheerfully. "Missed you at school on Monday, and at the Halloween party too. Did you bail out early on me?"

I gulped. Surely, Leon would have seen him come in here. Surely. "Oh, uh . . . yeah . . . yeah, I left early. Didn't feel good."

He nodded. "I'd imagine not after that little treat I slipped in your drink. We could've had so much fun." He took a step forward, and I took a quick step back, which made him laugh. Was he serious? He was going to admit to drugging me that easily? "But instead of a night wrecking your drugged-out ass, I ended up in police interviews for six hours, trying to explain everything I know about why *dear old Dad killed himself*." He put big air quotes around that last bit. Shit. This was bad. My eyes darted toward the door at the far end of the market, ready to make a run for it.

But the guy I'd seen staring at me from the end of the aisle stepped into my path.

Shit. Shit, shit, shit.

"I suppose I should thank you and that traitorous demon of yours," Jeremiah said. "For finally getting my father out of the way. Spending every waking moment trying to convince your own dad not to choose you as his human sacrifice will really fuck with your head." He shrugged. "But in the end, Rae, I have to admit that I'm still pretty pissed off about it. All the fucking *condolences* and the *I'm-so-sorry-for-your-loss* bullshit. It gets so old pretending I'm in mourning."

He thought Leon had killed Kent. He thought *I* was somehow responsible for his father's death. I darted forward, trying to dodge around them, but Jeremiah and his buddy blocked me easily.

"Aw, Rae, not trying to run away from me again, are you?" Jeremiah chuckled, circling me. My back was to the freezers, and I still had hope that I could slip around them. Until Jeremiah yelled, "Lock it up, Tommy!"

I threw my basket toward him and bolted for the door. A loud, metallic clattering jolted adrenaline through my chest, but I couldn't stop, I had to make it to the door.

The metal security gate had been rolled down over the entrance. I stopped, panting, my heart beating painfully hard as the checker—whose name tag said *Thomas*—grinned as he locked the security gate into place.

"I don't think my father made the reality of the situation clear to you, Raelynn, so let me elaborate." I whirled around as Jeremiah sauntered up, his other friend close behind. "Abelaum belongs to the Libiri. It always has, and always will. Sure, you'll find some poor naive souls like Inaya." He rolled his eyes. "But your classmates"—Thomas grinned at me—"your neighbors, the sweet old couple you walk by on the street, they're ours." Jeremiah paused, and chuckled softly. "Or, I should say, they're mine. They're all *mine,* Rae. And so are you."

"No." My voice came out as a whisper, weak with

terror. Leon had to have seen them lock this place down. He would come. Any second now, he would come.

Glass shattered behind me, followed by a roaring and a sound like stone colliding with metal. Jeremiah didn't look surprised, but his friends' faces fell, their eyes widening as they stared at the monster trying to break in behind me.

My monster. The *only* monster I belonged to.

"I thought Nick and Will were supposed to distract him, J," Thomas said, his eyes flickering nervously to Jeremiah as another bang came behind me. I didn't dare turn my back to them, but the screeching sounds of ripping metal told me that Leon was almost through.

Jeremiah slipped out of his jacket, tossing it carelessly to the floor. "They did. Their job is done. They had to be real dumbasses to not realize they were signing up for a suicide mission." Jeremiah glanced over at Thomas, a wide, unnerving smile on his face. "Don't be a fucking dumbass, Tommy."

Tommy looked like he was going to be sick as a strip of torn metal flew over my head, crashing into the shelves and sending bottles of liquor shattering across the floor. There was a rush of heat, and Leon's arms were around me, enveloping me, holding me close and safe in his arms. His shirt was damp, stained with blood, the metallic scent of it sharp in the air.

I could guess what had happened to Nick and Will.

"Oh, bravo, what a show, Leon." Jeremiah clapped his hands. "A little slow there though, I actually expected you"—he glanced at the watch on his wrist—"nearly a minute ago. Damn. And here I thought you *cared* about your precious little human fleshlight."

Behind him, Jeremiah's nameless friend chuckled. "You should give her up to someone who'll use her better—"

Leon's arms left me in the same moment that the man's head left his body. The headless corpse swayed for a moment, blood spurting, before crumpling into a heap. I clapped a hand over my mouth, nausea overwhelming me. Thomas began to scream, the sound ringing hollow in my ears until it choked off with a liquid gurgle; Leon's hand wrapped around his throat from behind, squeezing tighter, tighter, crushing his windpipe and then—with an audible crack—his spine.

My head was light as I stared at the carnage. Leon rolled his shoulders, moving himself back between me and Jeremiah. I pressed against his back, despite the blood on his shirt, whispering frantically, "Get me out of here, please, let's go, let's go, please."

"Easy, baby girl." He pulled me around under his arm, kissing my head. "Sorry I took so long."

Jeremiah shook his head. "Damn, you've really got that sweet, caring monster act down to a science, don't you? It's pathetic how much she's fallen for it, honestly. Impressive, Leon. I'm going to have to punish you for killing my father, but after that, I might still give you the opportunity to serve."

Leon laughed. "Punish *me*? You're about to go the same way as your father, boy."

This time, when Leon left my side, I managed to

preemptively cover my eyes. I expected a scream, a spray of blood—I didn't expect the sounds of struggle.

Leon had Jeremiah pinned on the floor, his veins bulging thick in his arms, his sharp teeth bared as they grappled. *Grappled.* Jeremiah was matching his strength, somehow holding back those claws from going through his throat. It should have been impossible. It *was* impossible. No human could match a demon barehanded. I'd seen what Leon could do.

But something was *wrong* with Jeremiah.

His eyes were glazed, like fog had seeped over his irises. He was expressionless, the only real sign of his struggle being the bulging muscles in his arms and twitching in his legs. As Leon leaned down with his jaws open wide to bite, a drip of dark, thick liquid seeped from the corner of Jeremiah's mouth.

They tumbled, a sudden flurry of movement before they clashed again and skidded apart. Leon rose slowly, his eyes narrowed, as Jeremiah remained crouched on the ground, panting.

Jeremiah was *laughing.*

Leon pushed me back, toward the ruined metal security gate. Jeremiah raised his head, coughed, and more thick black goop dripped from his lips. He wiped it away with the back of his hand and stood, clenching and unclenching his fists, gazing at his arms as if in wonder.

"Goddamn," he said softly. "Oh, that is a gift . . ."

His eyes darted over to us, slowly deepening to their normal color. I was torn between running outside, and staying close to Leon, but then Jeremiah spoke. So softly

I could barely hear him, he said, "God chose me. It *chose* me." He laughed again, nearly hysterical in pitch. "I made my sacrifices. Two, *two* in my name." He held up two fingers as if to drive the point home. "God rewards sacrifice. God rewarded me."

"Get to the truck, Rae," Leon said. "Now."

I backed away, stumbling and nearly falling on the ruins of the security door, my shoes crunching on broken glass. The cold air outside smacked reality into me as I jogged toward the trunk, trying not to stare at the torn, broken body lying on the concrete, or the second corpse splattered against the side of the market.

What the hell just happened? How could Jeremiah be that strong? *How?*

I climbed into the truck, clutching my head in my hands, and jumped when only seconds later, Leon was getting into the driver seat. The tires screeched as he backed out and he slammed on the gas as he hit the road, pushing the truck to its limit. He avoided Main Street to take the long way home that curved along the bay.

"What happened?" I gasped, trying not to scream—or cry—or keep replaying the gore I'd just witnessed again and again. "Leon, how . . . how—"

"Jeremiah gave himself over to the God," he said grimly. The words didn't make sense, but they tightened that knot of anxiety inside me until I thought I might vomit. "That strength isn't his. It's God's."

41

RAE

I'D REALLY WANTED those chips and cookies.

But Thomas's screams, and the decapitated body of the nameless man, lingered in my mind and curdled in my stomach until it was all I could do to hold down the little I'd eaten that day. Just as haunting was the memory of the cold, pale fog in Jeremiah's eyes, the black liquid seeping from his mouth. It was as if something was rotting him from the inside out.

Jeremiah's reward for the sacrifices he'd made was supernatural strength that his mortal body could barely contain.

"A human isn't meant to have strength like that," Leon said. "Mortal bodies begin to break down from the effort of maintaining it, so Jeremiah won't survive like that forever. But that doesn't make it any less of a problem."

"Who was the second sacrifice?" I was pacing in the house, unable to sit down, afraid that if I didn't keep myself distracted, I'd break down entirely. I'd seen Leon kill monsters before, but never humans. Watching humans die was something else entirely, even though it was for my own protection.

I could watch horror films all day and love them. I could revel in gore when I knew it was fake. But this was real. Far too real.

"The sacrifice must have been Victoria," Leon said. He was in the bathroom, washing the blood splatter from his hairline. It was only at my prompting that he was bothering. He didn't really seem to notice when he was spattered with gore. "One of the Hadleigh children is destined for death. Considering Jeremiah is walking around with the God's favor, I'd say he made quick work of his sister." He shrugged and turned off the water. "The only thing left on his list is you. You'll get his full attention now." He frowned, prodding curiously at his tattooed arms. They couldn't be seen through the ink, but I'd heard him grumbling that Jeremiah had bruised him.

I could hear sirens faintly in the distance. When I'd briefly scrolled Facebook earlier in an attempt to distract myself, it hadn't taken long to see someone post that Food Mart was on fire.

Would they find the bodies? Would there be security footage of what happened? Maybe if the police could just see what Jeremiah had done, maybe . . .

No. The police couldn't help me. It was me and Leon—and somewhere out there, Juniper and Zane were still out for vengeance against the Libiri. The bloodbath wasn't over.

It was only just beginning.

Emerging from the bathroom, Leon snatched me up and carried me to the couch, settling me onto his lap in front of the TV. He tugged my thumb from my lip—the nail of which I'd absolutely destroyed by chewing on— and held both my hands secured in one of his.

"Look at me." He tipped my chin up, running his thumb over my pouting lower lip. "A man like Jeremiah isn't allowed to spend this much time on your mind. Who do you belong to?" I pouted a little more, and his hand moved from my face to my breast, teasing gently over the piercing there. "Who do you belong to, baby girl?"

"You," I said softly, and despite the anxiety pressing down on my lungs until I couldn't breathe, I smiled when he kissed my forehead.

"You're mine, and I don't let what's mine get taken away from me. I protect what's mine. Is that clear?" I nodded, and he settled me against his shoulder. "Jeremiah is still just flesh and blood. He may be strong, but he's mortal. He tried to take you and already sealed his own death for that."

A few moments passed in silence. I never wanted to leave that place, that feeling: the absolute safety and comfort of his arms around me. The knowledge that he would fight for me, that he was prepared to take on any-thing for *me,* made my heart ache.

There were words my brain wanted to say but my tongue refused to form. Words like *I want to take your deal* that really just meant *I want you to have my soul,* because he'd already gone against the deal he'd offered. The price for his protection wasn't paid, but here he was. Even when the danger was greatest.

I really hated planning for the future, I hated thinking of big, scary decisions, but this? This didn't feel so scary anymore. It felt right. It felt like safety. It felt like opening a door to the greatest adventure I'd ever take.

I wanted to say it.

There was something else I wanted to say too, words that set me on fire and settled me at once, words that terrified me. Three simple words that rang true in my heart but balked before they could leave my mouth.

But I could be brave.

"Leon—"

The house creaked, and he tensed. The ground shook, the beams overhead groaning and the lights flickering. Cheesecake scrambled out of the kitchen, bolting upstairs to hide under the bed, his tail puffed up.

The shaking stopped. Only the flickering lights remained.

"Earthquake?" My voice sounded too loud in the silence that followed. Leon shook his head, staring at the light above. It flickered faster, faster, the electricity audibly crackling until—

The bulb burst, raining glass onto the floor, plunging the house into darkness. Leon got up slowly, his eyes bright in the dark. I could hear him sniffing, every exhale creating a cloud in the rapidly chilling air.

Goose bumps went up my arms. The temperature had dropped so low, so rapidly, that I was shivering. Leon's arm was still around me, my only heat as I watched the window panes frost over.

"What the hell is happening?" I whispered. "Leon, what—"

A cry, a *howl,* filled the night. It carried through the forest, a scream from the darkest depths of oblivion, both too bestial and too human. It wasn't the cry of an Eld, or the snarl of a Gollum. This sounded . . . *bigger.*

"A Reaper," Leon murmured. "He summoned a god-damn Reaper."

There was another cry, and I had to cover my ears as my stomach lurched at the sound. It was so unnatural, so viciously primal and alien. A sound like that shouldn't exist on Earth, it shouldn't be heard by human ears. But there wouldn't be a single person in Abelaum who didn't hear it. Whatever this thing was, it wasn't even attempting to hide.

"You need to get out of here." Leon was handing me my keys. I hadn't even realized he'd moved to get them. "Get the cat. Start driving. Don't fucking stop. Not for anything. Get as far away from here as you can."

I stared at the keys in my shaking hand. Leon was at the door, staring off into the trees. The yard's motion light flickered on as three deer ran across the yard, fol-lowed closely by a possum with her babies clinging to her back. Squirrels scurried over the deck and away, and crows were cawing overhead.

The animals were fleeing.

I dashed upstairs, and dragged Cheesecake out from under the bed. I barely managed to get the terrified cat into his harness before I dashed back downstairs. Leon was still exactly where I'd left him, shirtless as he stood on the deck, his claws out and his back tense.

"Leon, I'm ready, let's go."

He turned back to me, and something on his face made my heart plummet like a stone. "Give me five minutes to make sure it's distracted. Then start driving."

I gulped, shaking my head. "No. No, you're coming with me."

"Five minutes, Raelynn. You need to do as I say." His face was grim, the cocky determination I was so used to seeing there utterly gone. I felt sick. I was so cold.

"Then you'll catch up with me," I said firmly. "I'll start driving first, and you'll catch up with me. Right?"

He turned, walking back inside. His bare feet left steaming prints on the freezing deck. He reached into the pocket of his jeans, and pulled out a folded piece of yellowed paper.

"When you're far away from here, try to summon me back." He held out the paper, and when I couldn't bring myself to take it, he forced it against my chest. I put Cheesecake down, holding onto his leash, and unfolded it.

I recognized it immediately.

"This is your mark." My eyes were stinging. "From the grimoire. You said . . . you said you hadn't found it yet . . ."

"If the Reaper doesn't kill me, you can summon me again." He grinned, but it didn't reach those smoldering eyes. "I've never given anyone permission to summon me. But if you can, bring me back to you."

I knew what this was. I didn't want to acknowledge it, because it hurt so bad, but I knew.

If the Reaper doesn't kill me . . . but he didn't believe that. He was saying good-bye.

He was saying good-bye, and I . . .

I threw my arms around him, squeezing as tightly as I could. I didn't want to let go, he couldn't make me let go, but he wasn't holding me back either. He was gently—so very gently—pushing me away.

"I'm sorry." The stinging in my eyes was welling over now. He couldn't do this. Not like this. "I'm so sorry, Leon, please, please don't—"

"Don't say you're sorry." His voice was just a whisper as he backed away, putting distance between us as if he was afraid I'd cling to him again. "No human is ready for forever, and forever is all I have. But you gave me a part of your life, when mortal lives are so short." He laughed softly. "I suppose saving your soul could be as good as owning it, so you'd better fucking survive." He glanced back at the trees, as a freezing wind ruffled his hair and another cry shattered the night. As the awful sound faded away, he said, "You should know that I love you, for whatever that's worth. Stay alive. Don't waste that mortal life."

That was where he left me, standing there in the door with tears streaming down my face and his name in my hand.

LEON

THE GROUND WAS crawling with insects. Centipedes and creeping spiders fled beside mice and rabbits. The birds had been roused from their roosts, taking flight with a rattle of leaves and flutter of wings. A fox and her pups paused when they saw me, then hurried on, heads low as they ran.

Only I went against the tide. The youngest plants—little seedlings, sapling trees, fresh grass—were withering and dying. The air was sharp with the scent of blood and mold, cloying in my nose, like a butcher's slaughterhouse.

There was a hierarchy in Hell: demons, Archdemons, and Reapers above all. They were once executioners, having made a delicate pact with the Archdemon royals to only kill those demons who had been outcast.

But Reapers couldn't be trusted. Demons hunted

souls, Reapers hunted death. They craved it, hungered for it. They were as old as the Gods and nearly as dangerous.

I'd heard legends of magicians attempting to summon them. Kill enough people in offering, and maybe you could get one to show up. They couldn't be contained like demons, nor commanded as we could. Offer them an intriguing enough task, and maybe they'd take it.

Or maybe they'd kill you for bothering them.

The forest had gone deathly silent. It was as if the world had been draped in a heavy cloak, smothered and breathless, the air eerily still. I paused, breathing deeply, my ears straining for the slightest sound.

It had to be close.

A twig snapped, and I whirled around, claws outstretched—nothing. Just that empty, dark forest. Would it pass me by? Would it head straight for Raelynn? She would be driving by now—so long as she didn't get any foolish, hardheaded ideas. Fucking hell, she had to obey me this time. She had to.

But it was likely the Reaper wasn't here for her. It was here for me. It was here to get me out of the way, permanently, and leave her vulnerable. Once I was dead, the Libiri could go after Raelynn without fear.

I'd fight death as long as I could if it meant giving her more time to run.

The Reaper didn't arrive with snapping twigs and howling. It arrived with an ice-cold breath on the back of my neck. I turned, slowly, raising my eyes to the otherworldly beast looming over me.

A black shroud obscured its features, except for the pale, ghostly glow of five blinking eyes. A collar of jagged bone, antlers, and claws guarded its neck. Massive black wings stretched from its back, and it towered above me on long skeletal limbs garbed in armor of blackened metal and stone.

It raised a hand, taut with gray skin stretched over long boney fingers adorned with black rings. Strings of teeth, bones, and shriveled bits of flesh hung from its chest. It was a walking amalgamation of death, rot, and pain.

"Demon." Its ancient voice rattled through me. "Have you come to submit to death?"

I smiled. My veins throbbed black and tight beneath my skin. Strange how the most alive I felt was in the moments before death. "Never."

"Oh good." A rumble, its booming laughter, shook the trees. "I do like it so much better when you struggle."

I didn't expect its speed. One knock from the back of its hand crushed the air from my lungs, and in the seconds it took my dazed brain to realize what had happened, I was lifting my head from the ground hundred feet from where I'd once been standing, the tree at my back splintered open from the force of my impact against it.

I dodged away, darting among the trees, circling, looking for an opening. The legs—thin bones, breakable—a weakness despite their armor. I lunged for it, but it anticipated my attack. Its claws tore down my chest, digging deep into my skin and burning like acid.

my mouth and nose, a smell like sweet acetone flooding into my head.

I stumbled, my muscles going limp and my limbs refusing to obey. My head swam, my vision faded—the last thing I saw was Jeremiah smiling as he approached, Leon limp on the ground behind him.

RAE

GOD WAS CALLING my name.

The voice sounding in the dark, in the cold, stroking its subtle influence around my skull was not just calling me but *summoning* me, demanding I answer. It was the voice I'd heard for months, the one that haunted my dreams, my nightmares. It was louder now. It was close.

I couldn't wake up, but I couldn't truly sleep. I was trapped in my own body, screaming wordlessly when I heard movement around me, when I felt the pinch of a needle in my arm. They were keeping me unconscious, keeping me helpless. It felt like an eternity had passed . . . or maybe it was only hours.

All I knew, with a certainty that made every inch of me feel cold, was that I was going to die.

Whatever drug they'd given me kept me calm, but the

panic was there. I knew I had to fight, somehow. I had to get back to Leon.

I had to hope Leon had survived.

Slowly, I began to realize I could move my toes again, then my fingers, then, at last, my eyes. I was lying on something hard and smooth—metal, perhaps a metal table. My body was strapped down and something was pulled over my head, so even as I opened my eyes, all I could see was darkness.

The panic, held back by the now-faded sedative, slammed into me and I began to scream. I struggled against the straps holding me down, but it only exhausted me to strain against something so immoveable. The immediate shakiness in my limbs told me that it had been at least a day—probably longer—since I'd eaten. Screaming made me breathless, so I fell silent, but adrenaline was rushing through me in painful bursts, my body tingling, my heart racing, my fight-or-flight activated without the ability to do either.

I wriggled around, and realized that I was still wearing all my clothes, including my boots—which my dagger was still tucked into, pressing against my ankle. My phone was no longer in my back pocket, but my lighter was still there, and, if I wasn't mistaken, the page torn from the grimoire was still there too.

There was still hope. I couldn't give up yet. I was still armed. I just had to be patient . . .

But hope and patience were becoming more difficult by the second.

There was a creak, and somewhere in the distance a

door slammed shut, followed by heavy footsteps. The steps came closer . . . closer . . . there was the soft beep of digits being pressed into a keypad . . . and the door that opened next sounded as if it was right beside me.

"It's time, Raelynn. Are you awake?"

The voice wasn't familiar; it wasn't Jeremiah. I immediately began to struggle again, wrenching against the straps that held me down. "Help me! Help me, please, please, he's going to kill me, please—"

The voice laughed softly, chidingly, as if what I'd said was silly. "You don't need help, Raelynn. You're going to rest with God. This is a joyous day."

Cold, sickening dread slammed into me. "No . . . no, no, no, you can't, please—"

There were hands on me, and metal pressed around my ankles and clicked into place—some kind of shackles. One wrist was unstrapped, only to be bound in metal cuffs to the other. I kept struggling, but I was still thoroughly restrained when the straps were removed and I was tossed over a hard shoulder, strong arms carrying me, moving up stairs, through more doors, and finally outside.

The fresh air was a relief, even through whatever cloth bag they had pulled over my head. The few drops of cold rain that hit my skin grounded me, and I finally stopped struggling. I had to save my strength. There were crickets chirping, a car engine running—another door opened and I was shoved across smooth leather seats into the warm interior of some large vehicle.

When we started moving, that same fight-or-flight panic gripped me again. I had to stay calm, I *had* to. I tried to keep track of the vehicle's turns, I tried to count the minutes as if that would help me figure out where we were going. Whoever was in the vehicle with me wasn't speaking; Chopin was playing through the stereo, which would have calmed me if I hadn't been so certain I was being driven to my death.

The memory of Leon lying there, bloodied on the ground, haunted me. He was by far the strongest being I knew, but how could even a demon heal from that? Even at the end, even with no strength left, he'd still tried to fight them off me.

I curled up a little tighter into the seat, biting back the tears. If he lived, would he come for me? Or did Jeremiah have him bound somewhere too, enslaved again, back in that awful concrete room he hated so much? Or had Jeremiah left him there, to die slowly and alone, without the strength to get up again?

The thoughts knotted up my empty stomach, and despite my efforts, tears slipped down my face, dampening the cloth over my head.

We drove for so long that I nearly dozed off, weak with hunger and shaking. The rain was pouring now, pattering against the outside of the vehicle when we finally came to a halt. The engine turned off, and panic flooded me again. I was already struggling when the doors began to open, and someone dragged me out across the street to throw me over their shoulder again.

I screamed as loudly as I could. I yelled, thrashing, struggling until the metal on my wrists and ankles cut into my skin—all of it was useless. I was carried through the rain, the scent of pine and damp earth heavy in the air. Then came the scent of smoke, like a woodfire, and then the sound of a door scraping, wood on wood.

There had been a murmur of voices, but they abruptly fell silent. For a moment I thought I was falling, instead I was set gently on the ground, my legs folded beneath me, and the bag covering my head was pulled off.

I blinked rapidly as my eyes adjusted, taking in the dusty wooden floor beneath me, the leaves scattered around, the dim light—this place was familiar. I raised my head, and my heart felt as if it was clenched by a fist. I was kneeling at the end of a church nave, staring down at two long lines of white cloaked figures in stag-skull masks. At the end of the two rows, standing between them, was Jeremiah in his white suit. He stood before a pulpit covered in lit white candles, their wax piled up in dripping heaps around them, adorned with those familiar little trinkets made of fishbones and twigs.

They'd brought me back to St. Thaddeus. The rain poured down through the broken ceiling above, pooling behind the row of silent onlookers. I tried to get up, tried to scramble backward—only to run straight into the legs of the person who'd brought me. He was hooded and cloaked like the rest: faceless, utterly uncaring as I began to scream again. I struggled against him as he forced me to walk between the rows of figures toward Jeremiah. He watched over it all serenely, the one smiling face among so many skulls, somehow the eeriest of all of them.

"You can't do this!" I was forced to my knees at his feet, my guard holding me down and then wrenching my head back, so I was forced to look up at Jeremiah's face. The calm expression, the utter disconnect from any emotion—he may as well have been looking at a bug struggling at his feet. My mouth was too dry, or I would have spit in his face.

"Let me go, Jeremiah." I was breathless, my voice hoarse from the struggle and lack of water.

He just shook his head. "It's almost over," he said softly. Then, louder, "Brothers and Sisters, it's almost at an end! Our long struggle, the culmination of our devotion—before an eternity of faithful devotion to our God. The end of the Age of Man is here. With this, our final sacrifice, we give Earth back to God."

"Back to God," the crowd murmured in unison. Jeremiah turned toward the waxy altar behind him, and when he faced me again, he had a slim knife in his hands. He crouched down, and pressed the tip of the knife up under my chin.

"Now, there's no need for me to hurt you unnecessarily, Raelynn," he said softly, so softly only I could hear. "But if you struggle, if you fuss, this knife might slip, and this will all be a lot worse than it needs to be."

"Fuck you," I hissed, then yelled. "Fuck you! Fuck all of you!"

Jeremiah smiled patiently, then roughly grabbed my shirt, slicing through it with the knife so quickly that the sharp tip nicked my flesh, leaving a long thin line of welling blood down my chest. My guard's grip on me tightened as I began to squirm, protesting as Jeremiah grabbed my bra and sliced through that too, leaving my chest bare and my ruined clothes hanging off my shoulders.

Goose bumps spread over my skin. I glared at him as he smirked at me, and tried to flinch away as he reached out and flicked one of my tender nipple piercings. "How cute," he mocked. "I knew there was a freak in you. It really is too bad, Rae. We could have had so much fun, but . . ." He shrugged. "You're promised to another. It's a shame I can't keep you."

I was promised to another, but it wasn't him and it wouldn't be his evil God. He raised up the knife again and pressed it into my skin. I held my breath, my head going light as I tried to ignore the pain, the dragging burning sensation of him slicing me open.

"*Dominus dedit, Dominus abstulit*," he said, and the crowd echoed him: "*Dominus dedit, Dominus abstulit!*"

I tried not to look down, but I couldn't help it. The sight of the blood streaking my skin made my vision blur. But I wasn't going to scream, I wasn't going to give him the goddamn satisfaction of knowing it hurt. Lines and circles, runes, a language I couldn't understand— he etched them all into my skin, just like I'd drawn that summoning circle onto these floorboards once. It seemed so long ago now. A lifetime.

Back when I'd thought I was invincible. When I still thought my greatest adventure would be to catch a ghost on camera.

But now, no one would believe what I'd seen. No one would believe the way it was all going to end.

Jeremiah stood, and as he stared down at me, he

licked my blood from the edge of his knife, and smiled. "Brothers and Sisters, it's time. Unchain her, so that she may walk to God."

My guard gripped me by the arms as another masked figure stepped up and unlocked my wrists and ankles. The freedom renewed my struggling, but between my hunger, dehydration, and blood loss, my fight was weak. I was hauled to my feet and forced to walk, Jeremiah close behind, back between the rows of white-cloaked figures, who closed in and followed behind us. Out the doors of the chapel, into the rain, into the woods. Up a narrow path through the trees, the absolute silence of those following me chilling me to the bone.

The path evened out, and there, set into the hillside among the trees, were the old wooden beams of a mine shaft. More of those fishbone trinkets had been hung around it, words I couldn't read etched into the wood of the entrance. Jeremiah took my arms and led me away from the guard. His masked followers gathered around, watching as he dragged me toward the entrance, and it was as if the forest itself held its breath.

The shaft was dark, plunging down into nothingness. I stood at the edge, pressing back against Jeremiah, shaking my head.

"Please," I whispered. "Don't. Don't do this."

I shuddered at the touch of his breath on my ear. "Good-bye, Raelynn. Go now, to God."

He shoved me down, into the dark.

RAE

I HIT MUD, tumbled, slipped off a ledge, and fell until I plunged into icy water. It was so cold that I choked, my muscles cramping as I tried desperately to swim. I broke the surface, flailed, and realized my feet could touch the thick mud below. I trudged forward, utterly blind, my arms outstretched in the dark. The water grew shallower, and I crawled out onto wet, pebbly ground.

My glasses were gone, lost in my fall. Above me, the entrance I'd been pushed through was a pale gray square in otherwise total darkness, dripping rain into the pool I'd just climbed from. As I watched, even that pale light began to disappear with the sound of hammers.

They were boarding up the shaft. They were sealing me in the dark.

Shivering, watching my only source of light disappear, I let myself cry.

I sobbed, despair gripping me so hard that for a moment, I only wanted to curl up there and wait. Wait to die, to waste away in the dark or be taken by whatever monster lived down here. I wept until the hammering stopped, and then the silence was so much worse.

I was alone. Completely and utterly alone.

Leon must have died in those woods where the Reaper left him. My protector was gone, his life given up to protect mine—and for nothing. The Libiri had made their final sacrifice. The God was going to be set free. Perhaps it was better this way, that I would die before I could see what became of this world under the rule of an evil God.

But as my tears stopped, and the minutes passed, I realized I couldn't just lay down and wait to die. Not when Leon had fought so hard for me. Not while I still had some strength in me. Not while I still had a weapon.

I fumbled at my boot, reassuring myself that the dagger was still there. It was just one small knife with unknown magical properties, but it meant I wasn't entirely helpless. My vision was shit without my glasses, but I tugged my lighter out of my back pocket and after a few tries, managed to get it to light. The cavern around me was a blur of dark shapes with few defining features, but at least now I'd be able to see enough in front of me to know if I was about to walk into a pit.

In the flickering light, I realized there was something lying in the mud beside me, half-submerged in the murky water. I held the lighter a little closer, frowning—

And realized I was looking at Victoria's muddy, naked corpse.

I scrambled away, and gagged but there was nothing in my stomach to come up. There was a tunnel at the back of the cavern and I stumbled toward it—anything to put distance between myself and the body. Leon had been right: Jeremiah had killed his own sister, and thrown her down here to rot in the dark. I was shuddering violently, and had to lean against the mouth of the tunnel to swallow down my panic. Even knowing that Victoria had intended to kill me, seeing her dead was horrifying.

I'd eaten with her, drunk with her, laughed with her. Villain or not, I'd once thought she was my friend.

I had to pull it together. I had to keep moving. Somewhere, surely there would be another way out. I wasn't going to end up like that. I wasn't going to be a forgotten corpse abandoned underground.

No. Fuck no.

The caverns were eerily silent. The shuffle of my boots echoed as I trudged down the narrow tunnel, with only my lighter illuminating the way. I paused at two branching tunnels, trying to steady my rapid breathing. There was a trick to this, wasn't there? Something like, if there was a breeze coming from one tunnel, then that was where the exit was? But I held up my lighter to both paths, and neither seemed to make a difference.

I went to the right.

The tunnel was so cold, my clothes were soaked, and I was shivering uncontrollably. The smell down here was odd: damp and musty, fungal, and faintly oceanic. The tang of brine was in the air, and so was the pungent smell of rotten fish. The deeper I went, the more I felt as if I was wandering through one of my nightmares again. These black tunnels seemed endless. With every step, I feared my flickering flame would illuminate something in the dark. With every breath, I feared I wouldn't be able to get enough oxygen as I went deeper, and deeper.

The tunnel narrowed, and sloped steeply downward. I edged myself down the slope, slipping to a halt as my boot touched water. The way ahead was flooded, the water too murky to see how deep it was. If I wanted to go on, I'd have to swim, and completely submerge my head.

I had no idea how long this tunnel was, or when I'd be able to surface again. If it kept leading deeper, then there was a chance the rest of the way was entirely underwater. It wasn't worth the risk, it would be too dark to see. I'd have to double back, take the other branching tunnel and hope it led me further up instead of down.

I turned to go back, and abruptly stopped. I could hear something moving in the tunnel behind me. Sniffing the air, walking slowly—stalking.

I held my breath, too frightened to make a sound, and held out my light. It barely penetrated the dark, the blackness beyond its glow utterly complete. But slowly, a long, thin, boney limb stepped into the light. A skeletal canine head. A rotten, fur-covered body.

The monster opened its mouth and howled, and I had no choice. I shoved my lighter into my pocket, and plunged into the water.

The water was freezing, seizing up my already cold body. I had to fight the painful cramping as I swam, my flailing arms and kicking feet bumping against the narrow tunnel walls. When I opened my eyes, only darkness greeted me. My lungs were aching, and I released a little air. I had to swim faster.

Something brushed against my foot and was gone when I frantically kicked out at it. Shit, shit, shit! My heart beat harder and my lungs began to scream for air. I couldn't turn back now. The tunnel had narrowed so much that I was crawling more than swimming, unable to spread my arms because the walls and ceiling were so close. Claustrophobia set in as I frantically wiggled my way forward, terrified that at any moment the tunnel would grow too narrow to move at all. My lungs were begging for air, burning to release the carbon dioxide sitting stagnant in them.

Come to me.

Panic made me release the last of my oxygen. It felt like a weight had been set on my lungs, slowly crushing them under the pressure. I was frantic now. I had to dig my nails into the dirt to pull myself along, because the tunnel was too narrow to kick my feet to propel myself.

Come . . . come . . .

The voice was a whisper in my ear, a vibration in the water, an invasive, pervading thought that echoed in my head. I pushed it away, trying to wall my thoughts with a determined internal mantra: *Just keep going. Go. Go. Go.*

The tunnel opened. I swam up through open water toward a faint, silvery glow. I burst to the surface gasping, coughing, my lungs frantically taking in every bit of oxygen they could. It was dim, but there was light here: everything was gray and pale. I could see a dark shore and swam for it, hauling myself up onto the damp stone where I lay on my back, staring at the stalactites high above as they dripped icy water onto my face.

Only when my lungs stopped aching did I sit up. The chamber I found myself in was large, the source of the pale gray light impossible to determine. There were old wooden boxes stacked against the far wall, and in the center of the room was another pool. It was perfectly black, like spilled ink. Beyond that, a pile of rubble had collapsed out of another tunnel entrance.

There was no way out. Only back, through the water, toward the monster that waited on the other side.

There was no way out.

I sat there in silence, staring at the dark pool until my eyes ached. My stomach growled, and my mouth was so dry that I sipped some of the murky water from the tunnel I'd just swam through, but it tasted bitter and muddy, and did nothing to quench my thirst.

This couldn't be it. It couldn't. No one would ever find me down here. My parents . . . Inaya . . . they would never know what happened to me. Cheesecake would never understand why I didn't come home. I'd rot away in the dark, never buried, lost like those miners over a century ago.

I dug into my back pocket, reaching around the light, and my fingers shook as I pulled out the torn, dampened page from the grimoire.

I couldn't read the Latin on the page. I couldn't remember the circle I'd drawn to summon Leon, no matter how much I tried to recall the details of it, nor did I have any chalk to draw it with. The chances of him still being alive were slim. I could only guess that days had passed since I'd been taken, and if he hadn't found me yet . . .

Then he wasn't going to.

My soul was meant for him, not a God. I was certain of that. My soul was meant for the one who'd protected me, who'd given up his immortal life for a mortal one. I should have offered it to him sooner. I doubted it would have made things any different, but at least I would have the hope that, maybe, when I left this life, I'd find him again.

"My name . . . in your flesh . . . and . . . blood . . ."

I knew it was too late now. It was too late for regrets, too late for useless symbolic gestures. But even so, I carefully laid out the grimoire page in front of me. I pulled off my boots and peeled off my soaked pants and laid them aside, my bare legs covered in goose bumps. Jeremiah had marked me for the God—but I didn't belong to his God. If I had any choice in where my soul was to go, there was only one being I wanted to have it.

I was so cold that I didn't even feel it when I sliced the knife along my thigh. I followed the curves and lines of Leon's mark, recreating it in my skin. It tingled, but it didn't hurt like Jeremiah's blade had. It was just smooth pressure. When it began to bleed, I wasn't scared.

I didn't really care if I bled anymore, so long as I bled for this: for love. It was the only thank-you I could offer—my final devotion he'd likely never even know I gave. But at least my choice was clear now. My soul was Leon's, even if the God stole it. It was his, always, as was I.

I lay down the knife, feeling calm and small as I stared at the mark on my thigh. It was a comfort, a defiance to the ugly cuts across my chest. I scooted myself back against the cavern wall, pulling my legs up to my chest with a heavy sigh.

"My soul is yours to take, Leon," I whispered. "If you're still alive . . . if you can hear me . . . it's yours."

I closed my eyes, as tiredness settled over me like a heavy blanket. I wanted to sleep now, sleep until this was all over. But as my blurry eyes grew heavier, right before they closed, I saw that perfectly still black pool *move*.

Something was emerging.

LEON

JEREMIAH PEERED DOWN at me, his blue eyes bright. He nudged me with his boot, and scoffed as I groaned. "The Reaper broke you. Useless now, aren't you?"

"Fuck . . . you . . ." My voice rasped over my aching throat. I wanted to tear him open, but I had no strength left. They'd taken Rae. Taken her away screaming. And I did nothing.

I could do *nothing*.

"Leave him here to rot. I have no use for a broken tool."

The words echoed long after Jeremiah had gone, long after Rae's smell had faded from the forest around me. It had been hours. Maybe days. Time didn't pass with the ticking of a clock, but with the cracking of my bones as they slowly knit back together. Muscles and sinew re-forming, blood pumping painfully through my veins, my heart pounding so hard that despite how weak I was, it kept me awake. I couldn't sleep.

I could only lie there, cold as the rain fell around me. Creatures came near, sniffing curiously, but not one of them dared to scavenge.

I wasn't dead.

Not yet.

All I could think of was her. As I lay there, immortal magic molding back together this fleshy body, her face remained in my mind. She had come back. She had come after me. Damned stubborn woman. Couldn't obey to save her own life. But she'd come back as if she . . . as if she could protect me. As if she could fight beside me.

That alone made a little warmth come back to my chest. She was foolish as hell, but she—she loved me.

She'd said it.

It was almost laughable, because why would a woman so vibrant, so alive, love a monster from Hell? Why would she risk her life to come back for me, or offer her soul when I'd already given all I could to protect her, when I had nothing more to give in return?

Love. Because she . . . loved me.

How simple and silly that sounded. A four-letter word wasn't enough to describe the desperation in me, the craving, the *need* to get back to her. It wasn't enough to describe the absolute fury I'd turn on those who had taken her from me, who had dared to put their hands on her. And if they'd killed her . . .

I'd destroy them all. I would hunt them down, every last one, every human who'd ever dared to give allegiance to the Libiri. I'd make them all beg for mercy, and give none. The murders that had earned me my reputation would be nothing in comparison to the slaughter I'd unleash on them.

I had to believe she was still alive. I had to believe I still had time to save her.

The downpour was heavy, but I could finally move my fingers and toes. Everything ached, but my movement was returning. I was just so weak, so goddamn *weak*.

The rain smelled like the ocean, and that made me afraid. The God's influence was growing. If It didn't already have her . . . It would soon.

Something brushed against my mind, soft, almost like the call of a summoner but gentler somehow. It was a feather's touch in comparison to a summoner's deep, piercing hooks. A nudge, a caress against my deeper being.

It took me a few moments to realize it was my name being called in the way that only a demon's hidden name could be: someone was writing it.

I'd given it to Rae, and although I had no guarantees that Jeremiah hadn't found it hidden in her clothes and taken it, something told me that this wasn't Jeremiah's doing. It was too tender, like the touch of her hands on my chest when she'd cleaned my wounds, or the way her eyes looked up at me from the bed, or the way her lips curved in that eager smile of hers. It was soft, like outstretched hands, like a whisper. *"My soul is yours to take . . ."*

My eyes opened wide. I was . . . warm.

Not just that, but my blood was on fire in my veins,

my heart like a coal in my chest. I was breathing deeply again, even though my lungs ached. I was getting *stronger*, somehow.

"*. . . if you can hear me . . . it's yours.*"

I tried to get up too quickly, and my legs buckled under me. I knew it was her, and knew it was her hands writing my name. I tried again, and was able to get to my feet, gasping as my healing accelerated painfully, and I could feel every new cell as it formed, every interlocking fiber of muscle pulled tight.

I knew what this was. I knew why I could suddenly feel her touch my mind as I could touch hers, why I could hear her voice, feel her as if she was right there.

She'd done it; she'd given her soul to me. Every passing second bound us more tightly together, locking her vibrant mortal soul into mine. I could feel her like a thread, binding tighter and tighter around me and tugging, desperately tugging, trying to draw closer.

She was alive. She was out there and alive.

And I wasn't going to lose her.

With every passing second, I was getting strong. Strong enough to walk, then to run. Strong enough to find her scent, strong enough to follow the tug of her soul on mine. I'd steal her from the hands of God Itself if I had to.

RAE

"YOU'VE COME TO me at last, Raelynn Lawson."

My mind couldn't comprehend what my eyes were seeing. Despite not having my glasses, somehow what lay before me was perfectly clear. The being that had arisen from the black pool was both incomprehensibly large, and only as tall as a man. It was constantly morphing, growing and shrinking, an amalgamation of color, light, and absolute darkness. It should have been impossible; no Earthly being should have been able to take that form. When It spoke, it was with a voice that was as ancient and cold as bleached bones.

It was the voice that haunted my dreams. The voice of God.

And God was both painfully beautiful and horrifying beyond words.

The sound of Its feet padding slowly across the damp

stones toward me made me shudder, and I had to cover
my eyes because I couldn't bear to look at It. I wanted
to run, to hide. I would have flung myself into a pit if
it meant being able to get away. But I couldn't move.
Even raising my hands to cover my eyes felt like an enormous effort, and keeping them covered was even worse.
I couldn't bear it. My hands fell back trembling to my
sides, and my burning eyes wouldn't close even when
tears flooded down my face.

It stood before me, enormous, all-encompassing. The
cavern around us had expanded indefinitely, the walls
hazy, unable to contain the true mass of the being within.
Its nearness made me sick, but It also flooded me with so
much pleasure that I could hardly breathe.

Within the rapidly changing, unnamable colors that
made up Its being, I could see something like a human
face, as pale as mist, with numerous eyes that slowly
winked open and closed as It spoke.

"A mere century ago, I spared three of your kind to
go back into the world, to prepare it for me, to spread
the word of awakening. Three lives spared, must one day
be returned. The work is done. The oath is fulfilled. Look
at me, mortal."

The longer I looked, weeping, my chest aching as if I
was drowning, the more Its misty face solidified. It could
have been carved in marble, It could have been painted
by Michelangelo, or created by some computer algorithm
with unwavering perfection. So beautiful it was terrifying, so overwhelming that I thought I would melt away
and become nothing just from having Its gaze on me.

"I've waited for you, Raelynn Lawson. I have called to you, even when you wandered so far from your home. But you returned to me, as you were meant to."

I tried to shake my head, but my movements felt so slow. "No," I whispered. "I'm not yours. I'm not."

There was a glitch in Its perfection. Beyond the beauty, I could see gray, slimy skin. I could see a massive form, with coiling tentacles, covered in dozens of blinking pale white eyes. I could smell rotting fish. I could smell the ocean.

God smiled, with perfect white teeth. Like static cutting through a television screen, for a moment those teeth were jagged, curved and sharp, like some predator from the deepest parts of the ocean. Then it was gone, and it was as if a switch was flipped in my brain and I forgot how to be afraid.

"Do not fear your fate." Its voice reverberated around the cavern, rumbling deep in my bones. "Always, you were meant for me. Always, you were meant to return. This place called you back, and you answered willingly." There was another rumbling sound, deeper and darker that made the hairs on my neck stand on end. God was laughing. "You came to me. You left your family behind. You followed my voice in your dreams. Even as you wandered in the darkness of this deep place, you chose the path that would lead you to me."

I wasn't here willingly, I *wasn't*. But as It spoke, my protests died with barely any fight. It reached for me, and I wanted so badly to cringe away, to scream and fight but I just . . . couldn't. It touched my face, but Its fingers didn't feel like flesh and blood at all. They were cold, thick, and slimy, and wherever It touched me my skin was left numb.

Then It pressed Its palm against my forehead, and it was as if my skull was being split open, cracked like an egg. Memories, as bright and vivid as if I was reliving them, flashed before my eyes. I was a child, running through the trees with bare feet, climbing over fallen logs and hauling myself up onto mossy stumps. I'd heard a voice calling me, and I thought it was my fairies. I ran and ran, like it was a game and they were hiding from me. Then I paused, knelt, and pressed my ear against the dirt. The voice was down *there*. I dug my tiny fingers into the earth, as if I could dig my way down to it.

Then the memory was gone, and I was in another time, another place.

The California sunset was pale pink and bloody red over the ocean. My feet dangled over the edge of the pier, swinging above the water. I stared down at the swirling foam, at the waves crashing against the pillars of the pier, and imagined sinking into those dark depths. I imagined that if I went deep enough, everything would be silent. In the back of my mind was the constant feeling that I had forgotten something, that there was something incredibly important I was meant to do and yet, no matter how hard I tried, I didn't know what. I was restless, so restless. Maybe if I sunk beneath the waves, maybe if I went deep enough, the restlessness would stop.

My head split wider. It was unbearable, overwhelming. I knew my body was violently twitching, and I was screaming, then seizing, but I couldn't stop.

My parents were talking about Spain again. They wanted to move, they wanted to buy a house and retire by the coast. My dad looked at me and asked, "So what's the plan, sweet pea?"

I knew, right then, that I wanted to go home. Home, to Abelaum. Home, to the trees and the rain, to my childhood ghosts. Home, to the place that had never stopped calling me. Maybe if I went back, the restlessness would stop. Maybe I'd remember what I was meant to do.

I'd fallen to my knees. The stones were so cold, and I was sobbing, my tears mingling with the puddles of water at God's feet. It was agonizing but it was joyous. It was the deepest, truest terror I could imagine, so awful I wanted to die.

It all made sense. I was meant to be here. I was meant to come. Every step I'd taken, every choice, had led me here. Even when I'd been fighting so desperately to get away, I'd run back into danger.

My sense of self-preservation hadn't just been bad— it had actively driven me to this place, to this cold cave deep underground, to fall at the feet of my God.

"You see, my child? Your soul is mine, to be bound into an eternity of exquisite suffering among all those who have come before. Marcus Kynes, Victoria Hadleigh, and now you, Raelynn Lawson. The sacrifice is complete. As I escape this place, and the world changes beneath my hand, you will see it all. You will feel the agony, the pain, the righteous fear of humankind. Such is the fate of my chosen ones, to be blessed to suffer for me forever. To feel such pain is beauty. It is the final, ultimate purpose of your soul."

I looked up, into the face of God, through the watery haze of tears. "Am I going to die?"

"Never," It said. "Your flesh will rot, consumed by my servants. But you will go on, with me, forever. There will be no end. There will be no rest. There will be no respite nor comfort. Only perfect, holy suffering."

In the shadows beyond God, I could see the Eld waiting, I could smell the deathly stench of them. They watched me hungrily, thick saliva dripping from their jagged teeth. I wouldn't even be dead yet when they tore into me. I'd die slowly, ripped apart until my soul abandoned this body.

God grasped my jaw, forcing my gaze back to Its beautiful, awful face. "You are mine. Forever awaits you. The time has come."

The sensation of my head being split again made me scream. It was as if cruel, cold fingers were pressing into the cracks of my skull, pulling it apart. But it wasn't memories that I was forced into this time. The swirling colors that made up the God's being had surrounded me. I didn't know if I was falling or floating, if I was being pulled into pieces or compressed so tightly that I would soon cease to exist. It hurt to look, it hurt, but I couldn't close my eyes. Within the myriad of colors, I could see shapes, structures made of iridescent light. It was so blindingly bright and so cold.

Then came the screaming.

Not mine, but the screams of dozens, if not hundreds, *thousands* of voices. Screams of true agony, the kind of sound that made me sick just to hear it. My screams melted among them, and I realized that it would never end. This raw feeling in my throat would go on, this pain would go on, this ripping feeling wouldn't stop. This was the endless, holy suffering God spoke of. This was the fate of my soul.

But no matter how much It ripped at me, no matter how shattered my mind became in Its grip, I was tethered and my soul wouldn't let go. God couldn't take me, because I'd bound myself to another.

To Leon.

And when I realized that, the colors around me suddenly vanished and I was struggling, thrashing, then tearing away from God's hold, screaming, "No! No, no, *no*! I'm not yours!"

I scrambled back against the stone wall of the cavern, gasping, my vision sliding in and out of focus. God's perfect face was twitching, morphing rapidly between beautiful and vile. The illusion was breaking, and it was as if I could see both at once: the horrifying reality of Its massive tentacled form, and the too-perfect mask of a beautiful being.

"You can't take me!" The louder I shouted, the more I could breathe, the more I could move. The control It had over me could be fought against, and I fought it viciously. "You will never be free from this place because you'll *never* have your last sacrifice!" I laughed hysterically as I laid my hand over Leon's mark on my thigh, the cuts still tender but no longer bleeding. Somewhere, Leon was still alive. He'd survived. When God had tried to take me, tried to separate my body and soul, I'd felt my tether to him pull taut and hold me back, refusing to let go.

Every path I'd taken, every seemingly inconsequential decision, had led to this moment. The choice between two eternities, a choice that was mine alone. I'd chosen. I knew to whom my soul belonged, and it wasn't to a merciless God.

It belonged to another monster, a monster who had found me and protected me despite his darkness. It belonged to a demon who, even now, I knew was trying to reach me. To protect me, to save me. I stood up a little taller against the wall, even though I had never been so afraid.

Maybe this would be the day I died. Maybe this really was my fate. But in the end, the choice had still been mine. I'd found the deepest depths of this darkness and looked upon true horror. I'd fought every step of the way.

If I was going to die, then I would die still fighting.

RAE

GOD'S FURY MADE the very stones in the cavern walls crack. Everything shook, the ground rolling as if with an earthquake. I tried to run, but the strength had gone out of my muscles and my knees buckled. A massive tentacle wrapped around me as I tried to crawl away, right as my fingers closed around the handle of my dagger, and jerked me up into the air.

"What have you done?" God's voice slithered inside my ears like cold, sharp wire prodding my eardrums. "*What have you done?* You offered your soul to another! You betrayed your God!" It roared, and the cracks in the cavern walls spread, chunks of stone beginning to fall. The Eld howled, panicking as the cavern began to collapse around them.

God was beautiful no longer. It looked like a beast that had crawled up from the deepest, darkest ocean

depths. Its gray flesh was so pale it was nearly trans-
lucent, run through with a spiderweb of blue veins.
Numerous tentacles, dozens of them, coiled around the
cavern, up the walls and into the water, and tightened
mercilessly around me. They were covered with white
eyes, blinking among the suckers, looking around with
wild anger. God's face was no longer mist and swirling
colors, but gaunt with wide, bulbous eyes, and gills fluttering along Its too-long neck.

Its tentacles wrapped tighter and tighter. The cavern
had completely collapsed in, and we were sinking down
among mud, rock, and water. We were falling into nothingness, the dirt and stones vanishing into the abyss as
darkness stretched out around us in every direction.
Lightning flashed in the distance, and the air filled with
thick white fog. The silhouettes of massive beings, briefly
illuminated by the lightning, sent adrenaline coursing
through my veins.

"You are mine!" Its voice was guttural and distorted,
as if a hundred voices had all shouted at once. "You cannot take my sacrifice from me!"

We plunged down, into dark freezing water. All I could
see were the numerous eyeball-covered tentacles spread
out around me, a monstrous web in the water. Deeper and
deeper we went. The pressure was building, my body aching under the weight of the water pressing down.

"You cannot escape me, mortal. You are meant for
me. Your Earth is meant for me."

My fingers ached as I gripped the dagger as tightly
as I could. I was determined to hold on, no matter how

deep we went, no matter how much it hurt. My body was being squeezed, slowly crushed in the grip of those tentacles and the pressure of the water. But my arms were free.

I swung back the dagger and plunged it down, as hard as I could, right into one of the pale eyeballs in the tentacle gripping me.

A nauseating shudder went through the water, and there was a roar of fury that nearly made my eyes roll back. I pulled back my arm and stabbed again, the dagger sliding in up to the hilt. The volume and horror of the sounds the God made were beyond words. Such wrath needed no language. It was palpable, wracking my body with pain as I was dragged deeper and deeper into the depths. I stabbed again, plunging in the knife and leaving it there when the pain made it impossible to retain any more conscious thought.

The tentacle's grip on me loosened.

The water swirled, tumbling me, sucking me down, down, down. Water rushed into my lungs. Everything burned, everything ached. I couldn't tell what was up or down, left or right, air or water. There was only darkness.

Darkness that seemed to go on for eternity.

I WAS DYING.

Death felt . . . cold. Uncomfortable. But not as terrifying as I'd thought it would.

The silence was nice. The cold . . . after a while . . . felt nice.

There was catharsis in acknowledging that I wasn't going to make it. I made peace with it.

Maybe I could drift for a while. Maybe I could sleep.

I wanted to sleep. Just sleep. I was so tired. But . . .

There was a silver thread in the dark, glowing bright and beautiful, and it wouldn't let my eyes close.

I stared at it, numb at first and a little irritated. Why was it here? Disturbing my darkness, refusing to let me drift. Then I felt it tug. Just a little trembling tug that seemed to pull on all my ribs at once. It made my heart lurch. It made my brain wake up.

"Raelynn!"

That voice . . . so . . . soft . . . so far away. I'd have to swim forever to reach it. I didn't want to swim. I wanted to drift.

"Raelynn! Keep going! Don't you fucking give up!"

Where? I wanted to ask. *How can I reach you?* The voice was so familiar, but so far away. I wrapped my hands around the silver thread, using it to pull myself through the darkness. I didn't know if I was in the water anymore. I wasn't breathing. Air didn't seem necessary. But it was cold and thick and strange. Would it be like this forever?

I didn't want to be in the dark forever. I didn't feel ready.

I clung tighter to the thread. It was pulsing, beating like a heart under my hands. It was the only light, at first, but the further I went, I began to see a glow above. Faint and golden, like the sun behind the clouds.

"You're almost there, baby girl!"

Leon . . . it was Leon.

I was tired. The depths had been soft, and everything hurt worse here. I could look up now, and see the surface of the water, and the gray clouds, and the rain dimpling the surface.

Then I was splashing, trying frantically to surface, and my fingers brushed against dirt and I realized the water was shallow. It was the shoreline. My head bobbed up and I could see the trees.

Warm arms snatched me up, dragged me from the water and pounded my back until air was forced into my lungs. Oxygen rushed to my head, making it light, and I blacked out for a moment as my head kept swimming while the rest of me hit land. There was dirt, there was wonderful solid earth under my hands. I could smell the pines and the rain, citrus and smoke.

"Fucking *breathe,* Raelynn, fuck, please!"

Breathing hurt. Everything hurt. But if it hurt, that meant I was alive.

I was still alive, and Leon was holding me, cradling me like a baby with my head beneath his chin, murmuring in my ear, "I'm so sorry, baby girl, I'm so fucking sorry. Just breathe. Breathe for me. I've got you. You're okay."

I was too tired to keep my eyes open. I was weak with hunger, dehydrated, and my lungs were burning. But somehow, I'd never felt so happy.

I pressed my face against his chest, taking in his scent, warm as a summer bonfire, sharp and dark as the pines. "They tried to take me from you," I muttered, only half-lucid, somewhere between a dream and that deep darkness I'd swam out of. "They tried, but . . . but I'm yours. I'm yours."

"You're mine, baby girl." His arms were so tight, so strong, as if they hadn't been broken and bleeding the last time I'd seen him. "You're mine, and nothing is ever, *ever* going to take you from me again."

I DRIFTED IN and out of consciousness. Leon had tugged his shirt onto me and held me close against him to keep me warm. I still didn't fully feel real, as if my body wasn't sure if it was flesh and blood or still drifting in that awful, screaming *other* place.

Thunder cracked through the soft sounds of rain and I jolted, my eyes flying open.

"Shh, you're alright." Leon's fingers stroked over my arm, easing the fear out of me. We were walking through the trees, and I was cradled in his arms. I felt so heavy and achy, and my head was pounding.

Muffled, as if from a great distance, I could still hear a voice in my mind, screaming in fury. *"Raelynn! Raelynn, you're mine!"*

I shuddered, pressing my face closer against his chest. I knew there were more scars across his skin now, scars still pink from having only just healed. I wanted to kiss them, to thank him somehow, but I was so scared that my head felt like a balloon that was about to pop.

"God is calling me," I said. "Still calling me. Leon, it won't stop."

"It will stop," he said. "It can't take you, Rae. It can't take a soul that's been willingly given to another."

I looked up at him, even though his face was blurred without my glasses. "I thought you were dead, Leon. I thought the Reaper killed you." The thought made me choke up, the memory of him lying broken and bloody.

"I'm not going to leave you that easily, baby girl." He smiled, and his fingers tightened around my arm. "There's no getting rid of me now. You're stuck with me."

The God's voice grew muffled as we walked, until it was only a faint murmur. Then it was gone completely, and thunder rumbled again as lightning lit up the skies.

Leon chuckled. "God is furious. Such a storm."

"Will It give up?" The thunder was so loud it hurt my ears. "When will It stop?"

"You injured It," Leon said. "It's weakened. The witch, Everly, told me she intended to kill the God. With It injured, perhaps now is her chance."

"Everly . . . is a witch?" I thought back to that soft-spoken girl, who'd looked at me as if she could see my very soul, who'd drawn cards to warn me of my fate. I remembered that she'd felt wild, even though she was so quiet. A feral being, forced to pretend she was domesticated.

I closed my eyes again. I was completely soaked, but Leon's body heat kept me from shivering. "Do you think she can do it? Can she kill a God?"

"Her mother was one of the most powerful witches I'd ever met," he said. "Her daughter carries that legacy. If anyone can kill a God, she can."

I couldn't imagine how a being so great, so incomprehensibly powerful, could be destroyed. Thinking about it made my head hurt, and I groaned softly into his chest. "I want to go home."

"I know, baby girl. We will. But I'm going to make sure no one ever takes you from me again."

I wanted to ask more questions, but tiredness won out. Exhaustion wouldn't allow me to stay awake another second. I drifted off to sleep in the arms of the Killer, *my* Killer, as he carried me away to spill more blood in my name.

49

LEON

NOTHING HAD EVER felt so right, so complete, as holding Rae in my arms. Limp with exhaustion, twitching in her sleep, but back with me. Back where she belonged. Battered and scarred but alive.

I knew that nightmares would torment her for weeks, and that the memories of this would never fade. It would stay with her, always, like the cuts on her body that would become scars. I couldn't forgive myself for it, for not fighting hard enough for her, for having just laid there, broken, when Jeremiah and his minions took her.

But I was going to set it right.

With Callum by her side, I believed that Everly would destroy the Deep One, even if it killed her too. I've felt it in her, that wild magic that, once unleashed, could destroy empires, worlds, and even Gods.

That was her story, her fate. Perhaps I'd never know if she made it out alive.

It didn't truly matter to me. Only Raelynn mattered. Keeping her safe, making sure nothing ever took my baby girl from me again, mattered more than anything else.

I looked down at the cuts Jeremiah had carved across her chest and was filled with so much rage I couldn't see straight. He'd marked my girl, and for that I was going to break his hands, crush his fingers one by one until every bone shattered. As I walked, I fantasized of every gruesome thing I'd do to him. His God was dying, and he was merely mortal. The strength God had rewarded him with was only temporary.

He was going to die, slowly and agonizingly, and I would enjoy every goddamn second.

I stayed deep in the trees as I walked, to ensure no one driving by on the road would get a glimpse of me. It would surely be a sight to behold: my jeans were torn, my chest was bare from having given my shirt to Raelynn to cover her, and the injuries the Reaper had left me with were only barely healed, still pink and angry. I was too furious to disguise myself, so my claws were out, my eyes were bright, my teeth sharp and ready to rip apart any member of the Libiri I managed to find.

I smelled the fire long before I saw it. The ashen scent of burning was strong in the air, the smoke carrying even through the rain. As I reached the tree line at the edge of the Hadleigh property, I could see the flames.

I hated to leave her for even a second, but I laid Rae down at the base of a tall pine, where she could lie hidden among the gnarled roots. She sighed softly as I laid her down, curling her arm around to cushion her head. The ache of looking at her was almost too much, the sweetest pain in my chest as I brushed her hair back from her face before turning to leave her.

Love. What an odd thing.

I crept beyond the trees. The grass sloped down, to where the Hadleigh's house was entirely engulfed in flames. I could feel the heat of them, the scent of the smoke sharp in the air. The rain wasn't enough to put the fire out, despite the downpour. All the glass had burst, the ground around the house shimmering with its shattered pieces.

This was no natural fire. I could smell the gas in the air. There was a crack, and a massive section of wall collapsed inward. The house would be reduced to nothing more than its concrete foundations soon enough.

A little further down the lawn, two figures sat in the grass side by side. I recognized Zane immediately, covered in ash and bloodied. Beside him, Juniper turned toward him and whispered something too softly for even me to hear. A shotgun lay in the grass beside her and her face was bruised, but when Zane reached out and cupped her cheek, she leaned into his hand. She closed her eyes, and they sat there silently, watching the house burn.

I watched with them, trying to figure out the bizarre feeling of melancholy that overtook me. I knew nothing was alive in that house. I knew that if Jeremiah had survived, Juniper wouldn't be sitting here. She'd still be hunting him down.

They stood and turned to go. But when Juniper caught sight of me standing there, she raised the shotgun immediately, aimed and ready to fire. Zane laid a hand on her shoulder.

"Easy, Juni," he said. I put up my hands and slowly, nervously, Juniper lowered her weapon.

"You beat me here," I said. "Got to have all the fun before I could, eh?"

Zane smiled and shook his head, but Juniper came closer. The bruises on her were even worse than I thought, furious purple blossoms across her skin. She looked me over cautiously, her eyes narrowed with suspicion, but she didn't raise the weapon again.

"Where's Raelynn?" she said.

"Close by," I said. "Hidden. She's safe."

She nodded. "We left no one alive. The Hadleigh family is gone. The Libiri are gone."

The leaping flames had died down now, but the ashes still smoldered. "Jeremiah, too?"

"He died like a coward," she said. "You would have loved to see it."

"I would have loved to do it."

She laughed, and slung the strap of her shotgun over her shoulder. "I sold my soul for revenge. It was mine to take. But it's over." She glanced back toward the house, the reflection of the flames making her eyes almost as golden as mine. "It's over."

Faintly, the distant wail of sirens began. Zane came up, and tugged lightly at a few strands of her hair. "We should go. This place will be swarming with people soon."

She nodded, turned as if to leave, then suddenly turned back and held out her hand. It took me a moment to realize it was a handshake. Strange human comradery thing. As I took her hand, she said, "I forgive you. I really hate to say that, but I do."

I'd never really cared about forgiveness. It was only meant to ease guilt and bring closure. But as they left, and the sirens grew louder, I took one last look at the smoldering ruins and realized that I *needed* closure.

I needed to know that all this was finally over.

WE ONLY HAD a little time.

Rae was still sleeping as I carried her through what remained of the house. The flames were almost entirely out now, leaving only the charred skeleton of the house behind. There were several bodies I came across, but I didn't care about them. There was only one I was looking for.

When I found Jeremiah, he never would have been recognizable to human eyes. He was just a blackened husk, lying among the splintered glass and burnt wooden beams. But I knew him. Even dead and burned, I felt hatred looking at him.

It really was over. Nothing remained but ashes.

Rae squirmed a little in my arms as I made my way back out through the rubble, her eyes blinking slowly open. I felt her stiffen as she looked around, and I said softly, "Don't be afraid, baby girl. You're safe."

"Where are we?" She tried to turned her head to look

around. She was missing her shoes, so I wasn't about to set her down.

"The Hadleigh house."

"Did you do this? You burned it? How long was I asleep?" Her voice was deeper when she was sleepy, and a little raspy. It was so damn cute.

I almost lied. I almost told her that I did burn it, that I killed Jeremiah, that I made him pay for what he'd done, that I'd taken vengeance for her. But I couldn't lie to her, even though I felt as if I'd failed her somehow.

"I didn't do it. Juniper and Zane got here first. She got her revenge." I could see flashing lights on the road. The fire trucks had arrived. I quickened my pace, jumped down from the back of the house and slipped away into the trees. Rae's eyes were on me the whole time, watching my face even though it must have been a blur to her without her glasses.

"And Jeremiah?" she whispered. There was fear in her words, and it made anger boil up inside me. She didn't deserve to feel afraid. I wished I could kill her fear. I wished I could rip it apart and burn its remains.

"He's dead, baby girl. I wish I could say I'd done it, but they got to him first."

The rain had slowed to a drizzle, dripping slowly down through the trees. I paused under the shelter of a thick pine, and let Raelynn stand on her feet for a few moments. She was wobbly, and leaned against me for support, her arms wrapped tightly around my chest. Feelings of comfort were relatively foreign to me, but holding her as she clung to me was easily the most comfortable thing I could imagine.

"I'm glad you didn't have to do it," she said, rubbing her eyes. "You've already had to kill enough. I know you're tired." She pressed her face against me again. "You deserve some rest."

I frowned. "You think so?"

"Mmhm." She reached her arms up, around my neck, and I scooped her up again. Through her yawn, she said, "I wanna go home and sleep. We can sleep for days, like you did before . . . and you don't have to be angry anymore, because Jeremiah is gone and Kent is gone, and . . ." Another yawn. She was going to pass out again at any second. "We're safe now. We're both safe."

Safe. What a strange idea. I hadn't felt safe in over a hundred years. And I hadn't seriously thought I could rest in nearly as long, at least until I met her. But now, as her eyes drooped closed again and I carried her toward home, I realized that I didn't feel so angry anymore. The knot of hatred that had kept me going through all those years was loosening. Suddenly I was thinking of rest, I was thinking of calm and quiet.

I wanted to hold her in my arms, wrapped up in all her blankets, and sleep with her scent surrounding me. When we woke, I wanted to prove to her that she was safe again and again until there was no more fear in her voice, and all this was just a distant memory.

And I would. I'd keep her safe for eternity.

Epilogue

RAE

THE STORM THAT hit Abelaum was unlike anything the town had ever seen. The rain poured for days, an unending torrent that flooded the streets, with wind strong enough to knock out powerlines and leave half the townspeople without electricity. The cabin was dark, but Leon lit candles and kept me wrapped in blankets. Warm, safe, and never out of his sight.

When the storm finally ended, more destruction was reported. The soaked soil had caused the White Pine mine shaft to become a massive sinkhole, caving in on itself and completely demolishing what remained of the old tunnels. St. Thaddeus still stood, but its roof had caved in completely, and town officials began to talk of having it demolished despite its historical significance.

Without Kent Hadleigh around to protest it, the decision was made: the church, too, would be destroyed.

Jeremiah's burned body had to be identified via dental records. The event was called a tragic accident, the fire supposedly started by the lightning that had accompanied the storm. Rumors that the fire had been set on purpose swirled around campus for weeks, but nothing came of it.

Some of my professors looked at me warily, almost bitterly. I would never know for certain, but I had to wonder if any of them had been in that church, hidden behind stag-skull masks as Jeremiah cut me. I would always wonder who among them had eagerly awaited my death, but I hoped that every time they saw me walk in, alive and well, it burned them up inside.

I no longer dreamed of the mine's dark tunnels. I didn't hear the God call my name. The bruises from Its massive limbs squeezing me faded, but the marks left by Jeremiah's knife became scars. Leon told me that if I wanted to try medical treatments to fade them, then money wasn't an object.

I was beginning to suspect he had piles of gold hoarded away back in Hell, but he just laughed and wouldn't confirm if it was true. He said that would be a surprise for when I got there.

His mark on my leg scarred too, but that was one scar I didn't want to remove. He would trace it with his fingers, kiss it with his mouth, murmur the filthiest things as he ran his tongue across it. It was his mark of ownership, one only I could give him. A willing promise.

My soul was his to take, to love, to own—forever.

Bonus Chapter

RAE

ONE YEAR LATER

OAK TREES FRAMED the old ivy-cloaked chateau. The house was surrounded by an overgrown lawn, stretching acres in every direction. It was isolated, reachable only by a long, narrow dirt road that led deep into the French countryside.

Yet, despite how far we were from the nearest town, I had the feeling we weren't alone.

Leon had noticed it long before I did. As he drove at terrifying speed down the country road with the windows down, wind whipping through the cab, he'd taken a deep breath and declared, "This place is infested with spirits, you know. *Infested*."

I hadn't been able to resist letting out an excited squeal.

After I graduated, Leon and I were eager to finally get out of Abelaum. There was a strange hollowness to that little town, an echo of wickedness that had me looking over my shoulder everywhere I went. So we'd spent the last several months in Spain with my parents—with Cheesecake along for the adventure, of course.

Introducing the demon who owned my immortal soul to my parents was nerve-wracking. Especially considering that this demon hated nearly every human he met. But he hid his claws and golden eyes, and he made a clear effort to be polite.

My mom was enamored with him, of course. She'd always had a *thing* for possessive, protective men, and Leon was certainly that. My dad was delighted to have someone to talk to who seemed to share his love for European history—to Leon, such chats were simply a recounting of his early life.

But we had no plans to live with my parents permanently. After a few months of visiting and traveling around Spain, I was eager to start exploring Europe and finally put my camera back to work. I put together a long itinerary of haunted places to visit: castles, dungeons, graveyards, old houses. With Cheesecake safely with my parents until we could find permanent housing, I was able to focus on growing my skills as both a paranormal investigator and a videographer.

It was Leon who insisted we visit this old chateau. No one had lived in it for several years. Ivy had grown over the windows, and moss carpeted the ancient stones. The big iron gate guarding the property had been unlocked, but the front door was not.

"God, what I would give to live in a place like this," I said, sighing dreamily as Leon fiddled with the lock. "Big old house, full of ghosts. My very own haunting. Imagine the video content I could get, living in a place like this!"

"People would think you're faking it," Leon said. "As mortals so often do when confronted with things they can't explain."

"I'd find a way to prove it." I stared at one of the upper windows, certain I'd seen movement—or perhaps the shadows were just playing tricks on me. Leon cursed, glaring at the locked door with his fist pressed against it, and I frowned. "Maybe we shouldn't break in. It's private property, isn't it? We could contact the owner and come back—"

Leon smiled slyly. "Since when have you had an issue with trespassing? I'd hate for you to miss out on your ghosts."

"Well . . ."

With a sigh, he straightened up and slammed his fist into the door, sending it flying off its hinges and into the entryway with an explosive bang.

"We'll replace it," he said gruffly, as I stared at the door in horror. He sniffed the dusty air, peering around the dim entryway with narrowed eyes. "That certainly got their attention."

"Did it? Oh my God. Are there ghosts here? Like, right now?" I edged around him through the doorway, but he grabbed me with one arm and lifted me, preventing me from going any further. Not to be dissuaded, I pulled my cell phone from my pocket and started recording as I called out, "Hello? Is anyone here with us? My name is—"

"Baby girl." Leon's voice carried a warning that made me instantly fall silent. "Not yet. Names are precious things; don't give yours to the void so easily."

"Oh, right, right." He slowly set me back on my feet but didn't remove his arm from around me. He'd been trying to teach me more about how to safely interact with ghosts and other preternatural energies. Key word: trying. My excitement usually got the better of me. "Can I at least set up the cameras though? If something happens, I don't want to miss it!"

He kissed the side of my head. "Give them to me, and tell me where you want them."

LEON SET UP the cameras, following me from room to room. On the first floor, we could hear soft footsteps from above. On the second floor was a pungent smell of floral perfume. In the cellar, shadows flitted away at the edges of my vision.

The sun was setting when I decided to give it a rest and eat. This was going to be a long night; I had yet to capture anything on camera, but I *knew* spirits were here. It was fortunate Leon didn't have a need for sleep; he didn't mind my late-night expeditions and terrible rest schedule.

"Do you ever wish you could eat?" I said, my mouth full of a granola bar. We were seated on the floor in the dilapidated kitchen, lit by a portable electric lantern. "I mean, I guess you *can* eat, but don't need to . . . so do you ever crave food?"

He chuckled, comfortably leaning back on his hands. "Sometimes. It's the smell that gets me. Especially when it's savory. Something I could bite into and taste it bleed . . ."

He was suddenly crouched over me. It made me giddy when he did that, using supernatural speed to move faster than my eye could follow. I nearly choked on my food as he lowered his head, bringing his teeth close to the curve of my neck.

"Salty and sweet," he murmured. I forgot about my food entirely as he traced his tongue along the shell of my ear. "Tender. Succulent, one could say."

"Oh, please don't eat me, Mister Demon," I teased, setting aside my food and watching him coyly. He arched an eyebrow, rocking back to crouch on the balls on his feet.

"Are you taunting me?" His voice lowered dangerously. "Do you think that's wise?"

I giggled. "When have I ever been wise?"

"I'm suddenly starving, doll." His wide, sharp smile grew. "Didn't I once tell you how much I love a good chase?"

My heart sped up. My palms began to sweat. Delicious fear, hot and heavy, slithered through my veins. Slowly, never breaking eye contact, I got to my feet. He remained crouched, watching as I backed away and he was slowly consumed by shadows.

Only his golden eyes remained, staring at me from the dark.

Then they disappeared, and I felt hot breath on the back of my neck.

"*Run.*"

His snarl sent me sprinting. My feet pounded across the old floorboards, racing through tall doorways and ducking around corners until I found the stairs. Leon was never far behind. He could catch me easily, but like a cat with his mouse, he wanted to play before he moved in for the kill.

No horror movie I'd watched, or haunted house attraction I'd walked through, could ever come close to the thrill of my demon chasing me. My body perceived danger while my brain knew I was safe. I nearly slipped on the stairs and clambered up them, sprinting into a large room on the upper floor. The remnants of a library, the vacant shelves strewn with dust and cobwebs.

Haunting laughter echoed around me. Darkness swirled around my feet, shadows brought to life by my demon's power. I couldn't see him, but I could feel his unmistakable presence.

"Poor little doll, fallen prey to the darkness yet again," he crooned. "Your fear is so sweet in the air."

Phantom hands caressed my thighs, shoving them apart as ghostly touches pinned me to the wall. The evening shadows, spilling through the open windows, morphed around me, becoming looming specters that extended clawed hands toward my face.

"*Tellement délicieux . . .*" Fingers wrapped around

my throat, a tattooed arm webbed with black veins reaching from the darkness. "Mine to consume. Mine to take as I please . . ."

I groaned as I was lifted from the floor, strong arms cloaked in shadow wrapping around me. The room vanished, replaced with swirling darkness that crackled with silver threads of energy. The scent of woodsmoke surrounded me.

The sweet cocktail of fear and arousal made my body flush with heat. My panties were ripped, torn off me and flung away into the darkness.

"Will you beg for mercy?" His forked tongue licked my inner thigh, making me shiver. "Or do you surrender to wickedness?"

His hot breath tickled my parted thighs, and I barely refrained from whimpering.

"I surrender," I said, and my remaining words were snatched from my mouth by his kiss. He held me close as his tongue swept over mine, the hard bulge in his trousers pressed against my belly. One hand remained wrapped around my neck, the other hooked behind my back.

He stole my breath, squeezing my throat, and my head swam blissfully.

"That's my girl." He lowered me to the ground, where I sank limply to my knees. Golden eyes peered down at me as he tipped my head back, gripping my hair and hooking two fingers onto my jaw to wrench it open. He spat on my tongue, laughing at me when I swallowed. "Such a desperate little human, aren't you?"

"Take me," I begged. "Use me." I squeezed my thighs together, need knotting in my stomach. "Please, Leon . . ."

"*Please,*" he mocked, pitching up his voice. His grip left me, and his eyes retreated deeper into the shadows, across the room. I could barely see the high-backed silhouette of the chair he sat in. "Prove your need. Crawl to me."

I obeyed, palms scraping across the dusty floorboards. My skirt brushed against my bare backside, arousal making my thighs sticky as I reached my demon's feet. He was splayed in the chair, massive cock jutting upwards as he stroked it slowly in his hand. He'd discarded his clothing so quickly, it was like the garments had simply vanished.

"On your knees for a demon," he growled, squeezing his shaft at the sight of me. "You are truly damned, aren't you?"

Leaning forward, I took him in my mouth. He barely fit. His hand came to rest on the back of my head, guiding me down only a few inches before I was struggling to breath. But he held me there, my eyes watering as my throat convulsed around him.

"Shall I fuck you, Rae?" he said. "Shall I show the curious spirits in this house what a filthy little whore you are for me?"

I barely managed to nod. He curled his finger, encouraging me to my feet, and grinned as I straddled him, my skirt brushing the head of his cock.

"Hold your skirt up," he ordered. "Let me see you."

As I lifted my skirt, he tore open my blouse, sending buttons flying. He flicked the piercings through my nipples, making me moan as he toyed with the jewelry.

As I slowly lowered myself onto him, he talked me through every inch.

"Fuck, you're gorgeous, baby girl." He spoke from between clenched teeth, every muscle wound tight with pleasure. "Take it deeper, I know you can. That's it. I love how you sound when it hurts."

Deeper and deeper I took him, until he was sheathed inside me and I was gasping. He consumed me from the inside out, ravenous demonic power pulsating through me as he thrust his hips and I fell against him. He gripped my jaw, tipping up my chin so he could watch my face.

"Ride it, pretty thing. Let me see you suffer for it."

Every thrust ached deeply, deliciously. I lost myself in the rhythm, one hand braced on his shoulder as the other grasped my skirt. Ecstasy sparked through every nerve, drowning me. He toyed with my breasts, leaned his head forward and took my nipple in his mouth. Suckling, flicking the jewelry with his forked tongue.

"Are you going to come for me?" he murmured. I nodded mindlessly and caught my breath as he suddenly gripped my hips, holding me in place as he fucked into me.

"Ah—Leon—" I couldn't speak, couldn't think. As if I were imploding, shrinking down to a microscope point of pleasure, pain, stimulation. As the orgasm washed over me, I could feel him throbbing inside me, his thick cock swelling even more.

His claws dug into my hips when he came with a snarl. His arms wrapped tighter around me, drawing me close.

"Now these ghosts know exactly what kind of horny fucks they're dealing with," he said. He kissed me slowly, deeply, until my trembling muscles were limp in his arms.

"I'm sure they'll be pleased to get rid of us," I giggled. Leon's forked tongue moved slowly over his lower lip, as if savoring the lingering taste of me, but a little smile remained.

"They won't get rid of us that easily," he said.

Leaning tiredly against him, I said, "What do you mean?"

His clawed fingers caressed over my thigh, where his sigil was scarred into my skin. "You like this place, don't you?"

"I love it," I said, confused as to what he was getting at. "I've always dreamed of living in a place like this."

He was still smiling, and I swear his golden eyes smoldered like coals.

"All that you want out of this life will be yours," he said. He lifted his hand, and dangling from his finger was a large old house key. "I will make mortality your playground, in every way I can. I will see you consume every last drop of pleasure this flesh can give you. Just as I will consume you." His head ducked to my neck, lips and teeth giving pleasure and pain in equal measure as I gasped.

"You bought this house for me? *Really?*" My voice pitched so high, I nearly screamed as his mouth tickled my neck. "How—when, I—ahh —"

"I intend to luxuriate in my freedom," he growled, warm hands still exploring me. "By spoiling my woman in every way I can and reaping the rewards. So long as you wish to play in the dark, I will be there to protect you. I will be there to give you everything this wicked heart desires." He placed a kiss over the beating organ, reverent and possessive as he gripped me. "Beyond your wildest dreams, baby girl."

Shaking my head in disbelief, I looked around the room. We could fix up the old place, return it to its former beauty. I could learn the stories of its ghosts, study the supernatural. I would have all the time I desired to document a true haunting.

I met my demon's eyes once more and traced my fingers over his tattooed chest as warmth bloomed in mine. "I love you."

He caught my hand and kissed my knuckles. "Say it again."

"I love you." I kissed his chest. "I love you." I kissed his throat. "I love you." Our mouths met, his sharp teeth and forked tongue ravaging me for a few breathless seconds. "For eternity, Leon."

THE END

*Keep reading for a special excerpt of
the next book in the Souls Trilogy!*

HER SOUL FOR REVENGE

Juniper

After a cult tried to sacrifice me to their wicked God, I went on the run, doing whatever was necessary to survive. Until a demon offered me a deal: give him my soul and he'll help me claim the vengeance I seek. Blood will be spilled, and the monsters I once ran from will soon be running from me. But damning my soul was just the beginning—it's my heart the demon wants next.

Zane

I've been hunting souls for centuries, but she's the ultimate prize—vicious and feral, with a broken soul as dark as my own. I thought claiming her would be a simple game, but Juniper is far from simple. I chose to follow her on a path drenched with the blood of her enemies, but it's our blood that may be spilled next. As an ancient God wakes from Its slumber, neither of us may survive.

Her Soul for Revenge *is book 2 in the Souls Trilogy. Although all the books are interconnected, they are stand-alone and can be read in any order.*

ZANE

THERE ARE PLACES on Earth that are cursed all the way down to their roots. Places that hold pain, that tasted blood and can't get enough. Places where darkness grows, and even in daylight, they lie under a shadow.

Those places feel a lot like home, and I suppose that's why demons are attracted to them. Not to say Hell is some wretched, unpleasant place. To the contrary, Hell is endlessly fascinating, even to an immortal. It's vast, far vaster than Earth. It holds darkness, it holds pain and, in some places, misery and agony beyond words. But Hell is inhabited by those who have existed for centuries, for millennia. It has seen wars, uprisings, the growth and destruction of cities, of cultures. It is full of magic and memories.

Abelaum, like Hell, was built on a foundation of magic and memories. It was beautiful; it drew in curious minds and ensnared them, like a spider weaving its web. Some humans stayed there forever; others swiftly left.

But Abelaum had something not even Hell did: Abelaum had a God.

Gods and demons had never gotten along. We'd taken Hell back from Them, and They'd ended up on Earth, weak and asleep. But always, inevitably, curious little humans took things too far. Curious human hands went digging, and curious human minds woke something up.

Humans and Gods were a bad combination. Give a human knowledge, and he thinks he's wise. Give a human magic, and he thinks he's strong. Give a human religion, and he'll think he's right.

Demons were better off avoiding Gods, despite the intrigue a town like Abelaum held. Yet there I was in Abelaum, back again after several years away. I always came back, and I'd keep coming back, as long as Leon was there.

We demons didn't take our bonds lightly. When one of our own was summoned and held captive by some wretched human magician, we didn't simply abandon them. Leon and I had sworn our bonds to each other centuries ago, and that bond had never broken. It never would. We may not have been lovers as we once were, but relationships that lasted through hundreds of years had to ebb and flow like the tides.

"That fucking hurts," Leon hissed, baring his sharp teeth as I cleaned the burns across his shoulders. I didn't know why his summoner had punished him this time. Leon was volatile, and I couldn't blame him for that.

He'd always been unlucky, and getting summoned and kept captive by that wretched family—the Hadleighs—was just the latest in his string of terrible circumstances.

"You don't need to clean it," he grumbled. "It doesn't matter."

"It matters." I shoved his head back down when he tried to raise it to stand up. Even his blond hair was burned. His summoner wielded brutality like a weapon, using pain to force obedience. "I know you'll heal, Leon, but you can't pretend this physical body doesn't need to be cared for. You'll heal faster if it's clean."

"Fucking Kent," he muttered. "I swear I'll kill him. I swear it."

Kent Hadleigh—a man to whom God had given knowledge, magic, and religion. A dangerous trifecta, leading to a man who fancied himself untouchable.

"What was it for this time?" I tossed the bloodied rag away. I returned to Abelaum so often that I'd gotten a house here, and it was useful even outside of giving Leon a place to recover. Humans were far likelier to trust you if you had a house, a car, the illusion of money and grandeur. As a soul hunter, gaining humans' trust was part of my job.

"The girl," Leon said. "They let her out today. Three years later, and Kent's still furious she ever got away. Told me to find her . . . fuck him. Fuck his orders. She can run for all I care. He can break every bone in my body, but it won't bring her back." He chuckled bitterly.

The girl. I knew the story, only because Leon had told it to me: how Kent had his daughter lure the girl into the woods, how he and his followers had gathered in the old church, how they'd cut the girl before they'd thrown her down into the mine.

Their first sacrifice to their wicked God.

But the girl had escaped and run, and not even Leon had been able to catch her.

How the hell a fifteen-year-old mortal girl had managed to escape from Leon, I'd likely never know. How she'd endured her escape through the woods—bleeding, lost, and drugged—made no sense.

"Why did they lock her up?" I said. "Last I heard, the police were all over her case."

"She tried to kill Victoria Hadleigh." Leon leaned his head back on the couch, closing his golden eyes. "Kent has the cops under his thumb. Fucking humans. So goddamn easy to corrupt." He sighed. "They locked the girl up in some hospital, called her delusional. I don't think she was too upset about it. Kept her safe for the last three years. But now . . . she's out on her own." His voice was getting softer, weaker as sleep took over. Demons didn't sleep often, but when we did, it was because it was desperately needed. "The God has her scent. It'll keep hunting her. She's in for one hell of a wild ride out there." He yawned. "Going to rest my eyes. Just for a minute. Just a minute . . ."

He was out cold.

FROM CURSED PLACES come cursed humans. I was fascinated with them: humans who had been broken and survived; humans who had just turned out *wrong*. I liked to hunt oddities, souls with a heavy history and heavier scars. They fought the hardest, and that made it even sweeter when they eventually became mine.

This girl, the one who had escaped from Kent Hadleigh's cult—she was an oddity, certainly. But if being outcast from society didn't kill her, then the monsters hunting her certainly would. I could smell them lurking in the trees—the Eldbeasts. They'd be lured to the magic lingering around her, hungry for a taste.

She likely wouldn't even survive the night.

Since Leon was resting, I wandered. There was too much energy in the air, a tingling at the back of my head that warned me things were shifting. The boundary between Earth, Hell, and all the numerous other realms felt thin. That boundary waxed and waned like the moon, and some thought it would eventually disappear altogether, plunging reality into chaos.

I didn't know if I believed all that, but I did believe there were other demons in Abelaum, demons that hadn't been here only a few days ago. It was their scent that I followed curiously through the night.

It led me to an old diner perched at the water's edge, its blinking neon sign advertising that they were open 24/7. I lit up a joint in the parking lot, trying to get a good look inside through the windows. Three demons sat within, all apart from each other. Two I recognized as soul hunters, so I could only guess the third was the same. They knew I was there, shooting me wary glances out the window as they sipped their coffees and poked at plates of food they had no interest in eating.

What the hell were they here for?

As I smoked, the wind shifted. The skunky, herba-
ceous odor of weed wafted away from me, replaced
instead with a sharp scent of iron and rot. I turned toward the trees, staring back into the shadows. Deep
in the darkness, a howl pierced the night, the kind of
wretched animal scream that sounded almost human. I
took a long drag, exhaling slowly. First demons, and now
the beasts . . . all gathering here.

I wandered inside, and the other demons quickly put
their heads down. I'd been around long enough to have
made a name for myself, and I'd taken enough souls to
have earned a reputation as a hunter not to be trifled
with. These demons were young, inexperienced. Eager for
their first soul, perhaps, but whose?

I went up to the counter, tapping it to get the nervous
waiter's attention. His eyes were wide, his fingers twitching. He didn't know the guests gathered in his restaurant
were all unearthly creatures, but his primal instinct knew
and would be warning him of the danger.

"Coffee, no cream," I said, and watched his hand
shake as he filled a mug from the coffee pot. "Slow night?"

He shrugged. "Weird night. Something's not right
about it." He glared out the windows as he handed me
the cup. "Did you hear those howls out there? We don't
usually get wolves around here."

"It wasn't wolves," I said. I could hear someone
sprinting outside, distant but coming closer. Bad night to
be out for a run. "Make sure you don't walk to your car
alone."

"The hell is that supposed to mean?" he said. Suddenly his eyes widened even further, staring behind me. "What the fuck?"

The sprinting feet were coming closer, closer—

The door burst open, the bells dangling from its handle jangling erratically. I turned slowly, sensing the tension rising in the air. There, standing inside, was a young woman with long, messy brown hair. She was tall and lanky, wearing a backpack and muddy boots. All her clothes were stained with mud—mud . . . and blood.

She froze, scanning the room. Every eye was fixed on her, and three pairs of them were hungry. Her scent was intoxicating, sweet with lingering magic. But the blood on her wasn't her own. I knew the smell of it immediately.

It was the beasts' blood. She'd been fighting the Eldbeasts.

"Hey!" the waiter called sharply. "Hey, I know you! Juniper Kynes! You—you're supposed to be locked up! You tried to kill that girl!"

She took a deep breath, and wiped a splatter of blood from her face with her sleeve. She walked across the dining area, heading toward the corner where the bathrooms were. The waiter likely didn't hear her mutter, but I did.

"She tried to kill me first."

She locked herself in the bathroom. Every demon in the place was tense, their eagerness for her palpable. I chuckled softly, taking a sip of the steaming coffee. Young soul hunters like these were always desperate for easy prey, eager to make a deal with someone whom they didn't need to convince that magic and monsters were real.

This girl already knew. She'd seen the worst of it. But that wouldn't make her easy, no. Far from it.

"I should call the cops," the waiter said, staring warily at the bathroom. The sound of running water from within cut off, and the door opened again. Juniper trudged out, her wide eyes flickering around the room. She moved like a frightened animal on the verge of sprinting. Like a wolf . . . a little wolf, left without a pack, alone and hunted.

She really was fascinating.

She came up to the counter, eyeing me. "I need food."

The waiter shook his head. "No. No, you gotta get out." He was reaching slowly for the phone.

She whipped out a pistol and aimed at the waiter. With her other hand she pulled a knife from its sheath on her thigh, and pointed the blade toward me. I raised my hands innocently.

"Don't do anything funny," she hissed, her voice shaking. "Just give me some fucking food. I don't care what. Just put some food in a bag. Now."

The waiter nodded, his face white as a sheet as he disappeared back into the kitchen. Juniper kept the knife pointed at me, shooting nervous glances in my direction and at the demons seated behind me. She couldn't have known what we were, of course. We all wore our human disguises in public.

"You know he's going to call the cops while he's back there," I said. She jumped at the sound of my voice, her breath quickening as she looked rapidly between me and the door leading back to the kitchen.

"Fucking hell." She climbed over the counter and reached beneath it, hurriedly collecting bags of cookies and tiny packets of oyster crackers that she stuffed into her bag. She vaulted back over, right as a shout came from the kitchen, and ran out the door.

"Cops are on their way!" The waiter crept out from the kitchen. The cook stood behind him, a massive man with a frying pan wielded in his hands like a baseball bat. That vicious woman had really put some fear in them.

I liked that.

With their prey on the move, the demons were moving too, all of them heading out the door. I sighed, and gulped down the rest of the coffee. I wasn't interested . . . or at least . . . I *hadn't* been. But with so many other hunters after her, and that desperate, vicious look in her eyes when she'd brandished the knife at me, I couldn't help but feel intrigued.

I left the restaurant faster than I should have. To the confused waiter's eyes, it would have looked as if I simply vanished, leaving an empty mug behind. The hunters were in the lot outside, heading toward the road, laughing amongst each other and betting who would reach the woman first. I got ahead of them.

They stopped abruptly, their human disguises instantly slipping. Three pairs of golden eyes watched me cautiously, claws extended, and the hunter I didn't know bared her teeth. I smirked.

"Don't growl at me, darling, it's rude," I said, and the hunter beside her gave her a hard nudge in the ribs. "All this fuss for one little mortal woman, eh?"

"You know she'll be desperate for a deal." Amiria was the one who spoke up. I knew her to be a fresh soul hunter, yet to make her first bargain. She was hungry for it; I could see it in her eyes. "But we were here first, Zane. Let a novice get a soul for once."

I cocked my head, stepping toward them. With only one step of mine, they all jerked back. I chuckled at their nervousness. "I don't think I will. There's plenty of souls out there, fledglings, trust me. Find someone selfish, someone greedy, someone eager for life's riches with no care for the afterlife. *That's* an easy bargain. But this one . . ."

I let my body change. My veins ran black, like trails of ink beneath my skin, as my teeth grew sharper. I gathered energy around me, condensing it, creating a shroud of darkness. It was petty, perhaps, but it was a warning. It let them know how much power I had at my disposal: enough to destroy all of them, here and now, if they dared try to argue with me.

"This one is mine."

JUNIPER HAD COVERED a lot of ground in the time it had taken me to disperse the other demons. I spotted her along the winding road, her pistol still in her hand. She was walking in the middle of the road, her head jerking from side to side. The forest had grown right up to the edge of the asphalt, and thick blackberry bushes formed a wall of tangled thorns on either side. The trees loomed high, and beneath their boughs, monsters lurked in the shadows.

I could hear them scrambling through the trees.

The woman heard them too.

She turned, her weapon aimed. The bitter scent of fear surrounded her as adrenaline coursed through her. It got my heart racing, that pungent odor of terror. She faced the darkness, eyes wide. The stench of rot was in the air, growing stronger as the beast under the trees crept closer.

It fled the moment I drew near. One Eldbeast alone wouldn't face me.

"You need to shoot for the head. It's really the only way to kill them."

She nearly jumped out of her skin at the sound of my voice. She aimed the gun at me, clutching the small pistol with both hands, her extended arms shaking. "Who the hell are you?" she said, then, she narrowed her eyes. "You . . . you were in the diner. You followed me."

"You have quite a few things following you, little wolf, and they all wish you a lot more harm than I do." I looked off into the trees. More of the beasts were encroaching on our position, their silhouettes scurrying through the dark. They had long, boney limbs, and vile, hunched bodies. They resembled spiders as they moved. "You need to get indoors. If you're going to travel at night, use a vehicle."

She didn't lower the gun, but curiosity began to creep over the fear on her face. "Those things . . . do you know what they are?"

"Eldbeasts," I said. My golden eyes were hidden behind brown, and I had sheathed my claws. I would appear as just a normal human to her, at least for now. No point in scaring her even more. "They're elder monsters, from when the world was young. But magic can stir them from their slumber. Magic . . . and Gods."

Her face looked stricken. She cocked the gun. "You're one of them, aren't you? One of the Libiri?"

I shook my head. "No, I'm not part of Kent Hadleigh's little cult. I have no interest in sacrificing you to an old God. That would be such a waste of your soul." I looked her over, catching a glimpse of her scars at the neckline of her shirt. They were ritual marks, cut into her flesh as she was offered up in sacrifice. "And what a beautiful, damaged soul it is."

She began to back away. "What the hell are you then? What do you want?"

"For now, I want nothing at all." I let my eyes shift, and her entire body went tense. I let my claws come out, and my teeth sharpen. She nearly stumbled as she backed away, barely keeping her feet. "But someday, little wolf, I may want everything."

She fired the gun.

The bullet struck my shoulder. It felt like nothing more than a pinch. I looked down at the wound curiously, poking my finger in to dig out the bullet. She watched, in horror, as I dropped the bloodied bit of metal onto the ground.

"My, my, so flirtatious." I chuckled. "Do that again, Juniper, and I might think you want to play."

"What the *fuck* are you?" She was going to run at any moment. She was shaking her head, her brain unable to process what she was seeing.

"You'll see me again," I said. "Survive a few years, Juniper, fight for your life. I like fighters. They make better prey. Survive, and the next time you see me, I may have an offer for you."

"I don't want your offers," she said. "Stay away from me!"

I *tsk*ed. "You say that now. But as the years go on, and the danger keeps coming, you may change your mind. Or you may not." I shrugged. "The choice is always yours. But I *will* see you again. Now, get inside. Get away from the trees. Wait until morning to travel. Juniper Kynes . . ." I crossed the space between us in a second. I stood over her, her wide eyes defiant and terrified as they looked up, and I smiled with a mouthful of sharp teeth. "Run."

She did run, sprinting down the road. The Eld would keep following her, but I'd hold them back, at least for tonight. May as well give the little wolf a fighting chance.

She had more viciousness in her than I'd thought. So much fire, for a human so burned. I'd hunted enough souls to afford to be picky, so I could hunt by my whims rather than necessity.

She would be a fascinating hunt, indeed.

**Look for *Her Soul for Revenge*
coming soon in paperback!**

ACKNOWLEDGMENTS

To my husband, my man, my partner, my muse, to whom this book is dedicated. Thank you for being my biggest supporter, my voice of reason and sanity, that calm presence when I am absolutely losing my shit. Thank you for not judging me when I talk through dialogue scenes in the shower, and for always being willing to help me "test" positions before I write them.

To my kitties: Luna, Gizmo, and Azura. Thank you for trying to help write this book. Unfortunately, you're not very good at spelling. But I know you were really trying all those times you walked across the keyboard.

To Zainab, thank you for helping make this book shine. Thank you for encouraging me when I thought I'd written absolute trash. You're amazingly skilled and this book wouldn't be what it is without you.

To my readers, every single one of you who has given love and support to a new author trying to find her way in this very wild publishing world: thank you. Dear God, thank you. You've changed my life. I cannot even say how much that means to me. But you've given me hope for a dream I've clung to since I was a little kid.

To everyone who has made it here to the end of the book, thank you for giving me a chance. You picked up this work and gave your time to it. Keep reading, keep seeking the next big adventure, always dare to go on.

Until next time,
Harley